VALES GATE

THERENIA

ISONIA

PORT CLEAR

LEROLIA

INGILIA

URNSY

MYNSE

QUARY

SIRAL

RHOB

EAL B

BARROWS

UPPER (NURNSEYS) GREENWOOD

TUSCIA MOUNTAIN

SHERIDAN

THE VALE

NORTH SHYLSEY

SISTERS OF RHOB

UPPER

LITTLEVALE

GREENWOOD—CHAS

DOCKSIDE LOWER

VERNIST-ON-CONTIF

LOWER (NURNSEYS) GREENWOOD

SHYLSE

SENTRY ROCK

CONTIF MOUNTAIN

BEYOND THE GATE

Terri-Lynne DeFino

HADLEY
RILLE
BOOKS

BEYOND THE GATE
Copyright © 2013 by Terri-Lynne DeFino

Cover art © Jesse Smolover

Cover design © Hadley Rille Books

Map of Vales Gate © Ginger Prewitt

ISBN-13   978-0-9892631-0-8

Edited by Kim Vandervort and Karin Rita Gastreich

Published by
Hadley Rille Books
Eric T. Reynolds, Publisher
PO Box 25466
Overland Park, KS 66225
USA
www.hadleyrillebooks.com
contact@hadleyrillebooks.com

For Casey, keeper of the pages.

"…walking on the sea is very peculiar business, I've heard. You walk out of time, you walk out of the world, you find yourself in strange countries…"

~*The Changeling Sea*, Patricia McKillip

Acknowledgments

This is the one, that book of my heart. Though both *Finder* and *A Time Never Lived* reside in their well-deserved places in my writerly soul, *Beyond the Gate* was actually written first. It has taken six years, two books in between, and more revisions than anything else I've ever produced to get right. But it is, and has ever been, my favorite. Don't tell the others.

Without my editors Kim Vandervort and Karin Gastreich, this book of my heart would never have been made right at last. At *first* came my Viable Paradise buddies, Dave Thompson and Barbara Gordon, who graciously beta-read all nearly two hundred thousand words of the first version; and then Tracy Dickens, who beta-read a slightly less verbose version. My brother Michael, and his husband, Jon loved this story outside of a writer's perspective, reading it not once but twice, and urging me to keep at it until tamed. A tremendous thanks goes to Mark Nelson, who, in the midnight hour, discovered my "go to" word for BTG and kindly pointed it out to me. Once the edited, now the editor—you're the best. And always, there is Erin Turbitt, my beta-reader of the last dozen years, who read every single draft I pushed this manuscript through without ever losing the love and faith in it. I thank you all from the bottom of my sparkly heart.

I have to toss another wave of appreciation to Bill Pearson, who gave me some choice, shall we say, *salty expressions,* for the Everwanderers herein. My daughter, Jamie Kenney, gets a *huge* thanks for helping me wrestle my blurb material into submission. Thanks to all the artists, writers and thinkers in my Hadley Rille Books family who walk this amazing path with me; especially Jesse Smolover and Ginger Prewitt, for once again giving face and form to my world and its people. As always, without Eric Reynolds, our editor-in-chief, I wouldn't have the home I cherish for my work. Our association went beyond the books between us almost immediately, and grows by the day. Your sparkle-queen-curious-oyster-nudger thanks you.

And, as always, Frankie D gets the last words here that will never be adequate to say all I wish to say, all he deserves. He knows. That works for me.

—Terri-Lynne

Tassry, off Sisolo—2.19.1206

I was right. I did not want to be, but I was. The responsibility of that is nearly more than I can bear.

The archipelago is secure. Sisolo is once again the sentinel of Ealiels Bay. Everything Ben has accomplished for the love of Diandra and in her name now has a chance of true success. Time will have to decide if that is to be.

They celebrate here on Tassry and on Rilse. Even on Sisolo, where so much treachery was at work, those who knew nothing of the intrigue celebrate the annihilation of a royal house gone wrong. The Larguessa's head adorns the square, on a pike higher than her cohorts. Hers is decorated in violets, a crude and cruel mockery of her given name. I will never again set foot on Sisolo, or her islets.

I cannot celebrate with them. I cannot rid myself of the blood. The carnage was brutal. Magnificent. Clean. Again and again I must ask myself; am I capable of such butchery? Can I kill so gently? And I am left to believe that I must be, because I was the last one standing.

Ben's been to this room three times to bid me come. Each time he appeared, he was a little more drunk, a little less insistent. I believe he understands. I hope that he does. Even if he does not, he will forgive me. He owes me a life debt that even a king must uphold.

The blood waits for me somewhere. It will wait as long as it must for redemption, or reparations; right now, I don't know which. Ben is alive. Vales Gate is saved. That must be enough. That is what I will celebrate, in my own way, in my own time.

Dockside

"OH, LINHARE! HAVE YOU EVER SEEN such a thing?"

Fire danced on fingers, up arms and across shoulders. It leapt like toads aflame from mouth to mouth. The Thissian fire-eaters howled and twirled, feeding the flames that *whooshed* higher, sparked brighter, and died away just as the next burst flew from between smiling lips.

"Linny." Jinna nudged her. Linhare blinked but could not pull her eyes from the stage.

"No, Jin. I've never seen—"

"Linhare!" The nudge became a shove toppling her from the stone bench. Her friend pointed desperately to the aisle. Righting herself, the angry retort died on Linhare's tongue.

Oh, no.

Her heart bobbed like a ball from belly to throat and back again. She had successfully avoided him since returning home; and now there he stood: queensguard. Dakhonne warrior. Wait. Her hand moved to her pocket. Instead of reaching inside, she smoothed the front of her simple dress. He could not know it was there. No one did. Not even Jinna, and she knew everything.

"What do we do now?" Jinna leaned closer to whisper. On stage, the fire-eaters were singing, urging their audience to sing along.

"I don't know. Pretend we didn't see him?"

"And what are the chances that is going to work?"

Linhare sighed. "I knew we should not have stayed for the show. We made it through the whole day without getting caught. Why do I listen to you, Jinna? Why?"

"Oh, don't start that." Jinna waved her away. "It has been ages since we've done anything wicked. Your mother will understand."

"It has been ages since *I* have done anything wicked." *And it is not my mother I worry about.* "*You* are another matter entirely. Stay, Jin. No sense both of us missing out."

"Don't go, Linny. There's still the Vulgar Raven after the show. I can't go without you."

"Of course you can. You have been for years."

"Whose fault is that, eh? Besides, the Thissians invited *us* not me."

The old guilty pang was no less severe than when she first went up the mountain—without Jinna. Linhare patted her friend's hand. "A particular Thissian invited *you.*"

"Us! You're already in trouble! Just come with me!"

"I should not have stayed out so long. My mother needs me. This pregnancy is very difficult for her."

"Your mother is too old to bear. She should have listened to my mother and taken the proper precautions."

Linhare's body tensed. "Her husband wanted an heir. She knew that when she agreed to the marriage. It...it is his right."

"He's not the one who has to bear the little frog. Oh, please, Linhare. Come with me. I promise we won't stay long. And your *darling* sister Sabal is there if your mother needs comfort. Just look at my Thissian there." She pointed. "Isn't he the most delicious cut of flesh you have ever seen?"

The fire-eaters finished their song. The young man currently tickling Jinna's voracious fancy bowed low, his long hair now unbound and sweeping his boots. Jinna got to her feet with the rest, whistling and cheering. Wait was still there, at the end of the aisle. There would be no escaping him as she might have at least tried, when she was a girl. Such carefree days were over. She had changed; and so did life in the Vale. Father dead, Mother remarried and pregnant, her little sister a woman—none of that had been so when she left for university. It all happened without her.

Linhare stood up beside Jinna, touching her arm. She raised her voice above the applause. "Go to the Vulgar Raven with your Thissian fire-eater. Have fun for both of us."

"I'm not going without you," Jinna shouted back. Arms crossed and strawberry curls bouncing on fair and freckled shoulders, she pushed through the cheering spectators to the aisle where Wait stood, burnished golden in torchlight, attracting every female eye in the vicinity. Jinna's life goal was to see the man in all his naked, sinewy glory. Sabal giggled whenever he entered a room. Linhare understood the universal reaction to him. He was a heroic figure, handsome, brave and loyal. He saved a king, and all of Vales Gate in the process. She had been as smitten with him as the rest, until. . .

The secret in her pocket dragged her down. Linhare excused her way to him, henhairs prickling her skin. Wait's eyes, as blue-green as Ealiels Bay in summer, drew her, fixed on her and only her even if Jinna's finger wagged in his face. By the time she reached the aisle, Linhare could no longer hear the cheering crowds or Jinna's haranguing.

"Good evening, Linhare."

"Good evening, Wait."

An automatic response; a nicety ingrained since childhood. Linhare's face burned and not because she was caught outside the Vale without him. Her hand reached into her pocket. The cover, appropriately red and sufficiently scarred, was familiar to her fingertips; comforting and disquieting all at once. An adventure tale of some young man traveling the provinces of the main island, all her isles and islets, forging peace with a newly-made king. The author could have been any of his men; until the line that made it his.

—because I was the last one standing.

So many years in her possession, this secret, this betrayal, the temptation to delve further into his story was never as great as the need to stop at that treacherous line. One day, she would give it back to him. She had made that silent promise. One day. Not today.

Linhare straightened her shoulders, lifted her chin, and looked him in the eye for the first time since finding his secret stashed in a crevice behind a broken windowsill in the university library.

"Have you been here long?"

"Long enough. You do have a royal box at your disposal."

"I didn't want to be recognized." Plain enough to go unnoticed, pretty enough to blend in, Linhare was, on these occasions, glad she had not inherited her mother's rare beauty. Sabal's temperament was more suited to it. But there was no mistaking a man of Wait's size and fame. If her people did not know her by sight, they did know her queensguard; and now, whether Jinna liked it or not, the game was over. "I'm sorry for running off."

"No you're not." The corner of Wait's mouth lifted into something that might have been a smile, holding out his hand to assist her from the row of seats. "You're sorry you got caught. Come. I will escort you out of here."

"We don't *need* an escort." Jinna claimed his other arm. "We were fine all day, weren't we, Linny?"

"I know," Wait said. "You were fine when you stole the pony and cart. You were fine browsing the markets Dockside. And on the beach, the skewered meat stand and all through the show."

Followed. Of course. "Then why did you not simply fetch me home earlier?"

"And have you miss the Thissians?" Again that almost-smile. Linhare clamped her lips closed. Her fingers on his arm tingled madly. On the other side of him, Jinna was waving her free arm over her head.

"There he is! Wait, please. One cup at the Vulgar Raven and then we'll go back with you, meek as baby lambs."

Wait halted, gently extricating himself from Jinna's grasp. "Princess Linhare does not need my permission. I am queensguard. I await her command." He turned to Linhare, those serious eyes absorbing her like a sea-sponge. "Linhare?"

14

"Linny?" Jinna bounced on the balls of her feet. "Please, please, please? It is still early. We can be home before Ta-Diandra takes her bed-time tea."

Linhare bit her lip, her gaze lifting from Jinna's hopeful expression to Wait's quiet patience. At home, Mother waited. If she were lucky, her stepfather did not even know she'd gone missing. Yet. And if he did, Linhare knew who would bear the consequences.

"One cup," she said at last. "And I mean it, Jinna. One cup and we go home."

"Hurrah! I knew you'd see reason." Flinging herself onto Wait's arm, she jostled him as if a woodmouse could jostle an oak. "You'll have a cup too, won't you, Wait?"

"I don't drink fermented spirits," he told her, but let her keep his arm. Offering the other to Linhare, he said, "Your father was a well-known face in the Vulgar Raven."

"He was?"

"A man of the people. They loved him. They will love you, too."

"A man of the people," Linhare echoed. She smiled up at him. "Thank you, Wait."

"You are welcome, Linhare."

The crowd parted for them. Linhare noted the spectators now whispering behind their hands. Their future queen sat among them, and none had known. Now she smiled, nodded to those who dared meet her eyes, and wished. . .

There were no other carts or carriages on the road leading out of Dockside. Linhare's heart hammered. One cup became two, and two cups became bawdy songs sung with the Thissian fire-eaters. Somehow, Jinna kept talking her into staying longer and longer. The Vulgar Raven held her patrons tightly and close. Many told stories of her father, stories that made Linhare laugh even if a few tears escaped as well. Now, after midnight and long past her mother's bed-time tea, Linhare drove the stolen pony and cart out of sleeping Upper-Dockside. Wait's massive mare clomped behind. Jinna snored on her shoulder. Her breath tickled Linhare's neck. Six years had not banished the dear familiarity of the sound, the sensation. Comforting. Amusing. Beloved. It meant *Jinna*. Linhare rested her head atop her friend's, and let her stay.

The clomp of echoing hooves woke her. Linhare startled upright, blinking. Jinna grumbled in her intoxicated doze but did not wake. Somewhere between Upper-Dockside and the Gate, Wait had taken her reins, and was leading the pony and cart. Her cheeks warmed. How easily she fell into old ways, even after the safe independence of university.

15

Linhare waved to the guard at the mouth of the tunnel as her cart passed. The Gate separating Dockside from the Vale had been standing ageless for as long as history recorded life in the archipelago. It was older than all the cities on all the isles from Esher to Danessa. Folktales said it was fae built, fae protected. It needed no guards. As far as Linhare was concerned, it was a guard in its own right and far more effective than the bored and yawning boy she passed.

Her stepfather, apparently, thought otherwise.

Coming out of the tunnel and into the Vale, cobbles gave way to a well-worn forest road that muffled the *creak-clomp* of cartwheels and hooves. Gone was the briny scent of the sea and in its place, green.

The Vale smelled green. It tasted green. Even moonlight-doused, the eerie light glowed green. Crickets and nightbirds chirruped in canopy and brush. In daylight, woodland flowers splashed scarlet or curtsied white in some attempt to prove that there were other colors in the Vale, but the sunlight-dappled green swallowed them quickly. In such a light, it was possible to believe faefolk dwelt in secret places. In moonlight, it was impossible to deny.

"Wait," she called softly. The man stopped instantly, turned in his saddle. "I wish to go through Littlevale, please."

He only nodded, clucked to his horse, and continued on. Littlevale appeared like mushrooms in the forest mulch. A house, then two, then a cluster of homes mimicking but not identical to one another, lined the dirt road. Gardens thrived. Window-boxes overflowed. All windows were dark; the good people of Littlevale rose and slept with the sun.

Wait turned off the road and onto a familiar side track. Was he so attuned to her thoughts? Or had his traveled the same path? The track narrowed to the width of a single cart. Though few enough traveled it of late, the trees and brush seemed to know not to encroach any further.

The stone and timber cottage appeared as they rounded a familiar bend. The yard was all stakes and twine supporting vines bearing pods and peas and summer squash; beds of herbs and racks to dry them upon. Linhare did not have to see the potter's shed to know it sat slightly tilted in the yard. This was a place she knew as well as her own rooms. It meant comfort and peace and love. For that year after her father's return, of her mother's confinement and the birthing that nearly killed her, Linhare lived in all ways as a peasant girl with Jinna and Ta-Yebbe, in this forestwife's cottage in the wood, cleaning and weeding, harvesting and brewing. Many traveled the track back then, seeking remedies and wisdom. For that year, she was happier than in all her other years combined.

Ta-Yebbe stood on the front stoop, arms crossed, and trying to hide a smile, as if she had known all along they would arrive; as of course, she did.

16

"Jinna." She jiggled her friend. "Wake up. You're home."

"Hmm? What?"

"Home," Linhare told her. The cart rolled to a stop. On the stoop, Ta-Yebbe opened her arms. Linhare leapt out of the cart to embrace the forestwife as bony as Jinna was curved. Still fair and freckled, her cap of strawberry curls had dulled to a rich copper over the years; but she smelled the same. Lavender and mint. Linhare breathed her in.

"Ten days home," Ta-Yebbe said. "It's about time you got here."

"I'm sorry, Ta. I'm lucky I even get a few hours to sleep these days. My stepfather is determined to make my homecoming grand."

"I imagine he is." Yebbe let her go. "I see you have brought my wayward daughter home to me as well, and at this hour, that can't mean anything good. What mischief is she up to now?"

"It was my mischief this time," Linhare told her. "I made her come with me Dockside and I don't want her blamed for it if I get caught. I thought it best to leave her here with you."

Wait had dismounted and was trying to rouse Jinna, who was having none of it. He lifted her out of the cart.

"I won't pretend I don't know what this is about," Yebbe said quietly. "And I won't pretend I'm not grateful. But you cannot protect her from your stepfather any more than your mother can protect me."

"It's just that, with the baby coming and my return, things are so chaotic. It really was my idea to steal a pony and cart like we used to. She didn't force me to stay out so late. You know Jinna, always up for a lark. I'm the one who's not supposed to be out without an escort. She is free to—"

"Wait is with you." Yebbe hushed her with a finger to her lips. "You are to be queen, Linhare. Remember that." Removing her finger, the forestwife called to Wait coming down the walk. "Bring her in. I've a bed ready for her."

Linhare moved out of the way to let Wait pass. As he did, Jinna opened her eyes and grinned at her, then snuggled into the crook of Wait's neck, purring feigned slumber.

Yebbe led Wait further into the tiny cottage. He bumped his head or a shoulder on the low doorway she gestured him through. Linhare let them handle Jinna; instead, she stood in the kitchen that took up the rest of the cottage. It sparkled with moonlight coming through the enormous, Therkian-glass window spanning the far wall. Linhare rested her cheek to the rare glass shimmering muted rainbows wherever the light touched it. A priceless gift from her father to the woman who saved the lives of his wife and baby daughter, and the source of the never-ending gossip it sparked since.

17

"I am in your debt once again, Wait," Yebbe was saying as they entered the kitchen. "Can I offer you tea? Something to eat?"

"No, thank you. It's time I got the princess home."

"So soon?" Yebbe sighed and beckoned Linhare to her. Wait bowed to both of them and ducked out the door. The women followed more slowly behind.

"Do the villagers still believe you contracted with boogles to get your window?" Linhare asked.

"Of course." Yebbe squeezed her arm. "Just as I took a boogle lover to get Jinna. But better that than the other gossip floating around back then."

Linhare bowed her head, cheeks flushing. Those whispers linking the forestwife to her king, spoken behind hands and rarely louder, had resurfaced of late.

"I don't know what sparked such fascination with boogles." Linhare's voice wobbled only slightly. "Hairless, stumpy things. Why not a dark and handsome Drümbul Lord?"

"Because then other women would have to envy me instead of whisper about my fatherless child. Don't let wagging tongues bother you, poppet. Such silliness is a drawback of my trade. I am used to it."

You should not have to be. When my father was alive, your trade was honored. When my father was alive—

"How is Diandra?" Yebbe's softly spoken question halted Linhare on the walk.

"Not well," she said. "I fear for her, Ta-Yebbe."

"It is late in her life for childbearing." Yebbe shook her head. "But she is a strong woman, and healthy. It is more taxing for her, that's all. She will be fine."

"But when she gave birth to Sabal—"

"Hush now." Yebbe kissed her fingertips and touched them to her heart. "Don't speak of such things."

The screamed agony. Her father, who feared nothing, trembling and holding her so tightly it hurt. Young as she had been, Linhare remembered it all, including that moment Yebbe came out of the birthing room, a smile on her pale face and a squalling infant in her arms.

"Come see Mother," Linhare burst. "She would welcome you."

"Oh, child." Yebbe took both Linhare's hands in hers. "Of course she would, but no. The days a forestwife could call upon a queen uninvited are gone."

"They don't have to be. You said it yourself. I am to be queen. If I command it, my stepfather cannot—"

Yebbe grasped her by the arms. "If she calls for me, I will come. Nothing will keep me from her side. But she must summon me, not you. Understand?"

"Yes, Ta."

"Good girl." Yebbe kissed both cheeks. "Now go home."

Wait stood beside the cart, waiting to assist her onto the seat. Linhare took his hand and climbed in. He gave her the reins.

"Thank you, Wait," she said. "For everything."

Again that stoic nod, that hint of what might be a smile. Legging up onto his mare's back, he clicked her into motion. Linhare slapped the reins to her pony's back. She turned to wave to Ta-Yebbe, but, except for moonlit flowers and vines, the yard was empty.

Too soon, the sweeping lawns surrounding the timber and stone castle appeared through the trees. Linhare tucked the reins under her chin to unbraid her hair. Thick and wavy and the color of roasted chestnuts, it reached her knees. The mass of it was close to torture as Linhare could imagine during these hot summer months. She'd taken to braiding it at university, but her stepfather was having none of that now that she was back in the Vale.

"For mercy's sake, Linny, if you're not allowed to braid it then cut it and be done!" Jinna had stood, a hand on her hip and shears snapping the air. "Your father never meant for you to take that silly promise this seriously."

Tendrils floated like milkweed around her face. She licked her fingers and smoothed them down. A promise was a promise, and she would not break it to appease her stepfather's sense of fashionable propriety. Catching up the sides, she wound them loosely around the rest of the mass and bound the ends together at the nape of her neck, just as she had seen other young women do in Upper Dockside.

"We'll go around to the back," Wait reined in beside her to say. "Through the kitchens."

"And up the servants' passageway. I know, Wait. We've done this before."

"So we have."

Linhare laughed softly. "I imagine you did not think you'd still be doing so once I was a grown woman."

"No, I didn't. But I have to admit, I'd have been disappointed to be right. " No ghost of one this time; Wait's smile lit his face like sunlight on waves. That old, familiar shiver prickled henhairs all over her body; and sent her hand to her pocket, and the secret that ruined everything.

Give it to him. Give it to him now!

But Linhare's hand came out empty.

19

A yawning stable boy took Wait's mare and Linhare's pony. Perhaps he did not recognize her, because he didn't bow or in any way pay respect to his future queen. Linhare peeked up at Wait through her lashes. *Or perhaps he is accustomed to Wait bringing strange women home, late at night.* But even as she thought it, Linhare knew it was not true. Of all the rumor and intrigue surrounding the man, promiscuity was never part of the gossip. Quite the opposite. Linhare smiled in spite of herself.

Wait led her through the kitchen garden, a place that always put her back to those younger days when she and Jinna escaped on a nearly daily basis. They entered the castle through the scullery and took the servants' passages up and up, until they reached the suite of rooms her mother kept. Linhare halted Wait, a hand to his arm.

"Should we not let her sleep?"

"She's waiting for you."

"But it's so late."

"She is your mother, Linhare," he said, and knocked lightly on the door. It opened instantly.

"Did anyone see her?"

"Only a sleepy stableboy, and he didn't recognize her. King Agreth?"

"He only noticed her missing at dinner. I told him she was attending the performance at the arena. Fire-eaters from Thiss, if I remember correctly. He approved."

Wait nodded. The queen laid a hand upon his arm. Wait covered her hand with his own, then let it fall to take one proper step back.

"Good-night, princess," he said. "Sleep sweet."

"Good-night, Wait. Sleep—" *Sweet* would not fall off her tongue. "Thank you," she said instead. Another nod, and the queensguard left mother and daughter alone in the dim servants' passage.

"Inside, my girl." Diandra stood away from the door. Linhare, head bowed, entered the suite of rooms only to be clutched into an abundant bosom she knew as well as she did the clucking voice that went with it.

"You've worried your poor mother sick!"

"I'm sorry, Chira. I did not mean to." Disentangling herself, Linhare kissed both fleshy cheeks. Once her mother's nurse, then her maid, Chira had been in the castle longer than any other living soul.

"Goodness, me and my guiding star!" the old woman fussed. "Look at that dress! And your hair has been braided. You can't fool me. Tsk! A lady doesn't braid her hair like a common milkmaid."

"Hush now, dear." Diandra patted Chira's gnarled hand. "It is late. She is here. And now you must go rest, as you promised me."

Chira reached up to cup the queen's cheek as if she were a cherished child. "Of course, sweetling." Her other hand darted out to swat Linhare's bottom just as she used to when Linhare was little and naughty and too quick to be caught. "You mind your mother," she said and waddled out.

"I only went Dockside," Linhare said quickly the moment the door closed again. "And to see the fire-eaters, just as you guessed. Jinna came with me."

"A topic I will take up with Jinna when she returns from her mother's cottage."

"How do you know I left her there?"

Diandra, golden as sunlight on wheat and swollen like a kernel ready to burst, touched her daughter's face tenderly. "Because I know you, my darling. I knew you would make your escape eventually, though I did not expect you to be gone so long."

"I didn't, either. Honest. And—and Wait was with us all day."

"A fact you did not know." Diandra laughed. "Oh, sweetling. You've never been able to vanish without him finding you."

"I didn't see him," Linhare admitted. "Not even once. How does a man so large go unseen in a crowd?"

"He is Dakhonne," Diandra said. "He is not seen until he wishes to be."

"I fell off my seat when I saw him in the arena."

"Wait has that effect on women."

"Oh, mother!"

"Oh, Linhare," Diandra mimicked. "Don't pretend you have not noticed. Your sister certainly has."

She took her daughter's hand and led her to a lounging couch set near the window. There were no Therkian-glass panes here, but the less remarkable glass of Vales Gate. Gathered into her mother's arms, leaning against her swollen belly, Linhare closed her eyes and listened.

"It's a boy you know," she said. "I dreamed it."

"Did you?"

Linhare lifted her head to nod. "I did, while still at university. It was so real." She placed her palm to her mother's belly to feel the baby squirming inside. "A baby boy with hair as golden as his mother's and eyes so blue they glowed. I held him in my arms and he didn't make a sound. Not even a small whimper. So I know it is a boy. I suppose naming him Bennis would be out of the question."

"Why not take that up with Agreth?"

Linhare laughed at her mother's joke but even to her own ears the sound was artificial. Leaning into her again, she took solace there where she had been taking solace since birth. Between them, the unborn baby wriggled and kicked. Boy or girl, it was a vigorous thing. Despite her mother's pallor, Linhare's anxiety eased a little.

Diandra kissed the top of her head. "I know you were safe in Dockside, Linhare. But you are my heir. My concern is how your people perceive you. They want their queen to be just a little bit above them."

"That's dreadful."

"But true. It is an illusion they want, my darling. A wise queen understands that, but does not believe it herself. I have complete faith that you will be a very wise queen."

"I'm sorry for worrying you."

"You did not really worry me. I knew that Wait would watch over you and keep you safe should the need arise. No harm done; no fault bestowed. We will keep this between us. I see no need to upset your stepfather."

Linhare grimaced. Of course her mother had not been worried for her safety. There was no place safer than Vales Gate; no place safer than the Vale itself. Linhare realized suddenly that neither was her mother overly concerned about the people's perception of her, so much as her stepfather's.

"I have to insist that you choose handmaidens to attend you," Diandra was saying. "It is long past time. Jinna has ever been more playmate than helpmate."

"That's not true." Linhare feigned innocence. "She has helped me into quite a bit of trouble over the years."

"You wicked thing." Diandra laughed, then, "There are several Lerolian cousins vying for positions. You will choose at least three before Harvestide. I want you properly attended for the Darkday Balls."

"Yes, mother."

"You are not a little girl anymore," she continued. "Your father was a man of the people. His was as common a face in the Vulgar Raven as in the castle."

Linhare sat up. "That's what Wait told me."

"Indeed, but he was king. You are to be queen. It is my blood that gives you your place in Vales Gate. It is a fine balance you must strike, keeping the illusion of higher grace while being what he was to them."

Diandra straightened suddenly, her hands moving to her swollen belly, and her face paler than it had been moments ago. She leaned back into the couch.

"You are tired." Linhare leapt to her feet and poured her mother a cup of water.

"Thank you." Diandra took the cup but did not drink. "I am tired; and not as young as I used to be."

"Why not send for Ta-Yebbe? She would come. She told me she would."

"Of course Yebbe would come to me. I have no greater friend in life. But this is Agreth's child too, and he will have none of her woods-witchery, as he calls it."

"He is a fool, then!" Linhare fell to her knees and took her mother's hand to press it to her cheek. "Mother, please. Please send for her. You had such a difficult labor with Sabal and that was seventeen years ago. Ta-Yebbe's woods-witchery saved you both. Please. I cannot lose you, too."

Diandra gently pulled her hand from Linhare's. The gold of her hair, touched as it was by moonlight, made her pallor ethereal. Linhare shuddered, as if she already looked into the face of a ghost.

"I swear to you," Diandra said, "that if I fear for my life or my baby's, I will send for Yebbe. Please understand, Linhare, it is not for Agreth that I appease his idiocy, but for Yebbe. I'll not put her through any indignity because I am tired."

Linhare bit her lip but the words came out anyway. "Do you love him at all?"

Diandra's frail smile banished the ghostly pallor. "Agreth is handsome and he is charming when he is not thinking too highly of himself," she said. "We had our conflicts in the beginning but I have grown fond of him. I believe he's grown fond of me too." Diandra patted her daughter's cheek. "It doesn't matter. I will love our baby as I love you and Sabal. Fondness works, but love has nothing to do with this marriage. It was necessary."

"But, Mother—"

"Your father worked hard for the peace you have always known," Diandra snapped, then eased. "Three long years sailing the isles and islets, trekking the provinces to make promises and agreements, risking his life in those discontented times, all so that I could reign over a united nation rather than the fractured, bickering one inherited from my mother and her mother before her. Agreth is Sisolo's favorite son, and Sisolo is the key to ensuring all your father did remains secure. This marriage, this baby, binds Sisolo, Tassry and Rilse to us as no treaty ever could."

The journal in Linhare's pocket grew suddenly heavy again. Her mother had no idea how intimately aware she was of Sisolo's place in the archipelago, of the role it played in the past. For riches or for power, the Larguessa Violet conspired with Yerac'ia to overthrow the monarchy, to pull the archipelago into the greater nation to their east. Were it not for her father—*no, not Father; Wait*—the flag flying over the castle would be Yerac'ia crimson rather than Vales Gate blue.

Linhare rose to her feet, her hand pressed to the book inside her pocket. "Father promised to unite Vales Gate so you would marry him," she tried to joke. "He told me so a dozen times over."

"Your father loved me a great deal." Diandra laughed softly. "And he loved Vales Gate. I inherited the nation, but it was his work that made it great. History will remember him as the most significant king since Contif."

"And you the greatest queen since Tuscia."

Diandra pushed out of the couch, steadying herself before letting go. "You are a good daughter but no, I will never have a mountain named for me. I do not mind being in your father's shadow. A marriage can only sustain so much greatness. Now, my darling, I need to rest. I will have your word that you will not go running off again without Wait."

"You have my word," Linhare said. "My solemn word."

"There's my girl. Now kiss me and be off."

She kissed her mother's cheek, lingering there in the softness, and the sweet scent of her. History books veiled unpleasantness in the eventual victory. Linhare had grown up knowing there was no place greater than Vales Gate. Until finding Wait's journal, she took the peaceful prosperity for granted. What else did history veil?

Closing the door softly behind her, Linhare took Wait's journal from her pocket. She unwrapped the leather ties and flipped to that entry she read up to but never beyond.

That is what I will celebrate, in my own way, in my own time.

Her fingers trembled. She turned the page.

At sea off Enalia—3.11.1206

It has been a while since I have had the heart to open this book and take pen to it. Larguessa Violet's severed head still talks to me in dreams—

Linhare snapped the book closed. Her heart pounded. Her head lightened. Leaning against the wall, she wrapped up the scarred, red leather book, put it back into her pocket, and fled to her rooms where there was no snoring Jinna, no disapproving stepfather, no pale and weary mother, and mostly, no Wait.

Wait

THE THISSIAN FIRE-EATERS DID NOTHING for him. He had seen the splendors of the Corys Delta, Ealiels Bridge, and Sisolo's red tears. He touched a dragon that glittered like a hundred thousand jewels, but was softer than Lerolian wool.

As a boy named Calryan, he trekked up Mount Contif and received his Dakhan name—*Wait*. He descended into the deepest mines of Tuscia to extract the sheridans ore used to forge the sword at his hip. Wait had traveled with King Bennis when he was still just Ben, from the tip of Aughty to the promontory of Morle; from isle to islet; from Siys to Slarys. Wait had seen wonders, real wonders. The fire-eaters were a show. He was a little disappointed that Linhare was so enthralled; until he remembered she was still little more than a girl, all of twenty three, and far too innocent to view life the way he did.

Pushing off the wall he leaned upon, Wait moved into the next room, silent and unseen. It was his gift, he had been told while training on Sentry Rock, this vanishing in plain view, that few Dakhan claimed. Wait found it useful during his routine rounds, if not impressive, especially since his queen remarried.

He found King Agreth pacing around the table laden with breakfast fare. Wait held back, listened to the habitual, agitated muttering that had become more frantic of late. He did not like *frantic*; it too closely resembled *reckless*. Pulling his uncanny silence tighter about him, he was halted by a rustle of skirts and a hush of giggling. Agreth turned to the adjacent doorway; Wait's eyes stayed on the pretty, substitute king. His swift transformation unsettled Wait as much as the agitated muttering. Sabal entered, a gaggle of handmaidens in her wake.

"Father," she cooed, arms outstretched. Agreth took her hands and kissed both her cheeks. The handmaidens, pretty as nesting doves but pigeons beside Princess Sabal, giggled.

"Good morning, Daughter," he said. "I was awaiting your mother, or perhaps Linhare. It seems they have both forgotten about me. I am fortunate to have you, who did not."

"Darling Father, Mother always takes breakfast in her rooms. You know that."

Princess Sabal, blonde and fair as the queen, shooed her handmaidens to their corner and took her stepfather's arm. Wait disliked hearing her call Agreth *Father* and dote on him so fondly, but he forgave the young princess this; she was little more than a child when her own father died, after all.

"And where is your sister?" Agreth pulled out a chair for her.

"Oh, she went to see the Thissian fire-eaters perform last night. I suppose she was up late. Mother says it is important for her to go among the people now and again."

Agreth took his own seat and dabbed his fingers in the fingerbowl, dried them on his lapkin. "I see."

"Personally, I hate Lower Dockside. So mean and common. I hate it almost as much as..as..." She busied her hands. "...as I hate the thought of *university*."

"That is a silly thing to say," Agreth told her. "They are as alike as a jester is to a scholar."

"I only meant that I can't imagine actually *wanting* to go to either place." She leaned forward, her sweet, husky voice rising in pitch. "You won't make me go, will you, Father? You won't let Mother make me. Linhare's only just returned home and—"

"Go where, Sabal?"

"University! That dreadful, musty, dusty, cold university that I cannot even imagine myself being forced to live in."

Agreth put a forkful of eggs into his mouth, chewed slowly. Putting the utensil down, he dabbed at his lips. "I don't see the point of sending you away if you don't wish to go. Vernist-on-Contif is for those serious of mind and purpose."

Sabal clapped her hands. "I knew you would be fair. Mother doesn't understand. I just want to stay here in the Vale, happy as a little mollusk with my sorcery books and my dear maidens who dote on me. And now that Linhare is home—"

"Sorcery?" Agreth looked up from his plate, an eyebrow raised. "I thought Learned Garna decreed that you have no aptitude for it."

"Perhaps not, but I do enjoy it so." Sabal's childish giggle might have fooled Agreth, but it did not fool Wait. "I don't think it is fair that I cannot study magic because those single-minded Purists say one must show natural aptitude. I believe it can be learned."

"You'll be trying to conjure gobbets next."

"Oh, Father. Don't be silly. One doesn't conjure fae. One must simply be open to—"

"You sound like a child, Sabal. Bolleytales are nonsense."

"But Mother's family in Lerolia swears there are fae in the wood there. Oh, how I'd love to see a bolley or a gobbet or even a ghasty-haint. Could you imagine? Linhare said she saw one once."

"One what?"

"A ghasty-haint. She said—"

"Linhare is far too sensible to say anything of the kind." Agreth sniffed, pouring himself more wine. "You, on the other hand, are far more whimsical. At least it is not woods-witchery you are after. Branch-waving charlatanry. I'll not see my daughter among the Sisters of Rhob."

"Of course not, Father." Sabal waved an elegant hand. "I've no interest in the healing arts and herblore. Mother says that I should be more interested in affairs of state but I simply don't—"

"How does your mother fare today?"

Wait noted Sabal's pause, the frown creasing her soft features. The king cut off her words one time too many. Wait braced himself for the tantrum about to explode from her tiny frame, but when she spoke, it was with the same sweet huskiness.

"You've not seen her? She's as lovely as always, if a bit pale. That babe of yours is certainly taking its toll on her. It's going to be a big, healthy boy. I just know it."

"May the stars and starlight hear you," he said. "We certainly do not need any more females in this household."

"Oh, the things you say. You would think you've no love at all for your darling girls! And speaking of darling girls, did you hear about that actress we saw in Upper Dockside? The scandalous affair she denies but I just know is true?"

Sabal chittered on like a little squirrel, carrying the conversation by herself. If she noticed that Agreth was no longer listening, it did not show.

Wait had heard enough. Sabal's attentions uncomfortable, and Agreth's annoying, he moved as silently and unseen from the breakfast room as he had entered.

"I see that you are as impressed with the morning conversation as I am."

The voice was deep and rich despite the whisper, and one Wait knew instantly. Gripping the man's shoulder, he moved him away from the doorway. "You're here early."

"It's the only time I can get Diandra these days without having to endure her husband."

"If I did not know you are an honorable man, Ellis, I might be suspicious."

"Come now, Cal. She is your queen."

"And yours, too. Always has been." He grinned, then shook his head, chuckling. "You are the last person alive who still calls me that."

"Calls you what?"

"Cal."

"It's your name."

"Not since I was a boy."

"You were a boy when I met you," Ellis said. "You are still a boy, as far as I'm concerned. No matter how old either of us gets, I will always be nearly old enough to be your father." He wagged a finger. "Nearly."

Wait gestured, and the two started walking. Ellis's head bowed. Wait noted a few strands of white peppering his dark hair. Diandra was not much younger than her Mine Officer, and yet she was to have another child soon. Wait resisted the urge to kiss his fingertips and touch his heart; such wardings of his childhood had no place here in the Vale.

"I hear Linhare slipped out of the Vale without you. Quite a feat."

"I caught up to her quick enough."

"Did you not anticipate—"

"It won't happen again."

"Oh, it will." Ellis laughed. "I know that girl as well as I know her mother. She will slip away more times than you'll be able to catch her. Remember my words, Cal."

Wait chose to ignore Ellis' sidelong glance, the uncomfortable implication. "She's safe, here or Dockside. I'm a formality, not a necessity. This is not the best time to be Dakhonne in Vales Gate."

"Is it not? I wonder." Ellis stopped walking to stand gazing not so much at Wait as over his shoulder. Then he blinked, and smiled, and said, "I've been meaning to talk to you about something, my friend. A notion I had quite a long time ago. Ben and I used to discuss it, when you were far too young to care about such matters. But—"

"But?" Wait prompted when Ellis let his words trail away.

Again the smile. When Ellis finally spoke, Wait could have predicted the words. "But I suppose now is not the right time. And I've things to attend to before I head to the mines. Give Linhare my best, will you?"

"Why not stay and tell her yourself?"

"I am unwelcome here. You know that as well as I do."

"He's king, nothing more. We all worry too much about what he has to say."

"You know it's not that simple. Come now, Cal. I will be here this evening for the private little dinner our beloved king has planned for Linhare. Now I must be off before he finishes his breakfast and decides the Mine Officer of Vales Gate is his personal assistant and sends me off to buy bread for the party."

Wait stood like a tree, watching Ellis flitter away like a bird. So much changed after Ben's death. He thought they would, after a time, change in Ellis' favor; but Diandra married Agreth—or rather: Sisolo, and Wait hadn't the patience for either politics or heartache.

Giggling handmaidens signaled Princess Sabal's exit from the breakfast room. Wait cloaked himself quickly and vanished before either she or the pretty king saw him.

Duty

"**H**AVE YOU SEEN MY FAN?" Linhare pulled things from her drawer, searching for the fan she had left on top of her vanity table before leaving her room that morning. "Jinna?"

"Hmmmm?"

Linhare straightened. "My fan. The one with the blue flowers. Have you seen it?"

"No."

"Do you even know what I'm saying?"

"No."

"For pity's sake!" Shoving her things back into the drawer, Linhare slammed it closed. "Help me!"

Groaning, Jinna pushed herself up and over to the wardrobe. Dark rings smudged her eyes, love bites she made no attempt to cover up dotted her neck; evidence of all the time she'd been spending with the Thissians since the night they watched them eat fire.

"What do you need a fan for anyway? It's an evening party."

"It's not just the fan," Linhare told her. "I can't find the blue silk wrap my father brought back from Leftfoot or the book of Therkian poetry I borrowed from the university library, either."

Jinna's eyebrows raised. "You mean the book you *stole* from the university library. Unless, of course, you plan on going back up the mountain to return it."

Linhare tossed an underslip at her. Jinna laughed her snorty laugh while she rooted through a drawer. "Strange things are afoot in this household. Chira mentioned that she couldn't find that lovely pearl brooch of your mother's. And silver's gone missing from the pantry. We have a sneak-thief in the castle."

"Who would steal from us?" Linhare asked. "Our servants are too loyal."

"How should I know?" Jinna glanced at the clock. She stood up, hands on her hips. "You, my dear, are stalling. If you don't get moving you'll be late for your own party."

Linhare's shoulders slumped. "It's not a party for *me*. If it were a party for me, you and your mother would be attending."

"Wouldn't that be awful?" Jinna asked. "Agreth and my mother in the same room?"

"I wish you would change your mind."

"No chance." Jinna held up her hands. "I don't go where I am not wanted. Besides, my Thissian will be waiting for me. He is leaving for Lower Greenwood tomorrow."

"He has a name."

"I prefer to call him *my Thissian*. That sounds so erotic, doesn't it?"

"Everything sounds erotic to you."

"True." Jinna laughed. "After the Greenwood, he is off to the harlotries around Whilstley. I love Whilstley."

"Islets, Jinna." Linhare swatted her. "They are islets, not harlotries."

"Oh, well pardon me. I'd forgotten you are an educated woman now. We peasants still call them harlotries. If the nobility would stop gifting them to their spoiled children and privileged cronies like overused concubines maybe they'd earn a less vulgar name."

Linhare grimaced. She'd heard much the same thing in university when no one thought she was listening. "Giving Larguessi the power to reassign title of an islet is one of the provisions my father had to make when—"

"Linhare? Everyone is waiting." Sabal peeked around the door. Turning to the sweet and husky voice, Linhare could not dismiss the look of disdain creasing her sister's brow as her glance passed over Jinna; or Jinna's mimicked response. "Are you ready?"

"Almost." Linhare turned back to Jinna. "Are you sure you won't come to the party? Please?"

"She isn't attending the party?" Sabal cooed. "Oh, what a pity."

"If it means that much to you, Sabal, darling, I'm sure Linny has a gown I could squeeze myself into."

"Oh, don't change your plans on my account. Besides, I doubt there is enough powder in this whole castle to cover up those things on your neck."

"Sabal. Jinna. Please."

Sabal took her arm, giggling like a little girl. "You know how Jinna and I tease. I didn't mean to upset you."

"I'm not upset."

"And neither am I," Jinna said, but she looked at Sabal when she said it. Then she took Linhare's free hand and squeezed it fondly. "This isn't my sort of party, Linny. You know that. So, I'm going to take a nap on your bed and then I'm off Dockside."

Sabal tugged on her arm. "You heard her, Linhare. Come on."

"Look for my things again before you go," Linhare said over her shoulder as her sister dragged her from the room. "To make up for being so absent a friend this past week."

Whatever Jinna's response, Linhare did not hear it through the door Sabal shoved closed.

*　　*　　*

SABAL'S VOICE TWITTERED DOWN THE CORRIDOR. Jinna grimaced. Pesty as a child, Sabal had been annoying but tolerable. As she grew up and into her role as second born to the Queen of Vales Gate, Sabal became completely insufferable. The mild teasing Jinna used to consider an amusing if slightly mean-spirited pastime became all-out war. Sabal hated her, and Jinna hated her back.

"You don't hate her," Jinna's mother told her one rainy afternoon before Linhare's return. "You two are simply too alike to get along."

"I'm nothing like her. Sabal is a mean little cunny and I can't stand the sight of her anymore."

Yebbe said nothing after that, only pressed her lips into a thin, disapproving line.

Going to Linhare's wardrobe, Jinna opened the door peevishly. *Damn Sabal. And Damn Agreth, too.* But they would not keep her from Linhare the way they kept Yebbe from Diandra. If absenting herself from a party or two was the cost, so be it.

Flicking through the pinks and blues and yellows of Linhare's summer wardrobe, Jinna grimaced. Six years away from the Vale had done nothing for her dearest friend's sense of style. She was almost glad Linhare could not find that tired old blue wrap; and fans had gone out of fashion ages ago. Still, Ti-Ben gave Linhare the wrap. Jinna felt obligated to try and find it for her.

Rummaging through the chest of drawers beside Linhare's bed, Jinna found little more than smallclothes, and keepsakes from childhood. Stuffing everything back in, Jinna felt something hard. Something squareish. Reaching into the jumble, she pulled out a book.

Jinna's face flushed instantly. How long since she'd held that scarred, red thing in her hand? Linhare used to carry it around like a talisman. Close and secret. Thoughts she would not, could not, share with Jinna; or so Jinna had believed.

Pushing it back into the drawer, Jinna took the time to fold the other things in there and place them neatly. She pushed the drawer in; the click of the charm she wore around her wrist bumped against wood. Sitting on the edge of the bed, Jinna held it up to watch it twirl.

"It is the only thing I have that is truly mine and mine alone," her Thissian had said. Long black-silk hair passionately disheveled, his eyes bright and his cheeks glistening sweat, he'd taken the little charm from around his neck and wrapped the cord around her wrist. "I want you to have it, Jinna. I want you to remember me when I'm gone."

"Where are you going?"

"The Greenwood, first. Then Whilstley. Unless, of course, you wish to come with me."

31

Bright eyes softened then and Jinna saw it as clearly as if he had spoken the words. *I love you,* they said. *Come with me. Never, ever leave me.*

Jinna pressed the charm against her lips; a simple oval with raised letters that read, *Egh Ahl Fo.* She did not know what the words, if they were words, meant. Neither did he, or so he told her. It was his name, and perhaps nothing more than that.

Pushing off the bed, Jinna left Linhare's room. Her Thissian was waiting in the Vulgar Raven. She promised him an answer before his evening's performance, and she was still not certain what she was going to say.

"IS THAT WISE?" Sabal asked the moment they were on the other side of the closed door.

"Is what wise?"

"You are missing things from your room and you leave Jinna alone in there?"

Linhare sighed heavily. Sabal was shorter by several inches and slight as a bird; she took two steps for every one of Linhare's.

"I've probably just not unpacked them yet."

"This is why you need attendants." Sabal caught her arm, slowing her down. "You are to be queen. Your things should have been unpacked *for you* within an hour of your homecoming."

"I am used to doing things on my own."

"Another reason not to go to university." Sabal sighed dramatically. "Honestly, Linhare. I just do not understand you. Mother says you are just like our father."

"Good," Linhare told her. "He was a great man."

"I suppose I don't remember. I shall take your word for it."

"You don't have to take my word for it; his deeds are recorded if you would only—"

"If I would only open a history book and you would allow attendants all the problems in the world would vanish." Sabal laughed. "Oh, Linhare, it is good to have you home."

Linhare squeezed her sister's arm affectionately. "It's good to be home. I wish my homecoming was to be celebrated a bit more privately, though."

"Whatever for, you silly, ungrateful thing? Mother and Father went to great lengths to arrange this party for you."

Linhare stiffened. Sabal had been calling Agreth *Father* since the first time she met him, on the day he wed their mother. It had not gotten any easier to hear in the years since.

"I suppose I have never really enjoyed the more courtly things the way you have."

"I suppose they don't teach you that in Vernist-on-Contif, either. But you're home now. Mother and I will teach you. Father, too, is quite skilled in the courtly graces. We'll have you polished in no time."

As they approached the arches leading outside, Linhare took a deep breath in a small and futile attempt to ease the sudden pounding of her heart. The sun setting beyond Mount Tuscia perfectly lit the terrace; the tall, standing candles more resembled slender and spectral guests. Flower garlands lined the low walls overlooking a profuse garden. The table was laid in white linen and Therkian glass. Her mother, stepfather and several local notables, some of whom Linhare recognized, most of whom she did not, chatted on, unaware that the guest of honor had arrived. There was only one person who noticed, and he did not move from his place behind the queen.

"I'll leave you here," Sabal said, kissing her sister's cheek. "You must make a grand entrance. And I must claim a seat beside that scandalous actress Mother and Father invited to please me."

"No, no. Sabal, I don't want—" But Sabal scurried out onto the terrace. Linhare listened to the whispering, her heart pounding in her ears. These people gathered not to welcome a young woman home from university; they gathered to assess their future queen. Slipping into the safety of shadows behind the arch, Linhare leaned against it and closed her eyes.

"Linhare, my dear. Is something wrong?"

Agreth's voice soothed and unsettled her. She grimaced. It was not his fault her father died. It was not even his fault he married her mother. The Vale had to marry Sisolo. It was as simple as that. Yet when he touched her arm, it was difficult not to yank it away from him.

"No, sir. Nothing is wrong. I'm just a bit nervous, I suppose."

"There is nothing to be nervous about," he said. "We are your family and friends, wishing to give you a proper welcome home."

They are not my friends. They are yours. But Linhare smiled, biting her lip when it trembled. Agreth put a finger under her chin, tilting her face up. "You have grown up so much, my dear." His finger moved back and forth along her jaw. "Grown so beautiful."

She tried to laugh. "Sabal is the beauty."

"Sabal's beauty is obvious. Yours is more eloquent. Do not underestimate yourself. Now then, are you feeling ready to be greeted by your guests?"

Agreth took a step back and offered her his arm. His warm smile reached his green eyes. He was handsome and dashing, and for her life Linhare could find no reason for the way her skin crawled. Taking her stepfather's arm, she did her best to smile sincerely.

"Yes, sir. I'm ready."

"Sir?" He sighed. "It has been several years, Linhare. Will you never call me *Father*?"

His charming smile strained. It was not an unreasonable request; and not the first time he requested it. Linhare opened her mouth to speak the words he wished to hear.

"Forgive me," she said instead, her voice trembling. "I cannot think of you as my father."

No anger. No frustration. Agreth's soft laughter took her by surprise. He took the hand resting upon his arm and brought it to his lips.

"Darling Linhare," he whispered against her fingers. "Then you must call me Agreth."

Invisible

WAIT KEPT TO HIS PLACE behind the queen, trying to forget that Ben would never have suffered him standing while he and his guests ate and drank. In this court, no one addressed him. He was invisible, and not because of any Dakhan abilities, common or uncanny. Aside from Diandra's apologetic glances, only Linhare and Sabal acknowledged his presence, which suited him fine. He would rather stand like a serving man behind his queen than endure the arrogant banter of Agreth and his cronies.

Near midnight, the party wound to a close and Wait breathed a sigh of relief. He was not tired, only bored. At least Linhare's first step into queenhood was a success. Gracious and genial, she won over Agreth's hand-selected gathering. As unassuming as Sabal was pretentious, Linhare, he was certain, unaware of her success.

"Sabal," Diandra, whose pallor had gone from ethereal white to ghastly grey, called to her younger daughter. "Would you be so kind as to take my place, escorting our guests out? I'm afraid I've overdone it this evening."

"Gladly, mother." Sabal stood taller, her glance passing haughtily over her sister before turning back to the scandalous actress she had fawned over all evening.

Agreth stood over his wife, put a gentle hand upon her shoulder. "Are you feeling unwell, my dear?"

"I tire far too easily." She placed a hand upon her belly. "Do you mind Sabal standing in for me?"

"Surely it would be more appropriate for Linhare to do the honors."

"Perhaps. But I'm afraid Sabal's enthusiasm over the mad success of her evening will send me raving. I would be much better off with Linhare seeing me to my rooms. You will save me, will you not, Agreth?"

Behind his stony expression, Wait grinned. How many times had she used the same theatrical distress ploy with Ben? Only with him, the words were cooed and she called him *darling*.

Agreth chuckled softly. "I shall endure her chatter as I always do, my dear." He straightened and called to Linhare. She placed a small hand on the Larguesse from Quary's forearm, leaned in close to say something that made him laugh before bowing his leave. Linhare did not seem to notice the admiration in the Larguesse's eyes.

"Yes, Agreth?"

Wait stiffened. When did he go from *sir* to *Agreth*?

"Would you escort your mother to her rooms?" he asked. "Sabal and I will see our guests out."

Linhare's smile melted as she hurried to Diandra's side. "Are you all right, Mother? What is it? What hurts?"

"Nothing, sweetling," Diandra told her. "I am fine. Just tired. I am unaccustomed to staying up so late these days."

"And listening to your sister ramble might send her raving," Agreth added, gesturing to Sabal, who now had the actress by the arm. "A fate my stronger constitution will save me from. Do you mind, Linhare?"

"Of course not."

Agreth kissed his wife's upturned cheek and left them. As grateful as he was being spared the exchanging of pleasantries with the man, Wait was nonetheless irritated when the king walked away without even a nod in his direction.

Once all the guests paid their respects to the queen and to Linhare, Agreth and Sabal led them from the terrace. Some, like Larguesse Lorre, would stay in the castle, while others, like the actress, would be put in carriages and taken back to Upper Dockside or Littlevale or Sheridan. Wait had a list of those remaining and those leaving; not that it mattered. Nothing resembling intrigue happened in the Vale since Diandra took her throne.

"Goodness, that was a long evening," Diandra leaned back in her chair. "Did you enjoy yourself, Linhare?"

"I did, truly."

"Was she not magnificent, Wait?"

Hearing his name startled him, but Wait moved to stand on the other side of the queen. "She was."

Linhare lowered her gaze, her blush spreading from cheeks to throat, and across bared shoulders. When Linhare looked up at him through the dark fringe of her lashes, Wait clenched his jaw tight lest his mouth fall open.

"Ah, you are still here!"

Wait's attention turned to the arches, and Ellis hurrying through them. Diandra's pale face pinked slightly. Linhare flew to his open arms. "Where have you been? Mother told me you would be here."

"The life of Vales Gate's Mine Officer is a busy one, as your mother can attest to. I have missed more parties than I have attended over the years. Forgive me, Linhare. You know I would have been here if I could have been. But I am here now, if only to say a belated welcome home to you. And to pay my respects to our lovely queen, of course."

"Always so charming." Diandra laughed softly. "Please, sit, Ellis. I can manage to stay awake a few moments longer."

"You don't look well, Di." Ellis took his queen's hand across the table. Wait dropped into another chair without having to be asked.

"This pregnancy is taking its toll." She smiled wanly. "But I am near the end. Seeing you makes me feel much better."

Linhare did not seem to notice the tender glance between her mother and Ellis; nor did she notice the intimate caressing of his hand covering hers. Or perhaps, Wait thought, it was only his own skewed perception. The past was impossible to forget.

"You know that if ever you need me," Ellis said, "send for me and I will come no matter what turmoil or chaos I am in."

"Of course I know that, Ellis. Of course."

Diandra paled by the moment, but neither she nor Ellis showed any signs of parting. They chatted about nothing, and Wait joined them. It felt good, like times long past and terribly missed; until the queen pressed her hands to the table, pushing herself wearily to her feet.

"I hate to say it, but I must get to bed."

"Let me help you." Linhare offered her arm. Diandra took it, leaning heavily upon her daughter, moving with the laborious slowness of a turtle on the sand. She rested a hand on Wait's arm. "If you would be so kind, I would like for you to escort Linhare and me to Yebbe Forestwife tomorrow afternoon. Seeing Ellis reminds me that I have not seen her in a very long time, either."

"Of course. I will see to the carriage."

"Good night, gentlemen."

Once the queen and princess left, the men sat as if by some prearranged agreement, heads bent over the table.

"I worry for her," Ellis said. "She is beautiful and spirited and brilliant beyond all the stars and starlight but Diandra is no longer young. She nearly died giving birth to Sabal. This child could well kill her."

Wait again suppressed that ingrained urge to kiss his fingertips and touch them to his heart. "Yebbe will attend her. She saved her in the birthing room once. She will do so again."

"If Agreth allows her into the castle." Ellis grunted. "I was here the day he threw her out, Cal. Diandra will never bring her back here again."

Wait shook his head. He was out on Sentry Rock, initiating a graduating class of Dakhanna and Dakhonne, the day King Agreth had the queen's oldest and dearest friend escorted from the castle; but he remembered how Diandra wept.

"I know she endures too much for this alliance," Wait said. "But once this baby is born—"

"—if it is born."

"Stop saying that."

"She asked you to bring her to Yebbe for a reason. She is frightened."

37

Wait took several deep breaths. "I know that," he said at last. "I'm not a fool."

"No, you are not." Ellis exhaled long, pushing fingers through hair still dark and thick. "Forgive me, my friend. Diandra is not the only one frightened. We lost Ben. The thought of losing Diandra is unbearable."

Wait could not force words past the thickening in his throat. When Ellis pushed away from the table, it was an automatic response to do the same.

"And I've not forgotten about that notion I want to discuss with you," Ellis said. "Only lacked the time."

"As you have said. I'm here, now. What is it?"

"This is not the place, and perhaps it would be a good thing to include Linhare in the discussion."

"Linhare? Not Diandra?"

Ellis reached up to clap him on the back. "It must be soon," he said, and left Wait alone on the terrace. The scullions hovered in the shadows, waiting for him to leave so they could clean. From those shadows, they heard everything, they watched everything, and then added decorative bits and pieces of their own to create the royal gossip that would soon be whispered from Lower Dockside to Esher. It was a commodity as priceless as sheridans ore, and traded with all the delicacy of Therkian merchants after too long a journey. Ellis was wise not to speak.

Taking a bunch of grapes from the tray of uneaten fruit on the table, Wait left them to their task. Whatever stories they told, he was fairly certain he was no longer part of them. He was one of them now, and just as invisible.

Conflicts

L INHARE REMEMBERED THE GARDEN POOL being bigger, and she certainly did not recall so many bugs dancing atop the water like tiny bolleys; but it was bliss to recline in the cool water, only her eyes and nose above the surface. She could listen to Jinna and Sabal squabble as if they were far away rather than in the water beside her. In the weeks since the welcome home party her sister had yet to stop chattering about, Linhare endured more than enough of their constant bickering. Floating, free, she dozed and dreamed of cool autumn, when the Vale became brilliant and momentary gold before hushing into bare and faded winter.

"Linhare. Linhare!"

Sabal's voice shattered the golden peace. Opening her eyes, Linhare startled to find her sister's face only inches from her own.

"For goodness sake, Sabal! Don't hover so."

Naked and pink, blonde hair darker for being wet, she was a nymph risen from the depths. "Will you tell Jinna that I really can perform magic? She won't believe me."

Linhare avoided her sister's eyes, glaring instead at Jinna, who smirked.

"I have seen her do quite a few tricks."

"Tricks? Tricks! Oh, Linhare! How could you?"

"Darling, don't be upset. I chose the wrong word. Jinna, stop teasing my sister."

"I'm not teasing her. I'm stating fact. If one is not born with the innate talent, one cannot become a sorceress. There has not been a true magic wielder in Vales Gate in centuries."

"You sound like one of those Purists on the mountain." Sabal crossed her arms over her small breasts and turned her back. "I have many words for you, Jinna, but I would never have thought of you as small-minded."

"Ladies, please," Linhare tried, but Jinna only talked over her.

"A sleight of hand is not true magic any more than a harlotry is an isle."

"Leave it to you to be so vulgar. And the Purists wield magic, as do the Sisters of Rhob."

"That's different. You're not talking about either form of magic. You think you're going to be able to rise mountains and split the sea."

"You have no idea what I can—"

"Enough!" Linhare leapt out of the pool and into the sheet being held out to her. Wrapping up in it, Linhare moved into a patch of sunshine and away from the hissed bickering behind her. She pulled her legs up to her chest, twisting the water from her hair. Jinna dropped down onto the rock beside her.

"Please, Jinna. No more fighting."

"I'm not fighting with *you.*" Jinna twirled a wet curl around her finger, her eyes flickering back and again to Sabal watching them both carefully. Jinna pretended to stretch. The love bites that had multiplied were fading now; just yellow bruises against the fairness of her skin. As if feeling Linhare's eyes on them, Jinna rubbed a hand along the curve of her throat and sighed.

"There is something I need to tell you."

"You're pregnant!" Linhare burst.

"Stars and starlight forbid!" Jinna groaned. "Why would you think that?"

Linhare shrugged, quelled the urge to glance at those love bites. "It is about Egalfo though, isn't it? Pardon me, *your Thissian?* Do you miss him terribly?"

Jinna let her damp hair fall in her face. "I miss him more than I imagined I could. I think I might be a little stuck on this one."

"Really?"

"He asked me to go with him."

"He did? What did you say?"

Jinna looked up at her, those infinite blue eyes close to tearing. "I'm here, aren't I?"

Linhare's skin prickled. "Oh, sweetling."

Jinna scowled. "For goodness sake, I could never love a man half as much as I love you. You should know that by now."

"But Jinna—"

"He is a man and those are ferociously easy to come by." Jinna laughed a little too vigorously and the snort so much a part of the sound came out as a snarl. "Where else would I ever find another *Linhare?* Though, I will admit, he was beautifully hung. That may take some searching to replace."

"Stars and starlight!" Sabal stood behind them, her face aghast. Linhare blushed like a little girl caught with her fingers in the honey, but Jinna howled like a wild dog in the Greenwood.

"If I could bottle your righteousness and sell it to the clerics out on Valishul I would be the wealthiest woman in the archipelago!"

"You would do well to take example of them. Chastity is not an offense."

"It's offensive to *me.*"

Sabal stomped her foot and turned to her sister. "Honestly, Linhare! I don't see what you find so appealing about keeping company with a harlot who spreads her legs like a bitch in heat!"

"Sabal!" Linhare gasped. "That is enough!"

Jinna rose to her feet, poised despite, or because of, her nudity, hands moving languidly along her curves. "Why would I deny myself the power I have between my legs or the pleasure it gives me? A woman's body is a mystery. The things it does. The secrets it holds. Some men spend their lives trying to discover those secrets." She moved closer to Sabal, whispering. "I like letting them try. But that is something you will only understand once you have a man throbbing inside of you." Closer. Softer. "When he is hunting for that release he can find only in the depths of you. You will feel that power, and then you will understand, *sweetling*. I don't expect you to now. You are just a little girl who still believes that nubbing is only for making babies."

Sabal's face paled but for two splotches of color in her cheeks. Jinna tilted her head to one side, smiling like an indulgent nurse. "So I will forgive you for trying to hurt me. And to show you I bear no ill will, I will educate you on one more point. A bitch doesn't spread her legs. She gets it from behind. Learn to use correct analogies before you start spouting."

"Oh!" Sabal flushed from cheeks to breasts. "You will pay for this! I am going to tell my father what you have said to me!"

Her stomping feet made slapping sounds on the wet rocks. Jinna shouted after her. "He is not your natural father! Remember that before you say anything that might arouse him!"

Linhare watched Jinna pick up a bath sheet and wrap it around her body. Her movements were composed but her hands shook just a little bit.

"I'm sorry, Jinna. Sabal is—"

"—a little girl who doesn't know the first thing about anything. Don't concern yourself about it, darling. She can't hurt me."

But my stepfather can. He banished your mother from this household. He can banish you, too.

Saying the words aloud was too much like prophecy. Instead, Linhare said, "You are right about Sabal being very innocent."

"In some ways. Be careful where she is concerned, Linny. I know she is your sister and you love her but—"

"But?"

Jinna used the sheet to rub at her hair. "I almost don't want to tell you now. It will look like I'm just trying to get back at her for what she said."

"Tell me what?"

"I did say I have something to tell you. You're the one who nudged me off my rope with asking if it was—"

"Oh, for goodness sake! Just tell me!"

Jinna wrapped the sheet more securely about her body, tucking it in with great care before she picked up her head again to say, "I caught Sabal slipping out of your room this morning. She had that little red book you're always carrying around."

"My book?"

Jinna nodded. "I asked her why she was in your room and what she was doing with your book, but she said you told her she could borrow it and—Linhare? Linny!"

Linhare was already running, Jinna on her heels. Servants looked askance but Linhare did not slow her pace. She was too frantic to care what they were thinking about two young women racing through the castle wearing only bath sheets clutched to their bodies.

She reached her chambers and yanked open the door. Sunlight slanted through the windows, illuminating a perfectly ordered room. Some frenzied part of her mind expected it to be in shambles.

Linhare searched, calmly at first. But the book was not in the drawer beside her bed, beneath years and years of essays she wrote as a child; or in her wardrobe beneath winter woolens; or in the trunk at the foot of her bed, under her mattress, hidden within the stacks of books on the shelf in her study, or any of the other places she had taken to hiding it over the years.

"It's not here. It's not here!"

"I'm sure she has it in her room." Jinna pulled a dress on over her head. "She must still be in there dressing."

"Damn! Damn! Damn!" Linhare spun in frantic circles. Her book. Wait's journal. If Sabal had it, if she read it—

Jinna grabbed her arms, steadied her. "Put some clothes on," she said. "I'll watch the door to make sure she doesn't leave. Don't worry. We'll get it back."

Linhare buttoned her dress with wooden fingers. She kept this secret for so long. Too long. All those years, knowing who the book and its secrets belonged to, and she kept it to herself. Kept it from him. Now it could well be too late to do what was right. Sabal would not stop at those words that Wait wrote when he was made a man too soon. She would continue on to Larguessa Violet's severed head and learn those things Linhare was too decent, or too frightened, to learn herself. Once she took it back, she would give it to Wait. She would not even read the rest before doing so. It would be as if she had done the right thing from the beginning.

Linhare swiped away useless tears. She went out into the hall where Jinna stood watch and knocked on her sister's door.

"Go away!"

"Sabal, it's Linhare. Open the door, will you?"

"Is Jinna with you?"

"She wants her book back," Jinna shouted. "The one you stole from her room this morning."

"I don't know what you are talking about!" But on the other side of the door, Linhare could hear sounds like drawers opening and closing. And then a loud *whump*.

"Please, darling!" Linhare shouted. "I'm not angry. I just want it back."

The door swung open. Sabal's face scrunched in disgust but her eyes darted from Jinna to Linhare and back again. "I would never suspect you would take her word over mine. I am your *sister*."

"How do you know she's done anything of the kind?" Jinna snapped. "You've given yourself away, Sabal. Just give the book back."

"I have no idea what she is talking about, Linhare. I would never take anything from you without asking."

"Then what was all the bumping going on in here." Jinna pushed past Sabal and into her room. "What's in the trunk? I heard it *whump* closed. I'm certain of it."

Sabal's submissive stance changed. Her shoulders went back. Her chin rose higher. And though the splotches of angry red on her cheeks did not fade, they changed as well.

"Nothing," she said. "It's empty. Look for yourself."

Jinna stepped aside, gesturing to Linhare. The trunk was massive; large enough to fit all three of them inside with ease. Many years and countless hands made the wood glossy. Silver fittings and hinges, it was nonetheless too plain. Masculine. An antique; or made to look like one. There was a lock but it appeared to have been pried open sometime in the past and broken beyond repair.

Sabal reached around her and threw open the lid. "There! See, I told you it's empty. I only just got it in that curious little antiquities shop in Upper Dockside. Mother and Father bought it for me the day they took me to see the play."

Jinna stepped around Linhare to look for herself. She chuffed like a horse with dust in its nose. "So it's not in the trunk. I know you have it."

Jinna started on the drawers, opening and closing them again. Every bang hit Linhare in the stomach, but her eyes did not leave the empty trunk.

"Search all you like," Sabal sang. "I don't care. Just be sure to put everything back where you got it. If anything is missing, I'll know who took it!"

Something was not right. Sabal too calmly, so happily looped her arm through Linhare's to tug her from the room. "I don't know what that lunatic is talking about," she said. "But let her search. I've nothing to hide. You know I would never take anything of yours. You are my sister."

"But," Linhare swallowed hard. "But Jinna would not lie to me."

"Of course she would. She lies constantly but you simply will not— oh, dear me."

"Dear you?"

Sabal laughed, tilting her head back so that her sweet, husky voice lifted to the high ceilings. "Oh, dear, *dear* me! Well, you can hardly blame me. I suppose there is a first for everything."

Linhare pulled her arm from her sister's. "What are you talking about, Sabal? Tell me this instant!"

"I know what this is all about."

"You do?"

"Red riding gloves."

Linhare grimaced. "Pardon?"

"Those red riding gloves of yours. Do you remember when you first came home and I asked to borrow them?"

Linhare did not remember. But she did have a pair of red riding gloves. It was possible that in all her endless rambling, Sabal had asked after the gloves. "Vaguely."

"I did take those from your room this morning. Perhaps Jinna simply mistook what I held in my hands."

A lie. Linhare knew that it was. And though she said, "Oh, that explains it," the words were sifted flour in her mouth.

Linhare started to go back, to do what, she did not know; but Sabal grabbed her arm and pulled her forward. "She won't be satisfied until she's checked every crack and cranny in my chambers. Why don't you and I nip down to the kitchens and see if we can coax something sweet from—"

"Linhare! Sabal! Oh, my girls, come quickly!"

Apron waving, Chira shouted from the far end of the hall. Both princesses froze. Jinna burst into the hallway. The journal, their argument, lies and fears and loyalties scattered. As one, they flew down the hall to meet Diandra's maid. Cheeks flushed, face streaked with sweat and tears, Chira leaned against the wall to catch her breath.

"What is it?" Linhare was first to reach her. "What's wrong?"

"It's the queen. The babe's coming. She's calling for you both."

"Isn't it too soon?" Sabal's voice trembled like pine needles on a fire. "Isn't it?"

Chira said nothing. Linhare reached for the older woman's hand but was not reassured by the answering squeeze.

"I'll fetch mother," Jinna said and was gone before Linhare could respond.

Dread

THE MAN WAS NOT HEARTLESS; Wait couldn't deny the pretty king's earnest worry, or the way his face paled and his hands clenched each time his wife's weak moans reached him through the closed door. For that glimmer of humanity, Wait did not toss him out the nearest window when Yebbe appeared in the corridor.

"Get her out! Do not dare let that woods-witch near my wife and child!"

Wait stepped forward when the other guards moved to seize her and they immediately stepped back. It took great control, but he managed not to smirk.

"We will ask the queen's wishes," he said, and knocked on the door. Yebbe came to stand at his elbow, giving Agreth wide berth. When the door opened, the forestwife pushed through and shooed the princesses from their mother's side. Lifting the sheet, she reached her hand up between the queen's legs.

"I forbid this!" Agreth shrieked, but Wait barred his way. In the corner, Linhare held her weeping sister, crooned softly. Jinna was strangely absent.

"It is too late to stop the birth." Yebbe spoke only to Diandra. "Your baby will be born today."

Diandra nodded. Chira pressed a wet cloth to the queen's forehead, as if that could somehow revive a body exhausted long before labor began.

"You have been forbidden from this house!" Agreth called from beyond the wall of Wait. "I'll not have this. Do you hear me! And you." Something like a poke jabbed between his shoulder blades. "You will be dismissed for this defiance!"

Wait kept his back to the king. "My queen, what is your wish?"

Pale beyond pallor, weak beyond death, the queen's head lolled to one side, her eyes only slivers of blue. "Please, Agreth," was all she said.

He could not see it, but Wait sensed the fight go out of the man like a shifting in the air just after a storm. Wait let his arm fall.

"All right," Agreth's voice quavered with that humanness Wait could not quite disregard. "All right, Diandra."

The queen held her hand out to him, and now that Wait no longer barred his way, the king slipped easily past. He took her hand and brought it to his lips.

"I am frightened, my dear."

"Yebbe is here. I am in good hands. And so is our baby."

"Woods-witchery is not true medicine."

"Yebbe delivered Linhare. She saved my life and Sabal's. There is not a physician in all the archipelago I would trust more than I do her."

"Then I will trust you," he said, and kissed her hand again.

Diandra's eyes squeezed shut. Her mouth opened but no sound came.

"All of you. Out." Yebbe shooed them; but to Agreth she spoke without quite looking his way. "I will call you in before your child is born. Until then, Diandra has a difficult task and she does not need to worry about how you are faring."

"Their lives are in your hands, forestwife." Agreth's voice quavered. "I hope you understand the full extent of that responsibility."

Diandra's wail of agony found its way past her vocal chords in that moment, and whatever response Yebbe had for Agreth was lost.

"Breathe, sweetling," Wait heard her say as he escorted the king from the birthing chamber. "Try to breathe. It is not time to push yet."

Turning back to assist the princesses, Wait found Linhare already guiding her weeping sister from the corner. He stood where he was, holding the door, watching them, watching Diandra labor in the bed. Linhare bent to kiss her mother's cheek, prompting Sabal to do the same. Then she led her sister away, whispering words that made the younger woman sniff and sputter but smile all the same. Again Wait was struck by how like her father she was. But in this light, in the way she moved and carried herself, she was Diandra.

The best of both, his own voice told him, and Wait felt the corners of his lips curling into a smile as she came nearer. Stepping away from the door she brushed against him as she moved past.

"Mother asks a word," she said, then turned her attention back to her sister. Wait rubbed a hand over the place where she had brushed against him but the tingling sensation lingered. He moved back into the room to stand at the foot of the queen's bed.

"Why did you not call for me sooner?" Yebbe hovered like a bee. "You promised, Diandra. You promised you would send for me the moment the pains started."

"It is so soon," the queen said. "I did not think it was true labor. I could not summon you here until it was necessary, not with the way Agreth feels."

"I will keep my tongue because he is your husband and this child is his."

"You are a good friend."

Wait shifted from foot to foot. "You asked to speak with me, my queen?"

Diandra held out her hand; he took it and knelt beside her. She was not much older than he, but looking at her then, Wait saw death's grey, papery shroud already claiming her face.

"I know a birthing chamber is not a place for a Dakhonne," she said, "so I will make this brief."

"My place is beside my queen, wherever that is."

"Of course," she said, and the small and weary smile brightened enough to chase the papery grey back to the corners of her eyes. "Ben loved you like a son, you know."

"I do."

"You have always been more than queensguard to this family. And now I ask you to continue that role for Linhare. She will need you more than I ever have. You and Bennis won the peace in which I have ruled. I fear for her, when I am gone. This peace is a delicate thing. Maintaining it can be dangerous for her. And heartbreaking."

"Nothing will harm her as long as I am alive," he said. "But you are not—"

"Let us not quibble over what will or will not be. I have not given up, but it will ease my mind to hear your promise. Please, Wait. Promise me."

"You never had to ask to begin with. I swear it upon my sword, upon my honor and upon the life debt that will be mine until the end of days, that I will protect Linhare."

Sealing his vow with a kiss, Wait trembled to feel how cold her cheek was. The hand in his moved to his touch his face. For how cold her cheek was, her fingers were icier still.

"If ever you choose to follow your heart," she told him, "alliances be damned, you have my sincere blessing and my deepest gratitude. I mean that, Wait. Truly and with all I am."

The queen's hand fell away and her head turned as pain ripped through her. Yebbe touched his shoulder and Wait rose to his feet. He closed the door behind him, closed off the sounds of birth and death and pain and being. In his head, brought forth by memories rattling at their chains, Wait heard other voices, other cries. He smelled the blood. When he looked down at his hands, he could see it.

"Wait? Are you all right?"

Only his eyes moved to find Linhare at his elbow, her tiny hand on his arm, her soft eyes gazing up at him.

If ever you choose to follow your heart—

Wait's hands fell to his sides. His shoulders straightened.

If ever you choose to follow your heart—

She asked again, "Are you all right?"

"Yes."

She did not believe him; he could see it in those soft eyes that undid him, in the way she pursed her lips. Sabal was still weeping. Agreth pacing. Her worries were enough. Taking his place at the door, he stood guard as if he could bar death as efficiently as he had barred the king.

AFTERNOON BECAME EVENING, BECAME NIGHT. Linhare paced outside the birthing chamber. She dozed on the couch that the servants hauled from one of the other rooms and set in the hallway. She ate the food brought up from the kitchens. She would not leave.

Somewhere near midnight, Sabal was taken to her own chambers. Weeping had exhausted her beyond waking when she was lifted and carried away. Agreth came and he went, never gone long, but often. He could not, it seemed, bear the sounds coming from that room any longer.

Only Wait stayed with her. Only Yebbe with Diandra. Even Chira, though she was forcibly taken, finally relented to slumber in a nearby chamber.

"I haven't heard anything in a long time," Linhare said aloud when the silence became unbearable. "What do you think that means?"

"I don't know."

As the words left Wait's lips, the door to the birthing room opened.

"Where is Agreth?"

"Walking." Linhare feared the grim abruptness in Yebbe's voice.

"Wait, fetch him. Now. Linhare, come with me."

On his feet before she could gain hers, Wait offered his assistance. Weary as she was, Linhare accepted it gratefully. Wait did not let her go.

"Hurry," Yebbe waved her inside. "Hurry, Linhare."

"Be brave," Wait said, squeezed both hands, and sprinted off.

Head bowed and frightened, Linhare followed Yebbe to her mother's side.

"Oh, Mother," she whispered. There was no Queen Diandra left, only an animated corpse; even the blue of her eyes had dulled to slate. "Hush, sweetling. It will be all right. Please don't cry. Our time together is short."

"You can't die. The baby—"

"We cannot both survive," she said. "I have known this for some time. But I tried, Linhare. I tried."

Linhare's body went cold. Drawing a deep breath, she sat on the edge of the bed. She took her mother into her arms, just as her mother always held her. Words would not come, only hushing sounds that did nothing but make noise. Diandra raised her eyes to Yebbe. "Is he here yet?"

"Wait went to fetch him."

"I do not know how much longer I can endure."

"He will come. He will be here."

"Not soon enough." Diandra's voice was so soft, almost serene. Resigned. Her head lolled towards her daughter. "Listen to me, Linhare. Agreth is this child's father, but I am his mother. He is a son of the Vale *and* of Sisolo. Make sure that he always knows that. He will keep the peace. He will keep you and Sabal safe."

"Hush, mother. Don't fret. He will know. I promise. We will all keep one another safe."

Diandra trembled. Her eyes fluttered and closed. She whispered, "Guide Sabal, Linhare. She is a good girl at heart. Tell her that I love her. Tell Agreth—tell him good-bye for me. And Ellis—" Her eyes opened. There were tears there that turned dead slate back to blue gems. "Ellis," she said, the final sound drawing out like a pebble thrown into a well. Linhare bent her head to her mother's. Yebbe placed two fingers to her throat.

"She is gone," Yebbe said. "There is no time to lose."

Linhare leapt off the bed when Yebbe yanked the sheet aside. She lifted the queen's shift and exposed her naked belly, prodding it gently but expertly with one hand. In the other, she held a sharp blade. Linhare threw herself across her mother's body.

"What are you doing?"

"Taking the baby. It is the only way, Linhare. Move aside. Hurry. There is not much time before the child dies, too."

Linhare slid off the bed. The body there was no longer her mother, but the child inside was still her brother.

"What can I do?"

Yebbe looked up from her prodding.

"Are you certain?"

Linhare nodded. Yebbe told her, "Put your hands here and here. Do you feel him?"

"I do."

"If you feel the baby shift, tell me immediately. Do you understand?"

Linhare nodded again. Yebbe raised the knife. She touched it to dead skin and sliced. Blood did not spurt, but there was blood. She cut deeper, through muscle, through the birth sac—

"You've killed her! You've killed her!"

Agreth flew across the room, bowling into Yebbe and knocking her to the floor. Wait was right behind him, pulling him off before he could strike her.

"Restrain him!" Yebbe shrieked. "Restrain him or the baby dies, too!"

"No!" Agreth strained against Wait's hold on him. "She has killed her! Don't let her kill my child! Please! Please do something! She is your mother! She is your queen!"

Yebbe scrabbled on the ground for the knife. Linhare's hands were still on her mother's bloody belly. She looked away when Yebbe plunged her hand into the gaping slash and felt for the child within. Raising the knife again, she made her final cut. She put both hands into the womb. The tiny being she drew forth was slick and bloody and blue. It did not move.

"It's a boy."

Yebbe stuck her fingers into his mouth. She scooped mucus from inside. She sucked it from his nostrils and spat it out. Still the infant did not move.

"Breathe, little one."

She flicked his tiny feet. She flicked them again.

"Breathe."

Linhare watched Yebbe work on the tiny baby boy, enticing him to breathe, rubbing his blue skin. No gasp of life. No cry. His tiny arms and legs did not jerk. Yebbe held him close to her chest, muttering soft words meant only for him. She kissed his gooey brow before wrapping him in a blanket and placing him in his mother's arms. She drew the sheet up over them both.

"You've killed him," Agreth rasped. "You killed my son."

"He was too small," Yebbe said calmly, but her whole body trembled. "It was too soon."

"You killed him!"

"I'd have sooner cut out my own heart!" Yebbe shrieked. "You wasted vital moments when he still had a chance! If anyone killed your son, it was you!"

"Seize her! Arrest her!"

"That will be enough."

Linhare did not have to raise her voice. A cool sort of serenity had taken over, a combination of exhaustion, grief and fidelity. She moved to her stepfather, gesturing for Wait to let him go.

"Agreth," she said. "I was here. Would I allow Yebbe to kill my mother or my brother?"

He choked on his own sobbing. "She's ensorcelled you."

Linhare took his hand. She brought him nearer so that he could rest his head upon her shoulder if he felt the need.

"She asked me to tell you good-bye. And to tell you," she swallowed hard, "that she loved you."

He raised his head. "Did she?"

Linhare nodded. The lie would not come out of her mouth a second time. "Ta-Yebbe did not take up her knife until after mother died. She tried to save the baby."

His eyes filled. "Did I—did I—?"

"Hush. No, you did not kill him. He was born too soon."

Agreth put his head onto her shoulder. Instinct put her arms about him, his around her. He wept. "A wife and a son in as many moments. I cannot bear it, Linhare. I cannot bear it."

Linhare soothed him as best as she could. Wet breath and warm tears were uncomfortable on her neck, as were his clutching arms and heaving torso. But she held him. She held him even though she needed holding. Even though she had lost a mother and a brother in as many moments.

Queen

SABAL SAT LIKE A STONE CARVING. The sedative Ta-Yebbe had been administering kept the keening at bay, but Linhare did not like her sister's slow dream-like movements.

Agreth moved continuously. Every detail, every morsel of food served to mourning guests, every flower arrangement and fold of curtain was made by his order, to his specification. This too, Linhare watched with concern. She feared that the sedative Sabal needed now, he would need later; and if that were the case, she would see to it herself.

Standing alone in the vast hall, away from the mourners filing past the bier upon which the queen and her infant son rested in eternal repose, Linhare could see only the long curl of golden hair Agreth insisted be draped just so over the flowers banked against the slab. Fingers brushed the back of her arm.

"How are you faring, sweetling?"

Linhare turned to find Ellis at her elbow. His eyes were bloodshot; his face, unshaven. The usual flush in his cheeks splotched patchy and wretched. And though he'd neatly combed his hair, his clothes clean and unwrinkled, he seemed disheveled.

"I am still upright," she told him. "And you?"

Ellis laughed, a mad sound that he subdued quickly. "I will be fine, Linhare. My worry is for you and for your sister."

"I will take care of Sabal."

"But who will take care of you?"

Linhare slipped her arm through his and rested her head to his shoulder. There was no one left to take care of her. Wait would protect her. Sabal would love her. Ta-Yebbe would look in on her. But her mother was gone. And Jinna had vanished as completely as had her fan with the blue flowers, the wrap her father brought her from Leftfoot, the stolen book of Therkian poetry, and Wait's journal.

"Your name was the last word my mother spoke," Linhare told him instead. "The very last word."

"Yebbe told me." He choked, but this, too he quelled. Ellis took a deep breath, exhaling it in a kiss atop her head. His breath, warm in her hair, smelled slightly of spirits. Linhare let go of his arm.

"Have you been to see her yet?"

"It is where I spent last night," he confessed. "I kept vigil. Agreth was not happy to find me there this morning."

"I'm sure he understood."

"He understood too well," Ellis whispered, his eyes distant. Then he looked down upon her and smiled sadly. "Unless you need me, I am going to go sleep a little while, if I can manage it, before the banquet tonight."

"Go," Linhare told him. "I am fine."

"You are, aren't you." Ellis' eyes filled. He opened his mouth to speak, but the words seemed to stick in his throat. "There is so much we need to discuss, Linhare. Things your mother, and I, would have you understand. But there is time. For now, please know that you will be a remarkable queen. I mean that with all my heart."

"Not until she is twenty four."

Ellis grimaced, his gaze going over Linhare's shoulder to her stepfather standing behind her, then beside her. Agreth kissed her cheek, but the smile he offered was not for her.

"Until then, Ellis, you and I serve as regents. Do you think the archipelago will survive the ensuing months until then?"

"I think we can manage until summer's end."

"Indeed. And we have Linhare to guide us."

Agreth slipped his arm about her waist and drew her gently to his side. Linhare quelled the impulse to spin out of his hold. Ellis' eyes narrowed. Over her head, the tension crackled like winter between wool blankets.

"Go rest." She touched the Mine Officer's arm, drawing his eyes to her. "I will need you by my side tonight."

"I will be there."

"As will I," Agreth said.

Linhare stepped out of his hold to embrace Ellis, who turned just so. When he let go of her, he stood between her and Agreth.

Thank you, she mouthed. He nodded, a smirk barely veiled on his lips.

"I must see to my guests," she said. "If you gentlemen will excuse me."

Both men bowed, but their eyes were on one another, not her. Stepping away, Linhare did not look back.

WAIT PUSHED OFF THE WALL, skirting the Mine Officer and the king still staring one another down. Whatever understanding Ben and Ellis had come to all those years ago, Agreth did not share in the arrangement. Since Diandra wed the heir of Sisolo, Ellis was as absent in the castle as Yebbe; and as unwelcome.

He followed Linhare as she floated among her guests, his tread silent and himself unseen. She consoled those who were there to console her. In her grief, she was poise and sincerity. In her grief, she became queen.

Climbing the dais to the velvet chair Sabal sat upon all day, Linhare bent to whisper in her ear. Sabal lifted slow eyes to her sister. She smiled a slow smile, gave a slow hand over to the footman who stepped forward to lead her away. Behind Sabal and her footman, Yebbe followed. Wearing the green robes of her station, the red sash of her rank and a Sister's white shroud of mourning, she was a specter among the grieving. No one spoke to her. Everyone watched her.

Already, rumors were spreading.

Those who had already filed past the queen and infant prince started through the tall doors that led into the feasting hall. Linhare held her place, nodding to those expressing grief and going no nearer the slab where her mother and brother rested. Wait watched her carefully, noted the strain of her smile and the grief pooling, yet never falling from her eyes.

"She is very strong."

Wait startled. There was only one person who could come upon him unnoticed. One person who could see him when he did not wish to be seen. He turned to face her, arms spread low, and bowed in proper respect for her kind. For her.

"Stronger than even I would have guessed. It's good to see you, Tuliel."

"Likewise, Wait."

As tall as he, she was slender where he was broad. Long hair, angular features, narrow shoulders and graceful arms all the color of moonlight on white stone, only her eyes gave Tuliel a bit of color. One evergreen, the other earthy; even among her own kind, she stood apart.

"Is Ellis here?"

"Somewhere," Wait told her. "Would you like me to find him for you, my lady?"

Tuliel laughed softly, a sound like birds taking flight. "Such formality. There are no barriers between us, Wait. No social niceties. Such artifice is unlike you."

"It has been many years since I've seen you."

"Years. Such flimsy things. But now is not the time for this. I must pay my respects."

"Will you attend the banquet?"

"No. I will leave. I came here for you, my friend. And for Ellis. Dark times approach. I wished to know for whom time will be darkest."

Bowing her lovely head, Tuliel did not wait for him to do the same before gliding away. She moved to the slab where Queen Diandra and her infant son rested. She placed a moonlight hand to first mother, then son's brows. None seemed to see her but him; and Linhare.

She stood apart, watching. Her mouth opened in wonder, but she said nothing. Her eyes grew wide, but she did not look away. Wait saw her fingers twitch, as if she would reach out to the Purist or slap her hands away. Tuliel inclined her head to the almost-made queen. Linhare bent a curtsey. From where he stood, Wait could see she was trembling. Long strides put him between the women, his hands reaching for Linhare.

"I'll escort you into the banquet," he said.

If Tuliel was still behind him, he did not feel her eyes on his back. He did not feel the bond forged in the darkest of all times. He did not feel her leave. Yet when he glanced over his shoulder before going through the high glass doors, Tuliel was gone.

Missing

THE LONG NIGHT PASSED QUICKLY; it left Linhare lightheaded. She rather enjoyed the numb weightlessness akin to a sensation she felt only once before. A locked cupboard, a stolen key, and a dusty bottle of cider shared between university friends was certainly more agreeable than blood and death and exhaustion, but the result was much the same.

"I want my mother." Linhare heard her sister's voice. "I want my mother!"

"Hush, sweetling." And now there was Ta-Yebbe's. "It will be all right. Put her there, thank you. Wait, put Linhare with her. They need one another now."

Linhare peeked up to find Wait's chin, the curve of his jaw and a long, thin scar she had never noticed before, his earlobe peeking out from behind a sandy curl. The hair on his face was lighter than atop his head, but up close, Linhare saw a day's-worth of stubble glistening there like little flecks of gold.

The steady thrum of his heart in her ear, the even hush of breath in his lungs soothed. He placed her gently onto the bed in Sabal's room, beside her sniffling sister. Linhare jammed her eyes closed and did not open them again until she heard his boots on the polished floor beyond the carpet, until she heard the door close behind him.

"Why does he pay mind to Linhare and not me?" Sabal whined. Linhare closed her eyes again, keeping very still.

"He is queensguard, sweetling," Yebbe answered. "Linhare is queen."

"She wasn't always queen. I want him to pay attention to me! I'm the one who is mad about him. Linhare never even speaks to him."

"Sabal, hush now. Drink this and let Chira attend you while I see to your sister."

Sabal's whine rose in pitch. Fists pounded the mattress. "I don't want Chira! I hate being second born. I hate being second in everything. I want my mother!"

Linhare bolted upright to take her distraught sister into her arms. "It's all right, Sabal," she soothed. "Hush now. Hush."

Collapsing into sobs, Sabal clung to her sister until she fell asleep, hiccupping and whimpering softly in her dreams. Linhare smoothed her hair from her face. She wiped tears from her cheeks. Once she was certain her sister truly slept, she eased Sabal out of her arms.

"It's the after-effects of the sedative," Yebbe whispered as Linhare slid off the bed. "She will be better come morning."

"I don't like having her sedated." She looked over her shoulder at her sister. "But I don't know how she would endure these days otherwise. I appreciate you staying on to help her, Ta-Yebbe. I know you would rather not be here with my stepfather."

"I'm fine." Yebbe busied herself with folding undergarments, her mouth a thin line. "I am sorry my Jinna is not here to be with you in this terrible time of grief. Merry and changeable as she can be, it isn't like her to be so remiss where you are concerned. I thought she would return when she heard Diandra died."

"Return? From where?"

"From the Greenwood. Or so I assume. You know she doesn't actually tell me anything, only leaves me hints to guess at while I worry. But it is all she talked about for days after the fire-eaters left."

"You have not seen her?"

Yebbe stopped folding and turned to her. "Not since the day you girls and Diandra came to my cottage, that day after your welcome home party."

Sabal rolled over, sniffled, but did not open her eyes. Taking Yebbe by the arm, Linhare led her further away, whispering, "Did she not come fetch you when my mother went into labor?"

"No. Word was sent by courier."

She let go of Yebbe to hug herself against the chills crackling along her skin. The chaos fallen since the incident at the pool played over in her head like a dream.

"There has been no time to think," she said aloud. "No time to put things together. It did not occur to me that you got to my mother only moments after Sabal and I did. Of course you were sent for earlier."

Yebbe touched her arm. "What are you saying, Linhare? Please, tell me before I scream."

Linhare pulled away from Yebbe's touch. Her voice trembled. "When Chira came to us, Jinna said she was going to fetch you. That was the last I saw of her."

"And you have said nothing of her absence? Why didn't you tell me?"

"Forgive me, Ta-Yebbe," Linhare whispered. "I have been so…and so many arrangements and decisions and…and *of course* she did not abandon me! Forgive me, Ta! I'm sorry!"

"I have been thinking ill thoughts of her behavior, too. You've nothing to apologize for." Yebbe ran a hand over her eyes. "I was certain she went after that Thissian boy and perhaps hadn't heard."

"Perhaps she did go after him," Linhare said, but Yebbe was shaking her head.

"Not if she knew Diandra was in labor. Never."

Panic seized Linhare's insides. She took short, insufficient breaths until the nausea eased. Yebbe did not speak, but her lips moved as if mouthing some incantation. Her freckles stood out like dark blotches against her pallor. Linhare put an arm about her shoulders, kissed her cheek.

"I will send a messenger to the Thissian company. There is a chance, however small, that she is with them. We will find her, Ta, and we will all laugh at whatever mad story she has to tell us when we do."

A message sent, a search made, all for nothing. Linhare's last hope was that Yebbe was right all along, and Jinna went chasing after her Thissian lover. And, there was evidence that someone had been in Yebbe's cottage on the night the queen died.

"Every cellar and loft from Lower Dockside to the Greenwood has been turned upside down." Linhare paced the terrace, chewing on a thumbnail. "Where could she be?"

"Oh, do sit, Linhare." Sabal set her teacup down with a clink. "I've not gotten three strung-together moments of your time in days. I sent all my maids off so that I could have this afternoon alone with you. Will you not sit and drink tea with me? Please?"

Linhare closed her eyes and counted until she could turn to her sister without scowling. She could no longer sit without documents being thrust in her face. Decisions she felt unqualified to make, policy she was forced to turn over to advisors to enact, Jinna's disappearance, and her own grief underlying it all kept her heart pumping too hard and her slumber full of troubling dreams. Sabal had not considered such things when she begged this afternoon together. She was young, so spoiled. As it was after their father died, their mother's death left Sabal's day-to-day life largely unchanged.

Sitting opposite her sister, Linhare took both her hands into her own. "I'm sorry, sweetling. I don't mean to ignore you. I've so much on my mind. And I'm worried about Jinna."

Sabal snatched her hands away. "I don't see why you should be. How you haven't come to the same conclusion I have is beyond me."

"Conclusion? What do you know that I do not?"

"Though I suppose it shouldn't be," Sabal continued as if Linhare hadn't spoken. "You always wanted to see the best in her."

"Best in her? For goodness sake, Sabal!" Linhare pounded gently on the table. "If you know something about Jinna's disappearance that I don't, speak!"

As the words came out of her mouth, Linhare regretted them. The satisfied malice curling her sister's lovely lips made her belly churn.

"She's not going to be found because she doesn't want to be. Can't you see what has happened? All the things missing? Your things? Silver from the pantry? Mother's brooch? Even some of my trinkets have gone astray, and I was too kind to mention it. She's taken them, Linhare. She's been hoarding them all this time and then used the chaos of mother's—of that night to run off after her Thissian lover."

"How can you say such things?" Linhare's heart hammered. Fingers clenched at the crisp fabric of the table linen. "She would never."

"But it all fits. Open your eyes! Jinna is a harlot and a thief, just like that boogle-loving mother of hers, and if you won't see it—"

Linhare heard her hand connect with her sister's cheek as a thousand echoes before realizing she had even moved. Her voice quavered. "If I ever hear you even whisper such slander again, I will have you whipped."

"You struck me."

"You have a wicked tongue. Ta-Yebbe saved your life! She was our mother's dearest friend. Whatever you may think of Jinna, how dare you say such a thing of Ta-Yebbe?"

"You struck me!"

"Go run and tell *Father*." Linhare pushed away from the table, nearly tripping in her haste to be away. "I'll not suffer another word out of your mouth!"

Sabal got to her feet, a hand still on her blazing cheek. "You are *not* my sister." Spinning away, her hair swept a golden arc that knocked teacups from the table. She ran from the terrace without turning back.

Linhare put her head in her hands. There was no time for tea, and certainly no time for tears. None of her mother's wisdom, and all of her responsibilities, Linhare felt the cracks splintering her composure. Too much was happening too fast, and the almost-queen of Vales Gate did not know how to stop it.

IT HAD BEEN A VERY LONG TIME since Wait visited the mines dug deep into Tuscia's innards. His absence was not accidental. The ponderous inviolability of the underground world hummed with an earthsong akin to the crashing of the sea. Soothing. Humbling. Sacred. These qualities prompted some long ago queen to choose the deepest sections of Tuscia's mines to house *The Holes*, a prison, legend claimed, boogle-dug. Rubble taken out of the mountain formed the Gate. Both were already ancient before humankind ever set foot in the archipelago.

No prisoners were reformed in The Holes. From the most disturbed offender to the politically unfortunate, hundreds died in the soothing black. Few were ever released. None ever escaped. The absoluteness of this prison drew Wait once, when his mind was not his own; it was also what brought him underground to search for Jinna.

"Nothing, sir."

Wait blinked back to sane present. "Are you certain?"

"All patrols have reported in. All prisoners are accounted for. No cell was left unsearched."

Wait bit at the insides of his lip. There were other, less dire jails and reformatories to search, but he was not hopeful. If Agreth was behind Jinna's disappearance, he would not want her found. The Holes would have been it.

"Report back to the castle," he said. "This search was never made. Is that understood?"

"Yes, sir."

"Be sure the rest understand as well. Dismissed."

Wait let his shoulders relax only after his subordinate left the cell set up as his headquarters. The search had taken nearly three days. He hoped his fear would be proven wrong. Now that it was done, he wished he'd been right. At least he would know.

"No luck, I gather."

Wait turned to Ellis standing in the doorway. He shook his head.

"I won't say I told you so." Ellis stepped into the cell. "Agreth's a bore, but he's not cruel enough to have the child imprisoned simply because he does not like her mother. What will you do now?"

"I really don't know," Wait said. "She's vanished as completely as anyone can vanish."

"Any word from the Thissians yet?"

"Not yet. It's still too soon."

"Then there is still the chance that Jinna is with them."

"Linhare doesn't think so."

"Of course she doesn't."

"You do?"

Ellis shrugged. "I don't know Jinna anymore. I really could not say if she is capable of purposely vanishing without a word, without a trace."

"She and Linhare have been friends since the cradle. And Diandra was like a second mother to her."

"In years past, yes. But Linhare has been away these six years. Jinna was rather coolly cut loose to earn herself a reputation that rivals the Divinities on Antillis. Is it impossible to believe she took the opportunity to bolt when it looked like life was about to get far too complicated?"

Wait stood up, rubbing at the back of his neck. Before Linhare left for university, his defense of Jinna would have been immediate.

"There's been a lovely vein of lavender hephista struck," Ellis told him. "Perhaps it would be a good time to bring Linhare down here. Get her out of that castle and among her people."

"Good idea." Wait grimaced. "What are the chances the regent king will let her go without him?"

"Then you've noticed his hovering, too."

"I have. I assigned extra guards to her, especially when I can't be there myself."

"Do you think that's necessary?"

"I don't know," Wait said. "And that's reason enough for caution."

"Better safe now than sorry later," Ellis said, kissing his fingertips and touching his heart. "Still, I believe that it's a matter of him wanting to be in the thick of things. He takes his title rather seriously, even if it's never been more than that."

"Pompous ass."

"Indeed. But he is king and acting regent until Linhare comes of age."

"As are you."

Ellis laughed dryly. "Yes, I am, aren't I. Quite ironic. Quite ironic, indeed. Well then, shall we say day after tomorrow? The area will be secure by then."

"I'll arrange it with Linhare. It will make her happy."

Ellis' furrowed brow eased. He looked up at Wait, a smile curling the corners of his lips. "You have such an old soul, my friend. I often forget how young you were when we saved the world."

"Pardon?"

Ellis backed out of the cell, eyes averted. "You see to Linhare," he said. "I'll take care of everything else."

Arriving on the terrace where Wait's precise schedule of his queen's daily activities said she was supposed to be having tea with her sister, he found it deserted. The tea service had been cleared away but the table and linens were not. An amber tea-stain looked something like a rabbit's head. On the flagstones, a shattered teacup. The chair opposite was tipped over.

Wait scanned the area. Out of the corner of his eye, he caught a glimpse of black skirt. Two great strides and he caught her.

"What happened here?"

"Gracious!" The maid gasped, dishes and cups clattering on the tray. "You startled me, sir!"

"Where is the queen?"

"Why, dead, sir."

"Linhare! Where is Linhare?"

"Oh, the prin-*cess*!" The serving woman balanced the tray on her hip to wipe perspiration from her brow. "She had a bit of a spat with the little one, nothing more. I'm not one to gossip, but Princess Sabal said some unkind things and Princess Linhare slapped her face for it. If you ask me, it wasn't far from the truth. I never understood our beloved queen allowing her heir to associate with—"

"Was anyone else with them?"

The woman's chin went up. Her tone cooled. "No, sir. Just the two of them. And the guard, of course. Now if you don't mind, I have a mess to clean and linens to deliver to the laundress before the stains set."

Wait walked purposefully back to the terrace. *Linhare slapped Sabal.* Whatever the younger princess said, it was bad enough to tip her even-tempered sister over the edge. The vein of hephista had been struck just in time. Ellis was right. Linhare needed time away from the castle. *I should steal a pony and cart for her. An evening Dockside might be even better than the mines.* But Jinna was not there to make mischief with, and the smile accompanying the thought faded.

Heading for the princesses' living quarters, Wait hopped the terrace wall, landing in the inner ward below. The high glass doors beyond the arcade opened to the fresh air. Striding to the solarium, where the flowers bloomed as fragrantly as they did out of doors, Wait ignored the familiar rush of dread coursing up his back as he passed the moldy, mossy rainwell. He ignored it, but he could not quell it. He could never quell it, no matter how much time passed.

The sound of weeping snatched his attention. Sabal stood just inside the glassed solarium. One hand upon the curved trunk of a sapling, the other pressed to her abdomen, her pose perfectly pitiful down to the rhythm of her sobs, Sabal gasped as if on cue.

"Oh, Wait. I didn't see you there."

Wait grimaced, but approached her. "Princess Sabal. Are you all right?"

Lashes lowered. Head bowed. "I'll be fine. Thank you."

He noted the two guardsmen he had assigned to the younger princess: faithful, but no more equipped to dry tears than he. "I will send for your handmaidens."

"I was supposed to be having tea with my *sister*." Her demeanor slipped, however slightly. "I've given my maids the afternoon to themselves. I wouldn't know where to begin looking for them. But if you would be so kind—" Sabal held out her hand. "—you could escort me to my chambers. I feel a bit weak from so much weeping."

"Of course, princess."

Wait gave her his arm. Her fingers rested lightly in the crook of his elbow. Sabal smiled up at him.

"Aren't you going to ask why I was crying?"

Wait kept his eyes front. "It is not my place to ask such questions."

"But you are like family." Sabal slipped her arm further through his, wrapping the other around as well. "My goodness, but you must be strong. I can barely get both my arms around one of yours."

"My lady exaggerates."

"Why do you not call me *Sabal*? You call Linhare by her given name. I've heard you."

Wait glanced down out of the corner of his eye, at the hopeful, besotted face tilted up at him. Eyes flicking forward again, he said, "Different situations call for different titles."

"And you feel the need to be formal with me?"

"Sometimes."

Sabal giggled and nuzzled closer. At the door to her chambers, he stood aside for Sabal to enter. At the end of the hall, her guard waited. Wait held up his hand. "Enjoy the rest of your—"

"Could I trouble you for one last favor?"

Wait stopped, and took a breath. "Of course."

"One of my windows seems to be stuck and it is so dreadfully hot. I am certain it is no match for you. Would you?"

Aside from the night of Diandra's funeral feast, when he carried Linhare from there to here, Wait had never been inside Sabal's chambers. He stepped reluctantly inside. "Which window?"

Sabal closed the door, her back pressed to it. She pointed. "That one there."

Wait crossed to it, slid the latch. It opened easily. The last of afternoon's sunshine wafted in on the breeze. Filmy curtains fluttered in his face and he busied himself with them rather than turn and face the young woman trying so hard to entice him.

"I knew that silly window was no match for you," she said. "Again, you are my hero. How can I thank you?"

"No thanks are necessary."

"But there must be something you want. Something I can do for you. Anything at all."

Sabal's infatuation was nothing new to him. Hers. Jinna's. Serving girls, chamber maids, women in general. Wait had never been fool enough or modest enough to pretend he was not desirable. Only one woman seemed totally immune to his looks, his position, his legend; the only one who mattered.

Turning at last to face the princess, Wait did not to react to the front of her unlaced gown exposing perfect, white breasts. Head tilted back, eyes closed, lips parted, Sabal held her pose while the moments dragged on. Wait remained at stoic attention. Dozens of boys already slavered for a glimpse of what she offered him, dozens of men who would not think

63

twice about her youth or her grief. But Wait was not such a man. And Sabal was not the one he loved.

"I'm sorry," he said at last. Sabal's eyes flashed open. Her posture wilted. Splotches of crimson stained her cheeks. Wait bore the agony of her expression without blinking, without turning away. When she turned her back to him, tugging at the lacings she had hastily undone, he walked calmly to the closed door even if inside his head it was a mad dash.

"Am I so ugly?"

Wait's hand paused on the latch. "You are very beautiful. And very young."

"If I were older then?"

The womanly and seductive voice from moments ago became that of a young girl; a very hurt and disappointed young girl. Wait opened the door, but he let his hand fall away. He turned back to Sabal. She held her gown closed with both hands.

"No, Sabal. Not even if you were older."

"But I love you!"

"I am not the man for you, princess. I am not what you think I am."

"I am not a smitten little girl." Sabal stamped her foot, but held tightly to her gown. "I am a woman and I know what I want. I know who I love. You said I was beautiful!"

Wait rubbed at the back of his neck. Should anyone wander by, the conclusions made would ruin him.

"I'm sorry to hurt you, but I can't be what you want me to be. I can't love you."

Sabal trembled. She shouted, "It's because of Linhare!"

Wait froze halfway to a bowed exit.

"You are in love with her."

She still clutched the front of her gown. Wait rose up to his full height. His jaw clenched.

"It's always Linhare. How everyone loves Linhare!" Sabal strode forward; Wait stepped further back into the corridor. "I'm sick of it. Do you hear me? I am far lovelier than my mousy, queenly sister. Everyone says so! *I* am the beauty! *Me!* But I can never have anything because it belongs first to Linhare! Fine! Love her! But she will be forced to marry someone more suitable than *you*. You are just a guard in this household. A servant! Nothing!"

Sabal stood still, trembling and spent and waiting for him to speak. He could not be angry. She was young. He had broken her heart.

Wait reached for the door. "I'm sorry," he said again, and closed it. The loud crash against the door did not startle him. He expected it. Bottles of perfume and delicate figurines were easily replaced. A vain and spoiled young woman's fancy, however, was not.

* * *

SABAL WOULD NOT OPEN HER DOOR TO LINHARE'S KNOCKING, would not speak to curse at her. The new queen trudged away feeling awful; because she had struck her sister, and because she was not really sorry.

Wandering the halls, trailed always by the guards Wait insisted accompany her whenever other duties kept him from her side, she made her way without realizing to her mother's vacant rooms. Motioning for the men to wait outside, Linhare pushed open the door expecting to find it grim and dark, but it was as light and fresh as always. She closed the door firmly behind her, leaned against it, gained her composure. The sound of sobbing caught her attention, and led her to the small, sunny sewing room her mother used to spend quiet hours in.

"Chira, oh, darling." She rushed to the old woman slumped in the overstuffed chair set by the window. Kneeling before her, Linhare put her head in the old nurse's lap. "It is going to be all right. Hush, now. You cannot weep forever."

"I can and I will if I want to." Chira sniffed. She smoothed a gnarled hand down Linhare's hair. "I am old. I should not have to bury one of my babies. It was her duty to bury me. With honors, at that!"

Linhare took comfort in the old woman's touch. Chira was ever Diandra's maid, but she had helped to raise Linhare and Sabal, even Jinna. The thought of her friend sent a stab of pain between Linhare's eyes. She gasped back a sob. Chira's gentle fingers lifted Linhare's chin.

"What is it, sweetling? There is something else wrong. Tell old Chira. Make her feel useful."

"Do you think Jinna abandoned me?" she burst in a rush of breath. "Do you think she ran off with household valuables, like Sabal said?"

Chira wiped the tears with her thumb. "Ah, sweetling, don't be listening to the things the little one says. She's always had a sting to her, even when she was a baby."

"But where could Jinna be?"

"Somewhere far from here, if she is fortunate," a new voice said; one that sent a shiver up Linhare's spine. Chira pushed her gently from her lap, gained her feet.

"My lord." She bowed stiffly. He did not motion the old woman to sit, but instead looked all around him, hands tucked behind his back.

"I haven't been in here since..." In the sunlight coming from the window, the dark rings beneath his eyes were less pronounced. He looked down at Linhare, shaking his head. "Linhare, please get up off the floor. A queen should not be at the feet of a serving woman."

She scrambled to her feet, pretending not to see the hand he offered her.

"Were you looking for me?" she asked. "Or seeking comfort in my mother's rooms, like I was?"

"Comfort? Here? Where my son should be sleeping at his mother's breast?" He chuffed. "No, Linhare-dearest. I was looking for you." He turned to the nurse. "Leave us, Chira. I would have a word alone with my daughter."

The old nurse's hands clamped down on Linhare's shoulders, fingers biting into flesh. Linhare turned quickly, kissed both her cheeks and whispered, "Go. Please."

Chira's gaze narrowed, but she nodded to Linhare and shuffled from the sewing room. Only when the door into the corridor closed did Agreth turn to face her.

"I've hardly seen you in these weeks since your mother left us."

His words echoed Sabal's; and Linhare knew precisely why he sought her out. "It has been very busy for me."

"For me as well." He sighed, slumped into the chair Chira had vacated. "I understand you and your sister quarreled this afternoon."

"We did." Linhare fidgeted. "She said some terrible things."

"So I have heard." Agreth smiled then, sadly, tapping his ear. "The servants in this household love to tell tales. You were wrong to strike her, Linhare."

"I have tried to apologize, but she will not speak to me."

"Give her time. She will. Sabal is far too in love with her own thoughts to keep her voice free of them."

Linhare laughed softly. "I suppose. Still, we are all fragile yet. I should have been more understanding."

"Sabal must learn to contain her...less kind opinions." Agreth rose to his feet and moved slightly closer; too close for her comfort. He took her hand and patted it when she feared he would kiss it. "Especially with you, who are never anything *but* kind."

Linhare tried to smile. "I think my sister would disagree."

"She is young, and changeable as a summer wind. I will have a word with her before my audience with Lorre."

"The Larguesse from Quary?"

"The very one." He let go of her hand. Linhare tucked it behind her back.

"I thought he left yesterday."

"I thought so too, but he requested to meet with me this afternoon. I suppose we are stuck with him at dinner again this evening." Agreth sighed. "I look forward to some peace, Linhare. My heart is conflicted. I need time to come to terms with many things."

She remembered the negotiations between the Vale and Sisolo, even if she only heard them as gossip on the mountain. Agreth had not loved

Diandra any more than she loved him; and Sisoloans were fiercely and notoriously devoted to their isle. Having lost the wife he made, and the child that would bind them, he was nonetheless obliged to the Vale as regent until Linhare came of age. In his heart, she suspected, he wished to return to his beloved isle.

"Of course," Linhare told him. "I understand completely."

"I wonder that you do," he said. "I wonder. Now then, off you go. I will speak with Sabal. Have no fear. She will again be your sweet sister by this evening."

"Thank you. *Agreth,*" she added quickly, and was rewarded by a smile that did not make her skin crawl—until he pulled her into an embrace so desperate, she did not know what to do. He whispered into her hair, "It is good to hear you say my name. *Linhare.* Oh, my Linhare. I despise that your mother had to die to bring us closer together, but it is a joy in the midst of all this sorrow."

She did not have the heart to pull even gently away from him. After all he lost, it was an insignificant sacrifice to endure when so small a kindness, so grudgingly given, lifted some of his sorrow. Neither could she bring herself to return his embrace, and after a moment, he let her go. He said nothing as he turned and walked from the room, but stopped in the doorway as if he might. Linhare held her breath.

Go. Please go. Oh, please.

And he did. Linhare sank into the chair, her mother's chair that still smelled of her perfume. She put her head into her hands and breathed deeply until warmth returned to her body, until she could stop trembling.

THE GUARDHOUSE HALL DID NOT GLEAM as did the castle hall. Long, narrow, the table and benches pushed up against one wall took up most of what room existed. The walls bore no tapestries. The pitted floors nearly blackened by thousands of boots over hundreds of years did not shine. It was a place of warriors and food and ale. It was where Wait felt most at home.

Listening to Firstman Oswin give his report, trying not to yawn, Wait forced himself to at least sit up straight. His recent lament to Ellis about the boredom of being Dakhonne at this time in Vales Gate history was taking its revenge. Duties as Captain of the Guard and queensguard conflicted. He found himself at constant odds about where he should be, when. With Jinna missing, his place was ever with his queen; but with Jinna missing, his queen insisted he be looking for her, following every lead. Personally.

"A messenger delivered this."

Oswin held out a slip of paper. Wait sat straighter, took the note penned on costly, heavy stock, in Ellis' extravagant hand:

Cal, It has been too long since we have seen one another. I miss you, my friend. As does Yebbe. Contact me with a time and place the moment you receive this, and we will meet for a cup of ale.

~Ellis

Wait tucked the note into his pocket. He saw Ellis only the day prior. Stranger still was the suggestion of a cup of ale when the man knew all too well that Wait did not imbibe. "Who delivered this?"

"I am not certain," Oswin answered. "I can find out if you wish?"

Wait tucked the paper into his pocket. "No need. Send a messenger to the Mine Officer and tell him I have received his message and will meet him at the *Barrel and Mug* in Sheridan in an hour."

"Yes, sir. And now that I have your attention…"

"I didn't think I was that obvious."

Oswin shrugged. "Formalities. I've already seen to most of what I just reported. This is about Jinna."

"You've news?"

A nod. "She was seen in the castle the night Queen Diandra died."

Wait leaned elbows to knees, let the information pool. "Who saw her?"

"Several of the scullery maids. They all agree it was her, and that they called out to her but she didn't hear them."

"When did you find this out?"

"Just this morning, sir. One of the girls came to me, scared out of her wits."

"Scared? Why?"

Another shrug. "Perhaps because they did not come forward sooner. Or perhaps they feared they'd be implicated, somehow. The minds of young women have always confounded me, sir."

"Interesting. Maybe she did run off with her fire-eater after all."

"I do not believe so, sir. He is out in the yard waiting to speak with you."

Firstman Oswin turned, motioned to a courier at the far door. The door banged open and the Thissian fire-eater nearly ran the length of the long hall. Average height and build, he moved with the grace of an acrobat. His clothes screamed elaborate shades of yellow and orange. His boots were high and polished and competently patched. As he came closer, Wait noted mended holes in the flamboyant shirt as well.

The young man bowed as extravagantly as he walked, the back of his hand sweeping the ground before he rose again with a flip of his long, dark hair. Brown-black eyes, femininely fringed, and skin the golden brown of caramelized sugar, the boy was no Thissian.

"Name?" Wait asked.

"I am Egalfo." His voice rang smooth and deep. "I have come to offer my services in the search for Lady Jinna."

Wait rubbed at his stubbled chin and realized he had yet to take a blade to it that day. "We were hoping she ran off with you."

"I hoped that as well, sir. But my lady is too devoted, too loyal to her princess. She would not leave her. It was with immense sorrow that we parted, but I promised her I would be back. When my uncle received your inquiry, I knew immediately that something terrible happened."

"Your uncle?"

"Yes, sir."

"Is he a Therk, too?"

Wait watched the conflict change the boy's face from flamboyant drama to angry despair.

"He is Thissian, as are all the performers in our company. Thissians are known from the Vale to the furthest harlotry of Esher for their—"

"Then you do not deny being a Therk."

"No, sir. I do not. I don't know exactly what I am so I cannot deny your slander."

"No slander," Wait told him. "Just sorting out the facts. I have nothing against Therks. I've been to your land. It is quite beautiful."

"It is a desert. Or so I am told. I am a foundling. My aunt found me hiding in a barrel on a ship she and my uncle bought. He says he wanted to toss me over the side." Egalfo smiled. "But she hit him in the head with a wooden spoon and I became part of the family. I was a toddler. If I had a name, I did not know how to say it. They called me Egalfo because of a charm I was wearing when they found me. My aunt thought it sounded exotic. And now you know as much about my origins as I do."

"Are you always so free with information? I only asked if your uncle was a Therk."

The caramel color of his skin deepened. Wait put the boy at no older than twenty. He asked, "Then you haven't seen Jinna since you left Dockside? No word from her?"

"No, to both questions. I anticipated a letter. At least, I hoped she thought enough of me to write. But the first word I received was that she is missing."

"And you came straight back here."

Some of Egalfo's posturing deflated. "I know that it was rash, sir. Leaving my family, my livelihood, but I had to do something. I love her."

Just what I need. Wait exhaled deeply. "The best thing to do is go back to your family. I'll find you a bed in the guardhouse for tonight, but there is really nothing you can do that we are not already doing. I give you my word that as soon as we find her, I will send a messenger to you."

"I cannot go back to them and wait like a maid pining for her sailor lover. I must search for her. Every port, every city, every forest and every—"

"You do that," Wait said, rising from his chair and stretching cramped muscles. The motion caused the desired effect, and the young Therk or Thissian or whatever he was paled considerably. "Firstman Oswin will make sure there's a bed available to you tonight. After that, you're on your own."

Stepping off the platform, Wait shouldered past Egalfo, motioning for Oswin to follow. At the door, he halted. "Did you get that message off to Ellis?"

"Moments ago, sir."

Wait nodded. "I'm heading out now for Forestwife Yebbe's cottage before meeting Ellis in Sheridan. Something's not sitting right with me."

"Is there anything else I can do, sir?"

"Make sure neither princess leaves this castle, and—" He glanced over his shoulder. "—keep your eyes on that one, just in case."

LINHARE MADE HER WAY TO THE SMALL, PRIVATE DINING ROOM the family used when not entertaining, wondering why that was so when the Larguesse from Quary was to dine with them. He was an acquaintance, nothing more, even if Linhare found him pleasant enough. As she neared the doorway, she also realized that the guard trailing her every step for weeks was not in attendance, either, and she sighed a small, relieved sigh. She understood Wait's diligence, but it felt good to have a little normalcy return. She was in her home with people she loved, who loved her.

Stepping into the dining room, Linhare was surprised to find it empty; not even a serving staff lined up along the walls like furniture. Two Therkian glass wine goblets, already filled, waited on the sideboard. Two table settings. Two chairs pulled close. Sumptuous aromas wafted from a wheeled cart of covered dishes, making her mouth water.

Lifting the lids, she found all her favorite foods. Brush hen swimming in pale, sweet wine and savory herbs. Roasted migichoke roots and caramelized onion. Fresh greens and squash blossoms. Her heart lifted, certain and surprised that Agreth did as he promised and sweetened her sister's anger. Had he arranged this dinner to amend the wrongs committed in sorrow? The sound of footsteps coming down the hall turned her to the door, a smile already forming.

"Linhare, darling."

Her smile plummeted. Agreth grasped her hands, pulled her in to kiss both cheeks.

"Good—good evening, Agreth." She pulled her hands from his, looked vainly beyond him. "Is the Larguesse not with you? Sabal?"

"As you can see, darling, it is just the two of us dining tonight." Holding out a chair for her, he tucked her back in with gentlemanly flourish before wheeling the cart to the table.

"I talked with Sabal. It was quite enlightening, in fact, but she would not consent to dinner this evening. She said something about her heart being sundered beyond repair, or other such dramatic nonsense. I cannot tell you how I regret allowing her to associate with that actress!" He lifted the lids, serving her himself before taking the chair opposite.

"And the Larguesse?" she asked.

"Ah, Lorre was called back to Quary this afternoon."

"Nothing is wrong, I hope."

Agreth's lips tightened just a little. "No, nothing wrong. Eat, Linhare. Enjoy this peace. Something tells me the coming days are going to be even busier than our last."

Her stepfather's exuberance softened her wariness. He was right; the days melted together since her mother's death. An unmolested evening, no documents to sign or dignitaries to entertain, was welcome, even if it meant being alone with Agreth.

Linhare nibbled, then tucked enthusiastically into her dinner. Agreth mimicked her zeal, eating and drinking as she had never seen him do before. He even laughed when he spilled wine on himself, raised his hand to call for a steward, and then lowered it again.

"Curses," he murmured, dabbing himself with his lapkin. "I forgot that I sent the staff off for the evening." His eyes were slightly bleary. Linhare glanced at the sideboard. Two bottles already gone. She grimaced behind her own goblet, the skin on the back of her neck prickling.

"Did you dismiss my guard as well?"

He froze, his hand mid-mop. "You seemed so unhappy, being constantly followed about. I am still king...*regent* king. My word is still enough for simple commands, especially in my own home, where my own daughter is concerned. I simply sent them off for one evening, to give you some peace."

Linhare did her best not to grimace. His words seemed sincere, rational, even kind. And yet...

"And Larguesse Lorre? He was not called back to—"

Agreth slammed his hand down onto the table, clattering the cutlery. "No! I sent him away! And he is lucky I did not have him tossed into the Holes instead."

"Why? He seems like a lovely man."

"Lovely? He is deluded. And ambitious. And—" Agreth straightened his jacket, smoothed his hair. "I hoped to spare you, Linhare," he said, sounding more like himself. "Lorre did not linger here in the Vale out of great love or sorrow. He had a purpose. More appropriately, he has a son."

"A son?"

"A son he thought fine enough for you. I told him he was mistaken, in no uncertain terms, and asked him to leave."

Linhare lowered her lashes, pushed what was left of her food around her plate. A son. A prospective husband. For her. This was not a conversation she wished to have; and certainly not with Agreth. He reached across the table. She snatched her hand away.

"I'm sorry," she said just as quickly, but Agreth leaned back in his chair, picked up his empty goblet, poured himself more.

"Don't be. I was as appalled as you are. You will be expected to marry well and soon, but Quary? For the Vale? You must wed Sisolo, Linhare, like your mother did."

Marry? Sisolo?

Agreth's face danced back and forth before her eyes. She blinked, sipped her own wine, tried to eat, but it all turned to sand in her mouth. The notion of marriage had not even once entered her thoughts, but the king, acting regent of Vales Gate, would have been thinking about the change of power since the moment his queen died.

"I—I didn't think about…"

"Of course you didn't, darling Linhare. You are young and thrust into this role you'd not expected to take up for a very long time to come. Let it settle now. There will be time to discuss your alternatives in the weeks to come."

"Weeks?"

"I'm afraid so." Agreth set his goblet down. Instead of taking her hand, he offered his own across the table. Linhare place hers hesitantly atop, unprepared for the way his fingers curled beneath it to gently stroke her palm. "I vow to you, my dearest Linhare, that you will have love. Perhaps even a love you have secretly, silently longed for?"

Her heart thudded. There were two men she silently longed for; but her father was dead and Wait…she sighed.

"So troubled," he laughed softly. "All will be well, Linhare, but I can see you are no longer in the mood for eating, even if I arranged to have your favorite pears poached and glazed. Perhaps a stroll to settle thoughts and bellies. Come."

Images of her father and queensguard still tumbling about, mixing and melding with marriage and Sisolo and a life suddenly far too burdened than she ever imagined it would be, Linhare took the arm he offered without thinking. Only when the cool evening air hit her face did she realize he had led her to the inner ward, and the gardens most dear to her. Something of the cool, or perhaps the shiver slithering up her spine, brought to mind the winter of her childhood when a rare, heavy snow fell on the Vale. Envisioning snow castles and snow battles and riding high on her father's shoulders, Linhare nearly smiled; but Agreth stumbled, and her instinct to catch him banished all else.

"Are you well?"

"Better than well," he said, and chuckled a high-pitched chuckle. "I am serene."

You are drunk, Linhare thought, but left those words in her head. "Perhaps it would be best if I called for your steward to—"

"Don't rush away." He grabbed her back when she disengaged her arm from his. "Let us listen to the crickets together. It is a glorious night."

She felt his words, deep and soft as a down pillow pressed to her face. Linhare tried again, more urgently, to pull away from him. "It's indeed lovely, but I am very tired and—"

"Linhare." He whispered her name like an endearment. He yanked her arm, forced her closer. He plucked at a stray wisp of hair, rubbing the lock back and forth across his lips. "So beautiful and soft. It was the first thing I loved about you. Is it true that you promised to never cut it?"

"My—my hair? Yes, as a promise to my father. Please let go. You are hurting my arm."

Agreth's grasp on her loosened only slightly. "Daughters and fathers. Fathers and daughters. Who is to know for certain but the mother herself? All right, darling. Your *father,* even if Ellis' name was the last on your mother's lips, as this gossiping staff was glad enough to tell me."

Linhare trembled, but she did not make the mistake of trying to pull away from him again. Agreth's eyes never left hers.

"Do you remember when first we met?"

"I—"

"You stood beside your mother, lovely creature that she was, but you...I remember Diandra leaned down to speak to you and you turned your head just enough for your hair to cascade over one fair shoulder. I was lost right then, Linhare. Forever lost. I would drape myself in your hair and be always content for clothes."

"You must not—" Words failed. She forced them from her mouth. "You should not say such things to your...your *daughter.*"

He let go of her hair, pulling her ardently to him. "No, not to his daughter. That would be wrong. But I cannot look upon you as my daughter any more than you can look upon me as your father. Oh, Linhare, Linhare." Agreth buried his face in her throat, kissing the pulse so violently beating she could not speak to scream. "I know you feel for me what I have felt for you all these years. Please do not to deny me. I beg of you not to deny me."

73

Agreth's mouth captured hers. His tongue searched. He tasted like wine. Linhare pushed against him, but the harder she pushed, the tighter his hold on her became.

"My Linhare," he said against her lips, between forced kisses. Despite the softness of his life, Agreth was strong. His hands were too fast, too skilled. The front of her gown was already undone. He pushed her up against a column. Cold stone scraped her bare skin. Agreth's lips were on her throat, on her breasts, pulling her nipples into his mouth like a hungry infant.

"My love. This is what was meant to be from the beginning. You and I, uniting the archipelago as it has never been united before. Did she ever tell you? Do you know it was you I asked for?"

Linhare froze; one stunned moment was all he needed. One hand grasped her wrist so fiercely that her fingers went numb; his other hand fumbled up underneath her gown, searching, searching. His breath came quick and hot on her face. His hand tore away the delicate material of her smallclothes. Fingers pushed inside her. His fumbling became spastic, urgent. His fingers went deep.

In her mind, Linhare was screaming.

Pain, and warmth. She felt blood trickle down her thighs and the silent screaming vanished. Linhare no longer struggled. She sobbed. Agreth kissed her, swallowing those sobs, licking them down his own throat, moving his fingers slowly, as if to somehow soothe the horror of what he had done.

"There now." His voice was tender. Loving. He took his fingers from inside her and let her gown fall. "I know it hurts. It is a maiden's lot, I'm afraid. Don't cry, sweet Linhare. It will make our wedding night all the sweeter to have this out of the way."

Linhare stopped hearing him. She slid down the column, the broken skin of her back smearing blood the way down. The scent of it stung her nostrils. Her stomach heaved. What he had done. What he had said. She would never forgive. She would tell. Everyone. She would watch Wait open his belly from groin to sternum. She would feel no remorse while Yebbe stuck pins in his eyes and chanted damning spells. She would laugh when Ellis put his dead body into the deepest pit in the Holes to rot.

Agreth grunted. His breath was coming in gasps. Linhare's gruesome fantasies fled. He was thrusting into his own hand, smearing himself with her blood. His other hand reached for her, shaking with his own efforts.

"Come, my love. Let me show you how to please me."

Revulsion welled up from her ruined maidenhood to her throat; fury trapped behind the horror he inflicted, the terrible things he said, erupted now into a bestial roar. Linhare leapt up from the ground and headfirst into his swollen, thrusting pelvis. Then she was running full pelt through the glass doorways, through the solarium, the corridors to her room. Her hand on the lever, she turned, instead reaching for Sabal's door. It would not open. Linhare pounded with the flat of her hand. "Sabal! Sabal! Please! Let me in! Hurry! Oh, please, hurry!"

Phantom or real, Linhare heard the sound of his boots on the polished floor. From the other side of the door, Sabal's sleepy voice answered, "Go away! I don't want to speak to you."

"Please, Sabal. I'm hurt. I'm terribly hurt. I need your help. Please, please, please!"

On the third plea, the door swung open. Linhare fell into the room, sobbing uncontrollably. "Shut the door. Shut it and lock it. Don't let him in. No matter what he says, do not let him in!"

Sabal obeyed wordlessly. The *snick* of the bolt sliding into place sent a tremor through Linhare's body and she screamed. Her sister took her into her arms.

"Hush, darling. You are trembling like a bedraggled kitten. Who has frightened you so?"

"Agreth!"

"Father?"

"He is *not* our father," she shrieked. "Fathers do not do that to their daughters."

Sabal's arms stiffened before loosening just enough to tilt Linhare's face to hers.

"What did he do to you? Where is Wait?"

The trembling overwhelmed. Linhare could not speak. She could only shake and weep. No Wait. No guard. Not even servants to witness. Agreth planned his evening well. Sabal held her gently closer. "I'm sorry. Oh, Linhare. My sweet sister. I thought he—I didn't know he would—"

Across the hall, Linhare's door slammed. Both sisters startled. Another moment, and he pounded upon Sabal's locked door.

"Open this door! I know she is in there!"

"Please, Sabal. I am sorry I slapped you. Please do not—"

"You think I would allow him to harm you? For that? Oh, Linhare."

More pounding. Demands. Agreth called for a key. Linhare hid her face in her sister's nightdress, whispering over and over, "I'm sorry." Then Sabal was removing her, gently. She squatted before her, took her shoulders into her small, cool hands.

"He will get in," she said. "The maid who takes care of this hall will come with the key. We will make him believe you are not here. Then he'll go away. I have an idea."

Rising, pulling Linhare with her, Sabal led her to the massive trunk at the foot of her bed. "Hide in there. I will open the door as if he just woke me and tell him you are not here."

"What if he looks in the trunk?"

"It won't matter. Trust me." Voices on the side of the door. Keys jingling. "Hurry!"

Linhare climbed into the trunk. The lid went down instantly.

"I'm coming," Sabal called out sleepily. The sound of the lock tumbling, the door opening, threatened to pull a scream from Linhare's throat.

"Where is she?"

"Where is who, Father?"

"Linhare! I know she is in here."

Their voices faded even if she could feel Agreth's rage between her sticky thighs. Linhare put her face in her hands and took several deep breaths. Consciousness faded. Her head detached first, then her limbs, her torso—the sensation left her nauseated and shaking. Then it passed as suddenly as it came upon her, jolting her as if she had fallen out of bed.

There was cool air.

There was sunshine.

Linhare fell and fell and fell.

Vanished

WAIT LET HIS MARE HAVE HER HEAD; she knew the way. It had been an exhausting day, a puzzling evening, and the night ahead already loomed long. Making the trek into Sheridan was frustratingly fruitless. Ellis never so much as showed his face in the Barrel and Mug. After waiting an hour, Wait went to the mines, only to discover that the Mine Officer had not been seen since quite early that morning.

. . .I miss you, my friend. As does Yebbe. . .

His trip into Littlevale was equally fruitless. He'd arrived at Yebbe's cottage in the wood only to find it locked up and tucked away as if in anticipation of being empty a long while. Ellis' cryptic words, Jinna's vanishing, now his and Yebbe's—were they connected somehow? Coincidence?

His blood had suddenly thrummed then, like the pulse in the Holes, an unsettling sensation, and one he rarely experienced. Such thrumming meant something was wrong, someone in his protection was in harm's way. It was an almost-constant sensation since Diandra's death. But this...

Spurring his mare into a thundering gallop, Wait leaned low over her neck. Her great hooves kicked up gravel, sparked on the cobbles. They ate up the road like some monstrous beast, but it was still too slow. Something was not simply wrong. Someone was not in harm's way. Someone was harmed, and that someone, he knew beyond all doubt, was Linhare.

Ahead, coming down the road towards him, a rider. Wait recognized Firstman Oswin instantly. Reining his lathered mare to a halt, he commanded, "Report."

"Princess Linhare is missing."

Wait's vision blurred. "How long?"

"Uncertain," Oswin said. "She was last seen having dinner with King Agreth. Alone. Unattended. I have already recalled the staff, and sent a small guard to the Vulgar Raven."

"Explain. Start to finish."

"Should we—" Oswin looked over his shoulder towards the castle. His mount danced under him. Wait's stood as motionless as her rider.

"Here. Now. Be brief."

"Yes, sir. Her disappearance was first discovered at the changing of the guard. All but the perimeter guard, including the men assigned to Linhare through the evening hours, had been dismissed."

"By?"

Oswin looked him squarely in the eyes. "King Agreth. The serving staff was also dismissed for the evening. The last Linhare was seen was on her way to the private dining room about three hours ago. Dinner had been prepared and left. Dinner for two. Linhare and Agreth."

"Lorre? Sabal?"

"Lorre went unexpectedly back to Quary. Princess Sabal has been in her rooms since the incident with her sister this afternoon. She is safe."

"What does she know?"

"I have not had her questioned. I placed a guard on her rooms and came to find you."

Wait's gut clenched. His blurring vision narrowed.

"Good work, Oswin."

"Thank you, sir."

Wait managed to loosen his grip on the reins, but his vision refused to clear. Nausea sent waves of heat chasing cold through his body. He breathed. Deeply. Gained what control he could. In the years since the sensation made him a hero to Vales Gate, he rarely needed the skill he called upon now.

"Sir?"

Oswin's image wavered, but Wait could see almost properly. Nudging his horse into a trot, then a canter, he said, "Question the staff. Someone knows something. They are always watching. I will question King Agreth myself."

The guard sent Dockside to search the Vulgar Raven had already returned by the time Wait reached the castle; he could have predicted their report: Linhare was not there and had not been seen. A formality done and set aside. Wait pounded the halls leading to the king's suite. He swept past Agreth's steward, an ancient, hunchbacked Rilsian brought in from Sisolo, and burst through the doors. The man hobbled after him, grasping the door frame, panting.

"The queensguard, Your Majesty." The steward sniffed in Wait's direction, bowed to his king and stepped backward out of the room, dragging the doors closed behind him. Agreth rose from his chair, an overstuffed thing set near an open window. Everything in the room, from the chair to the tapestries to the cover of the book he read, was the same pale gold of his hair. He set the book down.

"Queensguard." Agreth drew the word out. "Forgive me if I am misinformed, but does that not mean you are meant to guard the queen?"

Fury roiled under Wait's skin. "Linhare is missing. You are the last person she was seen with. If I were you, I'd be very, very cautious."

The sudden blanch of Agreth's complexion betrayed his cool. "Need I remind you that I am still king? I could have you killed for such accusation."

"You are a figurehead," Wait said. "And a son of Sisolo. Marriage got you a queen, but it isn't working in your favor right now. Sisolo's treachery hasn't been forgotten."

"That goes both ways, *queensguard!*"

Wait met his glare without flinching. In his mind's eye, Agreth was gloriously covered in blood. Wait's lip curled. "I know you arranged a private dinner with Linhare, and that you dismissed her guard and the staff. Why?"

"I do not have to explain myself to—"

"Answer me now!" Wait roared and the king cowered behind his chair. Wait forced control. "Or answer me in the Holes. It is your choice."

Agreth bowed his head; his finger traced the swirls of beige within beige.

"Lorre suggested that his imbecile son court Linhare," he began. "I told him no and we argued. He left. I did not want Linhare upset, but it was her right to know of his preposterous request. Much as it appalled me, I have no idea how she feels about the boy from Quary. Since Sabal was not feeling well, I thought it provided a good opportunity to tell Linhare privately. I asked the cook to prepare all her favorite foods and gave the serving staff the evening to themselves. I did not want her embarrassed. You know how this staff gossips. I could not bear it. Not after all she has been through."

"And the guard?"

"They were upsetting her, following her about every moment of every day."

"And had they been doing so this evening—"

"Don't you think I know that?" Agreth burst, his fist coming down impotently on the chair cushion. "Don't you think I have berated myself over and over for that?"

Wait's jaw clenched. The pretty king put on a good act, but something dark lurked behind the comely face. His answers were too quick, too rehearsed. "When and where did you last see her?"

"Just after dinner, in the formal gardens. I told her as gently as I could about Lorre's son but all my efforts to be kind were in vain. She got quite upset, and struck me."

"Linhare? Struck you?"

"Don't look so shocked," Agreth said. "She did the same to her sister earlier in the day."

"What did you do when she hit you?"

Agreth sighed, pressed fingers to the corners of his eyes. "I am mortified to admit it, but I did become quite angry. She struck me and ran off. I gave chase. My only defense is that I am unwound myself. I have lost my beloved wife and my infant son. I am left with two daughters not of my own blood, but whom I adore as I would were they my own. It cut me to my core when she struck me."

Vision narrowing. Gut welling. Wait held tight to the control fast unraveling. He took one step closer to the king, met the man's frightened eyes, asked, "And did you catch her?"

Agreth did not flinch. "No. I did not. I went to her chambers, but she was not there. I questioned Sabal, but she was not with her, either. I'm afraid I woke the child from a sound slumber. She was quite incoherent when I questioned her. Have you spoken to her yet?"

The waves of Dakhan rage receded, but did not vanish completely. The king knew more than he said, but Wait's instinct told him he knew no more about Linhare's whereabouts than anyone else did.

"No one comes or goes from this castle or grounds until Linhare is located," he snapped. "Any attempt to thwart this mandate is as good as an admission of guilt."

"I have no intentions of leaving here until my daughter is found. As queensguard, it is your duty to find her, as it was your duty to protect her. I hope you will prove abler at the former than you were at the latter."

"I'll find her," Wait said. "Make sure you are here when I do."

"Is that a threat?"

"Only if you are guilty of something."

Turning his back on the king without first taking that proper step backward, Wait walked to the doors, struggled to keep his steps cool and slow. He yanked open the heavy doors; the Rilsian steward fell into the room.

"Did you hear anything interesting?" Wait growled.

"I—I was only waiting for—"

Shoving him aside, Wait did not turn around to see if the loud *crack* was the sound of the hunchback's head hitting the wall or the floor. Whichever it was, he was certain it was the last sound the man would hear for a while.

You have failed her. Again.

The sound of his boots on the polished floors echoed the words, echoed the thrumming in his gut. This was nothing like those times she would slip away with Jinna. Wait had known then she was safe. It was part of being queensguard and Dakhonne. It was part of the bond joining him to this family. Linhare would vanish and in that instant before fear could take root, some inner instinct told him he would find her safe and contrite but not sorry. No such reassuring instinct comforted Wait now; rather, he felt strangely unbalanced. He had no sense of her at all. It was as if she suddenly vanished so completely, even death could not claim her.

Wait cut his familiar, stubborn path through the inner ward. He never altered his course to spare himself the memories that pooled even now, when his thoughts were so consumed. Tucked behind a hedge, the rain-well lurked. Spidery, wet, moldy. Hidden. Wait halted on the path, glanced in its direction.

You have no power over me.

And continued on.

Cool air blew through the gardens, making the cloisters whistle softly. Night-blooming flowers whispered lusty fragrances. Wait approached the glass doors leading into the solarium, closed against night's chill. Reaching for the nearest handle, he heard a chuff.

"Sir. Sir."

Not a chuff; a whisper that sliced into his thoughts. Wait followed the sound to the figure hiding in a clump of flowering bushes. It took a moment, but the riotous color of his clothes gave him away. "Egalfo?"

The Therk stepped out from the clump, brushing petals and bits of old leaves from his clothes and hair. "Yes, sir. Egalfo."

"What are you doing in there? Oswin was supposed to keep watch on you."

"Don't be too quick to chastise him, sir," Egalfo whispered, his eyes everywhere. "I suspect he believes he does have a full guard on me. I am a shadow when I wish to be. A puff of breath. A pair of eyes in—"

Wait shook his head. "I don't have time for this," he growled and pushed passed the young Therk.

"I know what happened to the queen!"

Wait froze, turned back. He leaned in close, impressed that, though Egalfo blanched, he did not back away. "How do you know anything at all has happened to her?"

"The guard, the staff. They are all whispering about it, sir."

"How did you hear those whispers?"

"I—I—I was conducting my own investigation of Jinna's—"

Wait held up his hand. Egalfo cowered, arms over his head. The fire-eater from Thiss or Therk or wherever he was from had freed himself from Oswin—no easy feat. Better to listen than to dismiss.

"You said you know what happened to the queen. Tell me. Now."

The young man lowered his arms. "I don't know, precisely, what happened to her," he said. "But I *saw* something here in the garden. Something very strange. Come, let me show you."

81

Wait followed the young man deeper into the gardens, to a column that was part of the arcade leading to the solarium. He pointed to a puddle in a divot of stone at the base.

"Water?"

"Not the water itself, but the fact that I saw a servant out here in the night, scrubbing at a column of stone. He was quite nervous, always looking over his shoulder. As I watched, he began to sob, then he threw the remains in the bucket at the column and ran off."

Wait touched the column. The thrumming pulsed once, twice, and subsided.

"The servant, was he old? Hunchbacked?"

"Yes, sir."

Wait let his hand fall away from the stone. Facts whirled in his head, tried to sort themselves into some kind of logic. None of it went together, but they were all connected. Too many pieces were missing. And there was still Sabal to question, a task he would have been more comfortable conducting with witnesses, under less dire circumstances.

"Tell no one else what you saw," he told Egalfo. "And thank you."

"I told you I could help." Egalfo puffed out his chest. "Is there any other way I can be of service?"

Wait debated then shook his head. "No. Go back to the barracks. I will speak with you again in the morning."

"Yes, sir," Egalfo said, "G'night, sir!" But Wait had already turned towards the solarium doors, and did not answer.

Wait approached Sabal's door cautiously. The guard standing at attention stood taller, stepped aside without meeting his captain's eyes, and opened the doors.

"Leave them open," he said, and the guard obeyed. In the dim light within, Wait could see the princess elegantly positioned in profile against the moonlit windows. Details he would have seen and discarded any other time blared: her white gown, a thin band of silver crowning golden hair loosely curled, more silver at her wrists and her throat. Sabal was a vision of perfection, as always, but the deliberateness at this late hour, under such circumstances, told Wait things he did not have room in his head to consider. Sabal floated down the short flight of steps like a rare snowflake from the sky.

"I must begin with an apology." She stopped on that bottom step, her hands clasped demurely and her head bowed. "I made a fool of myself in your presence yesterday. I apologize for embarrassing you. You, who were so dear to my father, and to my mother. You, who have protected and loved this family for so long and so well. It is that love my silly heart hoped to change into something between a man and a woman. But I am not a woman yet. I am a girl of seventeen, and that is the only excuse I can give for what I did."

Sabal's head came up slowly. The low lamplight further softened the humility of her cheeks. Her eyes filled and two well-timed tears rolled down her cheeks.

"I ask your understanding, if not your forgiveness," she said, "before we attend to the dire matter at hand."

"All right." Wait held up his hands. Her mature humility disconcerted as much as her seduction. "I understand. And I forgive you."

"Thank you." Sabal moved to the trunk at the foot of her bed. There she stopped, pressed her hands to the lid. Despite her cool demeanor, those hands shook.

"I know my sister is missing," she said. "I know, because I am the one who vanished her."

"Vanished—what?"

"You will not believe me, Wait." Her voice shook. "No one believes I can do anything. But I can, and I did, but I didn't mean to. She was hurt and I panicked and I thought—"

"Hurt?" Wait advanced, hands clenched into fists. "By who? When? Speak, Sabal!"

"Please! You are frightening me!"

Wait's narrowing vision expanded. He blinked. He breathed. "Forgive me," he said. "Go on."

Her shoulders relaxed. She gazed dramatically towards the window. "If you are to understand at all, I must start at the beginning. You must be patient. It is the only way to save my sister, if there is any saving her at all. Will you promise?"

Digging deep, Wait found a small store of calm; a very small store. "I promise."

Sabal again placed both hands to the lid. "My mother and fa—" She closed her eyes, swallowed hard. "—and Agreth, bought this for me when we went into Upper Dockside to see a play. It was just before Linhare returned from university. I fell in love with it, you see. It is old and it smells a bit odd, but it has such character. It felt so magical. I just had to have it.

"I never put anything in it. Well, I believed I *did* put things into it, but whenever I opened it, it was empty. At first I thought I was being forgetful. Then I thought it was Jinna, stealing my things, but—but perhaps this is what happened to Jinna, too. Perhaps she has suffered the same fate as my dear sister."

"Sabal." He said her name and his voice shook. He calmed himself. "Please, just tell me what has happened to Linhare."

Sabal's lip quivered. She bit it. "It would be better to show you." Lifting the lid, Sabal took the silver circlet from her brow. She placed it into the trunk, then closed the lid. Stepping back, she told him, "Open it."

Wait lifted the lid.

"What trick is this?"

"It is no trick," she whispered.

Wait pulled his compass out of his pocket. He tossed it into the trunk and closed the lid. One breath. Two. He opened it again. No circlet. No compass. Empty.

"This is impossible."

"Wherever my circlet and your compass are, that is where Linhare is," Sabal burst, pounding on the lid with both fists; it came crashing down. "I was trying to save her! I was hiding her from him! I didn't know! I didn't realize until it was too late!"

Wait pulled her away from the trunk, holding her arms down when she would flail at it again. "Sabal, stop! Save her from who? Tell me what happened to Linhare!"

Sabal choked down her sobs. After a moment, she nodded. Wait let her go, only to find himself trembling violently. The young princess opened the trunk again, looked into it instead of at him.

"She came to my chambers, disheveled and shaking," she whispered. "Her gown was—it was undone. She said he mustn't find her. Then he was pounding on my door, demanding to be let in. I told her to hide in the trunk. I told her I would convince him that she was not here." She looked up now. "And she wasn't."

Half-truths and outright lies. Flight and chase. A hunchbacked Rilsian scrubbing a column in the night. Wait had all the information he needed. Yet he held on to the small bit of control he retained, spoke through jaws clenched and grinding together. "Who? Tell me!"

She looked away. "I can barely—"

"Say his name, Sabal."

Agreth.

The name reverberated through his skull, a sound not her voice, not a word at all, but an intonation of hums, thuds and clatters that spoke to the beast awakening. Wait's hand curled around the hilt of his sword as warm in his palm as the flesh of another hand. The thrumming building and settling and building again became a rip current inside him, pulling him further into the fury that once saved a king. An image formed in that violent, frenzied darkness. Wait held on to it, coaxed it like a potter at his clay. He would find the image that went with the name making those sounds in his head, and he would kill it.

"Wait, no! Listen to me!" Something grasped his arm, held on so that he could not move without dragging it. "If you kill him now, Linhare

84

will remain lost forever. Please! You must go after her! Go into the trunk! You've already failed her once this night! Now you must save her!"

The words echoed in the silence suddenly between his ears. Wait could not move. He could barely think beyond that echoing truth.

You failed her...now you must save her.

Shame absorbed the bloodlust, shifted its course. He found her there, behind his lids. His queen. His beloved.

"Linhare."

Wait whispered her name, sealing it to the battle-lust that had left him the last man standing in Tassry. He sank into the horror, welcomed it with a mad roar that went on and on, searing his throat and stealing his voice. It echoed throughout the castle, into the Vale and beyond. Bound to it, bound to her, he would save her or die.

SABAL STOOD TREMBLING OVER THE CLOSED LID that knocked her backward when Wait dove in. She opened it, cautiously, and breathed easier to see it was again empty. It had been simpler than she thought to get him in there. More frightening, but easier. She touched her tender cheekbone; fingertips came away bloodied. The cut stung horribly. With any luck, it would leave a thin, righteous scar.

She walked calmly to the door, put her head out. The guard on the other side leaned closer.

"Did you send for him?"

"Yes, my lady."

"And you told him it was the queensguard called for him."

"Yes, my lady."

"Perfect. Knock softly when you see him coming down the hall." She ran a seductive finger along his chin, down his chest, gratified by the way he shuddered. He was no one, not even her sort of attractive, and would never have been the one she chose to give her most precious gift; but it had been necessary to bind him to the charm she devised, and he was the closest at hand. "You will be well-rewarded for your service. And your secrecy."

Sabal closed the door on him, leaned against it. She let the blood drip down her face, onto her gown. Smiling, she yanked at the neckline, tore the seam to expose one perfect breast, and giggled softly into her hand. Wait hadn't wanted what she gave the guard, but he would claim it nonetheless, even if he was never seen again.

"It's his own fault," she whispered, and though something like regret panged in her chest, Sabal would not turn back. Jinna was right; sex was not just for making babies. It was powerful magic that would help her get everything she deserved, everything that instead always went to Linhare.

The guard's summoning knock banished all thought. She grabbed the stool from her vanity. Dashing to the tall window, Sabal threw it through the glass, took a deep breath, and screamed.

Mound

LINHARE'S FIRST SENSATION was the fresh, sweet scent of nearby woods: thick, rain-drenched pines like the ones in Lerolia. *Fae Pines* her mother had called them. In those moments between here and there, Linhare found her mother's face and smiled before it all came rushing back.

She came up on her elbows, shielded her eyes from the sunlight. There, just a short distance away, stood the pines, the sun setting over them. Pushing herself up, she found herself atop a mound. Clothes and shoes, trinkets, books and toys. Linhare peered over the edge; the mound was higher than it was wide, and quite unsteady. Wiggling tentatively, she sighed relief when it held.

Turning over onto her belly to shimmy down, Linhare's hand landed upon something wet and squishy and cold. She pulled her hand back to find, held down beneath a silver candlestick, a bit of impossibly familiar blue fabric.

Linhare pulled it free. She gasped, lost her traction, could grab nothing that did not come away with her. She slid down the piecemeal mountain to land in a heap along with all the dislodged trinkets. Groaning to her feet, she brushed debris from her gown—the same gown she'd worn to dinner. With Agreth. Linhare shuddered. The front remained undone to her waist. Her fingers clenched, squeezing rainwater from the fabric still in her hand, and unclenched. She let go a deep breath, shook out the wet fabric, and held it up to the dying sunlight. How or why it was there did not matter; it was undeniably the wrap her father brought her from Leftfoot, the treasure she thought lost. Perhaps *still* lost, and she, only dreaming.

Or dead.

Touching her arms, her torso, Linhare did not feel dead. If her stepfather had discovered her hiding in the trunk and beaten her to death, she remembered nothing of it. If it was all a dream, it was the most solid and coherent of its kind. But this was *not* the Vale. Her stepfather was nowhere near. She was safe, for now.

And Sabal? Is Sabal safe? Or did you barter your own safety for hers?

"Oh, my baby sister."

Sinking to the ground, knees to her chest, Linhare curled into a little ball. She watched the sun set until it was a sliver of pink, crested by a crimson dusk, until she saw nothing but soft night and infinite stars. She clutched the damp wrap about her shoulders, surveyed the trinket mountain strangely less imposing in the dark, like remembering the vestiges of a nightmare upon waking. Linhare felt no fear; not of her surroundings or the night forest. There were lights within the darkened wood. They sparkled as she moved this way and that, lights from a cottage, or a small village. Someone there would help.

Her gown, ruined with repulsive memories, was also completely unsuitable for trekking through the woods. Pulling out whatever she could without tumbling the trinket mound, she collected garments more suitable for walking. A pair of trousers and a man's undershirt, both too large and terribly old fashioned, the clothes were sturdy, and did not smell horrible.

She rolled her wrap into a strip, using it as a belt to keep the trousers from falling. Her slippers, thankfully still on her feet, would have to suffice. The prospect of sliding her feet into any of the mismatched boots she pried from the pile was too vile to contemplate.

With no one to reprimand her, Linhare wove her hair into a milkmaid's braid, and tied it off with a bit of ribbon ripped from her gown. Leaving the garment in the grass where she had stepped out of it, Linhare started for the lights in the pines and did not look back.

The lights never got any closer; not after an hour, not after half the night. Linhare continued on, as certain that she could not find her way back out of the forest as she was that the lights she followed would vanish with the dawn. Dropping to the ground eons of pine needles made soft, she caught her breath. The first rumblings of hunger whispered in her belly. Walking in dancing slippers blistered her heels. She took them off, rubbed at her feet. Her muscles ached. Between her legs, she felt trampled and hollow. Linhare's lip quivered and she bit down on it so hard it hurt. She would not think of that. Not now. If she did, she would never move another step.

"You really oughtn't follow. They'll gobble you down if you catch them."

Linhare spun on her bottom, spun again. "Who said that?"

"I did, silly thing. Here. Me."

The voice was small and sweet but she found no one. No thing but a bit of fluff drifting on the air. A feather. Or pollen. It began to spin as if in a whirlwind, and floated to the ground…where it became a big brown cat.

"Are you a bolley?" asked the cat. "I've never seen a bolley big as you. But you're pretty as one."

Linhare's mouth dropped open. The cat's shoulders shook and a stream of giggles tumbled forth. "No, not a bolley. Not Drümbul, either. Far too small and bright to be Drümbul."

The cat rubbed up against her trouser leg, purring loudly. Bewildered, Linhare scratched between its ears. It pushed up into her hand, rubbing its face against her knuckles and behaving in all ways like an ordinary cat. Rolling onto its back, it offered a soft belly. Linhare gave it a good scratching. The animal held on to her hand with both its paws and gnawed playfully. Tickling the brown belly, laughing softly at her own folly, she said, "My mind is playing games with me, little catkin. I'm still in the trunk dreaming. Or maybe I really am dead."

The cat resumed twisting about her legs. "If you're dreaming, then I'm just a bit of a dream. And if you're dead, then so am I. Since I'm myself, and neither dead nor a bit of a dream, you can't be, either."

Linhare yanked her hand away. "How—who? Cats don't speak."

"Of course they don't, and neither would I, if I were a cat."

The cat became a frog, then a fawn, then a boy grinning wickedly. The boy bowed and as he did, stretched into a man, tall and handsome, his grin just as wicked. Another blink and there was the cat again, licking at its paw as if it had been doing so all along.

"What are you?"

"I asked you first."

"I—I am Linhare."

"Linhare." The cat rolled her name out, elongating it so it sounded like *Lin-hhaaaare.* "Lovely. I am Kish. At least, today I am. When I awoke this morning, that is what I decided." The feline turned round and round. "Do you like it?"

"I do," she said warily. "Very handsome."

"Exactly what I thought. Well, then, come along. I'll take you there."

"Where will you take me?"

"To where you need to go."

"Wait!" she called when the brown cat moved to bound away. "Please, can you tell me where I am?"

"In the wood."

"What wood? Where?"

The cat cocked its head. Linhare's head swam, but she held on to what remained of her sanity after asking a brown cat named Kish that had been a fluffy bit of pollen where in the world she was.

"You are here, Linhare. In this piney wood. If there is more to it than that, I don't know. Now if you don't want the ghasty-haints to gobble you up with the dawn, you ought to come with me."

Childhood fears slithered up her back. "Ghasty-haints?"

"The lights you were following."

Linhare's eyes darted to the depths of forest where the faintest lights still twinkled in the pale dawn. Scrambling to her feet, she followed after the big brown cat already bounding away, tail in the air.

"Come, drink from this pool. You will feel better."

Moments, hours, Linhare had no idea how long she followed Kish. Past all limits of endurance, she dropped down beside the water's edge, plunged her head into the crystalline water, cupped her hands and drank deeply. The water, sweet and icy cold, tasted better than the sweetest wine. A burst of laughter erupted from her lips, scattering birds from the trees.

"This is wonderful!"

"Refreshing, yes," Kish said. "Have a care you do not drink too much. Only just enough."

She giggled. Whether some property of the water or her exhaustion, Linhare felt as giddy as she had on the mountain, drinking stolen spirits with friends she could barely recall.

Enough.

The echo, as deep and musical as Kish's was sweet and jingling, lifted Linhare's dripping face from the water. A hand came down. Long fingers curled around hers, assisted her gently to her feet. Linhare's eyes moved up a pair of long limbs, narrow hips; up torso and shoulders to the face smiling down upon her. A handsome face, a kind one and framed by hair as long as her own and black as sheridans ore in the fire. He said, "Come now, dear one. Away from the pool lest you forget who you are entirely."

Sunlight warmed her face; or was it his smile? The warmth penetrated her skin and into her blood, soothing...something. Some horror. Linhare could not recall it. All she knew was the man's kind face, his smile warming her through.

"There now." The man wiped her face dry with a corner of his sleeve. "Are you refreshed?"

"I brought her, Beloël," Kish cried out before she could make herself speak. "I brought her, just like you asked."

The man bent to the cat, scratching him between the ears. "You did, loyal friend."

"The ghasty-haints tried to get her."

"Of course they did. It is what they do." Rising, he said to Linhare, "You have come a long way."

"I have?"

"A very long way. So much further than you think."

"How do you know how far I've come?"

"I know how far you've come because you are not fae. That means you are from Away, and this place is Beyond, outside of anything you know. Does that frighten you?"

"No." Linhare shook her head slowly and felt as if she were waking from a dream, into another dream.

"Then come."

He was as tall and as broad as...as someone she could not quite remember, even if she could conjure his handsome, somber face, but there all familiarity ended. Linhare could not recall where she came from, or why she had left, but she knew that wherever that place was, whoever was missing her there, it was nothing like here: This *Beyond* beyond what, she could not guess.

Memorystones

LINHARE WOKE TO SUNLIGHT, soft and new, a smile on her lips, and her heart light. Such dreams! A brown, talking cat, and a handsome Drümbul Lord coaxing her gently through the wood. She half-remembered the old tales of the Drümbul and forgetting pools and that one must never trust either; but this one had lifted her off her feet, the arms around her reminded her of Wait, and old tales lost their caution.

"Jinna," she murmured. "I have to tell you about my dream before it fades. Jinna?"

Rolling over onto her side, Linhare blinked away sunlight and sleep and—

Oh...no.

Rushing memory gathered in her head, spilled into sunlight whirling with pollen and dust motes dancing in the sunshine, giggling madly. Linhare tried to take deep breaths but could only gasp. Her vision blurred. Forcing a long, shuddering inhale, she held it until she could sit up without doubling over.

"It wasn't a dream," she said, and remembered more clearly the brown cat, Kish, and the Drümbul Lord, Beloël. They had guided her to this place, fed her, put her gently into this leafy bower suspended like a spider web between low branches. High enough off the ground to stay dry but low enough for her to descend without assistance, the flower-decked nest swayed with her movements. Wrapping up in her blanket, a soft thing like thistledown and milkweed silk, Linhare climbed out and into a cloud of gobbets drifting like insects. They danced about her head, their sweet giggling making her smile. Linhare felt herself propelled to a glade of large boulders seemingly dropped from the pocket of some giant, somewhere far from where they belonged. The giggling cloud dissipated. Upon a rather flat stone sat a bowl of water and another of fruit; a grainy loaf, wrapped in a bit of colorful cloth and warm with baking or sunshine.

"Thank you," she called. Gobbets swirled on the breeze. She ate and drank, bundling up what she could not finish. Tying the blanket across her chest, like the slings she had seen women in Littlevale carry their babies in, she tucked the remainder of her food into it. Despite her circumstances, Linhare felt a little better. She lifted her face to the dappling sunshine, and tried to make sense out of the nonsensical; but a puff of icy air opened her eyes. Sunlight seemed somehow dimmer. Gobbets floating only a moment ago were gone, leaving the air still, and getting colder. Curious and strangely unafraid, Linhare wound her way through the rock grove. She inched around the largest boulder.

Cold blasted her hard. She shielded her face with both arms, bending to keep from toppling, turning her head this way and that in some vain attempt to breathe without gasping. Then the blast blew out just as suddenly, though the chill lingered. Linhare lowered her arms.

Snow?

Joy trickled through her body, making her shiver. The Vale saw little of it, but it once blanketed her world, never melting before the next storm hit, crippling the archipelago for weeks. Lean times, if one happened to be poor, or adult. For her, Sabal, Jinna, all the children of the castle, it had been a bolleytale too wonderful to question.

Linhare lifted her face to the snow falling upon it. Little girls laughed. Linhare turned in circles, her slippers crunching in the fresh fall. An endearing snort turned her about, and there was little Jinna, a specter blooming in remembered daylight. And there, Sabal. They pelted the other children with fistfuls of snow. The fort, made to better play snow-battle from morning until dusk, sprouted out of the frozen ground. Her mother, young and alive and beautiful, stood in the solarium window; and her father—*oh, da!*—lifted a little girl, bundled but for the long brown braid escaping from her fur hood.

Linhare walked unseen among the battling children. She paused beside her father and listened to the muted sound of his laughter. The little girl he placed atop the snow-turret turned to him, laughing because he laughed. Her father waved across the ward. Linhare followed the gesture to Wait, who saluted in turn, immense and earnest and always there at the edge of it all. A man only halfway through his twenties, stoic and handsome, he seemed older. Careworn.

A warm breeze blew at her back. Wait remained, slightly older but no more and no less earnest, and not in the snowy inner ward. Linhare stood in the grand ballroom seldom used after the king's death, and most recently for Diandra's funeral feast. Wait was watching the dance floor, his eyes moving with someone there.

Linhare saw herself, dancing with her father and dressed all in white. Her hair, only partway down her back, curled into ringlets. A thin band of silver held those curls away from her face, clear and young and untroubled. King Bennis smiled softly, his eyes full of the sort of love Linhare had not felt shine upon her since his death.

This moment, unlike the snow fight, Linhare remembered clearly. Painfully. In that instant her father's body tensed, Linhare felt the pain rip through her own heart, saw the fear clutching him as he clutched his chest. And then the sensation of Wait whisking her back onto the dance floor, back into the dance.

He moved gracefully, his arms sure and confident. Nothing could be wrong, not when he looked upon her with that devotion and astonishment in his eyes. Her father had tripped, twisted his ankle, and Wait could not allow the midnight dance on her fifteenth birthday to be ruined. He was her father's greatest friend, his protector and hers. He was her secret longing. That had been enough for the younger Linhare, even if the future would prove the kindness of this lie.

"Halloo? Is anyone there?"

Linhare gasped. The specters of the past vanished. Snow and ballroom, too. She searched for the source, opened her mouth to call back and heard: "No more, no more, no more." Then a wail, furious and pitiful. "I will go mad!"

Ahead, just there where Linhare thought she could see a shoulder or a knee, something moved. It was a shoulder, attached to an arm, attached to a feminine hand that smacked at the boulder the woman hid behind. As she got closer, Linhare heard her cursing like a Dockside sailor. Mixed in with the cursing and sobbing, a familiar snort that sent Linhare's heart racing.

"Jinna?"

The woman bolted to her feet, spun about, arm pulled back and fist ready to fly.

"Jinna!"

Grasping her shoulders, Linhare did not care if she got hit or if the woman she embraced was memory or gobbet in the form of her dearest friend. And then Jinna was embracing her in turn, the two of them weeping and laughing and weeping again.

"How is it you are here?"

"I don't know that I am! How is it that you are here?"

"I don't know that I am, either!"

"I'm afraid to believe you're real." Jinna sniffed. "I have been so frightened, Linny. Me! Frightened! Can you imagine? But the wood is full of all sorts of ghouls and ghasts that teased and taunted me to this grove of rocks. I've been trapped in memories for hours and hours."

"Hours?" Linhare asked. "You vanished from the Vale weeks ago."

"Weeks? That can't be. I'd have starved to death by now."

"But it is. Was." Linhare shook her head, her face burning for all the ill she had thought of her friend. She gave her the food from her sling. "Here. You must be hungry. Eat. And tell me, Jinna. Tell me everything that happened after Chira came for us the day my mother died."

Jinna froze, bread halfway to her mouth. Her hand fell slowly. "Ta-Diandra? Dead?"

"Oh, Jin." Linhare's heart ached. "I'm sorry. I forgot…I mean, I didn't think about…" She sighed, swelling heart, welling tears. "There is so much to tell. Yes, Jinna. My mother died giving birth, and so did her infant son…"

*   *   *

Linhare told Jinna everything from Diandra's death to slapping her sister on the terrace, at which point Jinna laughed herself silly, and thankfully spared Linhare going into details of that night she would rather forget than relive.

"Oh, I would give all my molars to see the look on her face!" Jinna snorted. "Good for you, Linny."

"No, it was not good. She is a child, Jinna. Children say nasty things. But you haven't said how you got here yet," Linhare coaxed. Stalled. "Tell me, Jin. What happened after...that afternoon Chira came to fetch us."

Jinna grimaced. Tears glistened. She sniffed them back and said, "I went to fetch mother, but she was already gone when I got there. I rested a bit, then started back. It was late. The castle was quiet. I went to your room to change my sweaty clothes and..." she glanced out of the corner of her eye. "I'll admit it. I was obsessed with proving Sabal stole your book. I didn't think...I had no thought that Ta-Diandra was in any danger. I swear it, Linny! I saw the opportunity to search with impunity, and I took it."

"Oh, Jinna."

"Don't '*Oh, Jinna*' me. I was right." Jinna reached into a deep pocket of her dress and pulled from it something red and square, scarred and familiar. She placed it on Linhare's outstretched hand. "See?"

"Where did you...?"

"That's the next part, Linny. I was in Sabal's room, convinced she'd hidden the book in that huge trunk. It was empty, but the bottom sounded hollow when I kicked at it. I climbed in and the next thing I knew, the lid came down and I fell atop a—"

"—trinket mound in a meadow, surrounded by a piney wood."

"—where the book was sitting, pretty as you please, under my nose. I nipped it just before the nasty things in this place chased me off."

Linhare stared at the book she never thought to see again. She untied the wrappings, let it open where it would, but did not read the words she knew too well.

"How'd she get you?"

Jinna's words blinked Linhare back to the moment. She tucked the journal into her sling.

"I don't under—"

"Sabal! How'd she get you into the trunk?"

Hide in there. I will open the door as if he just woke me and tell him you are not here.

Linhare shuddered. "It wasn't like that. Sabal would never—"

What if he looks in the trunk?

It won't matter...

95

"Stop being a fool, Linny!" Jinna snapped. "She sent that book *and* me here. And now you. Playing the bereaved orphan, I am certain, making sure everyone knows just how she's suffering to have lost her mother and her sister so close together. Little snake. Dash her from the Gate!"

Jinna's cursing faded into a faraway buzzing Linhare could barely hear. Had Sabal stolen her book, sent it into fae? Could she have seen Jinna in the trunk and sent her away, too? If that was true, then she knew what would happen when she bid Linhare hide in it. But she couldn't have, wouldn't have, because Linhare had come to her hurt and weeping. Sabal had been so calm. She had known just what to do.

Trust me...

"Jinna, no." Linhare placed a gentle hand upon her friend's and the faraway frenzy of cursing ceased. She felt strangely calm even if tears were already forming. "You don't understand. It wasn't like that at all."

Rescue

WAIT TUMBLED. CLANKING, CLATTERING, dislodging trinkets and books and clothing; flasks, musical instruments crafted of wood and metal, small weapons, rusted eating utensils and dented cups. Porcelain statuettes shattered. Glass vases and dishes chipped. He plunged down a household piled atop itself after the building had turned to dust.

Rolling off the last of it and into the tall grass, Wait came instantly to his feet, sword in hand. The bloodlust still held him but the tumble and the shock tamed it somewhat. Bent over, hands on knees, he caught his breath and gained his bearings.

Sun dipping to the horizon. Pinewood. Meadow. Pile of discarded junk. Wait took it all in, assessed it, scrutinized it, came to his conclusions. Despite the extensive knowledge gained while traveling with Ben, this was no place he recognized. Wherever *here* was, Linhare was near. Dakhan instinct, life bond or love, Wait felt her presence as certainly as he could see the tree line.

Rising to his full height, eyes on the trinket mound, Wait moved closer to it. How long had oblivious owners put their treasures into the trunk that swallowed them down, only to leave them on this pile, in this place? By the look of it—centuries. Wait nudged at it with his foot. How much effort would it take to topple? Not much. One strategic yank and the whole thing would come down.

All around the mound, the tall, tamped down grass evidenced that someone had circled it again and again. And there, just to the left, a distinct trail broke away into the meadow.

Wait moved closer to inspect the ground. No tufts of hair. No droppings. No animal bedded there or made the trail. Pushing to his feet, he noticed a pile of clothing, some of which looked quite old. Using the tip of his sword, Wait searched the pile. There was nothing to suggest that Linhare pulled these things from the mound, but Wait knew she had.

A crumpled bundle of cloth there near the pile of clothes confirmed his instinct. The dress belonged to Linhare. Gathering it from the ground, he held it up to inspect. Wait noted the tangle of ribbon, the smears of blood. Fury began to narrow his vision again. His mind's eye saw the column, could almost see Linhare pressed up against it. There he cut it off. He would not imagine more, not if he was to keep his mind about him. Wait dropped the gown, watching it float to the ground and grasping at every bit of control he possessed to keep the roar inside his head.

A loud *whump* followed by clattering and cursing spun him about. Wait took stance, hunched and ready, when the tumble of dark hair and orange and yellow cloth came to a stop at his feet.

"Egaldo?"

"Egalfo, sir."

Wait hauled the young Therk to his feet. "What are you doing here?"

"I followed you, sir." Egalfo's hands raised to shield his head. "I saw. I heard. And I followed. Put that thing down before someone gets hurt."

Wait glanced at the sword he'd forgotten he held, and slid the weapon into its scabbard.

"Explain."

Egalfo straightened his clothes, smoothed back his hair. "I saw you go into the trunk, sir. I slipped into the room when the guard wasn't looking. He's a poor guard, I'll have you know. It didn't take much to distract—"

"Get on with it."

"Yes, sorry. Where was I? Right, I slipped in, hid behind a drapery and listened. She tried to seduce you once, didn't she."

Wait did not answer.

"I thought as much. Anyone else know about it?"

Probably most of the castle staff. Again, Wait did not answer. Egalfo shrugged.

"After you went roaring into the trunk, she spoke quietly to the guard. I couldn't hear what she said, because I was trying to see what that trunk was all about, where you might have gone. I thought maybe you were dead. I didn't get the chance, because she came back, quite pleased with herself I think, and ripped the neckline of her gown. Then she took a stool from her vanity and threw it through the window. When she started screaming, I made a dive for the trunk. The rest..." He spread his hands.

"She...it was an act?"

"She's quite good, I'll give her that. Jinna told some tales about the younger princess. I didn't really believe she could be—"

"It can't be true." Wait grabbed Egalfo by the front of his shirt. "Why would she...?"

But there were many reasons, not the least of which being his rejection. He let go of Egalfo. Gently.

"I'm sorry, sir. This must come as quite a blow. But there is a blue sky to this raincloud. If the young princess used her trunk to be rid of you, she did the same to your queen and my Jinna. We will find them, sir. You and me."

"What makes you think Jinna is here?"

"Because she said it. Princess Sabal did. Did you not hear her? She wondered, so innocently, if the same fate that befell her sister also befell Jinna. For a well-trained man, Dakhonne, no less, you are not very observant."

Wait pushed his fingers through his hair. The mystery left behind was beginning to unravel itself. Sabal said all the right things; but had she lied? The fury shivered through him. No. The ruin of Linhare's gown was proof enough that at least some of the younger princess' tale was true—the worst part. Whatever she was after, he was in no position to stop her; even if he were, Linhare came first. She was here, wherever here was. He would find her.

"Linhare went that way." He pointed to the trail through tall grass. "I am going after her. I thank you for what you have done, but she is why I am here. If you wish to accompany me, feel free to do so. Finding Jinna must come second to finding Linhare."

Egalfo grinned, hop-stepping after Wait. "Where you find one, you will find the other," he said. "They will be drawn together like north and a compass needle."

"Are you always this dramatic?"

Bowing low, Egalfo snapped upright with a leap. "I have been trained as a showman since my aunt and uncle took me into their family. What you see as drama, I see as polish. For you, sir, I will try to restrain myself."

"Try hard," Wait said, and started hacking at the tall grass.

"I CAN'T BELIEVE SHE NEVER TOLD YOU."

Jinna sat cross-legged on the flat boulder, torn between taking Linhare into her arms and honoring the strength with which she spoke of so much horror.

"I should have known," Linhare said, sniffing back tears. "It was all there, plain to see. She married Agreth to spare me. She risked her life to become pregnant so that I would be forever saved from marrying Sisolo. I was a fool. I should have seen and done the right thing. I am—was to be queen. I knew I would not marry for love."

"Those were choices she made, Linny." Jinna put a hand on her friend's knee. "You were to be queen, but she *was* queen. And your mother. You can't blame yourself."

Linhare wept softly. Jinna continued to pat her knee. All around them, fae sunlight twinkled. Jinna did not trust such twinkling. Lures were always pretty until the hook snagged in your lip. *Like Agreth, the bastard.* Jinna's own lusty fantasies when the pretty king first appeared in the Vale died quick deaths, but she never imagined him capable of rape.

Linhare coughed, sniffed, pushed back hair that had come unbound. "I just don't understand, Jinna. The way he spoke, the things he said…" She let her arms fall. "He was certain I wanted him, that I was in love with him. But I never once gave him any indication that I harbored any feelings at all towards him. Never once."

"Of course you didn't." Jinna took both her hands and kissed them. "Agreth wanted you, so he took you."

"I didn't—I couldn't even scream. I couldn't call for help."

"You were terrified. *He* was in the wrong, and if I hear you blame yourself in any way, I'll pinch you good and sound." She jostled Linhare gently. "But you showed him, sweetling. You probably broke that wand of his."

Linhare pulled her hands away to wipe tears from her cheeks. "What if he is doing the same to Sabal right now? What if I sacrificed her for my own safety?"

Jinna bit the insides of her cheeks to keep from fuming. Whatever Sabal did, for whatever reason, kept Agreth from getting to Linhare a second time. For that, Jinna would be forever grateful; but the younger princess was not suffering at anyone's hands, of that, she was certain.

"Hush now." Jinna ran a tender hand down the length of Linhare's braid. "Hush. Whatever I think about your sister, she is—" *Ambitious, selfish, traitorous, cunning.* "—she knows what happened, and will take the proper precautions. We are here, together. That has to count for something, right?"

"But where is here? How will we ever get home?"

"Perhaps home is not the best place to be."

"I am queen, Jinna."

"That's not really relevant just now though, is it?"

"I suppose not." She plucked at her clothes. "What would Chira say?"

Laughter bubbled up from Linhare's throat. Jinna knew where such laughter came from, and where it would end if not dealt with quickly.

"I wonder where all your friends from yesterday are," she said, sliding down from the boulder and pulling Linhare with her. "Do you think they're watching us?"

"I am certain they are. But they mean no harm."

"Maybe not to you. You've no idea what I've endured."

When Linhare laughed this time, it was sad and deflated, but not hysterical. "What did you do to them, Jinna?"

"I may have cursed at them some. Thrown a few rocks and sticks. No tall, handsome stranger came to *my* aid. I was frightened." Jinna offered a hand to Linhare. "It has been an exhausting morning," she said. "I don't know about you, but I could do with a nap."

Spreading out the sun-warmed blanket, Jinna laid down and held out her arms. Linhare fell into them without protest. Drawing the edges of the blanket around them both, Jinna fell almost instantly asleep, the sound of Linhare's soft weeping in her ear, or her dreams.

*   *   *

100

Her trail was not difficult to follow. The flattened grass led to distinct disturbances on the forest floor that Wait did not follow; he followed his own instincts tugging at him like the old childhood game, *Olly! Olly! Woo!* When he strayed from the path Linhare took, *Olly!* But when he found it again, *Woo! Woo! Woo!*

"Sir! Sir! Wait for me!"

Again Egalfo lagged behind. It was nearly dusk and they had made, in Wait's estimation, little enough progress. A sparkle like sunlight on water caught his attention. Wait noted a break in the brush, as if some hand had tucked it aside just so.

Woo! Woo! Woo!

"Sir! Please wait!"

Long strides put him beside the pool in less time than it took to think about walking. Wait closed his eyes. Yes, she had been here. There was something else on this place; something unsettling, yet soothing at the same time.

"Leave me if you must." Egalfo fell at his feet. "But I can't keep going."

Wait's hands clenched at his sides. On the ground at his feet, Egalfo panting like an excited dog. "I am fit as any athlete but I cannot keep up with your stride. And I am hungry, sir. I have eaten nothing, sir. Not since your Firstman saw to a meal for me this morning, sir."

"My name is Wait."

"Again, I apologize."

"Stop apologizing. Stop fawning. That is not what you followed me here for. You are not my servant. I'm not going to cut you in two for not bowing every time I speak, so stop."

Egalfo rose to his feet. His mouth opened, then closed again. "I—I will try, s—Wait."

Wait let out a deep breath. Dusk was settling into dark. He knew better than to attempt continuing blind.

"We'll make camp here," he said. "I'll find us food. You gather whatever dry wood you can find. I want it burning by the time I get back."

As promised, Wait found food everywhere. Berries on bushes. Tubers below-ground and greens above. There were mollusks in bunches along the shallow edges of the pool, and fish that did not dart away when the men speared them. Wait gathered what he could, wishing for one of the cooking pots he earlier saw on the trinket mound.

He placed the mollusks on hot stones to steam open, then used the shells to heat water enough to sip. He spitted the fish, then plucked the piping tubers from the ashes he'd buried them in, macerating them with the greens and the berries to sweeten the otherwise bitter mash. Egalfo, balanced on his acrobat haunches, had watched with interest. Now he leaned back on his palms, patting his contented stomach.

"That was a fine meal. As fine a meal as I've ever eaten."

Wait grunted but said nothing. He reclined on his elbows beside the snapping, popping fire. His eyes drooped to slits that saw only shadows dancing on and around the water. Those shadows whispered promises of peaceful comfort. *Come. Come. We will take away your cares.*

"I need to wash." Egalfo rose, heading for the water's edge. Wait was suddenly awake. He grabbed Egalfo so fast that he startled even himself. "Don't," was all he said, and let him go. The younger man dropped to sit cross-legged, his head in his hands and his long, dark hair shielding his face.

"You didn't have to scare the skin off me."

Wait tipped back on his elbows again, willed his heart to stop hammering. The surface of the pool still did not stir, not even with insects skimming the surface or fish snapping them down. Yet he knew there were fish in there; and he knew there were insects in the air all around him. Sitting up, he dug around in his pocket to pull out a handkerchief.

"Wash with this," he said, handing it to Egalfo. "Just stay well back from the edge."

"What is the danger?"

"I'm not sure. It just doesn't feel right. Not evil. Just not...right."

Egalfo stood up again, pulling off his flamboyant shirt and stepping out of his pants. Crouching down near enough the water's edge to reach it, he dipped the handkerchief into the water again and again.

"Wait," he said as he washed the back of his neck. "A curious name, if I may say. No stranger than Egalfo, mind you, but curious."

Wait sat up, gathering his knees in massive arms. "It isn't my real name," he said. "It's my Dakhan name."

"I really don't know much about your sect."

"No one does. It's best that way."

"Why?"

Wait shrugged. Egalfo dipped the cloth again, ringing it over his head. "May I ask the name your mother and father gave you? Is it against some code?"

"It's a name I've outgrown," Wait said. "But it's not against any code to tell you. My name was Calryan."

"Calryan." Egalfo rolled the name over his tongue. "Cal. Hmm. I like Wait better. It has much more—"

"—polish?"

Egalfo laughed. "Yes, polish." He sobered then, wringing the handkerchief tight. "I do not know what my parents named me. I suppose

I am like you; I received a name that would fit my new life. Whatever my first name was is lost, though. I envy you, knowing yours."

"Do you know where your aunt and uncle found you?" Wait asked. "Who they bought the boat from?"

"As far as I know, it was a dry-docked wreck for quite some time. Perhaps my mother or father or both were living in it and had to flee when it was sold. From what my aunt tells me, I was well fed, if a little frightened. Someone cared for me."

"And no one tried to find your parents?"

Egalfo shrugged, turning to dip into the water. Standing up, he scrubbed at his torso and down his legs, rewetting the handkerchief whenever it became too dry. "Dyonia is an obscure place," he said, "full of people who do not wish to be noticed. That is where I was found."

"I know it well," Wait told him. "I was born on Crones Hook. I lived there until I was ten or so. Dyonia was only a rowboat ride away. My father and I used to sell clams there."

"And your mother?"

"She died when I was still a boy."

"I'm very sorry. But there! There is something else we have in common—we are motherless boys. See, you and I are not so different."

Picking up his clothes, Egalfo came closer to the fire. He held up his shirt, sniffing at it and making disgusted noises.

"It seems a shame to befoul this lovely pool with my filth," he said. "But I do not think I can put these on again without washing them first."

Wait stood up and unbuckled his sword belt. He undressed to his smallclothes and edged around the pool while Egalfo dunked and dunked his garments in the shallows with a stick. Crouching down to scoop up water and splash it onto his face and neck, Wait resisted the urge to guzzle down the icy goodness. The shadows were gone, but not the instinct telling him to beware. He placed a hand upon the surface, opened himself up to what the water tried to tell him. He saw his mother's face, anguished and angry. He heard her sobbing, his father's pleas.

Slapping at the water, Wait started to his feet only to be drawn back again to the rippling surface, to a flash of something blue unearthed by the disturbed silt, and glowing as if with moonlight. He waited for the water to go still.

A...stone?

Wait pinched it from the water and let it roll onto his palm. Pale, blue, a nearly perfect oval, it resembled an old man's eye; iridescent veins like cataracts just beneath the surface appeared as it dried. Those veins seemed to pulse in the light coming from the fire. Wait could almost feel it, like a heartbeat. Closing his hand around the stone that fit perfect and warm into the center of his palm, he moved back to where Egalfo was hanging his clothes on a stick wedged into the soft ground near the fire.

"A trick I learned, living so much of my life on the road," Egalfo said. "I could do the same for yours, if you wish."

"No, thanks." Wait pulled his clothes back on, buckling his sword belt in place and tucking the stone into his breast pocket. "Get some sleep. I'll take first watch."

"First watch? Is it really necessary to set a watch?"

"We're in unfamiliar territory."

"Then I suppose you'll be waking me at some horrifying hour to relieve you."

"I suppose I will be. Good night, Egalfo."

Dropping down beside the fire, Wait unsheathed his sword. The blade was fine and black and perfectly balanced, the hilt crafted specifically for his hand. Like every Dakhan sword, a master smith of their sect had forged it out of the sheridans ore Wait mined with his own hands. During that time when most boys still threw sticks and rocks at one another in mock games of war, he was in training. It was all he knew, all he wanted to remember, of his youth.

Taking his whetting stone from the pouch at his side, he sharpened his already deadly blade. The steady *scrape-scrape-scrape* of metal on stone soothed him as nothing else could.

"Oooh. Prickly-spiky."

The small voice startled him, but Wait did not jump. He turned to the pool and found a small, furry head visible only from the eyes up.

Wait held the little creature's beady gaze, never blinking, never wavering, waiting for it to speak again even if his mind told him it could not have. The voice had certainly not been Egalfo's; the young man snored softly there on the bank.

The furry face rose higher out of the water, paddled for the shore and shook water from its grey-brown fur. Long-bodied and sinuous, almost like a fat, furry snake, it waddled toward him on stubby legs. Its fur was nearly dry already, downy soft and more brown than grey. The little animal nudged the sword with its nose. "Prickly-spiky," it said again.

There was nothing to do but answer. "It is a sword."

The animal looked up at him, its head cocked. "Bad. Prickly-spiky, bad."

"That depends on which end of it you happen to be."

The little animal rolled onto its back, chortling and cooing with what Wait took to be laughter. The same instinct that kept him back from the pool told him this creature meant no harm. He held out his hand and let it sniff him, then it slunk to sleeping Egalfo to sniff at him.

"Desert-boy," it came back to say. "Dakhan-man and Desert-boy."

"I am Wait."

"Dakhan-man," it insisted and lowered its soft muzzle into Wait's outstretched hand. It trilled deep in its throat, something akin to a cat's purr. Rolling onto its back, it offered Wait its belly.

"Dakhan-man, good." It purred as Wait stroked it. "Prickly-spiky, bad. Nice Dakhan-man. Good and nice. Waterfurry like Dakhan-man."

"How do you know I am Dakhonne?"

The waterfurry picked up its head, then rolled over so that it could clamber onto Wait's lap. Tiny paws resting on his abdomen, it nuzzled Wait's chest. "Long-gone, Dakhan-man. Sweet-gone. Long-gone. Why has Dakhan-man come? Why?"

Wait petted the creature, holding it against him. It trilled again, louder now that it was so close, dipping and ducking from hand to hand.

"I am looking for a woman," Wait said when it finally settled down to trill in his lap. "She was here at this pool recently. Maybe yesterday. Maybe today. Do you understand? Have you seen her?"

The waterfurry wiggled onto its back to gaze up almost lovingly. "Sad-woman. Hurt-woman. Water take sad-hurt. Drümbul-man come. Safe-woman, now. Happy-woman, now."

Drümbul? Wait tucked the word away. "Drümbul-man took her away from here?"

"Drümbul-man, yes. Sweet-sad, happy-sad."

"Where did he take her?"

"Away. Too far for waterfurries. Not far for Dakhan-man."

"Can you tell me where to find her?"

The creature slipped out of his hands and off his lap. It slinked to the water's edge and slipped beneath the surface only to pop up again. "Will find. No fear. Stay, Dakhan-man. Waterfurry find."

And it was gone. Not even a ripple in the water marked the place where it had been.

Faekind

WAIT SAT UP, his hand going automatically to his sword hilt. Blinking against the gentle sunlight dappling through the pine boughs, he found only the still pool and a sleeping Egalfo to face. He let his shoulders sag; his hand fell from his hilt. He rubbed at his eyes, dismayed that he had slept so soundly in this unfamiliar, unfathomable place.

Moving to the water's edge, he kneeled to splash his face with only enough water to wash the sleep from his eyes. The icy-coldness cleared his head. He scooped a little more, pushing it through his hair.

"Uh, Wait?"

Egalfo's hushed voice lifted his head. Wait palmed water from his face.

They were everywhere they hadn't been moments ago. In the trees. Skimming the pool. Lounging upon rocks and plants and boughs. Golden rays of sunshine broken free to flitter wildly against all habits of natural light. Smaller than birds, larger than dragonflies, the beings darted about on wings fine and nimble; Wait could barely make them out of the blur, but he could hear the tiny *flrrr*.

"Bolleys," Egalfo said, "according to the stories my aunt told me as a child."

One fluttered close, hovering in Wait's face. She—for she was most definitely female—had round little features gathered in her face as if some artist's hand placed everything too near the center. It gave her a cheerful quality. Cheerful and slightly dim-witted. Creamy, curvy mounds of flesh bulged behind the skimpy, nearly transparent material of her gown and Wait fleetingly wondered how the diaphanous wings held her aloft. But there she hovered so that the puffs of air from her beating wings dried the water from his face.

Wait raised a finger, offering her a perch. She alighted upon it, pointing away from the pool and to another gathering of fae, perfectly miniaturized people all colors of earth and bark—and effectively cutting off their retreat.

"Now what?" Egalfo asked.

"They don't seem to mean any harm," Wait answered. The plump creature still perched on his finger tapped his attention her way. Coyly and coquettishly curtseying, she made peeping sounds Wait supposed were words.

"I'm sorry. I don't understand."

The bolley scrunched up her face and stomped her foot before fluttering from his knee. She flew up into the air then dove like a seabird after a fish into the pool that did not even ripple when she broke its surface. A moment later, she shot out of the water again, shaking herself dry as she circled back to Wait's finger. She gestured to the pool and the furry head suddenly there.

Wait frowned. "I thought you might have been a dream."

"No dream-me. Real-me. Dakhan-man not like the help I find?"

Wait handed the bolley off to Egalfo to squat closer to the pool. "I'm not sure I understand."

"I find sad-happy-woman, the Little Queen, like I promise. Bolleys and freelings take you to her."

"Linhare?" Egalfo cried out. The bolleys fluttered wildly and the waterfurry dove and the freelings fell to their knees. Wait turned a stone-glare on him. Egalfo blanched, but nodded.

"Where is she?" Wait asked gently when the waterfurry poked its head up out of the water again.

"Rocks-and-boulders, now. Dreaming place, now. This dark-night, Princeling glade. Dakhan-man happy, yes?"

Wait drew in a soft breath, let it go slowly, his heart doing terrible and wonderful things in his chest. "Dakhan-man happy," he said at last, and to the scrunch-faced bolley now perched upon his shoulder, "Take me to her."

LINHARE WALKED ALONE IN THE BOLLEY FOREST. Ghasty-haints lit her path but did not entice her from it. Some part of her dreaming mind told her that they wanted to, but they kept their beckoning bright to themselves, and she was not afraid.

The forest floor was soft beneath her bare feet, as soft as the dewy, pine-fragrant air invoking the Pinelands of her youth. Ahead, the path widened. She quickened her pace. Whatever drew her waited there, just beyond. Linhare's breath came faster, her heart pumped wildly.

I'm coming! I'm almost there! Wait for me! Wait!

His back was to her. Massive. Hard. Rigid as ancient wood. She stopped there at the edge of the clearing and called to him. He did not turn. Linhare crossed the clearing. His face, hidden in shadow, did not look down and smile that soothing, thrilling smile.

I'm sorry, *her dream self said.* I should have given it back the moment I realized it was yours.

Wait held out his hand. Linhare gave hers, and suddenly she was in the ballroom again, in Wait's arms. No courtly crowd watched them; Linhare was not fifteen. She and Wait danced without music in an empty ballroom.

107

Wait touched her cheek, the tip of her nose, her lips. He kissed her fingers. Then he let her go, stepped back, and shadow took him. Linhare did not cry out. He was there, somewhere. She felt him.

Linhare sat up, fully awake. Beside her, Jinna still snore-snorted softly. Wait's journal sat on the blanket where her head had rested. She picked up the book, glimpsed a dream fading, and set it down again.

She stretched the kinks from her body. Despite the softness of the forest floor, it was not a bed; warm as the blanket was, it did not keep the chill from her bones. Linhare shivered. Pines whispered. Sunlight speckled late afternoon rays. Downy bits coasted along the shafts of light, dipping and rising. The air giggled, first by dozens, then by hundreds, into something akin to birdsong.

Linhare patted Jinna's shoulder. "Wake up. Wake up, Jinna."

One blue eye opened and closed again quickly. "No."

"You must. Look!"

Growling and groaning, Jinna threw off the blanket and bolted upright. Floating bits alighted upon her arms and hair. "Oh my," Jinna whispered, "they—are they?"

"Gobbets."

Several of the drifting bits began to twirl, alighting to the ground as creatures soft and sweet. Those that took form clamored into the blanket and over it, gamboling and chittering excitedly. Then Linhare saw Kish, sitting on the hump of a low boulder and grooming his rich, brown coat.

"Kish!"

Gobbets scrambled madly in all directions at the sound of Linhare's voice. She jumped to her feet, shaking off several that were clinging to her clothes. "Are you still Kish today?"

He looked up, head cocked. "I suppose I shall have to be. Beloël commanded it."

"They talk?" Jinna's whisper was a hiss in her ear; her grip like talons. "Stars and starlight! They talk!"

Linhare shook her off as she had the gobbets. "I told you that yesterday."

"You told me a lot of things yesterday. If you haven't noticed, I don't always listen."

"Jinna, this is Kish. Kish, Jinna."

The gobbet-cat giggled, but he bowed his head. "Pleased to make your acquaintance."

"Likewise, I suppose." Jinna turned then to Linhare. "So where is this Beloël?"

Kish yawned. "The Prince of Pines bid me lead you to his glade. A revel has been planned in your honor, Little Queen." To Jinna he said, "You are most welcome, too."

"Well, isn't that just fine as feathers. I get chased through the wood and Linhare gets a revel in her honor."

Kish hopped delicately from his perch, cat-stepping to Jinna and winding himself around her ankles. He purred. "Sister, don't fret. My kin meant no harm. It's all turned a-right in the end, yes?"

"I don't know." Jinna grimaced. "We're not at the end yet."

"Then I pledge my oath that it will be."

"What good is the oath of a little catkin?" Jinna lifted the suddenly boneless cat into her arms. "Then again, you are not a catkin, are you."

"I am whatever I wish to be," he said, his voice no longer silly and giggling. "Is there something you wish me to be?"

"How about our guide out of here?"

"Your wish is my duty." Kish wriggled and Jinna put him down. "It will take until sunset to get there, but it will be a pleasant walk. First, eat."

A crusty loaf of bread, a square of soft cheese, and a hollowed out gourd full of fresh water appeared on the same flat rock. Jinna dipped into the soft cheese, squealing delightedly. Kish curled up beside her, feline eyes closed to slits, purring a low, decidedly masculine purr.

Prince of Pines

THE GOBBETS TRAILING THEM through the day slowly vanished. Day creatures, Linhare imagined, fed by sunlight and soft breezes. Upon the darkling gloam, ghasty-haints drifted like fireflies summoned by the night. She could see them more clearly now that they ignored her; glowing candles of softened wax. Jinna did not seem to notice them at all, or, if she did, she was ignoring them as pointedly as she was being ignored.

Voices and firelight. The aroma of meat roasting and simmering spices. The promise of wine so sweet it would linger on her tongue for days. These things reached into the wood to draw Linhare forward. This fae wood. This Drümbul revel.

"The glade is just ahead," Kish told them. "Beloël is always gracious, but this revel shall top them all!"

Bounding ahead, Kish announced, "She is here! I have brought her. Queen Linhare of Vales Gate, and her handmaiden, Lady Jinna the Fair."

"Lady Jinna the Fair, eh." Jinna giggled. "You think we can make that official once we get home again?"

Home again. The words swished through Linhare's head but would not stick. Home was not home anymore. *Can it ever be again?*

Hand in hand, Linhare and Jinna stepped into the glade. The gathered Drümbul rose to bow regally, not submissively. Tall and slender, every one of them radiated beauty from pale, translucent skin to long, black-silk hair. The women wore gowns of emerald and sapphire and ruby; the men were dressed all in black; all men but one.

"Welcome, Little Queen."

Beloël came forward, hand extended. His clothes, from vest to leather boot, were a deep and luxuriant purple. He took Linhare's hand and brought it to his lips. A lifetime of royal training, and the lingering memories of her first encounter with this man, quelled the impulse to yank away from him.

"Thank you," she said stiffly, then let go a deep breath. "Forgive me, but I do not know how to address a Drümbul Lord."

"I am Beloël," he told her. "Nothing more is necessary."

"And I am Linhare." She pulled Jinna forward. "This is my friend, Jinna."

"Is she, now?" He let go of Linhare's hand to take Jinna's and likewise kiss it, his smile seductive and secret. He offered his arms; Linhare took one and Jinna, the other. Kish flung himself at their feet, weaving around and around them as the Drümbul Lord led the way to the long table aglow in fae light. Seating the women, Beloël took his place at the head. He nodded once and a new sort of creature arrived carrying trays laden with food. Jinna squeezed her thigh.

"Boogles!"

The hoary, leathery creatures milled about, serving food and pouring wine. They wore no clothes. Linhare did her best not to stare at their overly large wobbly bits, but blushed every time she was jostled by enormous breasts or elephantine genitalia. Already ripping into the succulently roasted bird on her plate, Jinna did not seem concerned. Kish perched on her lap, nuzzling the hollow between her breasts and vying for her attention. Jinna fed him morsels from her plate, offering him her fingers to lick.

"Are all your servants of boogle descent?" Linhare asked.

The Prince of Pines poured wine into her goblet. "Our races are mutually beneficial to one another. Boogles exist to serve. Drümbul exist to revel. But they are not our servants."

"Forgive me. I did not mean to imply..." Linhare sipped at the wine. "I meant. . . goodness! I meant exactly what I said. I'm sorry."

Beloël laughed, a sound that hit her so low in her belly it made her squirm. "Your kind is ever fond of assigning roles. Everyone and everything in its proper place."

Linhare looked away, cheeks blushing crimson. Beloël's long fingers touched her chin, drawing her eyes back to his. He held up his goblet.

"To a night of endless revels, Little Queen."

His eyes smiled seduction. Lusty stories of Drümbul Lords rushed ferociously into her head. Stories giggled beneath thick blankets. Stories women coveted and men dismissed. Stories that made even the oldest crones blush.

"My Prince!" Kish bounded onto the table between them, releasing Linhare from that dream-like seduction.

"What is it, Kish?"

"That. *That* is what it is. I have performed my task. Please, allow me to exile the cat."

Gone was the giggling-sweet voice and in its place something deeply masculine, tremulous and aching. Beloël laughed, his glance darting Jinna's way. "So be it, my friend."

The cat vanished and in its place, the drifting fluff. Up and up it floated, then down onto Jinna's shoulder. There it spun before rolling along her back to become a handsome youth sitting behind her, arms encircling; his hands cupped her breasts.

"Oh!" Jinna startled but did not jerk out of his grasp. He turned her gently so that she could see his face.

"I have had enough of this revel," he said. "Have you?"

"Kish?"

111

"Kish is a fat, brown cat," he said. "I am Liloat."

Vigorously handsome, Liloat evinced virility as the Drümbul radiated beauty. He wore only a pair of fitted breeches; no shirt to cover his finely muscled chest, or shoes on his hairy feet. Lush brown curls fell in his face, rakish as Jinna's responding grin.

"Where have you been?" she asked.

"Purring in your luscious lap. Eating morsels from your scrumptious fingertips. Liloat can do such things as well. Much more pleasingly, I swear to you."

Rising, Liloat wore his arousal as comfortably as the boogles wore their enormous genitalia. Linhare blushed and turned away, but Jinna took his offered hand and left the Drümbul feast without so much as a backward glance.

"She wears her heritage proudly," Beloël said, drawing Linhare's attention from her friend.

"Her heritage?"

"Her fae heritage."

Linhare blinked. "But—that's village gossip," she said. "Surely you can't mean to tell me that Jinna is boogle spawn."

Beloël laughed, deep and powerful. He covered her hand with his own. "Boogle spawn? Not lovely Jinna. Drümbul, perhaps, sometime in her family-past."

Linhare sipped her wine while her thoughts tumbled. "Is it really true?" she asked. "Those with red hair are boogle—well, fae spawned?"

"Again you use that term. Fish spawn," Beloël answered. "Fae do not. Not even boogles."

"Forgive me." Linhare blushed again. "There seems to be no end to my ignorance in such matters. The faefolk are stories where I am from. Legends told to frighten or enchant children."

The Prince of Pines leaned back in his ornate chair. Only now did Linhare notice what looked like antlers sprouting from the back, appearing to come from the top of his beautiful head. Carved into the wood like burnished gold were scenes of mating and mirth.

"It is that unawareness that keeps my kind alive in your world," he said, drawing her eyes back to his irresistible mouth. "It is that unawareness I find so endearing."

Beloël drew her in ways she did not wish to be drawn, in ways that made her remember, and wish to flee; and just as it had been then, she could not. The Drümbul Lord elicited not simply desire, but a command to desire she could not disobey. Her body was not her own. It responded against her will. The Prince of Pines rose to his feet, offered his hand, and Linhare could not resist.

"Come, Little Queen. Dance with me."

At the wave of the Drümbul Lord's hand, the music rose from fae instruments to fill the glade: a dirge of lost love. Drümbul voices, one masculine and one feminine, rose clear and magnificent above the mournful strings. Beloël led her into a swaying dance. His body moved against hers, soft and hard all at once. Linhare felt muscle through silk, through the odd bits of clothing she found in the trinket mound and only then realized she was still dressed in rags. She felt his eyes on the top of her head, felt those stirrings deep within her and knew them false, magicked. Agreth had taken; Beloël's seduction was but a gentler sort of force, and against her will nonetheless.

Linhare stopped dancing. She took a small step backwards.

"Forgive me, Beloël," she said. Lifting her chin and forcing herself to meet his gaze was all that kept her from fleeing the glade.

The Drümbul Lord did not fly into the rage she feared, but held her gently at arms' length. "It is of no consequence, Little Queen," he said, and bowed despite the disappointment marring features trying gallantly to smile.

COME EVENING, EVEN WAIT'S DAKHONNE STAMINA BEGAN TO WEAR OUT. Egalfo never complained, not like the day prior; neither did he lag, though he stumbled often, always refusing Wait's offer of assistance.

Agitation grew among the guiding faefolk just as Wait heard the first chords of music and laughter. Bolleys and freelings scattered, all but the plump creature who had first landed upon Wait's knee. She gestured him ahead, towards the music and laughter, before flittering away.

A Princeling glade.

Wait's experience with royalty was of the human variety and, he feared, mundane in comparison. Stories of the Drümbul, plucked from long-ago memories he could not trust, gave him nothing but uneasiness. He motioned Egalfo closer.

"You go that way." He pointed west. "I'll go the other. Keep just outside the perimeter of light. They're making enough noise to cover you. I doubt they're expecting company. I want to get a look at things before we blunder in. Meet me on the other side."

Egalfo nodded wordlessly, wearily. To Wait's keen ears, his shambling through the wood blared. The revelers in the glade did not seem to notice. Shrouding himself in his gifted silence, he peered through the branches to glimpse those within the glade.

He had never seen so many beings as tall as he. Majestic. Beautiful. Every one of them. They exuded a coolness he rarely experienced, the same unwitting superiority he felt among the Purists in Vernist-on-Contif. Some danced on the earthy-soft ground. Others feasted at the long table. Wait searched the ethereal faces, searching for one who was not pale as moonlight and tall as a sapling. Letting the branches fall, he kept to the perimeter, always wary of a guard or stray reveler. He peeked through branches now and again in the hopes of glimpsing...

Linhare.

Wait's heart seized. The battle-lust that sent him diving into the trunk, into fae, sent prickles of heat along his skin. She danced in the arms of a man dressed all in purple. She wore men's trousers and an oversized shirt that long-ago warriors used to wear beneath armor. Her feet were bare and quite dirty. Fabulously long hair swayed as she swayed, braided but coming loose in floating tendrils.

The man, the Drümbul Lord of this Princeling glade, held her tenderly. Wait recognized the look of desire. He noted the way the hand in the small of her back made slow circles there, pressing her gently closer. The man inside the Dakhonne pummeled for release, but the Dakhonne sworn by life bond kept him from diving through the branches and breaking the dancers apart. Then Linhare pulled away from the Drümbul Lord. Wait's blood froze, turning his heart into a block of ice. She spoke words Wait did not hear, but that caused the Drümbul Lord to take a step backward. The desire in his face became sorrow.

"Harlot!"

The despairing shriek silenced fae music and stilled dancing feet. Wait peered through those branches again to see Egalfo, Jinna and a mostly naked young man stumble into the glade.

"You said you loved me!" Egalfo was shouting. Jinna, wrapped in what might have been her own dress, hurried after him. Behind her trailed the stormy-looking youth.

"Come back, my darling," the youth whined. "Our pleasures have barely begun."

"Touch her again and I will kill you!" Egalfo roared. "By the stars and starlight I swear it!"

"Calm down, Egalfo." Jinna attempted to cover herself better.

"Calm down? You were nubbing him!"

"And?"

"You said you loved me!"

The naked youth grabbed Jinna's hand. "Come, my sweet morsel. You and he can settle this once our passion is quenched."

Egalfo dove into the youth's abdomen. Horrified gasps echoed from splendid mouth to splendid mouth. No one moved to separate the brawlers. Wait groaned. Letting go of his silence, he ducked through the branches and into the glade, grabbed for Egalfo and hauled him to his feet. The stormy, naked youth growled up at him, but his eyes went round, and with a *pop!* he vanished.

"Let go of me!"

"Calm down."

"No!"

"Wait?"

Linhare's voice loosed Wait's grip and Egalfo dropped to the ground with a hollow *whump*.

"Linhare."

He spoke her name like the last word of a spell and she came towards him, reaching into her voluminous shirt and pulling from it something small, something red. His failure to protect her became like venom seeping into his bloodstream. Wait dropped to his knees. The venom spread through his system, paralyzing him. Then she was standing before him, one hand on his shoulder.

"You are here," she said. "You came for me."

"Wherever you go, I will follow."

"Even here, into fae." No question. A statement of fact. Linhare's lips trembled into a smile. Wait grasped her hand, brought it desperately to his lips.

"I failed you," he said, "so completely."

"Failed me? How did you—?"

Her furrowed brow lifted, lips forming a perfect O. Eyes filled and her hand came up. Wait prepared himself for the slap; but Linhare's fingers were raindrops on his cheek, cool and soft and gentle.

"Wait." His name on her lips was beautiful, its meaning clear for that whispered moment. "You came for me," she said again. The fingers curled about his own let go to caress his jaw, to push through his hair. She pressed her small body to his in a desperate clutch, breathing deeply as if to draw him inside her. Then she stepped back, took his hand and pressed into his palm that something small and red. Retreating slow step by slow step, Linhare did not turn her back on him until she reached Jinna, grabbed her hand and hauled her running from the glade.

Wait became suddenly aware of the gathered beings still watching; of Egalfo slumped on the ground, cross-legged and head in hands. Sitting back on his heels, Wait nodded to the Drümbul Lord, who bowed low in response. He uncurled his fingers from around that small, red something Linhare had placed into his hand, gasped, closed his eyes.

It cannot be.

And yet there it sat, upon his hand, in this fae place he had no name for. Linhare put it there, and of course it was she to free the wretched thing from its rotting tomb. When he opened his eyes, the memory-stained thing was still there despite all his desperate wishing, clutched in his sweating hand; the reason Linhare had, he understood now, stopped looking him in the eye.

"Brother." The Drümbul Lord stood before him, raising him to his feet. "Welcome to my glade. It is an honor."

"Thank you."

"Come, sit beside me." He gestured Wait into an ornate chair crowned by antlers of an animal bigger than any ungulate he had ever seen in the archipelago. The man clapped his hands, and small, leathery creatures appeared bearing trays of food. A plate was set before him, piled high with roasted meat and baked roots and other things he did not recognize. Down the long table, the creatures likewise served Egalfo. Head hanging and fingers clutched around fistfuls of hair, his young friend paid no mind to the long and lovely fingers enticing him to eat.

"I am Beloël, Prince of Pines," his host said.

"I am Wait," he responded. "Queensguard."

"And Dakhonne."

Wait's nod elicited gasps and whispers from the exquisite mouths of so many exquisite beings. Placing the journal on the table, he imagined a bloodstain beside the plate of aromatic food. Frayed and cracking cords bound the covers that had been brilliant scarlet when Ben first gave it to him. A color that spoke of adventure and daring. A place in which to record such things. Wait had done so devotedly. Every escapade, every triumph and mishap along that three-year journey of his life, neatly recorded.

Are you a chronicler or a warrior, son?

Ben's ever-cheerful voice, even as memory, made him smile. His hero. His friend. There had been nothing Wait would not sacrifice for him.

Unfastening the ties, Wait let the journal fall open. His own boyish, too-careful script lifted off the page; wavering black lines across the creamy background; melding together in a scramble he could not decipher, until his vision cleared.

I was right. I did not want to be, but I was.

He snapped the book closed. Revulsion and madness and grief welled in him like blood from a wound.

"If yours was anything like Linhare's, you've had a long and strange journey. Eat." Beloël tapped the edge of Wait's plate, picked up a crystal decanter to pour wine into Wait's goblet.

"Water, please."

Beloël's eyebrow quirked, but he set the decanter down again and motioned a boogle forward. "As you wish."

Wait tucked into the food first cautiously, then voraciously. When his plate was empty, the leathery creatures appeared again to fill it, and Wait devoured that as well. Soon, exhaustion overwhelmed and even he,

116

Dakhonne and queensguard, could not resist the pull of slumber, its promise of oblivion.

Sunlight filtered through the white canopy of the treetop bower, speaking more of spider webs than of cloth. The impulse to roll over and sleep on disconcerted Wait. He sat up before he could give in to it, lowered the bower to the ground and swung himself out.

Habit stretched muscles that did not need stretching. Digging back into the nest-like structure for his sword belt and blade, he strapped them on before reaching again for the leather journal that lost some of its horror in the night.

Wait scanned through the days of his life from cover to cover. Within the well-worn pages, he found Ben. He found Ellis. He found comrades, both living and dead. Wait found the boy he was and the man he became. He found the blood and the grief of so many hallowed deaths, those innocents slaughtered along with the treacherous, because battle-lust did not know the difference between such things. He also found that the journal, if left to its own devices, opened to the same tell-tale page every time.

Tassry, off Sisolo—2.19.1206
I was right. I did not want to be, but I was.

Was Linhare so fixated, so disgusted, so enrapt by his darkest moment? Wait tucked the journal into the pouch at his waist, unwilling to dwell on this possibility. He found Linhare; his first duty was queensguard, his first task complete. Pushing away from the sleeping basket he leaned against, the sound of his name on gentle lips stopped him short.

"Wait?"

There upon the path stood Linhare. Small and dirty and disheveled as she had been the night prior, she smiled and his heart lightened.

"I was just coming to look for you," he told her.

"I suppose we had the same thought then. I'm—forgive me for leaving you so abruptly last night, without any explanation. It was—oh, Wait, we have so much to talk about."

"We do."

She looked around the otherwise empty grove of sleeping baskets. "Where is Egalfo?"

"Still sleeping, I suppose. He drank too much Drümbul wine last night."

"Then you understand where we are."

He nodded.

117

"Am I to assume you got here the same way I did?"

"Through the trunk? Yes."

Linhare's smile dissipated like mist in the sunshine. "There is time yet for sharing such details," she said. "When Jinna and Egalfo are present. What I must say now is between the two of us."

"All right, Linhare. Of course."

He gestured her onto the path, away from the sleeping baskets. Linhare walked with her head bowed and her lower lip between her teeth. "I want to explain about your journal," she said. "You see, I found it—"

"I know where you found it." The severity of his own voice startled him. "I'm sorry," he said. "Linhare, I'm sorry."

"It is nothing I do not deserve."

Wait took deep, even breaths. He tried again. "It was stuffed behind a rotted sill in the university library."

"Yes. I—I didn't know you had ever been to Vernist-on-Contif."

"Only the one time," he said. "With your father."

Her eyes asked questions her mouth did not. Wait did not know which to wish for: courage or restraint.

"And there it stayed," she said at last, "until I found it that winter after my father died."

His jaw clenched; the grinding echoed between his ears. "It must have been distressing to discover that the man you looked to for protection was capable of such horror."

Linhare moved to block his path, her hand grasping for his. "Never. Wait, never."

Never. Wait, never. Never wait. Never, Wait.

He could only stare at their joined hands, waiting for the implosion inside his skull to stop echoing.

"I saw your sorrow," she said. "I saw the man who saved my father's life and Vales Gate in the process."

"But the slaughter—"

Linhare tugged at his hand. Wait forced himself to look at her, to see.

"That terrible day is part of history," she said. "I cannot imagine the true horror of what you saw, what you did. You are a warrior. Sometimes warriors must do terrible things. Please, I am the one who did wrong. I did not give you back your journal when I realized it was yours. I read it at first because there was so much of my father in those pages. Until that passage you wrote off the coast of Tassry, I didn't know who penned the pages. Once I knew, I read no further. But I kept it, Wait. I read it over and over again. Every time I came home, every time I saw you, the shame was...it was appalling. Still, I never gave it back. I couldn't. And then I lost it. But it is found again and I have done what I should have so long ago."

Wait's body beaded sweat. He clutched the journal with calm, steady fingers. Unwinding the cords, he let it fall open to that entry.

"You never read past this?"

Linhare bit her lip, then said in a rush, "Once. But only a few words. I could not do it. It was too much like betrayal. To read further was no longer innocent. It was deliberately prying into things you obviously wanted no one to see."

Wait closed his hand, closed off the journal's fluttering pages. She had not read them. Those pages that repulsed and frightened him. Those pages of bloody despair. Of madness. She did not know anything of the real and desperate reason Ben took him to Vernist-on-Contif.

"Can you ever forgive me?" she asked. "I am so dreadfully sorry."

His love for her, his life-bound duty, twisted and heaved. Innocent and trusting, she read his words and thought herself a villain when it was he who had done so much wrong.

"Don't apologize." He tucked the journal into the pouch at his hip. "You read a book. You didn't do anything that needs forgiving."

"But I did. And I do. Wait, please. Tell me you forgive me or tell me you never can. I beg of you."

"Do not beg anything of me. You are queen. I am only your queensguard."

"Only?"

Trembling fingers reached for him. Wait stood perfectly still, unable to take her into his arms or push her gently from him. Linhare spared him from doing either; she stepped into him, gave his arms no choice.

"You came for me," she whispered against him. "It wasn't duty that brought you, Wait. It wasn't. I saw it. I felt it. Tell me I was wrong."

When she lifted her face to him, his hand came instantly to the curve of her cheek.

"You are not wrong," he told her, and she nestled into him with a contented sigh.

She loved him. Or thought she did. He could no more deny what he found there in her eyes than he could deny his own heart. But Linhare loved the sorrowful young man she found off the coast of Tassry. He was a lie Wait never meant to tell.

"You are forgiven of any trespass you believe to have committed against me, Linhare." He let her go, took that one, proper step backward. Linhare stumbled forward, but righted herself quickly.

"I—I thank you, but—"

"Then this matter is settled. I will locate our host. If you would, find Jinna and Egalfo and meet me in the glade."

119

Wait turned away before the impulse to take her back into his arms overruled his better senses. Selfishness was one vice to which he had never succumbed.

Ugly Truth

JINNA SAT CROSS-LEGGED in her bower, elbows to knees and chin on fists. Frustrated passion, shock, joy, and ultimately anger caused by the guilt she had no good reason feeling chased one another around and around her head the night long. Her eyes felt gritty. She knew there were rings around them without looking; and that Egalfo was waiting for her there just beyond the little grove. Growling under her breath, she called, "Stop skulking. I know you're there."

"I am not skulking," Egalfo called back. "I'm waiting. I deserve something, Jinna. Some explanation."

"Go away."

"No."

She pounded fists against the downy nest. The charm he had given to her and she still wore dug into the delicate skin there. Tears stung, but Jinna gave them no outlet. No tears of pain. No tears of shame or regret. No tears at all. She tore aside the draping, threw her legs over the side and got tangled in the gossamer fabric. The more she tried to extricate herself, the more tangled she became. Jinna fell with an uneremonious *thud* onto the forest floor. Egalfo did not come to assist her.

"You are no gentleman!"

"And you are no lady, so we are even."

"How dare you!" The fabric shredded in Jinna's hands. "Take that back."

"No. I can't take it back any more than you can take back what you were doing when I found you."

"And that makes me less of a lady than when my legs were wrapped around *you*?" Jinna, finally free of the draping, strode angrily towards Egalfo. "You pompous fraud!"

"Fraud? I am a fraud? You said you loved me! If a woman tells a man she loves him, he expects certain things. Like *not* giving a bit of a snug to another man's stiff!"

"He's not a man, he's a gobbet." Jinna heard her own words and cringed. Blood rushed to her cheeks.

"That makes it even worse!" Egalfo shouted. "A fae creature as much animal as he is man and stars and starlight know what else. That is…it's bestiality!"

"Don't be disgusting. It is nothing of the kind. I am sorry for hurting you, Egalfo, but I never promised I wouldn't look at other men."

"Look? Looking is done with the eyes, Jinna, not with…other parts."

"Do you know where we are, Egalfo? I didn't know I would ever see you again!"

"That should not have made a difference. I would have waited for you. Forever."

"I never promised that, Egalfo. Not even in Dockside. Never once!"

Her shout echoed into silence. Egalfo's face did terrible things, as if she had slapped him; as if he were trying not to weep. "What a fool I am," he said at last. "When I left Dockside, I left your life. It wasn't that you could not bear to leave Linhare. It was—" He looked down at his own trembling fingers. "You were never going to write me, were you."

"I never even got the chance. Sabal—"

"But you weren't." His voice chilled her. "Were you?"

Jinna studied her own fingers now. On her wrist, the cord wrapped around and around again felt suddenly constricting, too heavy to wear. She took it off.

"I care for you, Egalfo. I do. But I never said you'd be the only one. I'm sorry."

She held the charm out to him. A pang of something like regret made her wince. It was nothing of value; just a worn metal disc on a tattered leather cord. Egalfo took the charm from her, holding it up to the level of his eyes. Jinna's hand dropped to her side.

"I imagined you appearing around every bend in the road," he said, "in each town I passed through, telling me you could not live without me. A fool in love is as blind as an oyster and twice as stupid."

"You are not stupid."

"No? Then why do I love you still? Even now. I have loved you since the moment we met in the Vulgar Raven."

His words filled her, suffocated her. His sorrow nearly undid her.

"Don't you know that love is a myth?" she choked out. "No one truly loves anyone as much as they love themselves. It's all a lie."

"That's not true. I love you."

"Do you know how many men have told me they love me? After the fun and the sex and the adventure of it all, it shows itself for what it is every single time."

"You are wrong."

"No. I'm not. Believe what you wish. I won't be such a fool. I'm sorry, Egalfo. I'm sorry for hurting you. I'm sorry you followed me here to find this out. But I won't apologize for being who I am."

Egalfo did not look at her; instead he gazed down upon the charm Jinna's fingers had worried like a stone. She could still feel the raised letters.

Egh Ahl Fo.

Her belly churned. Egalfo loosened the knot. He tied it again so that it rested in that place it must have been for so many years before he met her. Jinna remembered kissing that place, the hollow of his throat.

"Very well, Jinna. I suppose I cannot blame anyone but myself. You did not ask me to come after you. Now I see, you tried to do me a kindness by sending me on my way back in Dockside. I imagine we'll be stuck together for a while, seeing that we're in this world with no idea how to get back. But I hope that we can at least be civil to one another."

"I've nothing but affection for you, Egalfo."

"I wish I could say the same."

Egalfo touched fingers to his brow and left her standing in the little grove of sleeping baskets. Jinna watched him go. She tried to feel relieved, but found something hollow and crackly instead. Pressing palms to her belly, she pretended the sensation was hunger, and followed the scent of breakfast down another path.

THE LONG, FOOD-LADEN TABLE of the night prior was now empty. Beloël, Wait and Liloat stood when Linhare entered the glade on Egalfo's arm. She had found the former fire-eater wandering aimlessly, but he smiled genuinely when she called to him. He was as pleasant and charming as he'd been in the Vulgar Raven that seemingly long-ago night Dockside. Linhare did not question him about Jinna or Liloat; there would be plenty of time for such matters to rise up and make them all ridiculously uncomfortable. And then there came Jinna, ambling into the glade and avoiding everyone's eyes, including hers. At Beloël's gesture, they all took seats.

"Wait tells me that you wish to leave here," he began.

"I cannot abandon my people," Linhare told him. "Or my sister."

"Understandable. There is, however, a problem." Beloël looked to each of them in turn. "I do not know the way back. I am not even certain there is one. I am sorry."

"No way back?" Linhare gasped.

"If there is a way *here*," Wait said, "there has to be a way *there*."

"Perhaps," Beloël told him. "But not on this island. Not now. Perhaps there was once, or will be again. I cannot say. These things change constantly, a matter of some concern, but that is my trouble, not yours."

"What about the trunk?" Egalfo asked. "It empties here. Can't you...turn it around?"

"No more so than you can go up a waterfall," Beloël answered. "But there are other places where Beyond and Away overlie, where a crossing is possible. I believe."

"Where?" Egalfo asked. "How far away? How do we get there?"

"I do not have those answers, but I know those who do."

"My lord, no!" Liloat leapt onto the table, smashing dishes and clanging cutlery. "Not the Everwanderers! You mustn't summon them. You cannot ask!"

"Everwander-what?" Jinna asked. "What's he whining about?"

"The Everwanderers," Beloël repeated. "Of the famed Siren's Curse. Surely even Vales Gate knows of them."

"I'm sorry," Linhare said. "Wait?"

He shook his head. Beloël's eyebrows rose. "Has it been so long?"

"Is someone going to tell me who they are?" Jinna asked.

"Pirates! Fierce, stalwart, ill-tempered." Liloat turned back to Beloël. "Don't let them go. Let us keep them."

"Hush, my friend."

"But Captain Hepheo will be cross. He is always cross."

"You exaggerate. Pay the gobbet no mind. The Everwanderers are the greatest of sailors, fae or otherwise. They've been sailing since the first rains filled the first seas. There is not a cove they cannot locate or a shore they do not know."

"Are they...safe?" Linhare asked. Beloël smiled, and then he laughed.

"No, Little Queen. They are nothing of the kind. But if they agree to carry you, you will be safe enough."

"Is there any other way?" Wait asked.

"I am certain there are many," the Drümbul Lord answered. "But Captain Hepheo and his Curse are your best chance."

"And if we decide against it?" Eglafo asked.

Beloël rose to his feet, gesturing to Liloat, who did not budge. "Then you are quite welcome to stay here as long as you wish. Another ship might appear on the horizon, though I cannot remember the last time one did. It is up to you, of course. I will leave you to discuss it. Be aware that a seven-day will see you to the coast, another day for the Siren's Curse to arrive. I await your decision."

"But—" Liloat protested. Beloël grabbed him by the nape of his neck and hauled him protesting away. Boogle servers came from the other direction, set down breakfast and vanished just as quickly.

No one spoke. Aromas beckoned them to breakfast. Jinna was first to pluck a honey-saturated bun from the tray in front of her.

"Well," she said between bites, "I vote we sail with the pirates, if anyone's interested."

The vote was unanimous and quick. Remaining in Beloël's Pinelands, while lovely, was not a real possibility. Captain Hepheo, his Everwanderers, and the Siren's Curse seemed their only hope of finding home again. The decision left Linhare satisfied, however wary. Despite her realm of islands and the sea, she'd never spent a great deal of time sailing; and the only talk she'd heard of pirates was from the far-off isles of Sisolo and Esher.

"That's settled then," Jinna said, brushing her hands together. "Now I want to hear how Sabal got the two of you into the trunk."

"Jinna, please." Linhare's throat constricted. "Let them tell their stories their way."

"I'm afraid Jinna is right," Egalfo said. "Forgive me, Linhare, but one way or another, your sister is responsible for all of us being here…"

Egalfo spoke for both of them, looking to Wait now and again for his nod or grunt. Jinna interjected plenty. Linhare—nothing at all. Her skin had become too tight to house her muscles and bones. It itched and it ached and she wanted nothing but to be out of it. Pressing fingertips to her eyes, she rubbed until she saw sparkles, watched them swirl like bolleys in a windstorm, like stars falling from the sky…

"There's something else," Wait was saying when she blinked her eyes clear. He reached into his pocket, pulling from it a folded bit of paper. "I am not certain how this connects, or if it does at all."

He handed it to Linhare. She unfolded the note, cleared the heaviness from her throat, and read, "*It has been too long since we have seen one another. I miss you, my friend. As does Yebbe. Contact me with a time and place the moment you receive this, and we will meet for a cup of ale.*' It is signed—*'Ellis.*'"

Wait took the note back, tapped it on the table. "I made arrangements to meet him that afternoon, but he never arrived. He hadn't been seen in the mines all day. I tried Yebbe's cottage earlier, but there was no one there, either." He fell abruptly silent. Linhare watched his fingers, tap-tap-tapping a staccato beat with the note. Then he looked up, looked her in the eyes. "That is where I was when Agreth raped you."

Linhare gasped. Her stomach hurt. Her head. Yet the honor of his blunt account did not escape her. She held his eyes, or he held hers.

"Ghastly," Egalfo exhaled the word. "Then do you think the king was behind the note? To get you out of the castle?"

Wait blinked, releasing her. "The timing is wrong," he said. "Ellis's message came before Linhare and Sabal's argument on the terrace. Whatever Agreth planned came after a series of convenient events that left him alone with Linhare. I don't think this note has anything to do with what happened that night, but I do believe it is connected to something bigger brewing." He turned to Jinna now. "When I checked your mother's cottage, it was locked up, as if she planned on being away a long time."

"What?"

Wait nodded. "I believe she and Ellis are together, wherever they are. And they were going to bring me into whatever is happening."

"Don't you see?" Jinna slammed her palm upon the table. Cups and cutlery clattered. "It's about *them!* Sabal and—and that monster!"

"That makes no sense, Jinna," Egalfo argued. "You heard what Wait said. The note came before—"

"And I heard what *you* said! By all the stars and starlight, Sabal manipulated Wait! She can make Agreth dance like a puppet on strings."

"You cannot believe that my sister—" Words caught in Linhare's throat. The ache in her belly sank lower. "You think she convinced him to do what he did?"

"No," Jinna said less vehemently. "Not even she is *that* evil. But I'll bet every hair on my head that she's the one who convinced him you were in love with him."

I talked with Sabal. It was quite enlightening, in fact...

Linhare pressed her palms over her ears. She shook her head, slowly. It could not be. Sabal had held her so gently, acted so surely...

I'm sorry. Oh, Linhare. My sweet sister. I thought he—I didn't know he would—

Tears rolled down her cheeks. Linhare let her hands fall to wipe them away. No one spoke; they only looked at her. Waiting.

"I wish to be left alone. Now."

"Linny, I'm sorry. I shouldn't have said—" Jinna began, but Wait was on his feet, and Egalfo.

"I will be nearby," Wait said. "If you need me."

Jinna kissed her cheek. Her lips were cold. "Are you sure?"

Linhare could only nod. They left her, looking over shoulders, Jinna and Egalfo whispering. When she was alone, she leaned heavily into her chair, stared straight ahead until the world blurred. She tried to let her mind empty, but it wouldn't. Sabal's words, Agreth's, even those things her mother said without saying whirled and whirled. Envy. Lust. Protection. Absence. Betrayed and betrayed by those she loved, by those she believed loved her.

What good is love when it can be twisted so?

Tears rolled down her cheeks. Linhare did not wipe them away. Her own culpability shoved its way forward. Was she also not guilty of betrayal? Years and years she kept Wait's journal, even if she hadn't read into those secrets he wanted kept. She knew they were there, hers to discover any moment she chose; and the power of that chilled.

"Oh, forgive me, Little Queen. I was looking for my luscious halfling. Have you seen her?"

Linhare blinked her vision clear. Liloat stood on the other side of the table, the sweet smile upon his lips turning down.

"You have been crying."

She sniffed. "Jinna left a little while ago. I'm not sure which way she went."

He nodded, but Liloat did not gambol off. He sat down in the chair beside her and took her hand. "What troubles you, Little Queen? Is it those cursed pirates and their unnatural ship? Beloël will not summon them if you—"

"No, it's not that. But thank you."

The gobbet-man patted her hand, held her gaze. "You have dimmed," he told her. "That is a sad thing."

"Dimmed? I don't know what that means."

"Your light." He gestured a circle around her. "It was so bright when I first found you. After the pool in the wood, it was a beacon all of the Pinewood fae could see. And now it is dimming. Why, Little Queen? Is it the Dakhonne? A fearsome creature, he."

"Partly," she heard herself say. "It is many things, Liloat. Many hurts inside me."

"Ah, that is unfortunate." He slipped off his chair and instead sat upon the arm of hers. "Yours is a brilliance I do not see here in this Pinewood. The Drümbul are full of dirges. The rest of us are too merry by far. But you, Little Queen?" He kissed the top of her head, rested his brow to the spot. Warmth spread along Linhare's scalp, down her arms, straight to her toes. "Do not allow these hurts to dim your beautiful light. That would be a shame. Such a terrible loss."

A puff of sweet air, and Liloat was gone. A feather or a bit of pollen rose into the air. Linhare followed its wafting across the glade, into the wood. It drifted into a shadow that was no shadow, but Wait. Her heart swelled, an instant reaction to him, to his presence even when she first found his journal, even now.

She waved to him. He startled, but waved back. Liloat's words still soothed from that spot he had kissed. The hurt within tried to swallow it, but Linhare took the gobbet's advice and held tight to those thoughts. Her cheeks felt warm and she looked again to Wait, anticipating that swell radiating like light through her body.

Rising from her chair, she made her way to him, pushed aside a branch, some bramble. She stood before him and did not speak. Linhare only looked up at Wait, his expression still as confused and flustered as a little boy caught breaking a rule he hadn't known existed.

"Is there something—?"

Linhare pressed a small finger to his lips and was nearly overwhelmed with the urge to kiss him, for him to kiss her; but she couldn't and he wouldn't. Not yet. She settled for the conjured kiss she had been summoning since girlhood, from the lips warm and soft beneath her finger, before Agreth robbed her of such innocent longing. She lingered in her conjuring until the force and fear faded, enough if not away. Wait's fingers, callused and gentle, tucked a stray curl behind her ear.

"I would take all your pain." His voice was thick and gentle and full. "I will, if you ask it."

Linhare caught his hand. "Walk with me," she said, and Wait fell into step beside her. She led him so easily into the wood. They walked together, hand in hand. Just Wait. Just Linhare. In a bolley wood.

To the Sea

THE PROCESSION OUT OF THE DRÜMBUL GLADE the following morning was a merry one. All manner of fae creatures flitted along the path. Wait hadn't names for them all; it was like trying to name every variety of bird in the Vale, every species of fish in the sea.

Mounted upon a horse more shadow than flesh, the Prince of Pines led the procession himself. A fair pageant of Drümbul lordlings and ladies followed behind, riding upon their own shadowy mounts. Tiny bells fixed upon harness and rein jingled with every step, beating out a rhythm like a heartbeat, or the tide. For Egalfo, Jinna, and Linhare, Beloël provided horses of a more mundane variety. Sleek and spirited and somewhat smaller, they were nonetheless fine. For Wait, a creature built like a bull, shaped as a horse and colored in fire. He did not pine for his mare left back in the Vale, fine and loyal a mount though she was. The wildness of this fae mount suited both him and the mood fallen upon him since Linhare took his hand and led him into the wood.

Bolleys lit their way, day or dusk, from piney wood to meadow to greenwood. Ghasty-haints twinkled through the nights. Each day of seven brought the sea closer; Wait smelled it before he heard the gulls cry. Upon reaching the sandy dunes, boogles erected pavilions and built fires while the Drümbul gentry played. Jinna and Linhare splashed in the water with Liloat. Egalfo sipped wine with the ladies enthralled by his charms. Wait tended his mount, walked a perimeter, then chose a high place where he could see in every direction.

"You will find no enemies here, brother."

Wait turned his head to see Beloël standing just behind him.

"Habit dies hard."

"And in it lies comfort, no?" Beloël laughed. "You ride with the Drümbul and yet you never drink our wine or sing our songs. You rarely smile. Are you always so solemn?"

Wait's gaze wandered back to Linhare splashing in the surf. "There was a time I wasn't quite so solemn."

"We were all young once. Like them."

"Your lords and ladies are as old as your Pinewood, and they play."

"Ah, but they are Drümbul, made for eternal reveling," Beloël said. "And you are Dakhonne, made for eternal conflict."

Linhare waded out of the surf. Her shift clung to her every curve. The pall settled upon her since her mother's death was gone. And though she would not speak of Sabal or Agreth, she did not linger silent and distant in her own thoughts. She laughed with Jinna, Egalfo and the fae following them to the sea, like she frolicked in the surf with them now.

She took Wait's hand often. She sat close beside him at the fire each night. And when she slept, she was always near enough to reach out and touch, which he never did. Wait could almost wish back the years Linhare could not look him in the eyes. It had been easier, then, to convince himself he felt only duty, only love born of loyalty. He could no longer be such a fool.

"You fight when you should not." Beloël's voice startled him. "She is a woman. You are a man."

"She is my queen. I am her queensguard."

"You boil like a storm under glass, my friend. One day, the glass will shatter and all you are, all your raging blood makes you, will erupt. Take my advice. Don't wait for it to shatter. Set it free or it will destroy you."

Patting his shoulder, Beloël left him to stand upon a ridge of rock and sand higher up on the beach. The last rays of the setting sun cast the Drümbul Lord in silhouette. Below, faefolk ceased their playing. Arms around one another, faces lifted to the last rays of the day, they began to sing in a tongue Wait did not understand, but like most Drümbul songs, sounded like a dirge. Beloël turned north, west, south, bowing in turn to each. Then he turned east. He held out his hand and a boogle came forward, handing him something that glimmered. Putting it to his lips, he blew a long, piercing note. Up and out it went, eastward, over the sea. When the whistling ceased and the dirge ended, the moon had risen to cast its pale glade upon the water.

"The Everwanderers will come," the Drümbul Lord called from his perch. "Tonight, we revel!"

A great cheer rose up. The dirge of moments ago banished; a rollicking tune of pipes and drums picked up instead. Wait rose to his feet, brushing sand from his pants.

"We revel every night." Her voice turned him around. Linhare stood shivering behind him, smiling that smile that undid him. He took off his shirt and wrapped it around her shoulders, rubbed her arms gently through the fabric.

"Lovely as it has been," she said through chattering lips, "I can imagine it getting tiresome."

"The Drümbul are made for eternal reveling." *And you are Dakhonne, made for eternal conflict.* "They can't help themselves. And you're cold. There's a fire—"

"I'm fine. I came to speak with you."

Wait let her go. Half-soaked and still shivering, she nonetheless held herself as a queen. He took that proper step back. He led her a little further from the gathered fae already dancing to the pipes. Jinna laughed, turning Linhare's head, and she laughed softly. Fondly. Her serenity bemused and heartened him. He had known those who succumbed to the darkness in their lives; his mother was his first and most damning example. Even he succumbed for a time. But Ben's death had not toppled Linhare. Neither had Diandra's. She was strong, for all of them, strong, and Wait was ashamed to fear, even for a moment, that a villain like Agreth could topple her.

"I hoped," she said, halting him, "that when I gave your journal back to you, things would be made right between us, but it only complicated things further."

Her words, so far from his own thoughts, unsettled him. "There is nothing wrong between—"

"Don't say it, Wait. Please don't say there is nothing wrong between us. There is a chasm, and it gets bigger day by day."

Linhare's head bowed. Wait placed a finger under her chin, gratified that his hands did not betray the trembling of his insides. She moved closer. He could feel her heat, smell the salt of her skin.

"There is no chasm between us," he said. "Only what needs to be there, to keep you safe."

"From you? That's ridiculous."

"You don't know who I am, Linhare. *What* I am."

She shook off his touch, glaring up at him. "I am not a silly child! I know exactly who you are. You are the man who followed me into fae. You are the man I love!"

Her words hit him in the gut. Wait hung his head. He had known, hadn't he? He had wished. Sabal's confession of love was easily, if uncomfortably, dismissed; but he could not dismiss Linhare's. He wanted it to be real. He wanted it to be deserved. He did not simply want it to be true, he needed it to be. He was Calryan. He was Wait. Dakhonne. Queensguard. And he was hers so deeply inside of himself, he was not certain he existed without her.

Reaching into his hip pouch, Wait pulled out the journal, unwrapped the cords holding it closed. He thumbed through the pages. Some of the edges crumbled. The words remained intact. Those terrible words. His horrifying past made into glory.

"Wait?"

Linhare touched his arm, brought him back with his name on her lips. She had said the words. She meant them. *Set it free, or it will destroy you.* Winding the cords around the journal again, he handed it to her.

"Once you know," he told her, "you can't *un*know. It will change how you see me. How you feel."

"No it will not." She clutched the scarred, red thing to her chest. Wait averted his eyes. it looked too much like blood. Then she was in his arms and he was holding her close against his chest, to his heart, her long hair free of its braid and tickling his skin.

131

"I will read it and prove that to you," she told him. "You will see, Wait. I swear it."

He held her and he held her; how long, Wait did not know. *It will,* he thought, *it will. And when you know the truth, I am lost.*

THERE WAS SOMETHING TO BE SAID for distraction. Liloat obliged, as did Beloël and any number of Drümbul lordlings still shadowing the journey. Jinna hardly noticed Egalfo at all. Not when he danced with the smooth and silky Drümbul ladies, not even when he vanished with them into the dunes. Despite her notion to finish what had been interrupted, Jinna found teasing Liloat far more fulfilling than succumbing to his seduction. Fondling kisses, drinking too much, dancing all night, the seven days' journey was enjoyable enough.

Now pale and eerie dawn gave ghost to the dunes, the sea. Faefolk slept where they finished making merry, leaning one upon the other or curled in the sand. She did not see Liloat, and though she certainly was not looking for him, Jinna did not see Egalfo, either.

Walking over the last dune sloping down to the surf, Jinna dropped into the cool sand. Legs drawn to her chest, mind wandering, she gazed out at the sea that went on forever. Somewhere, far from where she sat, were worlds she had yet to discover. To go, to seek, to find! Whatever existed out there beyond her ken. Jinna searched the beach for those white stones she and Linhare used to cast into the sea with their girlhood wishes but found none.

"Take me," she whispered instead. "Take me where you will."

Resting cheek to knees, she noticed Wait standing further up the beach, calf-deep in the tide washing in. He wore a shirt now, but last night it had been draped around Linhare's shoulders. Jinna had seen them locked in an embrace both desperate and desirous. Envious as she'd been, Jinna felt no jealousy. Wait belonged to Linhare and always had. Their embrace proved, at last, Linhare knew it, too.

Brushing herself off, Jinna joined Wait in the surf.

"You're up early," he said, his gaze barely flickering from the horizon.

"So are you. What are you looking at?"

"Do you see it?" He pointed. Jinna followed his finger to a point in the sky.

"That star?"

"Yes. But it's not a star. It wasn't there until a moment ago. Stars are supposed to blink out as dawn rises. This one appeared."

Jinna squinted at the horizon. "Is it me? Or is it getting bigger?"

Bigger, brighter, closer. Fast. Just as she was beginning to make out a shape, Wait grabbed her hand and hauled her up the dune faster than her legs could move. She heard a sound, like screaming horses barreling down upon her. Jinna's skin prickled. Her heart hammered. Behind them, the sun broke the horizon.

"What was that?" Jinna spat sand from her mouth. Wait tried to help her to her feet.

"I didn't think it was going to stop," he said. "I'm sorry, Jinna."

"Move, you blundering boulder! You inelegant scoundrel!" Liloat was suddenly between her and Wait, pushing at the big man as if he could move him. "Keep your brutish hands off my tender morsel!"

"Oh for pity's sake, Liloat!" Jinna shoved him off. Wait only shook his head. He might have chuckled, but Jinna wasn't sure. As she got to her feet, Linhare appeared on the rise of the dune with Egalfo.

"Look!" She pointed, slide-slipping down the dune and hauling Egalfo behind her. "Oh, Jin! Wait! Look!"

Jinna turned to the sea. "By all the stars and starlight."

A ship bobbed like a small city above the water, on a cloud of mist shrouding her underbelly. Great sails, gaily patched as a street-dancer's skirt, glowed a shade of white only the sea sun and air could paint them. From the siren figurehead fore to the lathed railings aft, she gleamed as if she were newly wrought of virgin wood, yet oiled smooth over a thousand years. She was every ship Jinna ever saw, somehow cobbled together; and she took Jinna's breath away.

"You have summoned us, Prince of Pines," shouted a raspy voice. Human in shape, not quite human, the sailor calling was a tall and lithesome creature. He bore none of the genteel elegance or air of merriment of the Drümbul, but instead a wildness, a jolly menace that shivered something like fear or excitement along Jinna's skin.

"Not I, exactly," Beloël shouted back. "But my friends. They seek your knowledge, and passage on your Curse."

"And are they prepared to pay the price?"

"What price?" Wait put himself between Linhare and the Siren's Curse. "You didn't say anything about a price."

"Nothing of any worth can be gained without repaying in kind." Beloël smiled. "Not even Beyond. Not even for you. But rest easy, my brother. The price is dear, but not hard to come by." The Drümbul Lord smiled kindly, his eyes moving to Linhare. "I would let nothing ill befall you, Little Queen."

"What is it to be, Beloël?" came the raspy shout. "Are the Everwanderers to have their due, or do we leave this little island for more stimulating waters?"

"What is the nature of this price?" Linhare called. "If you please?"

"Nothing much, my pretty lass. A sacrifice is all I ask, to take you from this isle."

Hearty howling rose from the Siren's Curse, scattering gulls into the air. Beloël and his faefolk laughed as well. Jinna grimaced, her pirate-ship-dreams scattering in the wind.

"I don't know what's so amusing," she said. A glance Wait's way proved he did not, either. Before the storm of his expression could erupt in anything unseemly, the Drümbul lord held up his hands and laughter ceased.

"Hepheo, you scoundrel!" he called across the water. Then to his guests, "A sacrifice does not have to mean blood and death. If you have learned nothing else during your time with us, you should have learned that we are far too merry to be bloodthirsty. Your sacrifice, my dear friends, must simply be something it hurts to give. Only then is it a true sacrifice."

"It would have been better," Wait said, "if you spoke sooner."

"Would it have?" Beloël bowed grandly. "Perhaps you are right. Forgive me, but what is done is done. Decide upon your gift if sailing is still your ambition. The Siren's Curse departs with the sun."

Everwanderers

At sea off Enalia—3.11.1206

It has been a while since I have had the heart to open this book and take pen to it. Larguessa Violet's severed head still talks to me in dreams. She does not curse me or Ben or the thwarting of her plot. She talks to me about mundane things, like how she likes to warm her wine and add spices to it on winter nights. It is one of the things she will miss most. Spiced wine and the mild cold of winter on Sisolo.

Ben is very careful around me. He does not think I have noticed. Ellis is not so naïve. But perhaps Ben isn't, either. He only wishes, and thus wishing makes it so. He is King, after all. I don't know what it is he is being so careful about.

That is a lie. I know. It was he who cleaned me of the blood. It was he who fed me spirits and solace in the days since. It is he who listened to me speak of Violet's severed head. But still I have the feeling that there is more to it, that there is more waiting for me...

SUNSET LEANED ACROSS THE DUNES. Linhare sat on the sand, knees drawn to her chin and arms wrapped about them. The day flew by too quickly. She could think of nothing of hers worthy of passage on the Siren's Curse. Jinna would offer her body. Wait—his sword. Egalfo had only his skills as an entertainer, but even they were more than Linhare could give; and yet the sacrifice had to be hers. She was queen, even if an exiled one.

Untying the wrap lost and found again, the one her father brought her from Leftfoot, Linhare pulled it from the loops at her waist. Tattered for its trials on the mound and since, it was not a worthy sacrifice. She lost it once already, and survived with little more than wondering where it had gone.

Wait's journal rested on the sand beside her. The proof of her love he would not accept until it was read from cover to cover; was there anything more precious to her? But it was not hers to give, and thus, not her sacrifice. Pressing the wrap to her face, she breathed the fresh sea air through its gossamer filter. Riches, properties, all the privileges royalty bestowed, and Linhare had nothing. For the first time in her life, the young queen of Vales Gate truly understood the difference between *treasures* and *treasured*.

Replacing the wrap, Linhare stood and brushed herself off. In the end, she would offer the wrap and it would be Wait's Dakhan sword Captain Hepheo would accept as payment. She lifted her face to the calm, continuous breeze, trying not to weep for so heavy a price he would pay. For her. For them all.

Tendrils of her long hair drifted about her head like gobbet fluff. Drawing the length of heavy braid over her shoulder, Linhare unraveled it from its weave, petted it as it were Kish. How strange, it had not vexed her since her fall into fae. She barely thought about it at all, tucked into the back of her thoughts along with all things Vales Gate. Her mother. Brother. Sabal. She shivered, closed her eyes.

"Agreth."

She spoke his name. Bile rose.

"Agreth," again. Tears welled.

Do not allow these hurts to dim your beautiful light. Liloat's words looped like a hymn in her head, over and over, until the hungering hurt lost the fight.

"You have no power over me," she told the wind; and louder, "You have no power over me!"

Linhare lifted her arms to the sky, she tossed the length of hair over her shoulder and let the wind billow it like a soft sail twisting and curling about itself. A daughter's promise. A father's love. Linhare reveled in the luxury of it, in the faded memory of a rainy afternoon, a scandalous new style, and her father, alive and laughing.

"Jinna says I should cut it, but I don't think it would suit me."

"What do you say, Linhare?"

"I don't know. What do you say, da?"

"I say such a glory of hair should never be cut."

"Never? So it grew and grew forever? To my toes?"

"Just as my love for you, sweetling."

"You will love me to my toes?"

"To your toes, to the sky and back again."

"Then I shall never cut it."

"Never? Do you promise?"

"With all my heart."

Tears streamed down her cheeks and Linhare laughed, remembering his tickles, the way his smile crinkled the corners of his eyes. The promise she made in jest as a young girl had become a woman's oath after his death. A daughter's homage. Keeping it meant more to her than just about anything.

Gathering a fistful, she brought it to her nose. She breathed in the floral scent of it, the wild sea. And then the exiled queen of Vales Gate laughed softly as she headed back to camp.

CAPTAIN HEPHEO ROWED TO SHORE ALONE. A body of freelings caught the rope he tossed, dragging the vessel up onto the sand. Hepheo stepped out, tall and lissome. He appeared to wobble, as if made of some rubbery substance; or waver, as if in some juxtaposed place between land and sea.

Wait looked up the dunes for Linhare, then back to the man coming up the beach. Whatever Jinna or Egalfo or even Linhare could offer, he was certain his would be the sacrifice accepted. A Dakhan blade was a priceless thing, even here among the fae. Perhaps especially so.

Beloël stepped forward to greet the captain. "It has been over-long since you've come to my shores, old friend."

"Not much call for it," Hepheo answered. "This is the edge of the world, Beloël. Nothing to plunder. Nothing to trade. And bolleys gristle my innards, all that peeping and flittering. Don't know how you abide it."

Several bolleys darted off. Several more fluttered about the captain's head, peeping and poking at him before following after their kin.

"Bolleys are not confined to my Pinewood."

"But they know their place outside of it. Here, they're too brazen." Hepheo turned brusquely to face Wait, Jinna and Egalfo. "Well, then. What have you to offer me?"

The raspy voice that had called from the ship early that morning seemed strangely muffled. Wait resisted the urge to pass a hand through the man's indistinct form. Instead, he stepped forward, sword hilt offered to the Captain of the Siren's Curse.

"If you will grant us passage, it is yours."

"A Dakhan blade, eh?" Hepheo eyed it greedily, but made no move to take it. "Generous indeed. Precious. Rare. Haven't seen one of these in a very long time, and even then it was the only one to be had from this Pinewood princedom to Alyria."

"Then you will accept it?"

"It is a worthy sacrifice," Hepheo answered. "One I know pains you strong. But I agreed to hear what each of you has to offer before accepting one. You," he pointed to Jinna. "What've you got for me?"

"You're looking at it."

Egalfo snorted. Liloat whined. Beloël laughed outright. But Captain Hepheo walked around Jinna, inspecting her as if she were a mare or a sow.

"I'm Kept. But the Unfettered crew might appreciate your offer. For the duration? Or for keeps?"

"The duration," Jinna told him. "And there will be rules. Understand?"

Hepheo did not answer. He cocked his head as if he might speak, then turned to Egalfo instead. "And you? Do you have something more compelling than Dakhan blade or bewitching body?"

"I have only this." Egalfo opened his mouth, his fingers sparked, and flame shot in an arc over his head. All the gathered fae cheered and squealed. "It is all I have to offer, for I am an orphaned Therk with no prospects of ever attaining a blade like Wait's or a body like Jinna's. But my services as entertainment are yours—" He bowed. "—while our journey lasts."

"Hmmm," the captain murmured. "All fine treasures, but only one worthy of passage on the Siren's Curse. I hereby accept—"

"Captain Hepheo!"

Wait spun about so quickly his heel dug a hole in the sand. Sunlight at her back made Linhare a shadow sliding down the dune, a hank of rope held out in her hand.

"Consider my offering," she said. "If you please."

He took the rope from her, turning it over and around. "What is this?"

"A daughter's promise." Linhare's voice was thick. "And a father's love."

The captain's eyes opened wide. Then he nodded, hanging the rope like a stole over his shoulders. "A powerful sacrifice. I humbly accept."

Linhare inclined her head, bowed and stepped back. The sword still in Wait's hand suddenly felt like a stone weight.

"Linny!" Jinna leapt forward as if pushed from behind. She reached for Linhare's hair. "What have you done?"

"Made my sacrifice."

Wait's eyes darted from Linhare to the rope-not-a-rope draped across Hepheo's shoulders and back again to find her fingering the tresses now clipped to her shoulders. Ringlets formerly weighed down to waves liberated the curve of her nose, the gentle slope of her brow, the dimples in her round cheeks. Wait's gaze stopped at her eyes, green as the Pinelands in Lerolia, as the Pinewood left behind.

"My da would approve," Linhare said to him. "Don't you think?"

"He would."

Reaching out to her, his hand stopped short of running down the short length that had once reached her knees, and Wait came as near to weeping as he could.

SUNSET CAME QUICKLY. Difficult as it was to say good-bye, Jinna was ready. To move on. To journey further. To sail upon a pirate ship that floated on a cloud. She was glad that her offering had not been chosen, though she would have followed through. Jinna could not remember having gone so long without the carnal intimacy she craved. Celibacy afforded its merits.

Saying good-bye to the gathered fae, to Beloël and his Drümbul court, took longer than the wave and *Thanks and good-bye!* Jinna preferred. By the time she got to Liloat, who fidgeted from foot to foot, she was not quick enough to evade his embrace, his kiss or his pleading.

"You mustn't leave me, fair Jinna. You must stay and be mine."

"You've a more fickle heart than my own." Jinna laughed. And though her eyes strayed to Egalfo, she told him firmly, "My place is with Linhare."

"The Little Queen does not need you. I need you."

"It will pass." Extricating herself from his arms, she kissed his cheek fondly. "Good-bye, Liloat. And good-bye to my fat catkin, Kish."

"It will not pass!" he called after her as she walked away. "You will return to me! You will!"

Jinna hurried to the rowboat being held ashore by a gathering of freelings. She understood little of their grunts and growls, but they were a stalwart bunch always willing to assist. Two young males helped her climb first into the boat; Jinna was certain they looked up her skirt.

"There's always a passage a'tween here and there," Hepheo was saying as he approached, "but they're never quite where you expect them to be. From here we go to Weir, to bind an Unfettered man to his Keeper. Can't be helped. His time's his time. You'll have to wait. Would've been there already if it weren't for Beloël's summons. A summons always takes primacy."

"Ask Danle to forgive me, and give him my warmest regards." Beloël clapped Hepheo on his diaphanous back, the sound as solid as old wood. "Good journey, old friend."

They said the last of their farewells. Liloat stood despondently apart. Jinna tried to ignore him, though she could not quite ignore the way Egalfo sidled up to her before offering a friendly salute the gobbet-man's way. Wait took one oar; Hepheo the other. They dipped as the fae folk thrust them into the gentle waves. A few deep strokes took them beyond the breakers and onto the tranquil sea.

Jinna leaned her elbows on the edge of the boat, watching Linhare finger the ends of her ill-cut hair. The sacrifice she'd chosen touched Jinna deeply, and impressed her more than a little. Reaching forward to grab a fistful of Linhare's curls, she said, "It looks marvelous, Lin. You should have done it years ago."

"I did it myself." Linhare frowned. "It feels a bit crooked."

"Only a little." Jinna dipped forward to kiss her cheek. "I'll fix it for you on board."

It did not take long to row out to the Siren's Curse. The rowboat bumped up against a ladder hanging down from the strange mist beneath the hull. Hepheo grabbed for it, steadying it against the swelling sea.

"Up, up!" The captain said. "Sunset's not going to last forever."

Egalfo went first, climbing the ladder like a spider in its own web. He vanished into the mist, its whirling funnels sputtering haphazardly. Jinna's climb was not quite as graceful as Egalfo's, but she made it up and over. Linhare and Wait came aboard almost as one, his arms on either side of Linhare, his body like a harness keeping her from toppling.

"Find someplace to stay out of the way," the captain shouted, scattering his Everwanderers to their tasks. "And hold on tight."

Jinna leaned over the side to gaze down into the swirling mist now chuffing like a thousand horses at their bits. The Siren's Curse lurched, sending her belly-first into the railing. She whooped and laughed and held on tight as the ship headed out to sea. Then it turned, banking hard to port.

"We're heading inland!" Egalfo hauled himself towards her, hand over hand against the pull of gathering speed. The Siren's Curse came about. It belched and bucked, sending Jinna toppling against Egalfo, who laughed but held her up on her feet until the lurching smoothed and picked up speed. A great cheer went up, then fell away as the Siren's Curse and all aboard her swept over the fae gathered on the beach. Braced against the wind, against Egalfo's chest, Jinna eased her grip on the railing.

"Look!" Egalfo pointed, and below, Jinna saw the shadow of their ship speeding over land, following the sunset as if looped into a tail of flaming rays. The Siren's Curse made swift work of the trek it had taken them days to ride. Over scrub and pine and meadow, even the trinket mound bathed in the last red rays of daylight. Beloël's domain stretched on and on, a blur beneath them. And then they were nearing another coast, this one owning sunset instead of sunrise; this one as rocky as the other was sandy soft.

The Siren's Curse leapt from a high cliff. Jinna screamed. Egalfo's arms tightened around her, his knuckles white where he gripped the rail. The ship did not crash to the rocks and the surf, but hit the water with a dancer's grace, a child's joy. She lifted again, buoyant on the mist created in her hull.

"That was marvelous!" Breathless, Jinna let go of the rail to clap her hands and spin about. "Spectacular!"

Egalfo said nothing, only leaned casually upon the rail as if they hadn't just taken the ride of their lives. The Curse no longer bumped and lurched, but maintained its extraordinary speed. Egalfo smiled smugly, long black hair blowing back from his face. Jinna quelled the tiny lurch in her belly and turned away.

"Welcome to the Siren's Curse!"

No longer an indistinct, juxtaposed figure, Captain Hepheo stood solid and robust on the deck of his own ship. His once gaunt face beamed ruddy as any sailor's Dockside. His clean-shaven chin cleft deeply. Overly tall and slim, he was not quite to Jinna's taste in bedmates, but he struck an impressive figure nonetheless.

"Supper's called in waves," he continued. "You'll be in the first. When you hear the bell, report to the galley, down that way." He pointed aft. "Moslo's the best galley-cook in all the Juxta Sea. Wouldn't be surprised if he made something special in your honor, Little Queen.

"My Keeper, Ezibah—" He jerked a thumb over his shoulder at a tall and willowy woman. "—will show you to your habby. I got to bunk you together. Got an Unfettered man trading his soul for a Keeper in a few days. Didn't have enough time to rearrange things."

"Hepheo, my love." Ezibah moved forward like a breeze before he could rattle on. "Perhaps it would be best if I saw to our guests."

Hepheo took the hand that came to rest upon his arm and brought it to his lips. Their eyes met along the length of her slender arm. Jinna did not need to know anything about love or desire to recognize the abundance between them. Then he let it go, and it was as if the Keeper had never soothed him.

"Siren's got a strict curfew," he barked as he backed away. "Everyone's below by midnight. Deck's off limits. No exceptions. Understand? Good." He turned away to call over his shoulder, "See you at supper!"

Jinna smiled behind her hand, hid a snorted chuckle in a cough. Captain Hepheo already barked orders and scattered sailors ahead of him.

"Forgive his frenzy." Ezibah laughed softly. "His is a busy life."

"And it looks like he makes everyone else's, too," Jinna drawled. Ezibah laughed again, showing perfect rows of white teeth, whiter for the darkness of her skin. Familiarity washed through Jinna like warm water on warmer skin. She looked from Ezibah to Egalfo, at the similarity of skin and eyes, nose and hair, but kept her thoughts to herself.

"I thought much the same thing when first we were bound," Ezibah said. "Now, then. If you will follow me."

They followed the Keeper along the deck, past sailors who were not too busy to stare. Most eyes, Jinna was frustrated to find, were on Wait no matter how she swayed her hips or flounced her hair. By the time they reached the stairwell, her mood had soured.

They went single file once they were below deck, the corridors being quite narrow despite the size of the ship. Directly behind Ezibah, in front of Wait, Linhare looked like a bolley among Drümbul. Jinna, then Egalfo picked up the rear. She swayed her hips despite her mood. At least Egalfo might be interested.

"Keepers and their Kept reside on this deck," Ezibah said over her shoulder. "As will all of you. The Unfettered crew bunks in a common room below this one. The galley is aft. I trust you'll have no trouble finding it."

"Listen for the bell, and watch the sailors scramble," Egalfo suggested.

"That will work, too," she said. "I suggest, for the time being, you keep to this deck and the upper. There are many, many chambers and storage places below. It is easy to become confused. And unless Hepheo offers, do not go near the Pilfer down in the belly of the Curse."

"Pilfer?" Jinna asked. "What's that?"

"Ah, here is your habby."

They came to the end of what seemed an extraordinarily long corridor. Ezibah took a key from the pocket of her dress. As she jiggled the lock, the jewels of a bracelet around her wrist sent red sparkles of light onto the door. In the dim lantern light, the gold was like burnished copper. The stones, all shades of pink and red, glittered like no jewels Jinna had ever seen. Ezibah turned the key and pulled it from the lock, tucking the bracelet into her sleeve. She handed the key to Linhare. "I hope you will be comfortable."

Jinna pushed first through the door into a room far more spacious than was proper on a pirate ship. Half a dozen lanterns lit the habby fragrant with recent cleaning. There were even portholes, for what they were worth; the only thing visible at this level was the mist buoying them up.

Four bedsteads tucked into the four corners, each draped in gossamer and sectioned off by tapestry partitions. Between the beds sat a low table already set with fine stemmed glassware shimmering a familiar rainbow hue, and a decanter of deep-red wine. No artwork on the walls, no flowers on the vanity or writing desk, it was as simple as it was luxurious, masculine without being stark.

"What's behind the folding screen?" Jinna asked, pointing to the slotted screen between the two beds under the portholes.

"A bathing tub," Ezibah answered. "There is always hot water on the Siren's Curse. A consequence of the Pilfer's workings."

"There's that word again," Jinna said. "What in bloody blazes is a pilfer?"

Ezibah's dark cheeks flushed. "The Pilfer siphons elements from its surroundings and turns it into the mist that keeps the Siren afloat. Nothing more, I assure you. Now then, you will find suitable clothing in the wardrobe. You are guests on the Siren's Curse. Paying guests. That will not stop Hepheo from putting you to work. If he overtaxes you, tell me and I will see to it." Bowing as she stepped into the corridor, Ezibah finished, "Make yourselves comfortable. The galley bell will ring shortly." And closed the door behind her.

Jinna flopped onto a bed near one of the portholes. Ezibah was hiding something. Jinna was too good at lying to mistake when someone

142

else was. At the moment, she didn't care enough to worry it through. Instead she rolled onto her belly to watch Linhare test the mattress of the bed nearest to hers, short curls bouncing.

"We should trim your hair before the dinner bell rings," she said. In that unguarded moment before Linhare's eyes came to hers, Jinna saw her composure slip.

"Yes," Linhare said, and a watery smile replaced the fear. "Yes, please. Do you think there are shears in here somewhere?"

"Egalfo, Wait," Jinna called. "Would you mind finding us a pair of shears?"

When Linhare was not looking, she shooed at the men looking at her as if she'd sprouted ivy out of her ears. Wait nodded. Egalfo still looked confused. A moment later, she and Linhare were alone. Jinna sat beside her on the bed.

"What is it, Linny?"

"What is what?"

"Are you still angry with me about what I said?"

Linhare looked up sharply, her hand falling to her side. "I was never angry. I do not wish to speak of that, Jin."

Sliding off the bed, Linhare went to the door and stuck her head out, then came back in to rummage about in the writing desk. Jinna watched her fidgeting, certain her forestwife mother would have something wise and appropriate to say, but Jinna had never been, either.

"I found a razor." Linhare held up the small, sharp blade. "Do you think it will work?"

Jinna held out her hand. She inspected the small implement, tried to gather words that might help, and found none. Tapping the razor on her palm, she forced a smile. "This should work fine. Sit over there by the window where the light is best, and I will make you look like a queen."

Siren's Curse

Valishul—5.26.1206
    The clerics have absolved me. It was Ben's idea. I hold no such faith in fallen gods of stars and starlight. I submitted to their rituals for him, because he is anxious for me to once again be his cheerful companion. I see how he fidgets now, when I tell him Violet's musings. They have gotten decidedly more gruesome since those mundane natterings of spiced wine and winter nights. She seeks blood; not my blood. Of me, she is most protective. I fear her cravings. I fear my obligation.
    Don't ask. Please do not ask it of me.

CLOSING THE JOURNAL SHE'D RESTED UPON HER CHEST, Linhare turned it over in her hands. Night and silence had hold of the Siren's Curse. Linhare liked these middling hours when Wait was near and sleeping. She could read the words he'd written in the security of his nearness and in the solitude of her draped bed, unafraid of the change in tone and handwriting when it was to Violet he wrote.

Five days aboard the Siren's Curse, and no other ships passed beneath them. No isles. Just an expanse of water far greater than Linhare ever imagined, and the occasional dark shapes that might have been whales or kraken or the shadow of the Curse itself.

"Six rises come, we'll put port on Weir," Hepheo had told them that first morning. "Work hard 'til then and I'll take you ashore. One way or t'other, Ezibah'll have her day at market."

Though Hepheo was mostly bluster, and Ezibah kept out a keen eye, Linhare learned to mend sails under the captain's growling. She joined in menial labor she never knew took such skill, or elicited such pride. Still, she was glad morning would see them in Weir for a day without toil.

Linhare slipped from beneath her blankets. The floor warm beneath her bare feet—another benefit of the Pilfer—and the journal clutched to her breast, she crossed to where Wait slept. Looking through the gossamer drape was like gazing into his dreams, and he was younger. The grim lines around his eyes eased. Underneath the pale, thick beard, for Wait would not trust a fae blade to shave it with, Linhare imagined him as her father knew him all those years ago. Eighteen. Eager. Optimistic. She knew from the journal in her hand that he had been all of those. Then she parted the curtain and without the softening fabric, he aged back from boyishness. Here was the man she knew, the man she loved. Linhare had not known the boy. Whatever Wait might believe, she loved whoever he became after the journal was written. It was not innocence she craved.

Linhare let the drape fall. She took the journal and herself to her own bed, turned down the lamp so that it was barely a flicker, and read until she fell asleep.

WAIT SAT ALONE IN SOME TAVERN ROOM, perhaps in a chamber above, sharpening his blade. It was no inn or every inn he had ever visited. Yet he sensed Ben nearby. And Ellis. In sensing them, he heard their laughter. Would they laugh so easily together once in the Vale? Once their brotherhood was again sundered?

The steady *shck, shck* of stone on metal soothed him, like the sound of the Pilfer soothed him. Still his hands shook when he stopped, raised the blade to eye-level, confirmed the sharpness his hands already assured. Rising, Wait did not put the blade into its scabbard. His trembling hands steadied. Something buzzed inside his chest. He was no longer alone.

"Come out."

The shadow, a lighter silhouette within a deeper gloom, snuffed out like a candle between licked fingers. Lunging towards that place where it had been, weapon raised, Wait stabbed into the dark, empty depth. Stepping back into the light, he found blood on the blade nonetheless.

Wait dropped the cursed thing. He backed away from it, face in hands, refusing to see. Refusing to know. He stumbled over the chair he had been sitting upon. The sharpening stone fell with a loud clatter as if it were vastly larger than the small bit of worn rock now at his feet.

"It has been too long since we have seen one another, my friend."

Wait froze. Ellis' voice sounded clear. He turned, and there where the room had been empty, stood his friend.

"It has. So much has happened."

Ellis picked up the chair and set it beside the fire within the any-and-all room. He sat, rubbing at his belly as if it ached.

"Indeed." He paused, still rubbing. "Diandra's pregnant."

"It was bound to happen," Wait responded. "Ben was gone nearly three years."

Ellis said nothing. He only rubbed. Then, "She swears Linhare is his. Can she truly know for certain?"

"Women do. Besides, she has Yebbe to detect such things. The child does look a lot like Ben."

"She has asked me not to tell him the other possibility," Ellis told him. The lines about his eyes, the silver in his hair

145

darkened as he spoke. "I do not know which is kinder. Which is right. Telling the man his daughter could be mine or keeping it from him."

"Diandra has asked that you don't."

"But he is my friend. Like my brother."

"Tassry made us all brothers."

Ellis nodded. Both hands on his belly now, he was suddenly pale. "I always do as she asks. No matter what it is. Except once, when it mattered most."

The front of his white shirt darkened, crimson blooming from behind his clenched hands like sunrise. Ellis moved his hands. They dripped blood. Wait dropped to his knees, head bowed.

"I'm sorry, Ellis. I didn't mean to."

His voice calm, as soothing as the shck, shck or the Pilfer, Ellis told him, "It has been too long, Calryan. Too, too long. We must meet for that cup. There are strange things afoot."

Ellis toppled. Wait caught him, caught nothing, because though his hands dripped blood, Wait's arms were empty.

Wait came awake. A dream fled. He could not remember, and somehow did not care to. The pale beginnings of dawn lit the misty porthole. Everyone else slept on. The lamp near Linhare's bed flickered spasmodically as the oil ran out.

He dressed in his own freshly-laundered clothes. After the first morning he found his garments neatly folded in a basket just within the habby door, Wait ceased to wonder about the many inexplicable events aboard the Siren's Curse. Fresh meat so far out at sea, clothes laundered while he slept, the insubstantial mist holding aloft a ship the size of a village. He decided that it was what it was, and what it was, was fae.

The curfew aboard the Siren's Curse was indeed strict. No matter what the game or task at hand, all hands went below by the midnight hour. In the Vale there was always something happening, some crisis to deal with, that kept him or woke him all hours. Mundane as the matters often were, they were nonetheless taxing. Being aboard the Curse gave Wait an opportunity he had not enjoyed since childhood.

A full night of unworried slumber.

Curfew or no, Hepheo had not forbidden rising early. Wait left the warm and silent habby for the decks above. The silent immensity of the Siren's Curse at rest struck him dumb. No crew scrambling about, no sunlight to squint the eyes, she was indeed like a city square waiting for morning vendors and milling buyers.

Walking the deck, Wait pulled the neck of his shirt closed against the unexpected cold. The mist that held the Curse aloft eddied and curled over rail and rigging, settling in corners and dewing surfaces. Enchanting. Enchanted. The last of the moonlight pricked shapes out of this mist. Wait could almost make them into figures.

"You shouldn't be up and about yet." Hepheo's voice barked from a denser patch of mist at the helm.

"I wasn't sure if that was part of the curfew," Wait called back. "I was awake; I figured you had something for me to do. Permission to step to helm?"

"There's always something to do on the Curse. I suppose it's a'right. For you, anyway. Permission granted."

Wait climbed the ornate steps. "Don't you ever sleep?"

"Some." Hepheo winked. He lifted his shirt to reveal a chain around his narrow waist, thin and silver and sparkling. "Ezibah sees to it I spend some time abed."

They stood together amiably, Hepheo at the wheel and Wait leaning on the rail while the Siren's Curse sailed smoothly above the restless sea; while the pale horizon pinked. Soothing silence brought back snippets of his dream. It made him remember again the note from Ellis.

Reaching for it now, Wait felt an odd buzzing, as if a bee had crawled into his pocket, and he found instead the smooth blue stone uncovered in the forest pool and quickly forgotten. He pulled it out, balanced between forefinger and thumb.

"Pretty thing you got there," Hepheo said. "Talisman from Away, is it?"

"No," Wait told him. "I found it in a pool outside of Beloël's glade. I'd forgotten all about it."

"So say you, now." Hepheo chuffed. "Mind if I have a looky?"

The stone crackled between his fingertips. Wait startled. The stone flew up into the air. Hepheo caught it.

"Ho, there, Wait. Steady."

"Sorry," he murmured, tucking his stinging hand into his pocket.

Hepheo held the stone up to the fading moonlight, rolled it in his fingers. He closed one eye. The faint marbling deep within glowed. Something of cunning, something of desire sparkled in the captain's gaze, but passed as quickly as it came. He held the stone out for Wait to take, dropped it onto his palm when Wait did not take it.

"That's quite a prize. I'd hang on to that if I was you."

"It's just a rock."

"Is it?"

Wait looked down at his palm. No glowing. No crackling jolt. He held the stone to the moonlight. The opalescent veins pulsed, as it had on the night he found it. He could almost hear that soft whispering of a heartbeat; or was it a voice?

Wait blinked. Hepheo hummed tunelessly, a sound more like moaning than song. The moon sat low upon one horizon. Closing his fist around the stone, Wait tucked it into his pocket. The back of his neck prickled. All along the deck, that swirling mist rose and fell. Like a child finding animal shapes in the clouds, Wait saw a group hauling a net there, at the rail. Another showed a cluster standing around a barrel, cups raised high. A couple walked arm-in-arm, heads close together. There were fish in the net now, and laughter around the barrel. Diaphanous lips kissed.

The moon dipped into the sea. In the east, the first round hump of dawn. Hepheo stopped humming.

A sound like wind through a drainage pipe, first a low moan then a shriek, washed over the deck, over Wait who braced instinctively as if the wave of sound could cast him overboard along with those amorphous figures. What looked like hands grabbed helplessly for railings and ropes. And then they were gone, swept up like dust into a bin and tipped over the side where they eddied and curled into the cloudbank holding the Siren's Curse aloft. The shriek was again a moaning sound, now more like a song, like Hepheo humming. Wait was drawn to it, to the deep tones of it, and then it too was gone. He looked to the captain, whose shrewd, amused eyes were already on him.

"And now you know," Hepheo whispered, "once a sailor signs on to this ship, my friend, it's forever."

Market

Isonia—6.8.1206

Our course is set. We are docked, as I write, in Clearwater. Come morning, we disembark to begin the overland trek through horse country. Ben is determined to find a horse to accommodate my sudden growth. I am now nearly a foot taller than Ellis, who jokes but watches me most warily. Another result of Tassry—I have come fully into my Dakhan heritage.

Hush, Violet. I will not do as you ask.

There has been word of a young mare, only just put to saddle, of tremendous size and temperament. She is the reason Ben has decided to journey overland rather than by sea. We should reach Ingilia within a fortnight, less if Ben has his way. Diandra and the little princess are so near. I do not doubt that he will make all haste to reach them sooner rather than later.

Violet. Violet. Leave me in peace.

THE SIREN'S CURSE DID NOT RIDE THE SUNRISE INTO WEIR, but rather pulled port an hour shy of noon, almost as any sailing ship might. Though it looked no different from the deck, the great vessel took up no more room in the harbor than any ordinary ship. Only the mist perpetually holding it above the sea remained to mark it otherwise.

Linhare stood at the rail beside Wait, with Jinna and Egalfo, waiting for the crew to disembark. The bright and windy day tossed up fragrances as like as they were unlike those Dockside. Whatever roasted in the pits visible from the deck of the Siren's Curse made Linhare's mouth water. Dressed in her favorite frock, deep blue and sleeveless and rife with pockets, hair only a bob on her shoulders, she felt luxuriously unencumbered.

"Once the Unfettered crew is ashore, we will disembark." Ezibah's voice came from behind them. "It won't be long."

"If you're not back by sunup, you're on your own until next market day!" Hepheo barked over the side. Unfettered men and the first of the Keepers and Kept waved over their shoulders, unconcerned. Ezibah hooked her arm through Hepheo's.

"A month's leave in Weir is not exactly a threat," she said.

"Aye, no. But they'll be back." The Captain looked at Wait and winked. "Ever'one of them."

The last of the crew disembarked. Ezibah shook her bracelet free of her sleeve. In the sunlight, it dotted glittering pinpoints of crystalline light on her dress, on Hepheo, on the deck. He lifted his shirt, offering her the silver chain at his waist. The end of this fine link hooked daintily onto Ezibah's bracelet, joining them by refined shackle.

"You four are in Weir under my authority," Hepheo was saying as they stepped off the gangplank and onto the dock. "Makes me responsible if you get into trouble. Understand?"

"What trouble could we possibly get into?" Jinna smirked, laughing when Hepheo glared at her.

"We know." Egalfo laughed. "You told us. Ezibah told us. Be wary. Watch our belongings. Bolleys are sweet, but fabulous thieves. If we go to the tents, stay out of the northwestern quarter. I've got it all memorized."

"Maybe we should stay together," Ezibah fussed. "I have a terrible feeling—"

"You got to leave it be now, woman!" Hepheo growled. "They're none of them babies. And do you really think Wait needs you henning over him like some dillywig-dandy his first time out of the nest?"

Ezibah's cheeks darkened. She busied herself handing around small, jingling pouches. "Indeed. Well, then. Take these. No arguing. You've worked hard aboard the Curse. Hard as any of the crew. Spend your dolies wisely. They won't last very long. Things are expensive here in Weir."

"Come along, Ezibah," Hepheo said, though gently. Putting his arm about her shoulders, he led her away with a barked, "Sunup!" over his shoulder; and then they, too were swallowed by the crowd, leaving Linhare and Wait, Jinna and Egalfo alone on the pier.

"I don't know about you," Jinna was first to speak, "but whatever is roasting in those pits smells delicious. Anyone joining me in a nibble?"

The meats, as it happened, were familiar: haunches of venison, boar, birds as small as brush-pips and large as autumn-fat rockabits. The vendor cut long strips of the succulent fare and laid them on crusty slabs of bread, drizzling some kind of herbed oil over the top. Linhare ate vegetables the vendor called *covabas* but Linhare called squash, skewered on sticks and roasted over the flames so that the sugars oozed out and caramelized. As Ezibah warned, things were expensive; by the time they finished eating and drinking, their supply of dolies had been cut in half.

"Well, I'm stuffed as a down pillow." Jinna pitched her last empty skewer over her shoulder. "What shall we do next?"

"I could do a bit of browsing about the market." Linhare jiggled her pouch of dolies. "I fear that's about all I'll be able to do."

Jinna wrinkled her nose. "We can shop Dockside any time we wish. What about the tents? We can game a bit. What do you think?"

"You'll lose every dolie you have left!" Linhare laughed. "And Dockside has never been anything like this. Think of what treasures we might find."

"How about we browse the markets this afternoon and head to the tents this evening," Egalfo suggested.

"You don't want to browse the markets any more than Jinna does," Wait said. "You two go ahead. I have no interest in gaming. I'll keep Linhare company while she hunts for treasure."

Jinna grinned at Wait, but she asked, "Linny?"

"You don't need my permission."

"I know I don't. Fine then. Off I go. Egalfo, you coming?"

Jinna was heading out of the pavilion before anyone could object, Egalfo on her heels.

"Jinna!" Linhare called. "Be careful!"

Her face burned. She pressed her palms to her cheeks, trying to quell the same ill-feeling Ezibah seemed to have.

"They'll be fine," Wait soothed as the two vanished into the crowd.

"I know, but..."

"She's been taking care of herself a long time. We'll meet up with them later."

"But how will we find them?"

"We will. And if we don't, they'll be on the Siren's Curse by sunup."

Wait rose from the bench and offered his arm. Linhare took it, eyes still trying to pick her friend's red head out of the crowd. An ill-feeling rumbled in her belly. She pressed a hand to it and, though she smiled up at Wait, she no longer felt quite as unencumbered.

"YOU DON'T NEED MY PERMISSION," Jinna mimicked under her breath as she shouldered through the crowd. Hot tears burned at her eyes, blurred her vision. Turning, Jinna could no longer see the pavilion in which they had eaten together, but she did see Egalfo, bobbing his way through the crowd.

"Wait for me!"

Jinna crossed her arms and obliged. Much as she hated to admit it, she would rather his company than be on her own. Linhare did not need her, in any case. It could not be more obvious.

"What's the matter with you?" Egalfo asked, out of breath.

"I'm bristly as a sea-urchin."

"Apparently."

"I just didn't want to go browsing."

"Neither did I. Don't worry about Linhare. Wait will see to her."

"I'm not worried."

"All right." Egalfo smiled and tried to hide it. "If you say so."

151

Jinna opened her mouth, a retort on her lips. She let it go with a long exhale. "So you want to try our luck in the tents?"

"I have a better idea." Egalfo flicked his fingers. Fire burst and extinguished so quickly she gasped. "A performance. We can put the dolies we have left together and purchase the things I'll need. You can be my assistant. What do you think?"

Jinna looked up at him out of the corner of her eye, at that smile as annoyingly genuine as always.

"All right," she said. "But I get half the take."

He clapped his hands and sparks flew from his fingertips. Passersby gasped and clapped. He bowed extravagantly.

"See that? There's nothing like an eager audience, Jinna. You won't be sorry. I promise."

WEIR WAS LIKE DOCKSIDE only as much as Beloël's pinewood was like Lerolia. It was a noisy, aromatic, bustling waterside market. The air of exotic revelry mimicked the homespun intimacy of fishermen returning from sea. In the closed archipelago of Vales Gate, there was no place to arrive from but another part of Vales Gate. On Weir, the visitors, indeed, the denizens themselves, came from all of fae.

Linhare saw no gobbets in their fluffy forms, but thought perhaps she could detect them in others. There was something of mischief about their race, a look in the eye always up to some trick that distinguished them. Of bolleys and freelings, there were plenty. Of Drümbul and boogle, there were none. But there were others that could have lived anywhere in Vales Gate and gone mostly undetected. Those made Linhare think of Yebbe, and of Jinna, of that same something that set them apart.

She and Wait walked the length of the port town that, after all, hawked the same sorts of wares one could find in Vales Gate. Linhare resisted the old women with cards and crystals; young men turning caterpillars into small, colorful birds. She avoided dark places spawning musky scents and darker places swallowing light. She browsed the stalls of vibrantly colored fabrics; of spices and herbs she was certain even Yebbe had never smelled before; lotions and salves for every purpose imaginable—some that made her blush; knotted jewelry made of colorful thread and glass beads.

She bought a rather large sack of dried fruit, in flavors new to her, and that Wait insisted upon carrying. He bought a flask of juice that the vendor claimed would restore even the weariest traveler. Streetside jugglers and musicians tucked their acts into alcoves and alleys in the marketplace, performing for whatever kind offerings clinked into their cups. As afternoon keeled towards evening, she and Wait found a shady spot to rest. Linhare sipped from the flask of juice, waiting for the sweet tang to restore her. She handed it to Wait.

"Well, it tastes good, but I don't feel any less tired."

Wait took a long pull. He smacked his lips. "Refreshing. But I don't feel anything, either."

"I suppose that even in fae there are charlatans."

Wait handed her back the juice. Linhare sipped, wondered what Jinna and Egalfo were doing. Probably something wicked. The thought made her smile, but it faded quickly. Jinna was angry with her when she stormed off. Linhare did not know what she had done or said, even if she was certain of the result.

"Something's going on over there."

She looked up to find Wait's attention fixed on a commotion she could hear, but not see.

"I can't see anything," she said. "What is it?"

"Looks like an auction," Wait told her distractedly. "Ah, there's Danle. I think...this must be his Fettering."

"Oh! I want to see!"

Wait shouldered a path through the crowd that grumbled, but upon seeing Wait, made way. He lifted Linhare onto a rain barrel. "Thank you," she whispered, looking apologetically at those still glaring after them.

"This is your ninth inquiry. You are still one shy." An older, quite-handsome woman sat in an ornate litter between the blocks, addressing a nervous Danle. His hair blazed as red as Jinna's. Fair skin freckled from the sun blanched as pale as Hepheo ashore without Ezibah.

"Begging your pardon, Mistress," Danle said, "but this is my tenth inquiry. I paid you the required tithes. See here? I have the marker you gave me. With all the tallies. In your own hand."

The woman took the red ribbon Danle held out to her. Holding it up to the light, she inspected it then handed it back. "I see," she said. "Neciel!"

The woman who stepped forward was tall, like Ezibah; dark, like Ezibah; but somehow younger, newer. And though the crowd murmured, *The Vespe. It's the Vespe Neciel,* her eyes never left Danle.

"I done what was asked," the Everwanderer said. "I come back every month and gave gold for her. Neciel's mine. You said."

"So I did." The woman held out her hand for the Keeper's, drawing her closer when she took it. "Have you the shackle, Danle?"

The Everwanderer handed her a bracelet that did not sparkle the way Ezibah's did, though few of the other Keepers owned anything nearly so grand. This one, plain silver, housed a round cabochon glowing green in the sunlight. After inspecting it, the older woman handed it to Neciel.

"Is it acceptable?"

Neciel held the shackle in her hand but did not look at it. Her eyes still held Danle's. "Quite," she said, and handed it back to the woman.

"So be it, then."

The matron rose and moved stiffly to a cage that Danle stepped willingly into. The Keeper, or the woman who would soon become his Keeper, closed the door. The shackle was secured around Neciel's wrist and attached to a fine silver chain about Danle's waist. The older woman held firmly to the other end. Through the bars, Danle took Neciel's hand.

Several young girls linked arms in a circle around the pair and began a rhythmic dance. They chanted words only as audible as the whisper of their slippers on the ground. The older woman bowed her head to Danle. She curtseyed to Neciel. And she let go of her end of the chain.

Danle's strangled scream erupted from his throat. His face purpled. The muscles in his neck became taut and veined cords. His body shook. Neciel stood beside his cage, her hand still holding his. She watched, anticipating. Then her head fell back. An orgasmic moan fell from her lips. For one instant, Danle in his cage faded ghostlike; then that instant passed and he was solid again.

"It is done."

The chain, now firmly linked between Danle and Neciel, pulsed like an umbilicus. Life-giving. Blood-taking. Opening the cage, the matron stepped back to allow the newly-fettered Keeper and Kept to embrace.

Linhare gasped, and only then realized she held her breath. "Have you ever seen anything so...so wonderful?" she asked, but Wait did not answer. He only looked up at her, smiling that almost-smile. She put her hands on his shoulders; he helped her down from the barrel, his grasp lingering on her waist. Linhare could not look away from his face, from the lips still smiling that almost-smile. Her belly fluttered. Wait's hand came up, his fingers brushing the curve of her chin. The fluttering twinged lower and she blushed but did not look away.

"Next!"

The old matron's call turned both their heads. Candidates hustled forward. Linhare's burning face cooled. And Wait's hands fell away.

"We should congratulate Danle," he said.

Linhare nodded. "Yes, we should."

But the press was too thick, and they stayed where they were, each avoiding one another's eyes.

Gianostalia

THE AIR STIFLED WITHIN THE TENTS. Densely packed, sectioned off, no sea breeze could find its way in. Jinna wiped the sweat from her brow, hoping there were no obvious stains under her arms or down her back, and ignored the smell.

Stripped down to the waist, Egalfo glistened. He blew flames from his mouth. He made fire dance along his fingertips, up his arm and across his back as would a juggler with a ball. Instead of tossing it up and catching it once it traveled its path, Egalfo snapped his fingers, blew the flame still dancing up into the air like a feather in a draft, and bowed while it snuffed out in a thousand tiny sparkles.

Egalfo, Jinna admitted, needed her only for her dolies and to hand him the few props he used in his act. She was strangely content with this role, enjoying the show as much as she had Dockside. But now she knew what those glistening muscles felt like under her hands, against her skin. Rubbing at the sudden tickle in her throat, Jinna joined him when he gestured for her, curtsying extravagantly when the applause turned to her.

"More! More!" the crowd shouted, tossing dolies of gold and copper, silver and brass.

"We need to rest!" Egalfo shouted over them. "Later! This evening!"

Bending to retrieve the coins tossed to them, Jinna dropped them into her pouch. When hers was full to bursting she filled Egalfo's, and still there were more dolies left on the ground. She laughed over her shoulder, "This is ten times what Ezibah gave us! We'll never be able to spend it all!"

Egalfo did not answer. Jinna turned to see him cowering slightly before a tall, pale, imposing woman. Her attire was plain, a uniform of sorts. Jinna had seen other such pale beings roaming about the tents. The law, she supposed, and hurried to Egalfo's side.

"…heavy fines for doing what you did," the woman was saying. "There are very strict regulations that must hold for any and all performers, no matter where they are from. Do you understand the chaos that would ensue should just anyone be able to put up a show? Especially one like yours. Fire in an enclosed area? And Weir as dry as a tinderbox?"

"Is there a problem here?" Jinna asked before the woman could launch into the second wave of her tirade.

"Apparently." Egalfo smiled wanly. "Jinna, this is Gianostalia. This sector of the tents is hers to patrol. We've broken some rules."

"It's what we do." Jinna shrugged, handing Egalfo his pouch of dolies. "Is there a fine we must pay? A sanction from some performers' guild we need?"

"Both. And because you were working without sanction and under no performer owning a sanction, I have no choice but to take you into—"

"Gianostalia." A cajoling voice turned all their heads. Coming towards them, hands outstretched in supplication, was a specter. A ghoul. While Gianostalia's pale skin seemed to be a natural thing, this man's spoke of abuse, ill-health, or iniquity. What once must have been a fine suit hung in tatters. Long, greasy hair mocked the refined manner, the grace of his outstretched hand, the timbre of his voice. He came closer, wafting the smell of a body unwashed for so long a thousand baths would not cleanse it. He asked, "Did my throg-boy not deliver the message I sent out to you earlier today?"

"What message would that be, Longee?"

"The one saying that, due to my pair of acrobats deserting me, I endorsed my awarded sanction over to this fine fellow and his lovely assistant. For a cut of the take, of course."

Longee held out his hand. Egalfo opened his pouch, but Jinna placed her hand over his. Smiling her most captivating smile, she told the ghoul, "We haven't counted the take yet. You'll get your money. Don't worry."

"Of course I shall." Longee's outstretched fingers curled into a fist before falling to his side. He turned back to Gianostalia. "So you see, there is no reason for you to be so upset, my dear. And no reason to haul my friends in to your superiors. Hepheo would be quite upset as well, don't you think?"

"Hepheo." Gianostalia grunted. "Brodic gives him too much room to strut."

"Better than having him and his ghostly Everwanderers overrun Weir, no? So are we settled here? Are my friends free to go?"

The woman's silver-coin eyes narrowed. They moved from Longee to Egalfo to Jinna. Her jaw clenched, but she said, "We are settled. But don't think for a moment I believe a fish's fart of that story you told. And you," she stuck a finger in Egalfo's face, "no more fire in the enclosed areas. Take it out beyond the tents."

"Yes, my lady. Law officer? Uh—?"

Gianostalia shook her head, turned on her heel and left them where they stood. Egalfo grabbed the greasy man's hand, pumping it like a well gone dry.

"Thanks for that. We owe you a huge debt."

"Greater than you think you do," Longee told him. "You chose the wrong sector to perform without sanction. Gianostalia cannot be bought, but she is wise. Bringing you in to her superiors was not worth angering Hepheo. I gave her the way out she needed, fished you from a barrel and made a few coins in the process. All in all, a good bargain."

"I can't thank you enough."

"Oh, you most certainly can. You see, my acrobats truly did desert me. And I really do have a perfectly good sanction going to waste. So if you're interested in doing another show later, you may use mine."

"For a cut, of course," Jinna drawled. Longee wagged a long finger at her.

"Of course, my dear. And what would your lovely name be?"

"I'm Jinna. This is Egalfo."

"Enchanted." Longee offered his hand. Jinna took it. Cool as a lizard and dry as an old bone, his grip crushed. Jinna pried her hand from his.

"We just made a small fortune," Egalfo said. "I imagine we'll do even better later, after word of our performance spreads."

"That is beneficial to both of us then. There are a few small matters to settle before your performance. Endorsing the sanction over to you, for one thing. Negotiating the terms of our agreement, for another. And, if you don't mind my saying, Jinna, I have a costume for you that will draw in the men as surely as the dancing flames upon our young Therk's fingertips. If you would come with me to my domicile, we can settle these matters before turning our attention to the performance."

Longee did not wait for a response, but started off in the direction he'd come. Jinna snatched Egalfo back when he moved to follow.

"I don't think we should go with him. Let's just take off now and get back to the ship. You heard him. No one tangles with Hepheo."

"Are you serious?" Egalfo laughed softly. "I don't doubt that this Longee helped us out because there's something in it for him. He's stuck with a sanction and no act. We're an act with no sanction. It's perfect!"

"That's what bothers me. Why take the chance? We don't need the dolies."

"It's not about the coin. We had fun, didn't we?"

"Well, yes."

"This is what I do, Jinna. It's what I live for. When will I ever have another opportunity to eat fire for an audience like this?"

Jinna bit her lip. The ill-feeling running up and down her spine now settled in her belly. "Let's just go back to the Curse, Egalfo. We've had enough excitement for one day."

Egalfo shook his head. "You're starting to sound like Linhare. Or Ezibah."

Jinna's jaw clenched. Yanking Egalfo's hand, she hauled him after Longee, who turned back to await them, a greasy smile curling his lips.

LONGEE WAS UP TO NO GOOD and the two young fools hadn't any idea. Gianostalia followed at a safe distance. The last thing Weir needed was Hepheo's fury. Bolley rebellions, boogle uprisings, freeling wars waged

157

and snuffed and waged again. In a hodgepodge place like Weir where so many races lived in such close quarters, all the disputes of fae intensified. Those lesser races had obviously forgotten their place in the scheme of things.

Gianostalia watched Longee hold aside the flap of his raggle-tag tent and gesture the halfling and the Therk inside. He yawned and stretched, doing a poor job of pretending not to scan the crowd for witnesses, before ducking in himself.

"Scab," Gia grumbled. "How does one fall so far?"

She had better things to do than watch Longee, and the two fools were not her problem. She headed back to the annex.

It was a relatively quiet part of the day within the tents. Noontide performers rested up for evening. Morning performers geared up for afternoon. Longee thought to make a killing with the fire-eating pair that evening, she was certain; but he had probably not taken into account the fact that their performance occurred during that lull between others. The disappointment awaiting him, if nothing else, lifted her spirits a little.

The annex was cooler than the suffocating tents. Purist magic held its advantages, despite the drain on one's body. Checking the seal on the dome of trapped glacial air, Gia added her own bit of protection to stop up the leak she found. Eminence Brodic was quite powerful, but even he could not spread himself thin enough to see to everything.

The rather small annex, especially in comparison to the command hub in Weir proper, belonged to her. How many seasons since she was only a deputy in Brodic's command? Gia could no longer count them, or the seasons since Brodic showed up in his old haunt; and yet finding him leaning against the wall when she entered did not surprise her. She had felt his presence as easily as the change in temperature.

"I heard there was some trouble with Hepheo's passengers."

"Not trouble. Not really," she answered. "How did you hear already?"

"Complaints came in."

"To you? Why not to me?"

Brodic smiled thinly. "Perhaps because Hepheo is involved. I was following the other pair of them from the moment they stepped ashore."

"Is it true then?" Gia asked. "Is he Dakhonne?"

Brodic nodded. "It was quite…tremendous to see him. Not since Dread King Pulos has there been Dakhan among us."

"It is not a good thing, Brodic," Gia said, "to have such a one as Pulos here in Weir. He and his daughter wrought havoc at the edge of the world for far too long."

"He seems tame enough. Nevertheless, the four of them are here on my authority, under my protection by an agreement I made with Hepheo. You need not trouble yourself."

"Oh, need I not?" Gia smirked. "How thankful you must be for those broad shoulders of yours to carry all the responsibility you do. I don't know how you would bear it if—"

"That will be enough, Gianostalia."

Gia's eyes narrowed. Her chin lifted and her jaw clenched, but she said nothing. As always.

"Should anything untoward happen," Brodic continued, "I will take care of it. I will be responsible."

Gia shook the tension from her shoulders. A brisk rapping at the door gave her the opportunity to walk away from him, to regain the composure he always caused her to lose.

"Thank you." She took the missive from the novate's hand. "Return to duty."

"What of the throg, Lady Superior?"

Gia looked over the novate's shoulder to the wretched form of Longee's slave sniffing at the cooled air.

"Give him something to eat and send him back."

"Yes, Lady Superior."

"What is it?" Brodic came closer as Gia closed the door. She unraveled the rolled missive.

"As I suspected. Longee's sanction signed over to the Therk."

"I am surprised you accepted it. You are not usually so—" He smiled a bare, mirthless smile. "—indulgent."

"What choice did I have?" She rolled it up again, sliding it into the proper slot on the wall. "You might want to go check on the situation within the tents. If you got complaints all the way in Weir proper, things might get ugly."

"Quite right." Brodic pushed away from the wall. "I believe I will pay Longee a visit as well."

Gia nodded and walked with Brodic to the door. Difficult as it was to feign indifference, she managed somehow. Brodic had not said so many words to her since leaving her broken, but healing with the Silent Sisters. He tapped on the dome of wintry air as he passed. "Still working, I see."

"It is."

"Excellent."

Waiting for and receiving his customary salute, Brodic crossed the outer room and left the annex. Gia closed her eyes. She breathed deeply. She counted to ten. Then, without a backward glance to the cool and the quiet and the sanctions waiting for her signature, she left the annex to follow Brodic into the tents.

It Begins

THE TENTS TURNED OUT TO BE not so different from the marketplace on the docks. Instead of stray performers on random corners, merchants pocked the crooked lanes. Every tent housed a different company: dancers, singers, whole choirs; jugglers and acrobats and trained animals of a sort Linhare had never seen before. There were bolley extravaganzas resplendent with sugar-glass bubbles blown by a machine that tinkled music. There were fortune-tellers; not just the crystal-bearing crones found at every fair in Vales Gate, but young and beautiful women conjuring spirits from locks of hair tied up in bits of ribbon. Linhare and Wait found many astounding things in the tents; what they did not find was Jinna and Egalfo.

"Do we go back to the docks?" Linhare asked. "Or look a little longer?"

"This area is a lot bigger than I thought it would be," Wait answered. "They could be anywhere. I say we go back to the Siren's Curse. They'll turn up."

But Linhare was not so easily appeased. Turning helplessly, searching, she noticed a man watching them.

"Wait? Look there."

He was as tall as Wait, and so pale that his skin glowed like white sheets left on a moonlit line. Linhare thought she might have seen others like him wandering about, but that was not what trickled from her memory; she was suddenly and again at her mother's funeral feast, watching a woman touch her mother's lifeless brow.

"Purist." Wait spread his arms low at his sides, bowing to the man still watching them.

The man came their way, bowing first to Wait. "I was unaware that you were here in the tents. It is a matter I shall take up with my buzzers. They were supposed to be watching you while I saw to a certain matter."

"You were watching us?"

"Of course. You are guests in Weir. It is not often we get visitors of your—quality. I assume you are looking for your friends."

"We are. You've seen them?"

The Purist smiled, a cold sight. "They've been seen," he said. "They caused a bit of a stir here earlier. Fire in an enclosed area. Performing without a sanction. That sort of nonsense."

Linhare sighed. "Do you know where they are now?"

Wintry eyes strayed to Wait, whose hand rested easily upon his sword hilt. Stance spread. Shoulders squared. Ready for a fight. The hair on the back of Linhare's neck prickled.

"Of course." The Purist's sudden answer made her jump. He held out his fist to Wait. "I am Brodic. Eminence here in Weir."

"Wait," he said, touching knuckles to knuckles. "This is Linhare."

Brodic bowed his head. "An honor. I was on my way out to pay a visit to Longee, the performer who spared them from being arrested. Come; we will see if your friends are still with him."

Linhare was not certain if it was her own heightened awareness or that Brodic drew them, but she was more cognizant of the others who were likewise pale from skin to eyes to hair. They were as much like moonlight as the Drümbul were of the night. With the Drümbul, she had felt at home. These Purists disturbed her.

"There," Brodic pointed to an enclosed but empty space wedged between an animal arena and a row of what appeared to be dressing tents, "is where they gave their performance. You can see why this was not such a good idea, yes? They are lucky they did not set the tents ablaze."

"I'm surprised Egalfo did not take better precautions," Wait answered. "He knows what he's doing."

"That space is sanctioned to Longee, the person I earlier mentioned. I have been told, and the story has been confirmed, his main act ran off early this morning and he was left with space and no act to put in it. Apparently, your friends came upon the open space and decided it was up for the using. That, I'm afraid, is not done, even in the northern sector of the tents. There are sanctions and regulations. It was their good fortune, and mine perhaps, that Longee came to their rescue before my subordinate could arrest them."

"I'll be sure to thank him."

Brodic laughed, or Linhare assumed the rustling sound was laughter. "As I heard, your friends took in quite a bit of coin. We get our share of fieries in Weir, but it is only so impressive to watch a creature of flame play with flame. I do not know that the tents have ever boasted a human fire-eater. You can be certain Longee saw a dolie to be made and took it."

The living area of the tents resembled a village. A very portable village. Grand pavilions of silken, brilliant colors stood alongside gale-sturdy canvas tents; four room palaces alongside animal hides stretched between stakes. Brodic led them to a dwelling once and apparently grand, now faded and worn near to tatters. Linhare grimaced at the sudden stale odor, though she managed to quell the impulse to cover her nose.

"Longee!" Brodic's voice, until then rich and refined, boomed like thunder echoing in a canyon. "A word. Now!"

Inside, something crashed, someone cursed. A moment later, a man as tattered as his dwelling pushed through the tent flaps. "Brodic, my friend. How good it is to see your face at my door. Has it been so long since my last purge? Or is this a friendly visit?"

"Where are the Therk and the woman?"

"Pardon?"

"The fire-eater and his assistant. The ones you endorsed your sanction over to."

"Ah, yes." Longee bowed extravagantly, his long hair sweeping greasy streaks into the dust on his mismatched boots. "His is an amazing talent. And she," he kissed his own fingertips, "so lovely."

"They were last seen with you. Where are they?"

"Are they missing?"

"Where are they, Longee?"

"I imagine Gianostalia, or your buzzers, would be able to tell you better. I've not seen them since they left here. We worked out an agreement, what my portion of their earnings was to be for giving them my sanction, and off they went."

Longee looked now upon Wait and Linhare as if seeing them for the first time. His small, elegant nose twitched. "You must be Linhare and Wait. Jinna told me so much about you."

"Have you any idea where they were going?" Linhare's voice chirped. She cleared her throat. "Hepheo was quite adamant about us being aboard by sunup."

"There are many long and profitable hours before sunup," Longee drawled. "Many hours. I expect to make quite a few dolies from the bargain I made with your friends. I only wish I could have talked them into joining my company. We'd all be rich in the span of a year."

"How long ago did they leave here?" Brodic asked. "Exactly."

"Oh, an hour perhaps? I've been napping since, so I'm not quite sure."

"And where are they to put on their performance?"

"I am not certain." Longee yawned, showing yellowed but straight teeth. "As I said earlier, Gianostalia would know better. She insisted they take their act out beyond the tents, considering there is fire involved."

"Do you mean to tell me—" Brodic shifted slightly forward. "—that you are expecting to make a good fortune on these two and you don't know where they're performing? That you trust them to come carrying your take to you?"

"I—of course. They are most honorable. Ask their friends if you do not believe me."

"Their honor is of no importance, Longee. You would not trust your own mother with such a thing. What are you hiding?"

"What could I possibly be trying to hide?"

"Then give me leave to search your dwelling."

163

"I'll do no such thing. There are rules about that sort of invasion."

"Rules I am quite aware of." Brodic's jaw clenched, but he inclined his head stiffly. "Very well. I shall obtain the proper warrant and question Gianostalia about the possible whereabouts of the Therk and the halfling. In the meantime, my Dakhonne friend here will keep an eye on you."

Wait stood taller. The broad expanse of his chest flexed as he pulled his blade from his sword belt. Longee paled considerably. The bump of his throat moved up and down in his effort to swallow.

"This is outrageous." His voice wobbled. "The authorities will hear of this."

"I am the authority in Weir. See to it you are still here when I return."

"Your friends were fools," Brodic murmured once they were out of earshot. "I've no doubt that Longee has done something with them. I am bound by the laws here. I cannot go into that tent and search. I've also no doubt that long before I ever return with a warrant, that greased snake will slither out of Weir. You, however," he looked to Wait, "are bound by no such rules."

Wait only nodded, and turned back to the tent Longee ducked into. Linhare's heart raced. She could barely breathe. What had those two beloved fools done?

A popping akin to a thousand stoppers being pulled from their bottles paused Wait in his tracks. The sudden swirl of wind pushed him backwards. Brodic pulled Linhare against him. That wind tugged at her clothes, at the tents all around her, at residents running frantically in all directions. Stakes pulled from the ground. Surrounding tents collapsed. Longee's expanded like a bladder filled with air, and lifted. Up. Up. Slowly up. Wait grabbed for a corner of tattered cloth, but the force of wind knocked him backwards.

"Wait!" she screamed and he was there, holding her against his chest. Brodic's pale face was chalk. Beads of perspiration erupted along his brow. His mouth moved in chanted words she could not hear. And then there was a woman beside him, pale and commanding as he, joining her voice to his.

Too late.

Not enough.

The tent launched. Blew up and away. Like a kite in the wind.

"THIS IS EXACTLY WHAT I WAS AFRAID WOULD HAPPEN. I warned you. I did warn you!" Brodic paced the deck of the Siren's Curse, his face everpale, yet furious. Wait kept his arm about Linhare's shoulders, watching the Purist carefully. Ready.

"Your buzzers were supposed to be watching them," Hepheo shouted back. "Once they left my ship, they were your responsibility."

"How very convenient, Hepheo! They were in your care. You insisted I let them go ashore, and like a fool, I allowed it! They had no sanction to work the tents."

"Well, I didn't tell them to go perform."

Ezibah, still attached to her Kept by chain and shackle, put her hand on Hepheo's shoulder. "Longee is not supposed to be capable of such magic any more. No one could have predicted this. Recriminations will not help Egalfo and Jinna."

Brodic stopped pacing. The ghastly shade of Hepheo's face diminished. He lifted the front of his shirt, releasing the chain from the bracelet, but kept close to Ezibah nonetheless. "None of this would've happened if Gianostalia hadn't let them off."

All eyes went to the Purist peacekeeper standing apart from everyone else, until a clutch of Unfettered men stumbling up the gangplank turned their attention. One unfortunate fellow nearly pitched into the dirty water, but for a slim, steady hand that pulled him back.

"Take him to our habby," his rescuer gently told the crewmen. "I will see to him presently."

Wait recognized her instantly, and would have were the drunken man she unshackled herself from not Danle. Like all the other Keepers, Neciel was tall and dark, poised and beautiful. But something marked her as unique and familiar. As she came close and bowed to them one at a time, Wait saw it was in the eyes: one deep brown, the other a startling green.

"I came as soon as I heard of the trouble. Longee," she tisked his name. "There is no end to his villainy. How can I be of assistance?"

"Vespe Neciel." Brodic bowed. "I understood that today was your Fettering. I did not wish to disturb you."

"This is my family now. It is my duty to help them." Turning from Brodic to Ezibah, Neciel bowed. "Greetings, dear Ezibah." Rising again, she turned to the woman still standing at attention. "And to you too, Gianostalia."

The Purist nodded curtly as Ezibah took Neciel into her arms.

"My little one," she said. "I wished to be there to witness your Fettering. The crone would not allow it."

"That is her way. You remember."

"I do."

"Can you help, Neciel?" Ezibah asked. "Can you consult the green? See where Longee has taken our friends?"

"I have already done so," she said, and turned to Brodic. "Longee is bound for Jaquewatten."

"That far." He thumbed his lip.

"We can use an imp," Gianostalia suggested, and was met with a furrowed brow. "He did."

"How far is it?" Linhare asked. "How long will it take?"

"Several days by horseback," Brodic answered. "Moments with imp-magic."

"I will gather our things."

Linhare took only a step before Hepheo stopped her, a hand to her arm. "Ho-there, Little Queen. Where do you think you're going?"

"After Jinna and Egalfo, of course."

Murmurs ruffled about the gathered Everwanderers. Ezibah and Hepheo exchanged a glance Wait found unsettling. "What is it?" he asked.

"Hepheo, no," Ezibah began, but he hushed her with a finger raised.

"If you go after them, our agreement is broken."

Linhare's face blanched. "Broken? Why?"

"You bargained with the Everwanderers to find you a way back to where you come from," he answered. "Break with that, you break the contract. Rules is rules, and that's just the way of it."

"Can you not wait for us?"

"That's not the way it works." Hepheo grimaced. "You and I bargained, Little Queen. It was your sacrifice I accepted, you I am bound to serve until our agreement is finished. You leave this ship, you have only until next sunset to return."

"Then I will return by then."

"I cannot guarantee that," Brodic said. "Imp magic or no."

"And I cannot abandon my friends," Linhare told them. She turned to Wait. "I speak only for myself."

"You speak for us both," he said. Linhare held out her hand and he took it. "We go with you, Eminence Brodic."

The Purist bowed his head. "If that is what you wish. Are you certain?"

"We are." Linhare turned to Hepheo, back straight and chin raised. "If we are not back by next sunset...if we do not..." She choked on a sob and hurried off. Wait moved to go after her, but Ezibah put a hand upon his arm.

"Allow me," she said. Wait bowed his head and took a step back. Hepheo moved to stand beside him. The gathered crew dispersed, but for a clutch including Danle and Neciel still being congratulated by other Keepers and Kept.

"It pains me to have earned her scorn," the captain said.

"I don't think Linhare is capable of scorn."

"Then her displeasure." He petted the braid looped through his belt. "Help her to understand, this is the Siren's Curse. Long a'fore I ever came to captain her, the rules was the rules. Breaking them isn't just forbidden, it's dangerous."

"I'm Dakhonne," Wait told him. "I understand about rules."

"That you are." Hepheo opened his mouth, as if to say more, then closed it again. Reaching under his shirt, he gave a firm tug. A small piece of the delicate chain he wore came off in his hand. He wrapped it about Wait's wrist. End connected seamlessly to end. "A parting gift. And a token of friendship."

Wait turned his wrist over. The chain sparkled where sunlight hit it. He could barely feel the weight of it at all.

"You break with my Curse, but not with *me*," Hepheo told him. "Consider that my continued protection, wherever your journey takes you. It will bind anything you have a mind to bind, for love or need or malice. It knows no difference between them, but will do what it's meant to do. Just give it a tug, and off it'll come."

Wait tugged at the chain round his wrist. It came apart easily, but it did not break. Winding it again, it connected end to end.

"Thank you, Hepheo," he said. "It is an honor."

"I will wait as long as I can, but come sunset tomorrow..."

"I understand."

Taking wrists as warriors, the men parted awkwardly. Hepheo joined Brodic, finally done with berating Peacekeeper Gianostalia. Wait leaned on the rail, leaned back into the silent obscurity at his call, and gazed about the ship that had become dearer to him than he knew until that moment. In another life, in another world, he could imagine himself sailing forever upon the Siren's Curse, even knowing what he did about the mist...

"Calryan."

The sound of his name startled him upright. Neciel stood before him, smiling.

"Can I help you, Vespe?"

"I saw you at my Fettering."

"Linhare and I were in the audience, yes."

"It has been long indeed since one of your kind has been seen in Weir."

"I hear that a lot lately," he said. Neciel held his gaze, searching. Wait could almost feel her fingers sorting through the folds of his mind. Memory whispered and spilled. She gasped. He tried to gather it up again, tuck it away into those places recently and too easily accessed. Wait's heart heaved inside his chest. *Please, no*, he thought he said, but Wait did not feel his mouth move, or breath leave his lungs. The Vespe smiled, gracious and grieving. She placed a hand upon his chest, stilled the frenzy within.

"Nothing will ever spare you your own memory," she said softly. "But know this—a life honorably lived cannot undo one ghastly deed; but neither can one ghastly deed invalidate an honorable life. Good journey, Calryan."

"Wait!"

Linhare's call surrounded Neciel's whisper so that the two names became one. Her hand fell away. Sound returned. Wait shook off the green truth or kind lie. From across the deck, the Vespe Neciel smiled his way and resumed her conversation with Gianostalia as if they had never spoken; as if she did not know him at all.

Jaquewatten

Rhob—7.9.1206

We are nearly there. The Vale. When I left it, I was a boy keen on adventure. I return as a man looking forward to simplicity.

Ben has pushed us hard. I am grateful to my gentle, stalwart mare for her patience and perseverance. She is worth a hundred times what Ben paid for her, despite my initial shock.

Ellis is less enthusiastic about the end of this journey. I would rather be ignorant of the reason; but as I am not, I do understand. He still watches me warily, often asks if I can yet remember anything of the horror on Tassry. Though I tell him I do not, I have other ways of knowing what I have done. I will spare him this, as I have come to spare Ben. *They cannot know. They cannot know!* I'll not be the cause of discomfort or anxiety. There are enough such things at hand.

Tomorrow, we reach the castle. For the first time in three years, I will be home. For the first time since earliest childhood, I have a home.

By all I have sworn, by Ben's blood oath, I will not succumb.

LINHARE CLOSED THE JOURNAL and slipped it into the front pocket of the gaily stitched bag Ezibah gave to her, sniffing back tears for Wait, tears for Hepheo and Ezibah. Parting had been tense; Linhare left the Siren's Curse as reluctantly as Wait, but she would not abandon Jinna.

She buckled the little silver buckle on the pocket, smoothed her hand over the oiled and waxed sailcloth as water-resistant as any of the Curse's sails. The bulk of Wait's journal seemed to press against her hand. It had occurred to her to leave it behind, claim she forgot it beneath her pillow in the rush to gather their things. It was a believable lie, but one she could not tell. She set the bag down.

The Purists hustled about the annex like bees in a hive, doing everything and nothing at once. Brodic consulted Wait as if he were a comrade of many years. Linhare might as well have been invisible.

Wandering out into the yard, she lifted her face to the fair and generous dark. Brodic's trace was visible in the darkling light. He had been able to bend it according to Neciel's prediction, redirecting the already expended magic. Instead of simply showing direction, the glimmering star-like trail would somehow tow them right into Jaquewatten. Linhare was not entirely certain she wanted to know how this towing would be accomplished. Bottomless trunks and flying ships—surprise held its advantages.

"Little Queen." Gianostalia was coming towards her carrying a trencher. Like her superior, she was tall and slender and muscular. Her long hair was white; her skin, like moonlight; her eyes were pale, silver coins. A small, dark mole at the corner of her lip accentuated their fullness. She thrust the food into Linhare's hands. "You must eat."

"I could not possibly eat a thing." Linhare tried to give the food back. "But thank you, Gianostalia."

"Gia," she corrected. "And I'm not asking you to eat, Little Queen. I am telling you to. Our journey will be taxing in ways your body is unaccustomed to. Sustenance will work to lessen the effect."

Linhare grimaced, moved the food around.

"Eat or I will force feed you."

"You will do no such thing!"

Gia's stern smile said otherwise. Linhare bit into a piece of meat as Wait approached, his mouth full and his trencher piled high. He gestured to Linhare's food. "Not hungry?"

"No."

"She must eat," Gia said. "And you, eat slowly. None of us here will be able to flip you over should you choke."

Wait laughed, and shoved more food into his mouth. Gia shook her head. "It will not be long now. I will go speak with Brodic."

Linhare watched her go, chewing slowly on that bit of meat making her stomach well. The moment she was gone, Linhare spat it out.

"You have to eat," Wait said.

"I did. Some. Honestly, Wait, I can't."

"You heard what Gia said."

"I know. I will. Maybe if I had something to drink?"

He looked at her skeptically but led her to the bench shoved up against an outer wall. "Sit here. I'll be right back."

The moment he stepped through the door leading in, Linhare scraped some of the food from her trencher into the overly full one he'd left behind. When he returned bearing her drink, she was placing a strategic bit of overcooked carrot into her mouth.

"Thank you." She took the cup, setting the half-empty trencher aside. She sipped, swallowing the carrot mash along with the sweet beverage.

Wait looked at her trencher. "You ate while I was gone?"

"Just a little." Linhare sipped again, hiding her half-truth in her cup. "I'm finished if you'd like the rest."

Wait looked at her trencher, then at her. "Give it here."

Linhare scraped the last of her meal into his. Wait scooped food into his mouth, barely chewing in between.

"I never knew you were such a glutton," she said

"When you're poor, you learn to eat when food is available. You never know when it's not going to be."

"You were poor as a child?"

Setting his empty trencher down, he wiped his beard clean on the back of his hand. "Aren't all fisherfolk poor?" He rubbed at his whiskery chin. "I've never worn a full beard before. Not on purpose, anyway."

"It suits you."

"You like it then?"

"Don't you?"

"It itches."

"I know you wouldn't shave with the blade Beloël gave to you, but perhaps Brodic can provide something you can better trust."

Wait let his hand fall. "I never held much store in the bolleytales told to us as children," he said. "But being here has given me a healthy respect for such things. The soldier in the story my pap used to tell was bound inside a boulder because he was pricked by a fae blade. Maybe there is no more to it than a children's tale, but a wise man doesn't take such chances after he's been dropped into fae through a trunk in a princess's bedroom. I'll live with the beard."

Linhare reached up, tugged playfully at his blond chin. The hair was fine and soft. The smile peeking out of it was broader than she was accustomed to. It reached his eyes instead of just the corner of his lips. Each day, each moment, made him more like that young man in his journal; or the man that boy might have become had Tassry never happened. His hand came up as hers fell away. Fingertips traced the dimple in her chin.

"The night is drawn." Gia poked her head around the doorjamb, startling them apart. She did not seem to notice. "It is time."

Wait gathered their bags and they followed the peacekeeper out into the yard.

"Rare and dear." Brodic held up what appeared to be a lumpy glass ball. "But sure and quick. The trace you see there will help me keep the imp on course. We'll find your friends."

Inside the ball, between thin strands of glass, crouched a tiny thing no bigger than the palm of Linhare's own hand. She squinted, moving closer, trying to see what manner of being could be inside, but saw only a creature like liquid light.

"Gia, the harness."

She handed Brodic a leather brace of bands and tiny buckles that he fitted around the glass ball. From that brace threaded two long straps, like reins on a cart-horse bridle. These Brodic held tightly. Within the ball, the creature writhed.

"Come. Put your wrist through one of these." Brodic showed them the loops along the span of rein. "And hold the rein tight. Once I break the glass, the imp will take shape. It might take me a moment or two to convince it to cooperate but it will. Just be sure you are hanging on tight when it takes to the sky."

"Takes to the—" Linhare cried out as Brodic broke the glass with a little silver hammer. The imp poured out, took shape. A doglike creature, fangs dripping. A serpent. A goat. Linhare's arm felt torn from its socket as the changeling imp bucked and bolted; and then when she thought she would pass out from the strain, Brodic convinced the imp to form. It fashioned itself into the brace, taking a shape no bigger than a pony, and leapt into the sky dragging Wait, Brodic, Gia and Linhare with it.

"SHE DID NOT EAT." Gia stood over the Dakhonne cradling his Little Queen. All around them, citizens of Jaquewatten pointed and murmured, but they stayed well away.

"She will be fine," Brodic said. "Purist magic drains her kind more than ours. We've not far to go. Bring her."

Wait's head came up slowly, his dread glare falling on an oblivious Brodic who pressed through the gathering crowd without waiting to see if he was followed.

"Come," Gia told the Dakhonne. "Brodic is right. She will be fine soon enough. The magic drains, but it does no damage. Wait. Wait, come."

But his attention remained fixed on Brodic. Gia reached out to touch his arm, to break his concentration, and discovered she feared doing so. Clenching her teeth, she flexed her fingers and braved a gentle nudge.

The Dakhonne's eyes rolled to hers as if he stood inside time and, somehow, slowed it. The fury within the calm possessed the capacity to kill with no remorse. The Drümbul were refined merriment. The Purists were cool power. But the Dakhan, their lost kin, were caged ferocity. Warriors like no others. Like this one on the ground before her, holding tight to his Little Queen.

"Wait," she said softly, proud that her voice did not quaver as her insides did. "Come. We will make her comfortable while she sleeps away the effects."

That slow glare held another moment. Sweat beaded his brow. Then Wait blinked; a breath burst from his lungs as if he had been holding it a very long time. He hefted the Little Queen higher in his arms, burying his face in the soft ringlets of her hair. He whispered words Gia did not hear. Then he nodded, and she led him to the annex.

"There." She pointed to the cot Brodic had set up. "She needs rest, and when she has rested, food. This is why I told her to eat."

"I thought she did," Wait answered. In the short walk from the square where the imp touched down and vanished into sparkled light, the Dakhonne had calmed considerably. Gia no longer feared him. He laid Linhare onto the cot, drawing a thin blanket up over her as tenderly as a mother swaddling her babe. Gia respectfully turned away to find Brodic coming towards them.

"You were supposed to see that she ate." His quiet words were no less angry. "It was a simple task, Gianostalia."

"I brought her food. I waited to see her put some of it in her mouth, and I left her with the Dakhonne. What did you wish me to do? Force feed her?"

"You always were more crude than courteous."

"A trait you seemed to enjoy at one time."

"That is enough!"

Behind her, she heard the Dakhonne rise. She whispered, "You're angry because I dared try to help you in the tents, not because of this."

"You've no authority to—"

"Only because you will not grant it! I have the ability. Give me the rank."

"I cannot."

"You will not."

"See it as you must." His eyes strayed beyond her to Wait approaching. "You always do. Tend to Linhare. Let us see if you can get it right this time."

"You leave me to play nursemaid?"

"I leave you guarding a queen," Brodic answered. "Or go back to Weir. Ah, Wait. I see that you've recovered from the journey."

Gia turned away. The fury seething was an old one, and easily tapped to life; less easily soothed as the years dragged by and Brodic did not bend.

You loved me once. You saw me through. And then your heart turned.

"The trail led to Jaquewatten, but the local annex did not see any such commotion as we just caused," Brodic was telling Wait. "I suspect he managed to get to Hoophollow or Brinnymeade rather than the city proper. I have already sent riders out to ascertain if that is so. If you will come with me, I will show you maps of the area and possible routes to the most likely places we will find them."

"What about Linhare?"

"Gianostalia will watch over her. We will only be in the guardhouse across the way."

Wait turned to her, a glimmer of that focused fury shining in his eyes.

"If she stirs, I will send for you."

The glimmer faded. He looked once to his sleeping queen before leaving, Brodic right behind him, calling orders to the annex peacekeepers who jumped to his bidding. Jaquewatten was a small town in a rural area that required little more than the notion of power to keep the citizens happy. The locals knew Eminence Brodic by reputation if not by sight; it was enough.

Gia returned her attention to her ward. The Little Queen slept peacefully, though her color was like yesterday's ashes. Running fingertips along her smooth brow, she found it clammy. Never a good sign where such expenditure of magic was concerned.

Rising again, she went to the adjoining room and began rifling through the medicinals there. Like all annexes, it housed a well-stocked infirmary. Seeing the compounds, tinctures, and infusions all distinctly labeled, dated, and arranged filled her with a familiar joy. Brodic had cajoled her from herbwife robes and into a peacekeeper's uniform, but he could not make her forget all she once learned.

She gathered essential oils of moonrod, sisterspurse and turtlefoot. Ground ordiroot to bind it all. She reached for a clay bowl to fill at the well, but halted before reaching the door. Water would do, certainly; but loesh better activated all the ingredients to their fullest potential.

Bolleybrew on the streets of Weir.

Dunk in Therk.

Fool's comfort in the lands of the west.

The substance boasted as many names as there were races Beyond. Gia knew it as *loesh*, its oldest name, for her studies in herbwivery. She kept none in her annex, though diluted and dangerous forms of it were found easily enough in a place like Weir. Here in Jaquewatten, in this meticulously kept infirmary, they would have it under lock and key if they stocked it at all.

Setting down ground root and herb, Gia took the bowl back to the shelves and cabinets so neatly placed. She ran her hand along the jars and bottles, reading the alphabetically arranged labels, just in case. Turning from the shelves, a heavy wooden locker drew her. A lock dangled from its lever.

Where would I hide the key? Setting the bowl beside the locker, Gia closed her eyes. She touched the lock. Her fingers tingled and her head turned. To the desk. To the top drawer. To the ring of keys left carelessly there.

On the second try, the lock clicked open. She lifted the lid. There were few items inside, but items Gianostalia Herbwife remembered. Dangerous, wonderful things the lesser beings of fae could not have access to.

The bottle of loesh was in the corner, carefully packed in fresh straw that needed to be changed frequently lest decomposition warm the tonic and destroy it. Lifting it from the locker, Gia held it up to the lamplight. Clear and cool, it cast a silvery sheen against her pale skin.

She gathered the ingredients, mixed everything together in the clay bowl. She uncapped the loesh; her hand shook only slightly as she poured. Gia stirred until her hands stopped shaking, then carefully and quickly returned the bottle to its locker, closed the lid, locked the lock and put the keys back in the drawer.

She carried the concoction to Linhare and carefully squatted down beside her cot. Gia eased her ward upright, encouraged her to drink.

"There now, Little Queen. Your Dakhonne will be back soon enough. I'll have you well before enduring fear in such a man's eyes again."

Gia lowered her back again when she was satisfied by the amount swallowed. Linhare sighed in her sleep. Her ashen complexion pinked. Even the corners of her pretty, plump lips curled into the hint of a smile.

Cross-legged on the floor, Gia stared into the bowl, at the mouthful left within. She swirled it around, watching the bits and granules spiral. Moonrod for easy dreaming. Sisterspurse to revive. Turtlefoot to strengthen. Loesh to combine it all, and give back what imp magic had taken. The Little Queen would thirst tomorrow, perhaps the next day, but never know what it was she thirsted for. And then it would subside and she would forget that there had ever been such a thirst. Gia knew. Gia remembered. And yet now, so many years later, she thirsted so badly that her tongue swelled and her vision blurred.

She set the bowl down.

She picked it up again.

She brought it to her lips and let the scarcest drop wet them, let that drop linger, licked it away. The slightly bitter taste made her mouth tingle. The tingle spread to her cheeks, her throat, and there stopped to buzz like a thousand bees droning underneath her skin.

Gia smiled. And then she wept. And then she poured the remaining concoction in the dirt outside the annex before cleaning away all evidence that it was ever brewed.

Hoophollow

SOBBING WOKE HER FROM DRUGGED SLUMBER. Jinna could not rouse herself enough to make out what the voice was saying, or whose voice it might be. And then came whimpering more pitiful than the sobbing, a soft keen of anguish that ached in her own heart. Beside her, Egalfo still slept. She sat up, stretched. Underneath and all around her curved smooth, cool glass. Strands rose up from the ground and down from the ceiling like the inside of a cave. She used one to help herself to her feet. Her bladder instantly made its presence known.

Legs crossed, and slightly hunched, Jinna turned to movement outside her prison. A feral, hopeful face loomed enormous, spread wide by the curve of her prison. She backed away, came up against a glass column.

I have seen that face. The throg. But he was small and I...

Jinna scrunched her eyes closed—and remembered. Everything. She opened them again to find the throg still far bigger than it had any right to be, and she the size of a bolley. Swallowing fear and disbelief, she called out, "Can you hear me?"

The throg cocked his head. He appeared more beast than human, though his eyes were guardedly kind. Jinna pushed away from the glass column.

"Can you release us?"

The creature backed away, looking over one shoulder, then the other. Backing further, he nodded, and was gone.

"Egalfo! Egalfo, wake up!"

"Hmm?"

"Get up! Help is coming."

Jinna nudged Egalfo with her foot. The hairy creature was already returning, crouched and cagey.

"Help—what?" Egalfo rubbed at his head but he wobbled to his feet, glancing about. Jinna steadied him. The face loomed wide again. He seemed to be sniffing at the glass prison. Egalfo grabbed Jinna's hand and hauled her behind him.

"That's our help." Jinna shook him off. "Not our captor."

"What is it?"

"Remember the pitiful creature that served us wine?"

"Oh, yes. The throg." He tugged at a glass strand, looked down at himself, up at the throg. "I'm not even going to ask."

The throg motioned them back, a little silver hammer in his hand. Jinna grabbed Egalfo and hauled him to the center of their prison. A musical clink, and the globe split in two, neat halves that could have been hewn by the finest blade.

"Thank you!" Jinna jumped up and down on tiny feet, clapping her tiny hands. She looked to the throg. "We're still the size of bolleys!"

"I've no magic." The throg's deep and lilting voice quavered. "I am able to free you, because the hammer is the magic that does so. But I cannot return you to your proper size. I am sorry."

"Blast! Fank-rattle Longee!" Jinna stomped and cursed. "I knew it was a mistake! I told you we should've just gone back to the Siren's Curse, but no! You wanted to—"

Egalfo tapped her shoulder, gestured to the throg cringing away from her. She grimaced, took a deep breath.

"Thank you for freeing us," she exhaled. "If you could help us down from here, we'd be even more grateful."

The creature moved closer, offering a grimy, tentative palm. Jinna stepped onto it. Egalfo followed, bowing grandly and sweeping the tips of his boots with his elegant hand. "You have my eternal gratitude, sir."

The pitiful creature smiled at that, lowering them gently to the ground. "Longee will not be back for some time. You must be hungry. I will find food for you."

"I need to, you know…" Jinna made a squatting gesture. The throg blushed but pointed to the sliver of light letting moonlight into the tent.

"Be careful out there," he said. "Don't wander. The size you are, a cat could make off with you."

Jinna fairly sprinted for the opening. Lifting her skirts, she squatted behind the tent stake and kept her eyes and ears alert for any shadow, any crackling of grass. Egalfo stepped outside and casually took care of his own business. They had been lovers, after all. She knew every inch of his body. He knew her inside and out. Thought followed thought to those lazy afternoons, those long nights spent in his arms…

"Do we trust him?" Egalfo's back was still to her. Jinna stood up, arranged her skirts.

"I don't know," she answered. "Do we have a choice? How far will we get in the state we're in before something makes a meal of us?"

"Well, we can't stay *here*."

Egalfo turned to face her, still tucking in his shirt. "Do you think Wait and Linhare will come for us?"

"If there is a way, yes. But we can't just sit and wait for them to appear."

"Agreed. Then what do we do?"

Jinna looked to the sky. "We'll figure something out. Let's get inside for now, where it's safe."

"Saf*er*."

177

"Just come on."

The throg was sitting cross-legged on the ground, offering them a wooden bowl full of tiny bits of food he had broken up.

"It is all that I have," he said. "Longee is as stingy as he is foul. He feeds me, but only enough so that I will not die."

"We can't take your food," Egalfo said. Jinna bit into a piece of dried apple as big as her hand.

"I think even he will not miss the morsels we'll eat," she said. "Don't be such a hero."

The throg watched her. He smiled, but there was something of sorrow about his eyes. Jinna tried to smile back, but the shiver running up her spine made it more of a grimace.

"Do you have a name?" she asked him.

"I did. Once. I don't remember it."

"What does Longee call you, then?"

"Terrible things. None of them I will honor by repeating."

"Why don't you run away?" Egalfo asked. "You said that Longee will not return for some time."

"I cannot. I am bound. But—" he looked down at his hands, "—I can save you from Longee, if that is what you wish."

"Of course we wish!" Jinna cried, startling the pitiful creature backwards. "Sorry. Yes. But how?"

On hands and haunches, the creature crawled away. What Jinna had mistaken for furred breeches was actually fur. His feet were not feet but paws. She nudged Egalfo, who shook his head and pressed his lips tightly together. The throg returned with a little leather pouch in his hand. Jinna eyed it suspiciously.

"What is that for?"

"To carry you in."

"Carry us where?"

"Away from here." The throg bowed his head. "Away from Longee, just as you asked."

Quicker than either of them could react, the throg snatched them up and dropped them into the bag. Jinna and Egalfo tumbled over one another, into debris like fallen leaves at the bottom of the pouch. A single eye blocked what little light reached them.

"What are you doing?" Jinna screamed. "Free us at once!"

"Forgive me." The bag muffled his voice. And all light vanished.

Brinnymeade

THE BARREL BRIDGE INN, in the small town of Brinnymeade, still slept. Shuttered and thatched, a fragrant curl of smoke rising like a question into the morning sky, it was as quaint and tidy as any such place Wait had seen in Littlevale.

"The area is secure," Brodic reported, as if Wait were the one in charge. "Reinforcements are posted. We await the signal that Longee remains in his stupor. The fool. Foul and foolish. He has made this far too easy. Still, it is good we left the Little Queen in the hollow. No need for her to witness this."

Wait's hand tightened on his sword hilt. He felt the phantom weight of her lifeless body in his arms, saw the pallor of her face. How like her mother she seemed. The image flickered like broken memory. Taunting. Fanning the rage he had barely suppressed. Wait took deep breaths, pushed them out slowly, kept his eyes wide open lest the blood waiting behind closed lids drown him.

"Are you unwell? Wait?"

Brodic's pale hand on his arm nearly broke him. Pain seared through Wait's body. He refused the fury, tamped it down. Linhare was safe. Awake and whole. She had thrown her arms around him only an hour ago and he had breathed in her sweet scent, his nose buried in the softness of her hair, his skin on fire with the feel of her...

Wait came slowly back to himself. Brodic's hand still rested upon his arm. The concern had only just left his lips. Time stopped nearly still when the rage took him, like it did on Tassry. Between one moment and the next, all the blood still waiting for him had been spilled; and Wait only blinked.

"I'm fine," he said just as the innkeeper's wife came out onto the porch of the Barrel Bridge Inn, casually waving her apron back and forth. Brodic answered with a gesture to those nearly unseen peacekeepers on the perimeter, and stepped onto the path. Wait followed behind, drawing his sword only when Brodic did. Up the steps, silent as the morning, they passed the mistress of the house, then the scullery staff poking curious heads around heavy doors. The innkeeper hissed and clucked at them. "If anything is damaged you will get a bill. I run a respectable—"

"If you do not hush," Brodic warned. "I will gag you."

The innkeeper drew back as if struck, but spoke no more. Heads poking around doors ducked back behind them. Silence, but for the snoring already audible as they neared the stairs.

Brodic seemed to know where he was going. His hand moved from door to door, stopping at the third. He touched the door-latch. It clicked.

The door swung silently open. Longee snored on. Naked arms and legs sprawled as if he had leapt from some great height and fallen trying to fly. A woman, dirtier and scrawnier than Longee, slept beside him.

Brodic nudged the sleeping man with his foot. "Wake up. I'll have a word with you."

Startled snores echoed the man's grumbling. "I've not asked for breakfast, woman." Pushing himself upright, Longee's eyes opened wide. He pushed the naked woman from his bed and drew the blankets up under his chin. She did not wake; the odor of strong spirits wafted off her like perfume. Brodic yanked the blanket from Longee's hands and covered her.

"The Therk and the young lady accompanying him," Brodic said casually. "Where are they?"

"I don't know."

"Yes, you do."

Longee's eyes flicked from Brodic to Wait and back again, his yellowed teeth bared in a grin. "What would I have done with them? I imagine you have already questioned my throg."

"Your throg was conveniently not there."

Longee's brow furrowed. "Not there? I shall take up his lack of diligence with him later. I will assume you searched my belongings."

"As is my right to do so under such circumstances," Brodic answered.

"Yet you did not find them, or you would not be here. And, as you can see," Longee spread his hands wide, "they are not here, either. I may be depraved, but I do not take my pleasures with an audience."

"That means nothing. They do not have to be here or in Hoophollow for you to know where they are. Did you command your throg to hide them away someplace?"

"You have seen my pitiful creature." Longee laughed. "Can you imagine the folly of having him force them anywhere? Guard over them?" He laughed harder. "Oh, that is amusing. The throg heard you coming and hid. You had leave to search unhindered and found nothing. I am innocent."

Wait gripped his sword so tightly his fingers tingled; but Brodic remained cool. Cold. "How did you obtain the imp you used in your departure?"

"I broke no laws," Longee answered just as coolly. "It is not forbidden to purchase such a thing. Only expensive."

"Why, then, would you use so costly a mode of transportation for a piddling engagement in Hoophollow when you supposedly made much more lucrative arrangements with the fire-eater in Weir?"

"I don't see what business it is of yours what I do with those things I purchase. Careful, brother. You are close to abusing your own laws."

Brodic's jaw clenched. "We are not brothers."

"Ah, Brodic. You know better. One cannot *un*-become Purist even if one can be stripped of the right to call himself so."

Wait looked from man to man, instantly seeing the similarities difference masked before. They were light and shadow. Loyalty and betrayal. Eminent and disgraced.

"You were banished. I am not your brother. Refer to me as such again, and I will kill you."

Brodic's voice did not change even if the sudden tension in the room crackled. Longee bowed his head. His eyes darted to the wardrobe to the left of his bed.

"Come willingly," Brodic said, "or be dragged, but you will come with us at once."

Longee's shoulders sagged; he glanced again to the wardrobe. The door hung slightly ajar, showing the man's belongings carelessly shoved inside.

"Very well," he said. "I see there will be no appeasing you. If you will give me a moment to dress, I shall—"

Longee lunged for the wardrobe and out his belongings toppled with the dull *ploof* of soft things hitting the floor. He grasped and grabbed, muttering sibilantly. Wait hauled him to his feet by his hair.

"Unhand me! Quickly!"

Wait pulled him struggling from his pile. A cheerful muffling of sleigh bells came from something within.

"Longee," Brodic whispered. "What have you done?"

A silver ball wiggled free like a pup caught beneath a blanket. It ringled and jingled across the floor, bumping to rest at Longee's bare feet.

"Wait! Let him go!"

Wait obeyed immediately. Longee fell to his hands and knees, scrabbling along the floor and clutching the silver thing in both hands. "It's too late!" he cackled. "Too late!"

"Cover your eyes!" Brodic shouted, and again Wait obeyed immediately, that split moment before the ringing silver exploded.

THE SHAPE OF HOOPHOLLOW reminded Linhare of the amphitheater Dockside. No white stone. No benches or booths or stage, there were only shaded hillsides and sentinel trees and the sort of acoustics only nature could provide. It amplified Gianostalia's colorful cursing so that Linhare heard it as if it were coming from the hills. She would share some of the less vulgar ones with Jinna when Wait brought her back, as he assured her he would when he reluctantly left her in the hollow that morning.

"I won't be gone long," he had said. "The area has been searched, and Brodic has provided a guard. Gia will watch over you personally. I don't want you anywhere near Longee."

"If you think that's best," Linhare answered, sighed girlishly, and thrown herself into his arms. He caught her and he held her, though she felt the tension in his body. She did not care if Brodic and Gia and all the gathered guard knew how she loved him. She wanted the world to know; she wanted *him* to know; but he was a warrior. Dakhonne.

And I am queen, she had reminded herself, and let him go to sigh again for the brilliance of it all. Once he and Brodic were gone, Linhare ate the food Gia gave her without fussing. The peacekeeper stood over her while she ate it, dosing her with water to combat the powerful, unquenchable thirst. Linhare hardly remembered riding the short distance from the annex to the hollow, or the search that turned up nothing but an empty tent; only that it had been a glorious morning, and promised to be a beautiful day despite the heavy fog. She was certain the sun need only to wake up a bit more before burning it off.

Gia burst out of the several-times-searched tent, gasping for breath. "It smells like something died in there."

"Could it be the throg you were looking for earlier?"

"I doubt it," Gia said. "He's hiding. Probably watching us right now."

"Gianostalia? Pardon, *Gia*. But Gianostalia is such a lovely name." Linhare sighed. "May I ask you a question?"

Gia nodded.

"What is a throg?"

Gia grimaced. She moved closer to Linhare, looked closely into her eyes. "You thirsty?"

"Very, but I'm afraid I've finished all the water in my flask."

"Here." Gia thrust a waterskin into her hand. "Drink mine."

Linhare uncapped the skin and squirted a long stream into her mouth. The water was sweet and cool but did little to quench her thirst.

"What did you hope to find?" she asked. "We already know Longee is sleeping off a night of debauchery in Brinnymeade." She grimaced. "By all the stars and starlight, who would...with *him?*" Then giggled behind her hand. "Almost as disgusting as having it forced upon you."

Gia shook her head, took a deep breath, and ducked back inside the tent. Moving away from the malodorous dwelling, Linhare sat cross-legged in the grass and less eagerly sipped at the waterskin. The ground was cool and slightly damp. She tried to imagine the extravaganzas put on here, and then how Egalfo would have astonished the rural crowd as he had those Dockside. She conjured Jinna cheering and Wait standing stoically in the aisle, watching her as he always watched her... *except for that one night.*

The ground shook underneath her. Linhare dropped the waterskin, steadied herself as the earth rolled. Gia was already running towards her, sword unsheathed and eyes everywhere. The ground stilled. Linhare got to her feet.

"What was that?"

Long moments passed. The guard Brodic left circled around them, waiting as Linhare waited.

"Come," Gia said at last. "Into the tent. The rest of you, tight perimeter."

Linhare did not protest, even if the smell was worse than Gia said.

WAIT COULD NOT FORCE HIS BODY TO MOVE. His eyes would not blink against the brilliance of the silent explosion. His lungs would not breathe; his heart did not beat. Yet he was not dead. His mind was working, for within it he could hear a dripping sound. He could feel cold upon his hands, his face. The pinpricks in his eyes showed nothing but chaotic light. Then the pinpricks slowed. The dripping ceased. The light retreated. Like sliding open a peephole in a door, the room and its muddle appeared.

Wait pushed himself upright. Brodic squatted on the floor beside the hired girl, checking her for a pulse. There was no sign of Longee, only his belongings still scattered on the floor and a pool of liquid like molten silver. Wait touched the sticky edge with his boot.

"Where is he?"

"Gone." Brodic's rasped answer betrayed his calm.

"Dead?"

The Purist rubbed at his eyes. "No, not dead. What you witnessed was forbidden magic. It was ever Longee's downfall, and the reason he was banished from the Commonwealth. He can no longer control such power; more the fool that he had it. But it does not matter. He is gone. Perhaps for good."

Wait shook his head slowly. "What was that thing?"

"A Point in Time," Brodic told him. "I do not know what time. In the past, or the future. A century or ten minutes. I doubt Longee knows, either. It is impossible to trace."

"Then he got away."

"He did."

"Jinna and Egalfo?"

Brodic lifted the no longer snoring woman and laid her gently onto the bed. He touched her forehead. "She will need to sleep. I'll make arrangements with the innkeeper to—"

"Brodic. What about Jinna and Egalfo?"

The Purist tucked the blankets around her. "We will return to Hoophollow. Longee is gone. His creature is free. Our only hope is finding the thing before he knows that."

The tight perimeter around the extravaganza tent pushed Wait's heels into the draft mare Brodic had conscripted from the innkeeper. Reining in, scattering the guard, he leapt down and swept so fast through the tent opening that the whole thing nearly toppled.

"Linhare." He said her name and took her into his arms before thinking. Letting her go gently, he held on to her shoulders, leaned down to look into her eyes. "What happened here?"

"The ground shook," she told him. "And Gia forced me in here. May I go out now? I don't know how much longer I can hold my stomach in place otherwise."

Wait held aside the tent flap. Brodic and Gia argued, hushed but frantic. They quieted as he and Linhare approached.

"We must find the throg," Brodic said. "He will know something."

"We already searched—" Gia began, but Brodic's glare silenced her.

"We will assume the creature knows it is free. Perhaps he has taken to the road. Or the river."

"Can we use a trace?" Linhare asked. "Like you did from Weir?"

"It takes time, Little Queen. Time we do not have. It was with the Vespe's assistance that we were successful the last time."

"I will lead the search at the river," Wait said.

"Gianostalia and I will start back to Jaquewatten. The rest of you," Brodic told the guard, "fan out. Leave no stump unsearched. You are under Wait's command."

"And what about me?" Linhare crossed her arms over her chest. "Perhaps you should leave me in that putrid tent with a hundred guards standing around watching their fingernails grow."

The Purists exchanged a glance, then mounted up, one behind the other. "We will meet back at the annex in Jaquewatten," Brodic murmured, his horse prancing. "Sundown, with or without the throg."

Wait watched them go, watched the peacekeepers from Jaquewatten fan out. Linhare's arms remained crossed. "I can't allow any harm come to you," he told her once they were out of earshot. "You know that."

"Allow?" Her arms fell to her sides. "Can you allow or disallow harm, now? Does it obey? Tell me, Wait, how is that accomplished?"

"Linhare, I—"

"No!" she fumed and he fell silent. "Mother tried to protect me, you left guards on me day and night when you could not be by my side, but none of that *protection* did a thing to stop my stepfather. Look where we are, Wait! You could not save me from falling into fae, either."

"I willingly bear the responsibility of my failure to—"

"It is not *your* failure!" Her shout echoed about the hollow. Peacekeepers peeked out of the wood. Wait steadied himself, steeled himself for more; but Linhare was taking deep breaths, eyes closed. When she opened them, the anger no longer flashed. She reached for him, and he closed the ground between them, but only just enough.

"Listen to me, please," she said. "I cannot do this anymore, not without losing my mind completely. I am a woman. I am *queen!* Stop treating me like a glass bird in a velvet box!"

"How?" he asked, as surprised by his question as she. "How do I do as you ask when everything I am compels me to do all I can to keep you from harm? When every time I fail you, it makes it that much more crucial that it never happens again?"

Linhare's mouth dropped open, and then her cheeks pinked. Taking his hands, moving closer to him, she said, "I understand that. I do. I read your journal—no, listen." She held tighter to him when he tried to pull away. "I read, and I want to put myself between you and the pain. I know that compulsion to protect, Wait, but we are in this together. I am capable. I can help. If you treat me like I am weak and useless, what else is there for me to be?"

Wait held her gaze, or was held. His heart buzzed like a bee in his pocket.

"I didn't mean for you to feel those things."

"You did not mean it, but now you know."

He nodded, and Linhare smiled a smile that stilled the buzzing.

"Then that is settled." She picked up their colorful bags, handed one to him and slung the other over her shoulder. "Let's go search the river."

He saw little of the guard from Jaquewatten and suspected most were already on their way to their homes. After what happened in Brinnymeade, he did not blame them. These were country guards accustomed to the occasional pig-snatching or drunken brawl, not Purist magic that shook the world.

The rush of the river got louder. Wait caught the scent of something unpleasant. He found a tuft of coarse hair caught on a bristly bit of stick.

"Linhare," he called softly. She halted. Wait pointed to the tuft. "Stay close."

The throg's trail was easy enough to follow. Scuffed leaf mold. Broken twigs. More tufts of coarse hair. Humankind stayed to the paths centuries-worn into the forest. The throg kept clear of frequented places.

And then there was the smell.

The river, narrow and slow and murky, appeared just beyond a break in the trees. Wait could have crossed it in three easy strokes. And there, squatting upon the rocky embankment, the boy-sized throg. Weeping, dirty, the creature's spine humped ridges under the skin of his back. He rocked slightly on furry haunches. Dark, dense hair sprang wild from his head. He concentrated on something held in his hands.

Wait motioned Linhare behind him, a finger to his lips. Drawing upon the silence that was his gift, Wait stepped onto the rocks. Closer. He heard the creature chanting. Soft words. Musical. The rich voice did not match the misused frame.

"Twirl it once and twice around; to the Chase Queen they be bound. Accept my tribute, oh-Dread Queen; these be tithes for you to claim, to free me from my master's chain."

The throg held a crude little bark and bit boat. He set it into the water. Steadying it with one hand he placed a small, floppy something gently into it. Then another. Wait leaned over, holding his breath to keep the warmth of it from the throg's neck, squinting to see what it was he placed into the boat...

"Their freedom for mine. Forgive me."

Wait lunged, capturing the throg that cowered and keened like a wild thing.

"Don't touch it! Let it go!"

"Linhare! Grab the boat!"

"What is it? Why?"

"It is too late. She has accepted the tithe. You mustn't—"

"Who has? Speak quickly!"

The little boat bobbed on the waves Wait created, into the current of the slow, narrow river. Linhare was wading out to it, reaching for it.

"No! Please! I beg of you!"

Linhare's fingers touched the boat, tipping it slightly, and then she vanished as if sucked into a riptide. Wait dropped the throg.

"Linhare!"

He leapt into the water, scrambling to the place where she had gone under, to where the listing boat still bobbed on the water. The Throg was shrieking for him to stop. Wait could almost grasp the bit and bark ship. He reached, toppled forward. As he fell, his fingertips brushed the tiny craft.

Beyond Beyond

LINHARE'S FINGERS BRUSHED the bark hull. From behind her came a tremendous roaring, like a wave cresting, crashing to shore. And then it was upon her, forcing her under and under. Her lungs screamed. She was propelled to the surface again as if sea folk pushed at the soles of her feet. Gasping, shaking the water from her eyes, Linhare saw blue sky. And water. No Wait. No little boat. No throg, no trees, no riverbank. She treaded water, spinning first this way, then that. A swell lifted her higher; she glimpsed a fair-sized ship.

"Stop!" she called. "Come back! Help me! Please!"

Linhare swam. The ship did not seem to be moving at any windblown pace; rather, it drifted with the current. Hauling herself through the water, Linhare kicked as hard as she could, kicked something hard, screamed when that something grabbed her foot. Swallowing water, going under, Linhare thrashed against the hand that reached down and hauled her to the surface.

"Linhare! It's me!"

She choked. "Wait? Oh, Wait! How did you—"

"Not now. The boat is getting away." Wait bit his shirtsleeve and jerked it up his arm, grabbing her hand at the same time. With his free hand, he yanked a piece of chain from about his wrist. The chain stretched, binding him to her and reconnecting again as if it had never been separated.

"Hold on to me," he commanded. Linhare climbed onto his back, arms around his neck. Wait took them through the water quickly, his strokes strong and long. And then the boat was just ahead; and then just an arm's length away; and then Wait was catching hold of a slapping chain that once might have held an anchor.

"Halloo!" Linhare shouted. "Someone? Anyone?"

"It's no use," Wait told her. "No one's going to hear you. Can you hold on to this if I let you go?"

Linhare nodded, and he handed her the anchor chain. Letting her go, Wait yanked at the chain binding them, freeing himself; but rather than freeing her, he wound it through a link in the anchor chain and round her wrist.

"Just hold on. I'm going to climb to the deck, then haul you up. Unless you think you can climb it."

Linhare looked up the hull of the ship. It was bigger than it seemed at a distance. Her arms ached from swimming. She shook her head.

"Just hold on," he told her. "It won't take me long."

Hand over hand, Wait scaled the hull of the vessel. He was up and over the side so quickly that Linhare hadn't time to worry about what might be in the water, drawn to her kicking legs.

"Wrap the chain once around your wrist," Wait called down over the side. "Grab it with your other hand just above where you are bound. As I pull, brace your feet against the hull and walk your way up."

She tried, but Linhare ended up bumping against the hull more than she walked it. As quickly as Wait pulled himself up, he did likewise for Linhare, and it was over before the pain in her wrist and hands became unbearable. She flopped onto the deck with a squish and lay there panting, eyes closed to brilliant sunlight washing-warm the deck. Beside her, Wait was doing likewise. For a moment, there was no other sound but the lapping of water on the hull and their breathing. Wait sat upright, unwound the chain from her wrist.

"What is that?" she asked.

"Hepheo gave it to me, broke it off from the one around his waist. I don't think this is what it was meant for, but it worked."

The chain did not seem long enough or sturdy enough, but if it could bind a pirate like Hepheo to Ezibah, it was strong indeed. Wait looped it about his own wrist. It shrank back to size and the ends again connected seamlessly. Linhare pulled her sling bag over her head, then helped Wait do the same. Though they sat in puddles of their own making, their bags were curiously dry. Linhare looked over her own, checking first for the journal buckled into the front pocket. Drawing it out, she found it as dry as the bag in which it had ridden.

"I'm not even going to wonder," Wait said.

Rising to his feet, he offered Linhare a hand up. They were alone on the deck of a ship two dozen paces from bow to stern, half that from starboard to port. There was no sail, no oar, no helm. It was a plain and sturdy fisherman's hovel set afloat, complete with a shade-giving but empty shack stern.

"What happened?" Linhare asked. "I was reaching for the little boat, and all of a sudden," she spread her hands wide, "I was here."

"I wish I knew."

Wait unbuckled his sword belt. He hung his weapon from a peg hammered into the shack wall, stripped off his shirt and hung it likewise before pulling off boots and dumping the water from them. Linhare averted her eyes quickly, hoping and dreading what he would do with his pants; but those he left on, though they stuck to him like a second skin. He did not notice her blush, or her sudden staring. Wait was pacing slowly, eyes on the deck.

"There," he said, pointing to a hatch door in the floor within the shack. It lifted easily, the iron ring fitting into a hook on the wall so that it would not bang shut again. A soft glow emanated from the expected darkness.

Linhare followed Wait down the ladder into the hold. She blinked until her eyes adjusted, until the blurs of light became candles that did not drip or flicker, illuminating the flower garlands and gossamer curtains lining wall to wall, ceiling to floor. At the bow end, counter-balancing the shack above, stood a bed fit for a royal pair. Upon this bed, two forms: she, a silk and ribbon vision of fae beauty; he, a velvet-clad rake reaching for her pale hand. A hallowed place. Bridal bower or funeral barge? Linhare was not certain there was a difference.

Holding Wait's hand with both of hers, Linhare tried not to balk when he moved toward the bed. He reached out, parting the curtains.

"Oh," Linhare whispered, her hand dropping Wait's to stifle the sound. Jinna and Egalfo reposed in perfect slumber. Slumber, and not death, she knew, because they breathed. Jinna even snorted a softer version of her usual snore.

"No," Wait said when she moved to rouse them. "Don't wake them. I don't think you can, anyway. Let's go back up. I'll tell you what happened in Brinnymeade."

JINNA DREAMED.

She smelled the pipeleafy, sweaty odor of the leather pouch; felt Egalfo bump and brush against her; saw the throg's enormous eye, heard his pitiful apology, saw the world go black. These things looped repeated moments until she could conjure them all on her own. And somewhere nearby, she could feel Egalfo, his breath on her face, his hand near her own, as if he had frozen still while reaching for her.

Somewhere beyond the cocoon of her present, Jinna heard Linhare's voice. And Wait's. She felt the rhythm of water all around her. She heard footsteps on boards. In dreams, Jinna discovered where she was, even if she did not know why or how.

She sat, for years or moments, in a dark vast place. A desolate seashore. A moonless night. While she knew that she slept, could even see her own body if she closed her eyes, Jinna was unable to wake. The sand under bottom and feet chilled. A breeze whiffled her hair. The coolness soothed. It cleared her mind and focused her thoughts. The calm of it all made her lethargic. Freedom from this dead place was another moment, or a thousand moments, away. Jinna was not really concerned.

She did not tire. She did not hunger or thirst. The still water beyond the cool shore reflected the stars, and she was content to watch them. Their light did not shine down upon her, but rather seemed to reflect up, as if she were in an enclosed place and the holes pricked into the casing.

Starshine, starshine, whence do you come?
From lovers' eyes, from dreamtimes, from wishing on a stone.
Starshine, starshine, how long will you last?
Forever, darling-dear-one, until today is past.

The old clapping rhyme played in her head. She remembered singing it with Linhare, even with Sabal when they were very young. In this mind-clearing place, Jinna remembered that the younger princess had not always been sour and aloof; that once she was much more willing to get into trouble than Linhare ever was. Pranks played on the scullery staff. Slithery things left for chambermaids. Lessons skipped, and dramas performed in finery stolen from Ta-Diandra's wardrobe. Linhare rarely participated in their mischief, and Jinna had forgiven the one-day queen. Then Ti-Ben died. Linhare took her sorrow up the mountain. Sabal's veneration became disdain. The hollow, invisible feeling of that time descended from that backwards starshine.

Closing her eyes, Jinna saw herself sleeping and opened them again. To see herself in slumber now looked too much like death. But she had also seen Egalfo there beside her; his hand reaching for hers.

Rising, she moved to where the water made the sand easier to walk upon. Seashells and pebbles lay scattered, haphazard as any tide-tossed onto the shore. But no surf rolled, only a gentle lapping that retreated from her as she neared. Jinna picked up a smooth, white pebble. *Wishing stones* she and Linhare called them as children. Their abundance made them no less special; it simply proved that little-girl wishes were endless.

The pebble hefted heavier than it should have, as if she held something three times as big in her hand. Invoking the magic innocence invented, she rolled it between her palms; once, twice, three times. She kissed it, and tossed it into the water.

"If Egalfo is here, let me find him."

Her own ghostlike voice came back at her as if from a vast distance. Listening to it whisper, Jinna started walking.

Consequences

PELVIS PRESSED TO BUTTOCKS, arms locked around his waist, bodies swaying with the horse's motion, Gia tried and failed to keep her thoughts from wandering into forbidden places. At least she straddled behind Brodic on the saddle. Pressing rather than pressed, clinging rather than being clung to.

Sending her mind into the surrounding trees, brush, grasses, Gia found no hint of desperation, no sign of fear. Brodic would be doing the same, though he would push further a-field. His mind would search the farms and outbuildings in the distance. She always took the near. He always took the far. So many years of such partnering made it reflex.

Jaquewatten. The annex. Within moments, the locals were banded and sent out to continue the search. Gia dropped into a chair, rested her head to her arms. Had it only been a few hours since dawn? It felt like an entire day.

"Perhaps we should concentrate on the Therk and the halfling." She picked up her head. "We had no luck with the throg."

Brodic looked up from the map he was studying. "There is no way to know where Longee left them. It could be anywhere between here and Weir. Finding the throg is our best chance."

"The imp brought Longee to the hollow. There is a better chance they are around here. Ask the locals. Are there caves? Abandoned farms? Perhaps Longee has some cohorts in the vicinity willing to help him."

Brodic was silent, his jaw working back and forth. Setting the map down, he strode into the next room and spoke to the clerk there. Then he was back again, his face the same stern mask.

"You did well," he said, his eyes once again on the map, "watching over the Little Queen."

"Thank you."

"It does not make up for yesterday's disasters."

"I am well aware of that. Nothing I do will ever make up for the past, as far as you're concerned."

His eyes remained on the map even if his attention did not. Gia smirked; he would not look up and catch her. He would not look at her until he could do so with that stony expression he reserved especially for her.

A clomp of hooves on the dirt road outside the annex lifted both their heads. Shouts. A loud keening. Brodic dropped the map and darted out the door, Gia fast on his heels.

"We found him on the road heading this way." The Jaquewatten peacekeeper lifted the boy-sized throg by the scruff of his neck. The pitiful creature curled into a ball, whimpering and mumbling.

"Put him down," Gia growled. "He's not a hedgehog, for mercy's sake."

The peacekeeper dropped the throg that did not uncurl to protect itself from the fall. Gia put herself between it and those who captured him. Bending low, she touched the dirty creature's scrawny back.

"We mean you no harm," she said. "We want only to ask you some questions."

He picked up his head, shuddered. Gia sat back on her heels. Before she could rise, the throg clutched at her arm.

"I am not a wicked creature," he wailed. "I did not mean any harm to them. I was desperate, you see. I tried to warn them, but they did not listen, and now they are gone. All of them gone. Upon the chase. To the Queen I begged to free me. Oh, what have I done? What have I done?"

Gia shook him off. He curled into a stinking, hedgehog-ball again, keening into his own knees. She looked to Brodic, his pale face blue with fury. Grasping the throg firmly by the arm, he shook him until his body uncurled.

"Tell us what you have done. Now and quickly."

Head bowed and whimpering, the throg obeyed.

A desperate slave. A forgotten legend. A tithe cast and accepted on the chase. Gia's mind buzzed with all the things that could go wrong, and probably already had. The chase belonging to the legendary queen existed beyond Beyond. The Therk and halfling were likely lost to them, but the Dakhonne and the Little Queen were not part of the tithe. They could be retrieved. If they survived. Gia could scarcely believe that it had all been devised by so wretched and weak a being as the throg still sniffling and coughing before her.

"I did not think it through," he whimpered. "I did not think at all. You do not understand the desperation. You do not understand the humiliation."

"I have known Longee a very long time." Gia placed a trencher of food onto the bench beside him. "I can imagine. Eat."

The throg choked on his sobs, on the food he tried to eat. She pitied this creature she'd been acquainted with for many years, but had never truly seen. Trade in throgs was a given. She could not recall ever seeing a free throg, any more than she could recall seeing a boogle without a master to serve. Gia assumed them content in their servitude. But perhaps, after all, there was a difference between boogles naturally compelled to serve and throgs forced to.

She looked over her shoulder, to the doorway leading into the chartroom where Brodic shuffled through maps for the fastest way back to Weir. Sitting beside the throg, she asked him, "How did you know the ritual? Few even remember the legend of the Chase Queen."

"My only solace has been in the few books Longee kept. I've read them many times. The legend is there, and the ritual."

"I did not know your kind could read."

"Slavery does not make one stupid."

She ignored his impertinence. "You've been to Hoophollow with Longee countless times. Why them? Why now?"

Wiping the tears from his face, leaving dirty streaks in their place, he answered, "Hoophollow holds no significance. Any chase, any stream, any creek can lead to her. I will not lie and say my first concern was for them, even if I could not bear to witness what Longee would have done to them. And he would have, my lady. He would have done them great harm. But it was for myself that I did this. It was my first and only chance of freedom.

"Longee has many things of value hidden away. All were denied me, because they were his. But the Therk and the halfling, they were not his. Not yet. They were things I could take. Things I could offer."

"But, if I remember the legend correctly, the Chase Queen is obliged to accept any offer made, if made in earnest."

"Offer her a stick or a bouquet of wildflowers in exchange for my freedom? There is a reason her legend has fallen into obscurity. The Chase Queen was Dread Queen before. The gift had to be worthy. It had to be mine."

"But they were not yours, any more than they were Longee's."

The throg's gaze fell. His shoulders hunched so that he was nearly bent over his own lap. "The halfling wished," he said. "I tricked her into saying the words that would make my treachery possible." He looked up now, his shoulders rolling upright like a wave racing backwards. "But I am not responsible for the other two! They were pulled in by their own folly, and not part of my curse at all."

"As you have said. The fact remains, you..."

Gia's skin prickled.

Not part of... "The Curse!"

Rising abruptly, she checked the cowering throg's bindings and walked a little too quickly to where Brodic still consulted maps that would do them no good. Gia took a deep breath, let it out slowly, and leaned upon the doorjamb, waiting lest she seem too eager, and yet...

"Was there something you wanted, Gianostalia?" He did not even raise his head.

"We need to get to Weir, fast. We have to—"

193

Brodic's head came up. "I do not recall asking for your assistance."

"You didn't, I know, but—"

"Then you are dismissed, Gianostalia."

Her jaw clenched. "You will sacrifice the Little Queen and the Dakhonne to your hatred of me?"

Brodic leaned against the table, arms crossed over his chest. "Hatred? Such a strong emotion. To hate you, Gianostalia, I would have to care something about you, and as I don't—"

"If you would just listen!"

"Guard your tone. You are a peacekeeper under my command and will respect my authority. You have more than your share of black ink in your column. Any more will get you stripped of your position."

"My column is clean," she said. "I paid my debt. I have redeemed myself to all but you."

"Redeemed?" He tapped his finger on the thick map. It made a hollow sound. "You have kept the vows you made before the Silent Sisters. You remain temperate. You serve. You obey. You have done all you were required to do. That is not redemption, Gia." He turned back to his maps. "It is restitution. No more. Dismissed."

She could not drag her eyes from his bent head, his pale hair and the way the silk of it caressed his cheek. The truth of his words gathered like gravel in her belly. All she did, she did for him, to earn his forgiveness if not his love; but Brodic did not bend, would never bend.

And neither shall I.

Gia stood tall, eyes straight ahead and chin high, hands crossed behind her back. "It is not yet sunset, Eminence Brodic," she said. "Captain Hepheo is bound to the Little Queen's sacrifice until then. If we can get back to Weir, back to the Siren's Curse, he will go after her. He is honor bound."

His pause nearly undid her. "Not even the Siren's Curse can sail that chase without being tithed."

"No, it cannot. But the Little Queen and the Dakhonne were not tithed to her. The Chase Queen has no leave to keep them. If memory serves, that means they will end up in—"

"Find the captain of this annex," Brodic commanded, scrambling to roll up maps, Gia knew, so he would not have to look at her. "Pull him from his supper if you must. We need an imp. He will know where to find one."

"As you command, Eminence," she said, saluted and turned sharply on her heel.

"What will become of me in Weir?"

The throg's deep and musical voice always startled her. Clean, dressed in clothes instead of rags, he had grown less wretched in the short time in her care. He made no attempt to escape even when Gia unchained him. Without a name he would give, she settled on *Throg* for the time being.

"I am not certain," she told him. "Brodic will bring you before Hepheo, and you will tell him all you told us."

"Captain Hepheo of the Siren's Curse?"

"Is there another?" She nearly grinned. Throg cowered and began to whimper. Gia placed a tentative hand upon his boney shoulder. "I will not allow any harm to come to you."

He picked up his head. "You won't?"

"I won't."

"Why? Eminence Brodic says I have done wrong, and that I will pay for my crime."

Her belly lurched. "Sometimes right and wrong isn't as clear as Eminence Brodic would like it. I will let no harm come to you. You have my word as a Purist and a peacekeeper."

Throg threw himself at her feet, pawed at her legs. "Thank you, my lady. Thank you."

"Stop that." Gia nudged him away. "Get up this instant. My name is Gianostalia. Gia is better. Or Lady Superior."

Sniffing, shuffling backwards, Throg nodded his head. He was so thin, so weak. The loesh packed away in the trunk beckoned. Gia ignored it firmly. Instead she handed him the rest of her bread and an apple from the basket on the table.

"Eat," she said. "His Eminence is not as familiar with the imp obtained. We cannot know how taxing it will be, and you are...not strong."

"I am stronger than I look."

"Gianostalia!"

Brodic's shout came from the yard outside the annex. Gesturing Throg ahead of her, she stepped into the last of the day's sunshine.

"We haven't much time left," he said unnecessarily. "I have amended the harness the best I can. Let us hope it holds. Come. Now. Before the sun sinks too low."

Gia looped herself into the harness reins, then secured Throg to herself rather than take the chance of losing him in the flight.

"Ready," she said. Brodic nodded, his face a somber mask of concentration.

"Do not interfere," he told her, and tapped the glass ball with the silver hammer. The imp formed, instantly and ferociously—a dragon great of wing and sharp of tooth. Throg cried out and clung to her, buried his face in her side. Gia's own heart did flips within her chest. She pressed

Throg against her hip, and held on tightly when the dragon took to the sky, shrieking angrily and still unconvinced to carry them.

Exhaustion nearly overwhelmed her when the imp finally dropped them on the docks and sparkled out of existence. Brodic's gray pallor frightened her, but he had fought the imp-dragon if not tamed it. He got them back to Weir in time to see the sun slanting its last rays on the boards.

"Quickly, Gianostalia."

Brodic's fingers fumbled with the knots in the harness. Throg hung limp at her side, unmoving and unresponsive. She tried to blink her vision clear and found Brodic doing the same, his shaking fingers almost useless.

"Help me," she said. "We will carry him together."

She put her arm around his shoulder; he bolstered her with his, holding Throg upright between them. A three backed, six-legged creature, they jogged and stumbled the length of the pier to the Siren's Curse bobbing on her mist. Gia might have laughed if she possessed the strength to do so. Grappling up the gangway, they fell upon the deck as one.

"Hepheo!" Brodic's voice boomed. Where he got the strength to cast it, Gia did not know. She toiled again at the knots. Someone handed her a knife, and she took it with a murmured thanks. It slit through the harness quickly. Everwanderers gathered around them. By the time Hepheo stomped their way, they were free.

"What is this? What have you done to the foul little thing, and why bring him to my—"

"Listen quickly, Hepheo." Brodic lunged at the pirate king, grasping his elbows. "The Little Queen has been cast upon the Chase Queen's chase. You must go after her. The sun has not yet set. You are honor bound."

Hepheo stood motionless, jaw slack and eyes staring. Then he shook off Brodic's grip, stepped to the throg lying all but dead on the ground at his feet.

"Longee's creature, no?"

"It is," Brodic answered. "It is he who sought the Chase Queen's favor. He tithed the halfling and the Therk. The Little Queen and Dakhonne were pulled into the spell while trying to rescue them."

"Longee?"

"Gone. He had a Point in Time."

Hands on hips, shoulders bent, Hepheo shook his head slowly.

"The Dakhonne . . . in *her* land."

Brodic nodded. "It is not without significance."

"And not without a whole lot of peril." Lifting his head, he stood taller, fingered the silken braid at his waist. "Fetch Neciel," he called over his shoulder, "she'll know what's best."

More Everwanderers gathered. Gia could barely stand upright. In her mind's eye, she leaned against Brodic, his arm supported her, pulled her close...

"What is it? What has happened?"

Gia startled out of the doze she had fallen into. Daydreams fled like scattering gulls. Straightening, she listened to Brodic again explain, this time to Neciel, Danle and Ezibah as well as Hepheo, and all the gathered Everwanderers from the youngest cabin boy to the ancient galley-cook, Moslo. Then the Vespe knelt beside the inert throg, she touched fingers to his eyes, then to his heart.

"What is it, Neciel?" Danle asked. "What did you see?"

"Death."

Gia gasped, dropped to her knees beside Throg. "He is dead?"

"No, not the throg," Neciel told her. "For Jinna and Egalfo, Linhare and Wait. One of them or all of them. Or perhaps someone else. I do not know. I cannot see clearly. They are beyond my vision, on the queen's chase."

The Captain circled the unfortunate throg, a pelican preparing to dive. Gia leaned closer to the pitiful creature, ready to pull him out of the way or put herself between them. Hepheo did not strike even if the air all around him crackled like lightning.

"The Curse can't ride the queen's chase, les' I gift her to the Dread Queen, and that's not something I will do. Not even for the Little Queen."

"Agreed," Brodic said. "But you can retrieve her, if she makes it out alive."

"Chances are sorry that she will."

"It does not matter," Brodic said. "You took her sacrifice. You are bound to ride the sunset after her."

Hepheo nodded, but he said, "There are no sunset rays to take us where we must go," and turned to his Everwanderers. "Make ready. We sail for Alyria."

The end of the world. The Glass King's domain. Alyria. A legend as old and forgotten as the Chase Queen herself. Gia pushed to her feet, dreaded the thought of lifting even she insubstantial weight of the throg. She had done what she set out to do; the Siren's Curse would do right by the Little Queen. Bending to gather her burden, she nearly toppled over when Brodic said, "How long do I have to make arrangements with my command center?"

"None," Hepheo answered. "You leave the ship, I leave you behind."

"Then I shall not leave the ship. Gianostalia?" He said her name and she felt it slice through her head like a skewer. "Return to the command center. Tell them what has occurred."

"You're leaving?" she asked. "Sailing to the edge of the world?"

"Do not question my order. Just do as you are commanded."

Her jaw clamped. She nodded stiffly. "What of the throg."

"He stays with me."

"I promised no harm would come to him."

Brodic narrowed his gaze, opened his mouth to speak, but it was Neciel who told her, "No harm will come to the creature. I give you my word, as you gave him yours."

"As you wish, Vespe Neciel." Brodic inclined his head. To Gia, he said, "Now go. I am counting on you to see to this matter. Let us see if you can manage to get it done without any more calamity."

Gia forced short, shallow breaths through her nostrils until she could move without trembling. Saluting her superior, she bowed to the Captain and his Keeper, turned smartly on her heel, and headed for the gangway. Something like pain, like joy nearly doubled her over. With him gone, the thumb pressed down upon her every day would vanish. She could rise, perhaps even to Eminence if she handled this last command correctly. He would likely never return...

Gia's balance wavered. She clutched at the rail just before reaching the gangway. Leaning upon it, she saw Everwanderers at their tasks, Hepheo and Ezibah, Danle and Neciel in earnest conversation. As she watched, men lifted Throg and carried him off. No one was looking her way. No one waved good-bye. No one but old Moslo.

I'll make you my Keeper if'n you give me a suck, the old man once cackled in her ear, so many years ago. Her glare had been steady. Her face, hard. The old man only chuckled and ambled away. Gia harbored a tenderness in her heart for him ever since. And now he stood watching her from behind a row of barrels. He bent and tugged at something she could not see, then pointed to whatever he had done. He stuck that same finger into his mouth, obscenely pushing it in and out before nodding smugly and walking away.

And still no one looked her way. Gia gazed down into the mist, beyond the mist to the pier, the docks, to Weir. The command center rose higher than the other buildings. White stone. Domed. Stirring her ambition. At the edge of the city, the tents. Her annex. Her sparse but comfortable home.

Or Brodic, and the edge of the world...

Her belly lurched. Her heart constricted. She slipped unseen to that row of barrels and found the hatch Moslo left open. Crates and more barrels—a storage space. Glancing over her shoulder, Gia dropped down into it, reached up and pulled the hatch closed.

The Chase

WAIT GAVE LINHARE THE DISTANCE SHE NEEDED. She stood at the rail, gazing out over the endless expanse of water that should have been a narrow river he could have spanned in three good strokes. How the throg-made vessel had grown so large and where they headed were questions as impossible to answer as how the river became so vast; but he did his best to piece together what he knew, even if it ended with her at the rail, him staring at her back.

Fish jumped in fresh water, not salt. They would not hunger or thirst. Aside from the shack and the old anchor chain, the deck was otherwise barren of rope and barrel, chart, chair and helm. While Linhare stared, Wait emptied the curiously dry sling bags that she had hastily packed to see if there was anything useful. In Linhare's he found clothes, a fistful of ribbons, the sac of the dried fruit she bought in Weir, and the scarred red journal that always startled him to see. He was grateful for Ezibah's hand in packing his, for aside from a single change of clothes, he found a sewing purse, eating and cooking utensils, a good knife, and a medicinal bag of herbs and gauze bandages. He would be able to fashion a fishing pole from scavenged wood from the ship, a needle from the sewing kit, strips of gauze. Coming from poor fisherfolk stock, Wait knew how to make do with bits and odds.

The sound of Linhare's soft weeping distracted him, made his skin feel pulled too tight. He found himself rising, moving to her side before thinking it through. He placed a hand on her shoulder. His fingers tingled; the sensation shot up his arm, to his heart that buzzed. Not his heart, but the breast pocket of his now-dry shirt. Then Linhare spun around, buried herself into his body, and his arms came instantly around her. The buzzing jolted still. He held her while she wept, until she looked up at him and smiled a sad and watery smile. She stepped away from him, leaving him suddenly chilled, to gaze out at the horizon again.

"Is it morning or night?" she asked. "Today or tomorrow? It feels so...so nothing."

Wait scanned the sky. A cover of white clouds diffused sunlight. There was little guessing where it came from.

"I really don't know," he answered.

"I'm so tired, Wait. It feels like days since I've slept."

"Rest then. I'll rig up fishing tackle. Catch us supper."

Linhare turned back to face him. "Supper? That is something I've only eaten in Ta-Yebbe's cottage."

The word had risen unbidden from childhood. Long days. Simple evenings. His father's chair leaned back against the wall of their shack

200

beside the sea. The aromas of pipeleaf and salt air and clams permanently embedded into his skin, his nostrils. "*Supper* is what Pap and I used to have at the end of a long day clamming," he said. "I guess *dinner* doesn't sound right out here."

"Supper it is, then." Linhare wrapped her arms about her middle; she rocked a little back and forth. "Do I remember correctly? You're from the province of Athesia?"

"Crone's Hook, to be exact. Why?"

"You've a northern accent. How is it I never noticed before?"

Wait cleared his throat, as if that would purge the peasantish curl he thought schooled from his voice when *Calryan* ceased to be, and *Wait* was born. But he had said *supper* and even his own ears heard it.

"I love a northern accent," she said. Linhare lifted a tentative hand, then touched his face so tenderly. Her brow furrowed, but her lips hinted at a smile. Wait held his breath.

"Wait." His name? Or a request? "Wait," she whispered again. Her lips parted. Her eyelids drooped. Wait's body ached. His fingers clenched. A kiss was all she wanted, all he longed to give, but it would not end there; he knew it even if she did not. Wait took a step backward and her hand fell away. She startled as if just waking.

"You should rest." He bore her disappointment stoically. Better that than regret. Linhare nodded and turned away. She curled up in the shade, head propped on her arms. Wait opened his mouth to tell her to go below, to sleep in the gentle darkness there, but he knew she would not, and in moments, she was fast asleep.

Wait built a makeshift fire-pit using the small, cast iron pan from his bag, fueled it with bits of wood hacked from the boat with his sword. They would have to use it sparingly, but Wait was confident there was enough spare wood to warrant a cooked fish or two, until Linhare got used to eating it raw. If ever he caught a fish at all.

Pap would be mortified.

Until spearing complacent bottom-feeders in the pool in the Pinewood, it was years since he fished, and then it had been with proper gear. Still, seeing the abundance of shadows hovering near the surface of the water made his failure even more embarrassing. Abandoning the attempt to hook one, he started for the hatch. Jinna and Egalfo would not miss the gossamer curtains of their bower; they would make an efficient net.

But the curtains disintegrated when he tugged at them. He tested the flower garlands; they crumbled to nothing. His hand passed through the candles illuminating the dark. Illusion. Fluff. Wait left that fragile room frustrated, afraid to touch anything else.

201

Back on the deck, in the watery light that seemed to be dimming, Wait wove an awkward net from the fistful of ribbons. The slow-moving shadows just below the surface, earlier unconvinced to hook themselves on his makeshift hook, proved easy to net. Hauling water up from the river in the little metal cups, he set them into the pan with the wood. Then he lit the meager fire, spitted the fish still slick and glistening, and left it all to cook.

Linhare slept on; he was not inclined to wake her. There was time yet before *supper* was ready. Instead he stood at the prow of the little vessel, looked from horizon to horizon. Nothing ahead. Nothing behind. He thought, perhaps, he could see thin and far-off humps of land, but conceded that it could be his wishful thinking.

Arms up over his head, Wait yawned and stretched, scratching at the bothersome itch so often upon his chest and felt the stone he kept buttoned safely in the pocket there. Recalling the earlier buzz furrowed his brow. Could there be something trapped within, like the imp in the glass ball Brodic used to get them to Jaquewatten? Digging it out of his pocket, he found bits of paper stuck to it. The note from Ellis, meticulously preserved all this time, was in tatters. He brushed the bits from the stone; Wait knew the words, if not their meaning.

"What did you want to tell me, Ellis?" Wait asked the shreds of paper left on his skin. The goings on during those days between Linhare's return from university and his dive into the trunk were nearly forgotten for the strange and unsettling present; but thinking now, Wait found the inconsistencies he barely marked then. Ellis hurrying off the night of the fire-eater's performance, his absence from Linhare's homecoming feast were both as unlike him as suggesting Wait meet him for a cup. Where had he been off to?

Wait absently worried the smooth, blue stone between his fingers and thumb. The action soothed. The knot in his chest uncoiled. His fingers warmed, the sensation spreading up his arm. A jolt in his fingers nearly made them drop the stone. That buzzing he'd felt before returned, and he recognized the itch always upon his chest. He opened his hand. The stone sat flat upon his palm. Faint purple veins running through it seemed to pulse, like blood. Wait's vision narrowed. Upon the pulsing. Lost in the blue. And then it was getting darker. Darker. Now black.

Wait did not panic. He knew he stood upon the deck of the enchanted boat, transfixed by the blue stone. Diffused sunlight warmed his face, the slight breeze teased his hair. His eyes saw it all, and yet they also saw another place. A familiar place. Dark and soothing and inescapable.

The Holes.

Clutches of people gathered in the torchlight. Men and women and children. And then there was Ellis, older than Wait knew him to be. Or simply haggard. He stood apart, his eyes downcast and his fingers kneading his temples.

How did it come to this? Ellis' voice cracked.

We both know how it came about. He could not see her, but Wait knew Yebbe's voice. His vision focused on Ellis, unable or unwilling to shift. *It is up to us to fix it.*

If only Linhare were—

But she is not! The monarchy is dead. We are on our own. You cannot succumb, Ellis. They all look to you. I look to you. If you lose your strength, where will I get mine?

Ellis looked up. Haggard, yes, but definitely older. The flecks of white at his temples when last Wait saw him now streaked snowy swales. The creases around his eyes and along his jaw dug too deep to be weariness alone.

I am tired, Yebbe, he said.

So am I. Her voice was softer now, and as haggard as Ellis looked. *We have many on our side, my friend. Many who will fight for us.*

And after we are gone?

We are not going anywhere yet.

Her small hand touched his arm. Part of him had watched Linhare approach, anticipated her touch. He blinked his vision back from the Holes.

"I'm sorry," she said. "Were you daydreaming?"

All he had seen still fluttered in his mind's eye. "I suppose. Strange dreams."

"There are no dreams here *but* strange dreams," she told him. "While I slept, I dreamt gobbets and bolleys and all manner of fae creatures were caught in my hair. I kept cutting them free but there was no end to them, and no end to my hair."

He bellowed laughter that startled Linhare, the kind of laughter he had not felt expand his chest in many, many years. "That is a strange dream."

"What were you dreaming?"

Wait tucked the stone back into his pocket. It buzzed only a moment, then became still. "I dreamt of the roasting pits in Weir."

"Don't remind me." Linhare groaned. She glanced around him, to the fire he could still smell, and the fish sizzling. "I see you made good on your word."

"I do my best," he told her. Offering her his arm, bowing his head, he asked, "May I escort you, my lady?"

Linhare laughed. "Certainly, sir."

203

She took his arm. Wait smiled down at her, choosing not to question his suddenly lighter mood, or why he took her hand from his arm and kissed it, or why Linhare's soft, arousing laughter did not elicit the frustration it earlier had. If she glanced up at him now with parted lips and lazy lids, he would give her the kiss she longed for; the kiss they both longed for. But she didn't, and the grateful part of Wait was not nearly as relieved as the other, wilder part of him was disappointed.

THE BEACH SEEMED AS ENDLESS as the water it edged. Jinna knew not how long she walked, or if she ever truly moved from her starting place at all. Eternal twilight followed her, preceded her. Surrounded her. She met no one, came across no other footprints, not even a gull's. Jinna became certain that without her persistent trekking, this slumbering, twilight world would stay forever so. Only she could wind time forward. Only she could wake it. By walking.

Whether it was so, or simply her own wishing, Jinna thought perhaps the sky began to brighten just a little bit, there on the horizon ahead. Focusing on that hope, she quickened her pace. Soon she was running. And yes, the sky was brightening, the pinprick stars fading into light. She could see someone. Something. Ahead near that brightening horizon.

Jinna ran faster. Her muscles throbbed. Her lungs burned. She pushed faster, got closer to the figure ahead. A woman. Coppery hair flickered in the blossoming light. She was running in the same direction. Slower. Jogging. Oblivious to Jinna's frantic sweep.

Mother. Oh, mother!

Tears blurred her vision now, but Jinna did not stop. In all her life, she never wanted her mother as badly as she did in this moment of finding her. She stumbled, caught herself, but stumbled again. Head over heels over shoulder and hip, she rolled to a halt. Picking herself up on her arms, she saw the woman-not-her-mother, turn.

Jinna did not scream. Neither did the other Jinna staring curiously back at her. Jinna remembered the doll her mother once made for her, with red yarn for hair and an old white hand linen for skin. *It's made in your image,* Yebbe said. *In the wrong hands, it could do you harm. Keep your poppet safe, my little poppet.* Jinna lost the doll in no time at all, and did not really think about her again. Until now. Until this double, this second, this other Jinna, and the single set of footprints between them.

"Did you find him?" the other Jinna asked.

"Find who?"

Poppet-Jinna rolled her eyes. Were those stitches there beneath her chin? "Egalfo. Did you find him?"

"No. I forgot I was looking for him. I thought you were my mother."

"You came all the way around and you haven't found him?" Poppet-Jinna dropped down into the sand. Crawling to her counterpart, Jinna flopped onto her back, still panting. Somewhere deep inside her head, Jinna knew there was something odd about running to catch up with oneself.

"We might have to leave the beach," she said to herself. "Go inland."

Poppet-Jinna nodded, her eyes fixed on the horizon, but said nothing. Muscles aching, lungs raw, Jinna covered her eyes with her forearms, blocking out the dim but brighter light in the sky. There in that darkness of her own making, Jinna saw herself in a gossamer bower, and dressed all in ribbons and satin and lace. Beside her, Egalfo's hand still reached for hers. She could almost feel the warmth of his fingertips.

The deceptive quiet almost made her mistake the murmuring voices for her own heartbeat. One deep and strong; the other higher, sweeter. Jinna knew the voices, just as she knew she could not call out to them. They were near, wherever she was, and that helped.

"We should go," her own voice said. Jinna lifted her arm from her face. Egalfo vanished. The voices. She was again in the slumbering but brightening twilight, lying in the sand beside herself.

Pushing upright, she took the hand offered and was hauled to her feet. The Jinnas left behind the circle of their footprints to head inland, away from the shore of unwound time, together.

Sibbet

The Vale—9.23.1206

Do we nothing but eat and drink? What is there to still celebrate? I am done. My head aches with all this cheer. These Larguessi who know nothing of what happened on Tassry believe peace can now be had. Fools. They only know the foiling of a plot. The saving of a king. Sisolo is cowed but not quelled. How long will it last, I wonder? The price paid was high. Highest for Larguessa Violet and her kin. How long until it comes around again? Long enough, I suppose. Perhaps it will be the little princess who will pay for this false victory.

I can almost remember. Almost. Don't make me!

Memories come to me as dreams that I would not try to recall even if I could. Ellis urges me to pull them out. Ben tells me it is best to let such things be. In all the nation, they are the only ones who know the truth, and neither will tell me, though I have not asked. I cannot ask.

Life is a lie I cannot abide.

Done once, done a dozen times. Blood and flesh. Flesh and blood. I smell it now, phantom on my hands, in my clothes. My hair. Is this not enough? Violet, you are cruel. To punish me for your crime. You should have gotten them out. You should have known. You left them for me. You left them to die.

LINHARE LOST TRACK OF THE DAYS. She and Wait fished in the river that floated them further from Hoophollow but seemingly no closer to anywhere else. They ate fish and the dried fruit from her dwindling supply. Wait no longer boiled their water before they drank it. Like her sac of dried fruit, unnecessary wood was dwindling, and still she could not bring herself to eat raw fish.

They moored themselves to the boat by their makeshift rope, to one another by Hepheo's bit of chain, but swimming lost its adventurous appeal. Despite the boredom, Linhare did not burn through Wait's journal like a spark in tinder. The entries were becoming more frantic. They made her heart ache, and she could not look at it again for days at a time. Tucking the journal into her bag, Linhare buckled the flap and set it aside.

"The air feels warmer to me," she said. Wait looked up from the ribbon net he was mending after a less than willing fish shook it apart.

"Stickier." He took out the compass that never settled on a point, put it away again. "Maybe we're getting closer to land. Or the sea."

"I will hope for land. I almost envy Jinna and Egalfo their enchanted slumber."

Wait resumed his mending. Linhare shuffled to the rail, leaned over it to glimpse at her watery reflection. She turned her head this way and

206

that, watching the way her bobbed curls bounced. They were wild, like a toddler's after arduous dreaming. Pushing fingers through, snarls capturing her fingers, she wished either she or Ezibah thought to pack a proper comb.

Jinna would be able to get the tangles out, comb or no comb.

Turning from the rail and the frustrating, useless thoughts already gathering, a flash of green upon the water caught her attention. Linhare turned round again, searching for and spotting a leaf. Broad as a dinner plate, it did not eddy or twirl but floated as if a tiny mimic of their ship. Linhare leaned over further, half expecting to see some new fae creature sailing the craft. It was just a leaf after all. But a leaf could well mean trees; and trees meant land. She called to Wait, "Come look."

Another leaf popped to the surface to join the last as if in flotilla, and then another. By the time Wait reached the rail, there were five; then six and finally seven in V formation, like geese on the wing.

"What do you make of that?" she asked.

"I'm not sure."

"Shall we jump in and gather them?"

"No. It could be a lure set for us to do just that. Keep an eye on them. I'll try to pull them in with the net."

It took the better part of an hour, but they managed to catch and haul all seven leaves up into their boat. Nothing appeared to deter or chastise. Linhare sniffed at them, rubbed the tough leaves between her fingers. "They smell...clean."

Wait held a leaf to his nose. "Rivertidy, I'm guessing. It grows thick like this in deep water. Finer in shallow, sunny spots. It's a staple in the Ealiels. The people mash it into a pulp and then form thin cakes to dry on the rocks, sort of like what coastal folk do with seaweed."

"Are you certain that is what it is?"

"Certain? No. If I were in Vales Gate I would be, but not here."

"It's so tough," Linhare said. "Almost like waxed canvas. I wonder if I could make a hat out of it."

Wait tapped her nose. "You are getting a bit freckled."

Her nose tickled where he touched her. "Snarled hair, browned skin, now freckles. Chira would call me a fishwife and command me to bathe in milk."

"I like your tangled hair and brown skin and freckled nose. You remind me of the girls I grew up with."

"Is that a good thing?"

Wait took her hand in his, traced the lines of her palm. Linhare inhaled deeply, drawing the sensation through her body. Their river journey was changing him in ways that thrilled and frightened her. He smiled, truly smiled, and he *laughed*. Still, he rarely touched her, even at night. Curled together in the shack, he did not hold her in his arms but rather sheltered her from the chill. Guardian. Guarding. Guarded. Until moments like this that took her breath away.

Linhare took his face in both small hands. His smiled faded, but Wait did not back away, not this time. Her body lit, thrilled and afraid; and she drew him to her anyway, kissed his lips, softly, tentatively, persistently. Fear dissolved into the sensation of his beard tickling her skin, into the taste of him, like wild air. Linhare kissed him and kissed him until he kissed her back. And then he let go a sigh like a groan and gently pulled her closer, held her like some cherished thing. There was no desperate grappling, no wine-taint upon his lips. She felt his body respond to hers and it aroused rather than repelled her. Linhare pushed her hands up inside his shirt, kneaded skin and muscle and hair. Joyful tears rolled from her eyes. She wanted him. So badly. She was not ruined after all.

"Yes, there! Ho, there!"

A hollow thumping accompanied the shrill voice that startled them apart.

"Help, please. Yes, please. For kindness given, kindness shown. Yes?"

Wait took a deep, shuddering breath, then moved to the rail. Linhare's whole body trembled. She wanted to laugh and shout, to dive over the rail and fly circles around their little haven. Instead, she joined him at the rail. A furry creature, much like the river otters back home, bobbed in the water below.

"A waterfurry." Wait's voice was thick. "Like the one that told me where to find you, back in the Pinewood."

"Out here?"

"Help," it peeped. "Pull me aboard. Please, Dread Sir, you accepted my leafy gifts. Haul me up before they catch me."

"Before who catches you?" Linhare asked just as the water rippled. Fearsome little faces broke the surface. The waterfurry squealed and clawed at the hull. The fishy things darted toward it.

"Oh, hurry!" Linhare cried, but Wait had already tossed the net down to the frightened creature. It caught on, grasping it just as Wait started to haul. Fishy faces bared sharp little teeth, clacked high-pitched screeches that stung Linhare's ears. Spindly arms shook tiny weapons. As Wait hauled the waterfurry over the edge, the nasty little creatures screeched their last and vanished beneath the surface.

"What were those things?" Linhare gasped.

"Flakers." The waterfurry squealed. "They wanted my sweet, juicy flesh, they did. Thank you. Thank you. Thank you for saving me."

"What are you doing out here in the middle of nowhere?" Wait asked.

"Same as you." The waterfurry made a sound like bubbles popping. It shook itself dry. "All upon this river ride to Chase Queen's land, to Dread Queen's hands. Like me. Like you. Like her. But I was taken by flakers for their nasty feast. You won't put me back in the water? To the flakers and their sharp sticks? Friends now. Boat friends. Yes? I gave you leafy-gifts."

"We won't put you back in the water," Linhare said before Wait could speak. "Of course you can ride with us."

"Oh, yes, oh, yes." The fat little creature wound circles around Linhare's ankles. It pawed and petted, jumping back when Wait took a step closer. Linhare looked to Wait, eyebrows raised, then bent to stroke the silky, already-dry fur. It put paws upon her knee, trilling in her face. "Oh, thank you, kind. Thank you, dear. Sibbet is grateful and helpful as well. I shall fetch for you. And clean for you. I shall comb my lady's hair. Do you like your leafy-gifts? Fine they are, yes? Best in all the chase. For you. For help. For passage to the Dread Queen."

"Dread Queen?" Wait asked. "Do you mean the Chase Queen?"

"They are the same, same, same."

"What are these?" Wait asked, holding up one of the broad leaves. Sibbet scrambled to his feet, head bobbing and small hands twittering.

"Leafy-gifts, Dread Sir. For you. For my lady."

"But what are they? What are they used for?"

Sibbet's little body quivered like jelly in a bowl. "Leafy-gifts," he said again. "Pretty, yes? Lovely?"

"They are quite lovely," Linhare came to his rescue. "I was thinking I would make a hat with them, to shield me from the sun."

"Oh, yes! Yes, dear and sweet. A hat to keep you cool and your skin lady-pale."

Sibbet rolled onto its back, trilling sweetly and offering its soft belly. Linhare pushed her fingers into his fur. She looked up at Wait. He shook his head. "Do you know how much further until we reach the Chase Queen's lands?"

"The chase is hers, Dread Sir. All upon it and in it are hers. You are there now. She is near. Ride the chase 'til she comes. That is all. All to know."

Wait nodded. He gestured to Linhare, halting Sibbet when he made to follow at her heels. Linhare looked over her shoulder to the creature sniffling and simpering.

"Why are you being so suspicious?" she whispered. "He's darling."

"There is something not quite right about that thing," Wait told her. "Be careful with it."

"Don't be silly. Sibbet is harmless."

"Just be careful."

"All right, Wait. All right."

He smiled then, ran a finger down the slope of her nose. Linhare bit her lip, wishing for more of what her new little friend interrupted, glad his presence prevented it. It was enough to savor the desire, the victory; better, in fact. Until the next time.

Squatting on her heels, Linhare held her hand out to Sibbet. It sat upon his haunches there where Wait had bid it stay, little arms gathered close to his fluffy chest. Beady brown eyes flickered nervously from her to Wait and back again, his nose twitching like a rabbit's.

"Come," she said, and he scuttled to her, wiggling and nuzzling and sweetly trilling.

"There now," Linhare whispered. "Don't mind Wait. He is very protective of me."

Sibbet curled into her lap, put his tiny paws upon her chest. "As he should be, Little Queen," he trilled softly against her cheek. "As he should be."

Chase Queen

THE DRY, COOL SAND GAVE WAY to scrub, then to earth and a piney wood of stunted trees unable to soak in enough sunshine or water in this world of diffused light to grow properly. Jinna walked beside herself, avoiding conversation at first, eventually realizing there was really nothing to say. Whether she followed Poppet-Jinna, or Poppet-Jinna followed her, one of them seemed to know which way to go.

A dog barked in the distance. Both Jinnas turned to the sound. Another bark, this one higher in pitch. Another. Several dogs. Baying now. And closer.

"They sound like they're hunting," Jinna said. "Run!"

"No." Poppet-Jinna grasped her arm. "Running will only excite them, make them come faster. If they are hunting dogs, there must be a hunter. Maybe one who has seen Egalfo."

"Or maybe one who will kill us."

"Do you think it is possible to die in such a place as this?" Poppet-Jinna asked, lips pursed, eyebrows raised.

Picking up a fallen stick to beat the branches with, Poppet-Jinna started shouting, "Halloo! Halloo!" Jinna hung back, just in case. The sound of the hunt came ever closer, the scratch of paws scrambling for purchase, then hounds leaping through the brush. Circling. Barking. Baying longer, louder notes. A huntress stepped into view, bow grasped in one hand, arrow in the other, as if she had just taken it from the string. Clutching at their sticks, the Jinnas nonetheless held their ground. The huntress approached, sliding her arrow back into its quiver.

Tall, and lean as her grungy dogs, she might have been lovely once. Too many scars crisscrossed her face. Her pale scalp showed through shorn hair. Bare breasted and only a scrap of cloth wound around her hips and between her legs displayed a body sculpted of the perfect combination of muscle and curve, though it, too was heavily scarred, dirty. She smelled of sweat and old blood.

Angry, cruel, merciless eyes scrutinized Jinna, top to toes. Something else, something ghostly about her face made Jinna cower before the woman ever moved. Only when she came close enough for her odor to overwhelm did Jinna realize that the huntress had no eyebrows, only scars; as if she burned them off, or scraped them out.

"Have you no manners?" The woman's voice mimicked her appearance. "Bow down to your better!"

Poppet-Jinna quickly complied. Jinna did not; until the woman leveled those bare, bald eyes upon her, only her.

211

"I am looking for someone here in your wood," Jinna said. "A man. My friend. He has dark hair and—"

"Everything here is mine. Nothing is yours. Even you are mine."

"Of course, huntress." Poppet-Jinna bowed lower. "I meant no disrespect."

"Trinkets and nonsense," the woman grumbled. "For long and longer, that is all I get. Tithes fit for a mouse or a bird, not a queen. Now an offering of living sacrifices. And two not tithed. Does he know what was sent down my river?" She laughed, a sound like gravel or thunder. "Did he send him? To do what he could not, dared not? What could he be up to now?"

"I assure you that my friend has nothing to—"

"Silence!" The woman called her dogs to her. A whistle and a gesture, and off they went bounding into the wood. "A man is there," she said, pointing vaguely over her shoulder. "You may go to him. I have other matters to see to. Bigger matters. Bide with him. I will decide what to do with the two of you soon enough."

Two, not three. Jinna looked side-long at Poppet-Jinna, curious and confused. The woman followed after her dogs, and did not look back. The smell of her lingered, but Jinna could not help taking a deep, relieved breath, even if she regretted it after. She stuck out her tongue.

"Bleh! I can taste her."

"Have you ever smelled anything quite so bad?"

"No. Never. You did well, though. Thank you."

"Despite what others think, I am not completely lacking discretion."

"I've never been partial to it myself," Jinna said.

"But it could save your life," the poppet replied. "Like it did just now."

Looking over her shoulder, Jinna could still hear the dogs bounding through the wood. The huntress's departure took with it some of her fear, and left irritation behind. Pushing past herself, she wove through the brush and scraggly pines in the general direction the huntress indicated. Egalfo was near, even if he was not a moment ago. Jinna could feel him, as she felt him while sitting alone on the beach. The knowledge had given her purpose. Now, in this place of dreamed twilight, it gave her joy.

She heard him humming a tune that brought back the sensation of spent and satisfied slumber. Following that hum, she found a clearing; within this clearing, a bower akin to those in Beloël's Pinelands; and within that bower: Egalfo.

Lying on his back, hands folded behind his head, he stared up at the sky through the gossamer curtain.

"Egalfo," she and Poppet-Jinna called in eerie unison. He picked up his head and shouted back, "Jinna!"

Scrambling out of the curtained bower, he ran towards her. Jinna ran, too. He scooped her up into his arms, laughing.

"I've been looking and looking for you." She breathed into his neck.

"I've been here all along," he said, and set her back onto her feet. Jinna's insides jiggled like winter pudding, but she managed to pout.

"Why didn't you come looking for me?"

"I don't know. I thought it best to stay put. Then she came and told me you were coming."

"She?"

"A woman. A huntress. There were dogs, so I assumed—"

"Oh, her." Jinna wrinkled her nose. "Vile creature."

"Vile?" Egalfo laughed. "I've never heard of such beauty being vile. But I suppose we all have our opinions."

"You found her lovely? I've never seen anything so hideous."

Egalfo laughed. "Perhaps jealousy has skewed your vision."

"Or perhaps we saw her differently," Poppet-Jinna said before Jinna could find a sufficiently scathing reply.

She grimaced. "In this place, it wouldn't surprise me," she said instead. "I mean, that the huntress could change her appearance."

Egalfo quirked an eyebrow, his eyes only on her—not the poppet— just as the huntress's had been. "This *is* a strange place. I don't doubt that such a thing is possible. Even probable."

"Yes, very strange," the Jinnas said. Egalfo smiled then, and nodded toward the bower.

"It's comfortable," he said. "Will you come sit with me? Maybe we can figure out what's going on."

Egalfo did not wait for an answer but returned to his curtained nest, held aside the gossamer fabric. Casual, relaxed, even cheery, Egalfo remained the same one she knew before falling Beyond.

If I am dreaming him, perhaps he is dreaming me.

The thought came and went but stuck in Jinna's head like a fact too plain to dispute. She looked to her counterpart but got no answering look, for she was gazing at Egalfo like a moonstruck fool. Gritting her teeth, Jinna pushed past her. She climbed into the bower, Egalfo right behind, only to discover that Poppet-Jinna already curled up beside him as if it were her right.

"Tell me what you remember," Jinna said. "Everything."

Egalfo took a deep breath. He cocked his head, grimacing. "I am not sure what I remember, and what I dreamed," he said, "but I remember the throg…"

Their experiences were similar, if not the same. Egalfo remembered the pouch, the throg's choked apology, and queer dreams. But while Jinna

213

found herself on a quiet shore, Egalfo had woken in the bower. While she trekked and searched the strange landscape, he stayed in the same place, waiting.

"Tell me," Jinna asked, "when you close your eyes, what do you see?"

"I see us," he said, "in a canopied bed. Our hands almost touching."

Jinna bit her lip. "That is what I see, too."

"I can sometimes hear Wait, and Linhare, though her voice does not boom as his does, and I can rarely make out any of what she says. There is also a smaller voice that might be a child's."

"I've not heard that voice," Jinna told him. "But I haven't closed my eyes in a while. It's too eerie."

"It is. Like seeing yourself dead."

"Exactly." Poppet-Jinna reached for Egalfo's hand, but it was Jinna's hand he took. His fingers curled into her own. Jinna smiled smugly. He said, "Until you got here, I've just sort of been—existing. Waiting. I didn't know what for. I might get slapped for saying this, but now you're here, I realize that what I was waiting for was you."

Jinna's muscles clenched even as her heart liquefied. Poppet-Jinna spoke first. "I'm glad you did."

"I've been doing a lot of thinking, Jin."

"And I didn't think at all. I just...*did*. You were here. I knew you were. And I had to find you."

Egalfo smiled. "Am I permitted to tell you how happy that makes me? Or have I again risked being slapped?"

Jinna could only look at him, wonder why she fought so hard against what her heart told her was true. He was kind and good, and he loved her. He had waited in this twilight for her to come, even as she searched and searched.

"I'm not going to slap you, Egalfo," she said at last. "I'm just glad I found you."

"I'm glad, too."

Jinna swallowed hard. "I am so sorry for hurting you. I never intended to."

"It did hurt. I won't lie. What is the point of lying here?" He laughed softly. "A large part of what happened was my own fault. Dockside wasn't real, Jinna. When I asked you to come with me, I meant it with all my heart. But we were strangers. Had I known you better, I'd never have asked such a foolish thing."

Egalfo stroked the hand in his. He brought it to his lips and held it there a moment before kissing it and letting it go. "We're not strangers now. And I am not making much sense."

"Yes you are." Jinna inhaled deeply. *What is the point in lying here?* She touched the pendant resting on his chest. She traced the raised letters.

Egh Ahl Fo.

He sat perfectly still.

Egh Ahl Fo.

"If I asked for this back—" Jinna's fingers brushed against the skin of his hairless chest. "—would you give it to me?"

"I told you it was yours forever."

"Yes. You did."

Poppet-Jinna faded out like the last of a shallow puddle on a scorching day. And then she was gone, as if she had never been; as in fact she had not.

You are sleeping. You are dreaming. Real as this seems, it's not.

There was no endless water, no pinprick stars. No dogs, no huntress, no poppet come to life. There was no Egalfo looking at her now, loving and loved. He was not leaning forward. He was not kissing her. He was not drawing her gently into his arms. He was asleep too, his hand reaching for hers.

"Tell me you want me, Jinna." He kissed the hollow of her throat. He unbuttoned her bodice. He tugged her dress open. Lips and hands that already knew how to make her ache and sigh found all the places that wanted him most.

Jinna kept her eyes open. She watched his muscles move inside his skin. They had done this before. Many times before. And never.

Tell me you want me. The words whispered on her lips, curled about her muscles and bones. He hitched up her skirt. *Tell me you want me.* Softer now, and breathless, and reckless. Egalfo fumbled with the buttons and lacing of his pants. Fingers teased her up her thighs, gently prodded them apart. He got between them. *Tell me, Jinna. Please. Tell me.*

Dreams were not real. Not even Beyond. And especially not in this place neither living nor dead. She and Egalfo were dreams themselves.

"I love you," she told him.

"Even better," he said.

Jinna's eyes fluttered closed when he pulled her hips up to meet his own. The sleeping forms so finely arrayed atop the canopied bed blinked past her lids, then vanished completely.

LINHARE WAS LIKE A CHILD WITH A PUPPY, playing with Sibbet all hours of the day and sleeping with it tucked into her arms at night. In turn, the creature fetched and fawned and told her stories until she fell asleep. Wait kept his distance. Something less than innocent made him wary of the creature. Though it claimed kinship to the Pinewood waterfurries, it was quite different. The sleek critter in the enchanted pool within Beloël's domain bore only passing similarity to the rounder, paddle-tailed Sibbet. Linhare's affection for the thing kept Wait's suspicions to himself. But he watched.

The steady rocking of the rudderless vessel no longer soothed Wait into slumber, but it was not because of the creature or his caution that he could not sleep. He leaned against the rail, looking out over that endless expanse of water and sky, up to those distant and fragile stars more like an idea of stars, ending at his hands. They knew too much now. Of her. The feel of her skin, the curves of her body embedded into each callus, each line of his palms, his fingers. They wanted to touch every hollow, every curve, every downy bit of skin. His mouth needed the taste of her. His body itched with the strain of wanting. So many years of careful control, obliterated by so small a woman; toppled by a kiss.

A bump against the hull lifted his head, scattered his thoughts. Wait leaned over the side. Nothing disturbed the lapping water. Wrapped in the silence of his own making, Wait went to the hatch leading to the bower below. He hesitated, but he opened it, latched it against falling, and descended into the eerie glow.

"Jinna? Egalfo?" Even as he whispered their names, he saw them asleep on the canopied bed, now in one another's arms. A silhouette stepped free of shadow; a woman, tall and slim, and silent as Wait himself.

"Rest easy, Dakhonne. I mean them no harm."

Her voice, deep and musical and menacing, lured him closer. Clad only in rolled cloth about her waist, the woman was a shadow within more shadow. A circlet of hammered gold banded her coal-dusting of hair. Lean and muscular, she brought to mind the powerful predator cats he once saw caged in Therk. Wait's hand moved to his empty swordbelt. His weapon hung from the peg hammered into the wall of the shack, where he carelessly kept it since first climbing aboard this rudderless ship.

"Chase Queen," he said, and bowed at the waist.

"Of course you know who I am. As I know you, Dakhonne. You were not tithed. How did you come upon my chase?"

"It's complicated."

"Did he send you?"

"Did who—"

"Is this some scheme to punish me further? Sending kin to slay me? To torment me?"

Agitation shook her words. Not fear. There was no fear.

"I don't know what you're talking about."

"I'll hear no lies!" She did not shout, though her words reverberated in his gut. "You were not tithed. I have no claims upon you, as he would know. But these two are mine."

"They were given to you by someone with no right to do so." Wait took a step closer to the ladder. "You can't have them."

"That is not the way it works." She smiled, and again Wait recalled those captive cats. Agitation smoothed away as quickly as it had come. "It matters nothing whence they came or how they arrived upon my river, enchanted in this bower. The tithe was made, the ritual performed and I have accepted the gift as I am required. They are mine."

"Then tell me how I can win them from you."

The Chase Queen approached, padding so fluidly and gracefully she seemed to float. The top of her head reached Wait's chin. She tilted her face up. Her eyes were chips of blue ice shining from the ebony of her face. Her full lips parted. Her breath was a cool breeze, fragrant with mint leaves. "I shall have to consider. For now, I welcome you and the Little Queen, for that is what royalty does for royalty. What kin does for kin. You will be safe in my house. I give my word. But stay upon this tithe ship at your own peril. And hers."

Her bared breasts brushed him as she slid past and grabbed on to the ladder. "Come along," she said to Jinna and Egalfo, and like puppets on strings they rose from their sumptuous bed to follow. The curtains, the bed itself disintegrated, a confection-castle in warm water. Candles snuffed out as they passed until there was only one left, this suddenly in the Chase Queen's hand.

"Do not linger." She ran a finger under Wait's chin. He jerked away from her touch. The Chase Queen laughed. She went up the ladder, then Jinna, then Egalfo. Wait gazed into the absolute darkness and for a moment thought he could see beyond it.

"No! No, you mustn't! You can't!" Linhare's shriek propelled Wait up the ladder. One stride put him between her and the Chase Queen.

"Stay back," he commanded, and the woman flinched. Face screwed up in fury, ice-chip eyes fixed on Sibbet, she pointed a long, elegant finger in its direction.

"You've no idea what you hold in your arms, Little Queen. Treachery. That is what you hold. Deceit. Foul, heartless creature. I'll not have that thing in my court. He was not tithed. I am not obligated. Toss him back into the river."

"Linhare," Wait said softly. "Maybe you should put him down."

"No!" Linhare held Sibbet to her breast. "The flakers will eat him!"

"Is that what he told you?" The Chase Queen laughed a sound like drums. "Is that how he tricked you into taking him aboard?"

"It was no trick," Linhare said. "I saw them with my own eyes."

"You saw their teeth and believed them vicious, but their gruesome smile is for gnawing tough leaves, not meat. You see that *thing*," she pointed to Sibbet, "so soft and fat and flattering, and you believe it is

217

sweet and playful. Open your eyes, Little Queen. See what is, not what seems."

Sibbet squirmed and heaved himself out of Linhare's arms. He waddled to the Chase Queen, winding about her legs even as the woman kicked at him.

"Sibbet! No!" Linhare lunged for her pet, but Wait held her back, and Sibbet paid no attention.

"Dread Queen, beautiful Lady, send me not away. I labored hard and long to return to you."

"That is your own stupidity." The Chase Queen kicked at it again. "And your doom."

"Doom was being parted from you!"

"Sibbet?" Linhare bent to the animal. "What is all this about?"

Sibbet did not answer. His little body quivered, but he did not simper, and Wait realized it was not fear but joy trembling him. The Chase Queen trembled as well, fury barely contained. Behind her, nearly forgotten, Jinna and Egalfo stood statue-still.

"I cannot abide this form," the Chase Queen said. "There is no honor in disposing of something so weak."

"No!"

Wait caught Linhare just as she lunged for the creature now folding in on itself. Its hair sloughed off. Pale skin stretched and bronzed. It was a boy, and then he was a man. Taller than most. Broader. Eyes as blue-green as Ealiels Bay, hair sandy as her beaches. Now it was Linhare who trembled. Wait pulled her closer.

"Perhaps this body is more appealing," the echo-Wait said. "Dakhonne, as no woman of this realm has touched or tasted since Pulos scourged its shores. Do I please, Dread Queen?"

"No true Dakhonne." The Chase Queen grimaced even if her gaze lingered. "I will have you quartered by dragon-chicks for coming here."

"I am yours to do with as you wish. You knew I would find my way to you. He parted us, but he could not keep us parted."

"You betrayed me."

"I did no such thing. It was he who betrayed you."

"You lie!"

"Make him change!" Linhare burst. "I cannot abide this!"

Sibbet turned to her, smiling Wait's smile first for Wait himself before offering it to Linhare.

"As my dear one wishes," he said. Echo-Wait bowed his head, folded in upon himself, and just as quickly as he had taken Wait's form, he took another. Half and half-again as high, there stood a freeling lad as red-capped as Jinna.

"Forgive my deception, Little Queen. Love knows no scruples. But I did enjoy being your pet."

"What manner of creature are you?" Linhare whispered.

"I am a sibbet."

"You said your *name* is Sibbet."

"Oh, no, darling one. Never. *You* said it was."

"He is a lie with no true form." The Chase Queen growled somewhat less ferociously. "If he has touched it, he can become it, whatever the living creature, whatever the sex. A talent I found most useful, until it was turned upon me."

"And shall find useful again," the lad said. "I've touched many in our time apart. The Dakhonne was only one. Let me show you. I vow you will not be displeased."

"Your vow is as false as the forms you take."

"I will prove otherwise."

"You can prove nothing dead."

"No. And if anyone can make good on such a threat, you, my Dread Love, are such a one. But I am still quite alive despite this fact. For all we once meant to one another, you at least owe me a chance to prove my love and my worth."

"I owe you nothing."

The boat gave a frightful groan, pitching as if suddenly kicked. Wait caught Linhare before she toppled. Standing beside the Chase Queen, Jinna and Egalfo did not totter.

"Come, Little Queen," she said, turning away from the sibbet. "You and the Dakhonne shall be my honored guests, accorded all such an honor implies. Now we must be away from here before the spell pulls apart completely. Come along."

The Chase Queen legged over the side and onto a dock that hadn't been there a moment before. A foot upon the boards and from the dock sprung a town all twinkling lights and muffled music. Jinna and Egalfo, like animated dolls, followed behind her. Neither they nor the Chase Queen turned back again.

"Go ashore," Wait told Linhare. "I'll get our things."

The freeling leapt off the vessel just as it lurched a second time. He stood on the dock, his hand offered to Linhare.

"Do not fear me, dear one," he said. "I am still your own sweet pet."

"I don't know what to believe anymore," Linhare answered wearily. Defeated. Wait took her elbow before she could grasp the sibbet's hand, assisting her over the side. The vessel lurched a third time, sinking lower in the water.

Two strides and he grabbed the bags Ezibah had given them, slinging them across his chest. Under his feet, the deck shifted like sand.

"Wait! Hurry!" Linhare cried. "The ship is—is melting!"

Like the bower bed dissolved, so too did the ship as the throg's spell unraveled. Wait tried to scramble across the non-existent deck. He grabbed for the wall. His hand went through. And then he saw it. His sword. Swinging from that peg hammered into the shack wall.

"Wait! Please! Come now!"

Leaping, reaching, Wait's fingers brushed the blade just enough to knock it from the peg dissolving with the rest of the ship. The wall gave way. Linhare screamed. Wait caught hold of a mooring rope hanging from the dock. Below, the water roiled, digesting the ship and his sword and all else left aboard.

His hand slipped. Linhare screamed. The rope burned his skin. She was leaning, reaching for him. "Please! Please help me!" On the dock beside her, the freeling lad grinned. And then there was no freeling lad but a fearsome thing of glitter and scales. Its monstrous beak plucked Wait from his doom as his grip failed. Away from the water. Up and up. So fast that his head swam and his fingertips tingled. And then he was lowered onto the dock as gently as a fine cup to its saucer.

Linhare plowed into him, clung to him. Wait held her close, trying hard not to fall. His vision wavered. Behind her back, the dragon chick folded in on itself and again the freeling lad emerged, grinning as he had been that moment before the change.

"You are most welcome," he said, bowed, and trotted after the Chase Queen, now just a distant shadow against the twinkling village.

Jungle and Snow

Linhare's eyes were everywhere at once. On the board walkway. On the swamp underneath. On the dripping vines and the sparrow-sized primates watching her from the trees so dense there was no sky. The Chase Queen awaited them just ahead, boogles lined up like servants at the board. Several huts, some large and some small, dotted the trees, the walkways.

"Refreshment awaits you in your chambers," she said. "You will rest. Tomorrow, we shall have a discussion."

A hump-backed boogle crone moved toward Linhare. Wait stepped in front of her. "She goes nowhere without me."

"I have sworn your safety and hers." The Chase Queen's eyebrow quirked, a storm already brewing in her eyes. "Do you dishonor my word?"

"It will be all right," Linhare said. "Wait, it will be all right."

Still he did not budge, did not blink.

"Such devotion. I know your kind, Dakhonne. Most intimately. Can anything here harm your Little Queen without suffering your wrath?"

He did not answer.

"As I thought."

"Wait, please." Linhare touched his arm. He looked down at her hand like it was some alien thing. She squeezed. "Remember what we talked about."

He covered her hand with his own, nodded. Stepping away from her, he faced their host. "I accept your word, warrior to warrior." He held out his hands, fingers balled into a fist. The Chase Queen stared at it, then touched her knuckles to his.

"Warrior to warrior."

"Come, Little Queen." The boogle crone's head was bowed, enhancing the mighty hump of her back. "I will show you to your quarters."

"Th-thank you."

Linhare looked once to Wait, tried to smile confidently, reassuringly, and followed the boogle to a nearby hut. Glancing over her shoulder, she saw Wait escorted to another quite near her own. She blew out a relieved breath and entered the hut.

"Refreshment is on the board." The boogle pointed to an abundance of food set neatly upon the small board. "A basin for you to wash there in the corner. When you sleep, be certain to use the netting so the bugs don't eat you alive."

"Thank you again. You are most kind."

221

The crone bowed her head, a purplish tinge staining her leathery cheeks. "If there is anything else I can do? Serve, perhaps?"

"No. I'll be fine."

"Very well. Sleep well, Little Queen. May williwisps bring you happy dreams."

Linhare pushed damp curls from her face. Away from the river, the heavy, wet air clung to her like a summer afternoon. Letting her bag fall to the floor, she leaned over the basin and splashed her face, neck and chest. The tepid water was at least cooler than her skin. She felt better.

Stripping off her damp clothes, Linhare pulled a dry shift over her head, but it was damp by the time she tugged it into place. It smelled of river water, but it was clean. She grabbed a long, thin, yellow fruit from the board, studied it. She bit at the soft but fibrous peel. Inside, it was soft and sweet. She sighed, delighted, a little shaky, and took another from the bowl.

Climbing into the netted hammock, Linhare finished her fruit and licked her fingers clean. The structure rocked pleasantly. Slowing. Stopping. She closed her eyes, but they would not stay closed. The foreign noises outside flimsy, woven walls, the vastness of the dripping land caught her in its enormous embrace. Enveloping. Suffocating. Nothing like this place existed in Vales Gate, but it did in Therk. She had read all about it in nice, safe books. Dense swathes of impenetrable land populated by fearsome predators and insects as big as a man's head; by half-naked humans and their gruesome hunts and the drums that meant death. Linhare found it all so fascinating once...

"Dear one! Little Queen? May I come in?"

Linhare bolted upright in the hammock that swayed precariously but did not topple her.

"Who's there?"

"Your own dear pet. Let me come in. I wish to make a'right between us again."

Linhare grimaced. Something growled outside, a scream of killing or being killed. She bit her lip, torn between maintaining her anger and needing company in this strange place. "Very well," she called. "You may come in."

The shutter opened a tiny crack and a sparrow-like primate swung through the window. He pushed it closed before scurrying across the floor and up the netting of her hammock. Parting the netting and scooting inside the tiny creature sat upon her knee. His coat was light but for the deep brown face, hands, feet and the long tail that curled like a question beneath him. Enormous golden eyes lowered; tiny eyelashes brushed round cheeks. It was all she could do not to reach out and stroke his coat.

"Am I forgiven?"

"You lied to me."

"A lie? If a fish does not tell you it is a fish, is it lying to you?"

"Only if it has taken the form of a hummingbird."

"And if no harm is done? You would simply see a hummingbird and think nothing of it. You must understand that I was desperate. I have searched the chase for countless years trying to find a way to my beloved. When I saw your little boat, I knew it was my one and only chance."

"You are changing the subject."

"The chase is vast," he pressed on. "The chances of us coming together were minute. It was meant to be, don't you think? And in the end, there was indeed no harm to you or the Dread Sir. Was there?"

Linhare grimaced. "I suppose not."

"And we were good friends, yes? We played and we petted?"

"But you—"

"You did me a service. I did you one. Something for something. That is the way of things, yes?"

"Yes, but—"

"Then I do not understand why—"

"Oh, for goodness' sake!" Linhare startled the primate from her knee. He looked up at her from behind her foot, his tiny hands clutching her toes; golden eyes wide and frightened. Linhare reached out her hand. He climbed onto her leg and scurried carefully to her lap. She said, "I'm sorry for frightening you."

"Treepiggins startle easily," he said. "I have taken this form. I am governed by such instincts."

Linhare stroked his tiny head. "Is it true what the Chase Queen said? You have no form of your own?"

"Not as you would comprehend it, no. Being confined to a single form is as close to death as a sibbet can ever be. I am all things and none, it is true. But I have been your good little darling. I have cared for you. Tell me that you forgive me. Tell me that we are friends again."

"We are still friends," she said after a moment, and the treepiggin squeaked and flipped on her knee. Linhare laughed, and he did it again. "But I have not quite forgiven you yet."

"Joy and more joy! I could weep with joy!"

"Settle yourself." Linhare laughed, catching him in both hands when he leapt again. She hugged the treepiggen—sibbet—to her cheek, nuzzling his soft fur. His tiny hands patting her cheek were like the softest leather.

"Ah, Little Queen. You are so very dear."

"Please stop calling me Little Queen. My name is Linhare. I am quite weary of being referred to as *little* wherever I go, especially by a creature smaller than I am."

223

"I am not always so small," he chuckled. "And you mistake the honor given you. You are Little Queen, because you are neither Great Queen of aged years nor Dread Queen of triumphant exploits. You are Little Queen in age and deed."

"Is that why?"

"Indeed it is."

"I would still prefer that you call me Linhare."

"Very well. Then you must call me Rodly."

"Very well. Rodly."

Linhare settled into her hammock, curling onto her side as she did so many nights on the river. The sibbet snuggled against her breast. Linhare stroked his buff coat. The sounds outside her hut did not terrify her so much now, but still she could not sleep.

"Tell me a story, Rodly," she said. "As you did on the chase."

"A story?" He made a chirping sound Linhare took as laughter. "Yes, a story. That would be wonderful. I have just the one. I think you will like it best of all."

Squirming up to her shoulder, he sat upon it, stroking her ear with his tiny, leathery hands.

"As so many tales do, this one begins with a boy and a girl. He was born of no great lines, no titles, no consequence. But he was comely as he wished to be, whenever he wished it.

"She was a gangly thing, all arms and legs, feet and hands. Born motherless to a Dread Warrior. Some claimed he was of Dakhan heritage, the only one of his kind to come Beyond when the fae turned Away. But that is not a tale for this telling. I speak of the boy, and the girl.

"They met and fell into instant dislike. He threw sticks at her. She threw mud at him. He had many friends. She had none. He grew older and more merry. She grew lovelier and more dangerous.

"He stayed with his kin in their bastion, for though he was born without titles, he was born of a race dying since it began. Mistrusted. Abused. She campaigned with her father and learned the ways of a warrior. When the Dread Warrior perished in battle, she mourned by eating his heart still warm with his blood.

"After many years, she returned to that place where she was born. All feared her. All loved her. Victories made her wealthy and powerful. Suitors flocked to her, attracted by such things but mesmerized by her Dread Beauty. Charm, she had little of; glamour, she had in abundance. Love, she had none.

"The boy, now a man, saw her swimming one day, in a quiet pool where they once threw sticks and mud at one another. The dislike of so long ago showed its true face. He threw a stick. She threw mud. They fought and then they kissed, and such-like followed such-like. When they left the pool, they left together and did not part again.

"They fought often, for both the boy and the girl owned wicked tempers. Trained at her father's side, it was her way to draw blood before forgiveness could be granted or received. He drew little. She drew much. The boy loved, but he feared. Her wrath. Her forgiveness. He feared losing her love most of all.

"Then came the soldier, a warrior with whom she once campaigned. The boy's jealousy first suspected they had also been lovers, then made it true whether it was or no. Every smile, every whispered touch seized him in agony worse than any inflicted forgiveness. The boy went mad with his own dark fantasies.

"The jealous, stupid boy devised a plan, to once and all be rid of this rival. Taking the guise of his beloved Dread Beauty, he went to the soldier as he slept. He kissed and he caressed, and as he suspected, the soldier loved his one-time comrade. Then he fornicated with that most hated one. He promised to be his and his alone, if only he would slay his rival for her affections.

"*'Go to him now, asleep in our bed. Strike him down! Make me your own.'*

"Engorged on his own passions, the soldier obeyed. The boy, abandoning his beloved's guise, got to the bedchamber first. He slipped into her bed with only moments before the soldier entered.

"*'Where have you been,'* she murmured sleepily. *'You know I cannot abide sleeping without you by my side.'*

"Before the boy could comfort her, the nettings were ripped aside. The Dread Beauty was her father's daughter. Her dagger came instant to her hand, deflecting the soldier's killing blows from the boy. She sliced and she slashed in those moments of confusion.

"*'Hold!'* called the soldier. *'It is I, your lover, come to slay my rival as you bid.'*

"The girl's weapon, raised to kill, fell from her hand. She looked to the boy still in their bed, a full knowing upon her face. Her comrade bled from the cuts she made. His face was ruined. He was missing an eye.

"*'What have you done?'* she asked the boy. He did not answer. There would be no blood-forgiveness this time."

Rodly's voice faded. "He was exiled. His darling made the soldier her own, in recompense and respect if not love. In time, they became known as Dread Queen and Dread King, for their exploits raged greater still; until he was lost in some battle somewhere. Lost or fled, no one truly knows. Such men make restless mates."

He fell silent then. Linhare caught her breath. She asked, "But the boy? What became of him?"

225

Rodly squirmed against her, wiggling to rest his furry face close to hers. "He was a comely boy with no title, no heritage other than being of a dying race," he said. "Nothing became of him. Nothing at all. But his story is not over yet."

Linhare stroked the place between his eyes; she was not so taken that she forgot the lesson she earlier learned. But she was suddenly too tired to ask how much of his story was true and how much embellished. They both drifted off to sleep. Treepiggen softness nestled against her cheek and wound about her neck like a stole. Treepiggen breath whispered, mingled with her own. Soothing. Sweet. Bonding.

PALE DAWN SLICED THROUGH SHUTTERS TO WAKE HIM. Wait lifted his head from his pillow. He'd fallen asleep in a netted hammock, woke now in a featherbed, and it came as no surprise. Nothing did, since falling Beyond. Not his breath blowing in clouds, not the downy blankets swaddling him like an infant, not the stone walls where woven reeds stood the night prior. Untangling himself, he rose from the bed and opened the shutters.

Ice and snow.

Wait dressed, his chilled body growing colder when he reached for his sword belt and remembered. Gritting his teeth, he stepped out into the dim hallway. A stout, pointy-faced chamberlain hurried toward him before he got very far.

"Ah! There you are. Come along. Come along."

From pointed ears to bare, knobby feet, the chamberlain's skin blushed pig-pink. Dark, spiky hair stuck up at odd angles, quivering when he spoke as if vibrating with the sound.

"Her Dread Majesty expected you long ago. It is never wise to keep her waiting."

He led Wait to a pair of massive doors. They opened of their own accord, and to a cavernous hall, before an equally cavernous hearth. Wait could make out a white-clothed table set with candles, sparkling silver, and, as he came closer, the distinct shimmer of Therkian glass.

"My queen." The hedgehog-man bowed low to the woman draped in furs as white as the snow outside. The contrast of raven hair, dark lashes and brows stood out against pale skin glowing like pearls under water. Wait did not recognize her any more than he did the room in which he'd woken; yet he knew her by the ice-chip eyes.

The Chase Queen did not rise, but gestured Wait into the chair opposite her. "I trust you slept well."

"Quite well, thank you." Several leathery creatures rushed forward with furs before Wait could pull his chair closer to the table. "That isn't necessary," he said. "I'm not cold."

"As you wish."

The fur-bearing boogles left, and food-bearing ones entered. Until smelling the hearty aromas, Wait hadn't realized he was hungry. He refrained, as protocol insisted, but the Chase Queen made no move to eat.

"I honored my word. Your Little Queen rests safely in her chambers."

"And the others?"

"Are no longer your concern. They are mine." She waved a hand over the abundantly laid table. "Are you not hungry?"

"I am."

"Then by all means, eat. I stand on no ceremony here. Least of all with kin."

Kin. Twice she'd referred to him as such. Wait cocked an eyebrow, picked up a two-pronged fork. He skewered a piece of smoked meat, broke open a large biscuit and slathered it with butter before slapping the bit of meat between the halves. One bite nearly finished it. He reached for another.

"I do enjoy watching a man eat," she said. "There is something exceedingly erotic about it."

Wait swallowed and piled more food onto his plate, tucking into it unreservedly. The Chase Queen watched, eyes narrow and appreciative. Wait bore that icy scrutiny as if he did not notice. Soon, she too ate, filling her plate as voraciously as he.

They ate in silence. Belly near to bursting, Wait skewered a round, fleshy and distantly familiar globe from a bowl of carefully peeled and pitted fruit. It did not swim in syrup like winter fruits in the Vale. It tasted fresh and juicy, as if it only just picked.

"Cozagga melon?" he asked.

"Freshly harvested yesterday."

"Your domain is an interesting one. Jungle yesterday, icy tundra today. Does it change daily?"

"Sometimes yes. Sometimes no. It is summer outside of my domain, is it not?"

"It is."

The Chase Queen nodded. "In summer, the terrain changes often. In winter, sometimes not at all."

"And you? Do you change with your domain?"

"Certain forms come to me in certain places, yes. I welcome the diversity. All are lovely. All but one."

"I find that hard to believe."

The Chase Queen's fine, black eyebrows raised. "Flattery? Perhaps I will visit you in your dreams and prove how unlovely I can be."

Clapping her hands, she did not speak again until all the dishes were cleared. Shooing her boogle servants away, the woman rose from her chair to stand with her back to him, her face to the warm fire. Beneath the furs, her thin white shift, clipped together at the shoulders by little golden leaves, reached only to the tops of her thighs. Raven hair met the hem. She did not turn to him when she spoke, but her head moved so that her tresses swayed hypnotically.

"My father was Dakhonne," she said. "Or so he used to tell me. Seeing you, I am more inclined to believe his blustery old tales."

"I thought the Dakhan stayed Away when fae fled Beyond."

"Fae did not *flee!*" She turned on him. "Why did you come on that tithe ship? Have you come to kill me?"

Wait met her furious, narrowed eyes without blinking. He said, "I've not come to kill you, Dread Queen."

She crossed her arms then, stretching the thin fabric against her breasts. She moved closer. Still Wait did not flinch, did not blink. He held onto those eyes, furious a moment ago and now smiling.

"*Dread Queen* is a title for less worthy tongues," she said. "You shall call me by the name my mother's dying lips gave to me. Saghan."

"As you wish. I am Wait."

"Wait." She rolled his name along her lips. "Your Dakhan name. What is the name your mother gave to you?"

"Calryan," he answered. "But I prefer Wait."

"Very well, Wait. You are a warrior. And you are Dakhonne. So I will believe you when you say that you have not come to kill me." Saghan dropped into her chair, leaned elbow to table, chin to the palm of her hand. "But now you will tell me how it is you came to be on that tithe ship when such a thing has never happened before. Keep in mind that though my father was Dakhonne, my mother was the village madwoman who spoke prophecy for a price. Speak truly, for I will know if you lie."

Wait recounted events from Diandra's death to his plunge into the tithe river in the terse, efficient manner taught on Sentry Rock. He spoke of Linhare as little as possible. And of the blue stone, of the Everwanderers' chain, he said nothing whatsoever.

"The throg was a miserable thing," he finished. "But Jinna and Egalfo were not his to offer you."

"And as I told you, the ritual was done. I accepted the tithe. It does not matter."

"You also said you would consider trading for them."

"Yes, I did." Saghan leaned forward. "Several of those considered trades are of a nature I do not believe will be acceptable to you, so I will not bother suggesting them."

She leaned in further, rising off her chair. The shift rode up her back, exposing the muscular roundness it had only barely concealed. Handsome. A warrior, like himself. Yet Sagahn's madness, barely contained, concerned him in ways he knew too well.

"You lost your sword to my chase, yes?"

"Yes."

"Then perhaps, Wait, in exchange for your friends, you would carry another."

Mad Queen

SAGHAN KNELT BESIDE A LOW, narrow trunk, her head bowed in silent reverence. Still dressed in the thin shift, her pale skin like moonlight in this dark, moldy grotto beneath the castle, the Chase Queen did not shiver.

"I am a warrior wronged," she said without lifting her head. "I was given the blame belonging to another, betrayed by those I loved. This is my fate, this chase and its tithes. I am banished to this nowhereland for all time, not even given the respite of death.

"I made a grave mistake in taking this." She held her hand over but did not touch the trunk. "A mistake I hope you will rectify. It should not be languishing in this nowhereland. My father would—he would—" Saghan's head bowed slowly, lower and lower until her forehead came to rest upon the trunk's lid. "Forgive me, father. Forgive me. I shall make this right."

She lifted her head again as if it were some great weight to bear. For all the emotion of her words, nothing of it existed in her eyes. "Never has anything but trinkets come down my river. Now I am finally offered companions to ease my loneliness, and with them comes a warrior worthy of carrying this treasure from exile. It is a terrible choice to have to make, but the only one I can live with."

She lifted the lid. Wait could see the outline of the sword beneath its silky shroud. Saghan waved her hand over it, caressing the air.

"My father's blade. I have not touched it since I took it from that last battle, still wet with enemy blood and wrapped in my own mantle. My husband thought it was his, but he learned better in the end."

"Your husband?"

Saghan nodded. "A soldier. A warrior, like my father. Like me. It was a good match, for a time. But I loved another. I kept him. The source of all my woe."

"The sibbet?"

"He is a man, when he wishes to be. And a pet, when convenient. My husband never knew of him the way I knew of all his lovers. I did not care. I had Rodly to love and my Dread King to mate. It was satisfying."

Saghan fell silent. Trembling. When she spoke again, it was through clenched teeth. "You came here and brought my past with you. A past that had grown cold over so much time and now burns in me as if it were yesterday."

Hands clenched and unclenched but still did not touch the weapon. She bowed her head, hair falling forward to hide her face. Saghan inhaled silently, exhaled slowly.

"It was Rodly who grew jealous. He took it upon himself to do something about my husband. Using my guise, he went to my Dread King's bed. He fornicated with him. And then he tried to kill him. He failed. And he fled. I was blamed despite my innocence and banished to the chase. I did not see him again until—" Again her hands clenched. Muscles pulled taut and corded across her shoulders, her neck. "Years of fury. Years of festering betrayal. Foolish creature. He came here knowing what must happen. That I must forgive him until he begs me to stop. Even then I will forgive him. Again and again and again."

Saghan's hunched shoulders jerked. At first, Wait thought she was weeping, but then the Chase Queen tilted her head back, white teeth like fangs. The sound of her laughter shivered through him.

"You ask me what you may do to win your friends from me," she said at last, arms raised as if in triumph. "This is it. Take my father's sword. Avenge this wrong as only a true warrior can. That is what I want. Is it a price you are willing to pay?"

Wait squatted down beside her. He reached but stopped himself, looking to the Chase Queen lest her apparent madness change tack. She nodded. Carefully, reverently, he pulled the shroud away.

Despite the pitted and scourged hilt, the blade was sound. No intricate craftsmanship swirled fine metal into a work of art. No etching scrawled words of power into its surface. Simple. Utilitarian. Much like Wait's own hilt had been. He ran his fingers along the face of the blade as sharp as it would have been the day it was forged. Sheridan's ore. There was no doubt. Mined Away when fae still resided there. It was as excellent a blade as Wait ever saw. More so, perhaps, for its antiquity.

"Take it," Saghan said. "This is what I ask of you. Warrior to warrior. Blood to blood. Do it and I swear that your friends are free. They will leave my realm without harm."

"And Linhare."

"The Little Queen was not tithed to me and thus, like you, can leave at any time. But I will swear that she too will come to no harm from anything in my realm."

His eyes shifted from idle sword to the mad queen as cunning as a pickpocket. But her father had been Dakhonne, the sword proved it.

"You knew what I am when you came aboard the tithe ship."

"I did."

He nodded. "It seems a coincidence that I lost my sword to your chase when you have this one you wish for me to take."

Saghan sat back on her heels. So close to her now, Wait could see the gooseflesh of her skin. Still she did not shiver. She did not flinch or avert her eyes. She said, "I could not let this opportunity pass," and that was all.

Wait nodded. Mad Queen Saghan. Wronged warrior. Cunning and desperate and fanatically loyal to the only scrap of honor left to her. Wait understood far too well. He grasped the hilt and rose to his feet, weapon in hand. The weight was as near to perfect as a borrowed blade could be. The hilt fit his palm as if made for him.

A shiver slithered up his arm, along his spine and spread out to his whole body. It buzzed at his heart. Suddenly powerful. Suddenly fierce. Wait remembered the feeling. Remembered it well. It subsided, with effort, into the lingering sense of zeal only a truly magnificent weapon could instill.

"You are very much like him." Saghan rose to her feet. She held a sword belt out to him. "I can almost see him standing before me. Dread Warrior. Dread deeds. Victories and blood. You could be him."

"But I am not."

Wait took the offered belt, strapped it on. He took that proper step backward to bow a proper bow. She inclined her head in answer, every aspect the queen; and madder now in her calm than in her frenzy.

"No, you are not my father. But you are Dakhonne. It is with great humility that I thank you for doing this deed so long overdue."

"I will do my best to live up to the honor."

Saghan's eyes strayed to the sword at his hip. Her fingers twitched, but she did not reach for it. Instead, she closed her eyes. Those twitching fingers curled into a fist. Bringing that fist to her heart, she said, "I am certain you will."

JINNA WOKE IN A FEATHER BED, swaddled-warm in down quilts. An incompetent fire crackled in the hearth. Sitting up, she found it colder than suspected, and Egalfo likewise swaddled beside her, still sleeping.

"Egalfo." She whispered close to his face, brushed the hair from his brow. The extravagance of eyelashes fluttered. "Egalfo, wake up."

Fluttering lashes parted only enough to show the thinnest sliver of white and black and deep, deep brown. He smiled. "I've been having the strangest dreams."

Jinna burrowed in closer to him. "Were they dreams?"

"I don't know whether to hope they were or that they weren't." He wiggled his arms out of his blankets to pull her close. "I think I hope they were."

"Do you have any idea where we are?"

"None," he told her. "But I remember the huntress, and then…a summer-place. Do you?"

"A little. I think Wait and Linhare are here. I saw them. Or heard them." She sighed heavily. "It's all so confused."

The door banged open. An enormously-bosomed boogle lass entered, carrying a silver tray. She hummed inanely, paying them no notice, across the room to a section of wall where the stones appeared no different from any others. A shove, a flick, and a narrow table dropped down. Placing the tray upon it, she reached into the hole and hauled out two low stools, brushed them off, and set them beside the table. Then she reached in a second time, leaning so far into the hole that her equally round and acrobatic posterior waggled atop the table like two humps of winter pudding. After an uncomfortable amount of grunting and farting, she pulled a single log from the space behind the wall. Flames rushed up the chimney the moment she threw in that bit of wood, settling quickly into a constant, contented blaze. The boogle lass wiped her hands together, nodded a satisfied nod, and bobbled back out the door.

"I don't know that I'll ever get accustomed to such creatures," Jinna said after the door closed. "But better the little farting boogle than the huntress."

Egalfo kicked aside his covers, legged out of the bed. Moving to her side, he unwrapped her like a gift, his eyes half-closed and arousing. Jinna lay unmoving, wishing and fearing he would not stop with the blankets. Though the boogle-fire banished the bitter cold, she shivered a little when that last blanket lifted away. He pulled her out of bed but did not let go. Instead, he wrapped a blanket around them both and held her close against his chest.

"What did you dream while we were sleeping?" he asked. Jinna nestled into the hollow of his throat.

I dreamed that I was searching. For you. And I found you. And I held you. And I loved you. I love you still.

But she said, "I don't remember," and twirled out of his embrace. She checked the door. Locked, as she suspected. They were fed, comfortable. Again, or still, captive.

Egalfo was sitting at the table, already tucking into the food.

"I'm ravenous!" he said, his mouth full. "I feel like I haven't eaten in weeks."

"Me too." Jinna took the other stool. The food looked filling and homey, like something her mother would make. While Egalfo piled his plate again and again, Jinna picked at the little she put in her plate. It was not just unsettling dreams robbing her of her appetite. There was something more. She could not remember. And it had to do with the huntress...

The door banged open.

"Fine morning, is it not?"

In walked a tall woman as beautiful as the huntress was hideous. She was buxom and muscular and scantily clad despite the frigid air. Her hair

233

swayed long and silky and black as the grave. But her eyes were the same cruel, ice-chip blue. Unmistakable and frightening.

Flopping over the armrest of the chair beside the hearth, legs spread wide and swinging, she stretched like a kitten after a nap. The thigh-length shift hitched up to her waist. Jinna grimaced.

"Who are you?"

"Formerly your mistress, now, thanks to the Dakhonne, your host. There is just one small formality I must perform."

"But who *are* you?"

The woman stared. Legs swinging. Lips grinning. Eyes glittering madly. Then she was on her feet again, approaching the table. She smiled, slow and feline. Jinna winced when the woman tugged gently at a lock of her hair, curling it around and around her finger.

"I am one who, if I wished it, could make you and the Therk couple, watch you get hair and hilt like beasts, or tenderly as the lovers you are, and then, when I am wet with watching, I could make you please me in ways you have never imagined. Or I could make you belly ride a dragon and bathe in your blood as it ripped you in two. I am the Chase Queen, Dread Queen, Mad Queen Saghan, trapped in this world of no time or place. And you, my delightful little halfling, were tithed to me, along with your handsome young Therk. However—" Yanking hard at Jinna's curl, the madwoman released her. "I have made other arrangements more pleasing to me. You are remanded to the custody of the Dakhonne. Until you leave my realm, you belong to him. Once you leave the chase behind, so too do you leave your slavery. You may thank the throg for that and not look at me so viciously. I did not create the rules of my realm; I am only compelled to obey them."

Jinna pressed her lips together so hard they tingled.

"It is a small matter now of releasing you," the queen continued. "Come to me."

Like a horse on the rein, Jinna was impelled off her stool to stand before the Chase Queen.

"You too," she said to Egalfo, and he did the same.

"Pity. I could have such fun, playing with the two of you. Ah, well. A woman does as she must to see justice done." She leaned in, blew into their faces, one at a time. Her breath smelled of winter and mint. Jinna's gut clenched tighter than her jaw. She could not breathe. One moment. Two. And then it vanished.

"It is done. You are free to do as you wish, or what the Dakhonne requires. You are no longer my concern."

Straightening, flicking her hair over her shoulders, Mad Queen Saghan headed for the door where there stood a little grey dog, wagging its stubby tail. The woman halted abruptly.

"How dare you come into my presence in so loathsome a form?"

The little dog in the doorway came up off its haunches, tail wagging ferociously. "It is a form you once loved. One you petted and stroked in times of worry and sorrow."

"A form I now despise, as I will any one you take."

"Even this one?"

The dog folded in on itself like a tent without its pole. Jinna's eyes opened wide. The dog's form shifted and grew. It reformed itself and there stood a man. A fine-looking man of middle years, his face was a sculpture of masculine beauty. His hair was dark, his body lean and sinewy and quite naked. Dark hair covered his chest, trailing thinner and thinner until it flourished again at his groin.

The Chase Queen hissed. "Betrayer."

"Never, my darling. Never."

"Liar!"

"Perhaps. But do you still not see, my most dread beloved, just what it is I have done? Can you not praise me for doing the impossible? Come, let us celebrate."

He grinned, taking slow, careful steps closer to the madwoman he taunted. The Chase Queen growled. Every muscle in her body tensed for battle. "Stay away from me."

"Then how shall I take you into my arms?" He advanced, pace by certain pace. "Or kiss you? Or love you? Come to me, my beautiful Saghan, and the pleasures you knew of me in my youth will be as sun shower is to tempest."

"You push too far."

"I do not recall that ever being a complaint."

Jinna could no longer see the man. Saghan's furious body blocked her view. Behind her, Egalfo tugged at her hand. She turned to him and in that same instant heard a sound like a whip snapping.

"I would first open to a boar's rut than to your foul appendage." Saghan stood over the man now on the floor. He was shaking his head slowly back and forth. Blood dripped from his nose. Jinna took Egalfo's hand. They began edging around the pair.

"You loved him in my own bed. In my own guise. You left me to pay for your crime."

The man smiled up at her. He did not wipe the blood from his face. Instead, he came to his knees before her.

"I tried to free you from him."

"You failed."

"But I am here now."

He reached for her, running his hand up the back of her leg. The Chase Queen shuddered but did not move. His hand slid up higher, under her shift, and her head fell back. She groaned. The man, still kneeling, purred. "Let me please you. Let me suck and plunge and prove to you my love. Forgive me, my dread beauty. Forgive me."

"You do not know what you ask of me."

"I do. You know that I do."

The Chase Queen stood over the handsome man, her body trembling violently. The room felt as if all the air were being sucked out of it.

"Forgive me, beloved," he said. "Forgive me and forgive me again. Forgive me for all the eternity before us. I beg of you. There is no pain worse than being parted from you."

Jinna and Egalfo were still too far from the door. The mad queen reached for the man. Her hand trembled. He grabbed it. Devoured it. She did not pull away.

"I will forgive you," she said.

"Run," Egalfo whispered close to her ear. They bolted for the door, grabbed the handle and yanked it closed, cutting off that first agonized scream.

The Vale—10.12.1206
The night is old. As old as the gate. Old as me. Ale sleep dreams nasty but keeps a body from rising up. Keeps hands still.

LINHARE SHIVERED. Waking to the cold was disconcerting even if it had not lasted long. She was becoming accustomed to accepting the fantastic as commonplace; as in fact, Beyond, it was.

The Vale—10.13.1206
Done and done and done. What is one more?

Waking alone, for there was no sign of Rodly snuggled into the quilts with her, she had gotten up, dressed, eaten the food left on the little table beside the fireplace and waited for someone to come for her. When no one came, she peeked outside her doors, only to find two very large, very hairy and quite malodorous guards. To keep her in? Or others out? Linhare decided she did not wish to know.

The Vale—10.14.1206
Small. Sweet. Trusting. One nick and it's done. I'll be free. She promised. Violet, you promised.

Leaving her finger in the page, Linhare leaned deeply into the high-backed chair pulled close to the hearth. Outside, the wind whipped the falling snow into a drunken bolley dance. She remembered snow from that long ago morning in the Vale, the one the memory stones had given back to her. Strange how she did not recall being so cold back then, when she was a child playing at war.

She looked to the door, willing Wait to appear and give her reason not to read the next pages. It loomed—the horror that marked Wait's life. The journal on one side of her finger was thick; on the other, sparse. So few pages left.

The Vale—10.18.1206
    No.
The Vale—10.19.1206
    No.
The Vale—10.20.1206
    No.
The Vale—10.21.1206
    Please.
The Holes—10.22.1206
    Blood on my hands. It burns. I cannot wash it away. It wells. A never ending flow of innocence. I hear you. I hear you. Call death from his hiding place but he will not obey. Go. Please go. Forget me. The hero is a lie. I am Calryan. Ma saw true when I was born. She saw the horror. She saw the evil. Pap would not believe. It would have been better if she took me with her into the sea. She left me to do this thing she saw. Why? Why did you not take it with you?
    I hear you call. I'm sorry. Ben, I'm sorry.

Linhare closed the journal, wiping away the tears blurring her vision. Her heart hammered. Dizzy, nauseated, she breathed deeply. Slowly. Calmer. She opened the journal again.

Vernist-on-Contif—12.30.1206
    It is the turn of the year. Tuliel tells me—

Linhare turned to the prior page. The mad scrawl scratched one passage; the neat hand flowed on the following. No pages stuck together. No sign of anything torn away.

Two months.

Gone.

Sitting straighter in her chair, Linhare sniffed. She flipped through the journal, checking dates. The mad, infiltrating scrawl spotted the pages less and less as she went back in time. And then came the page the book opened to automatically; the page that changed so much.

237

Tassry, off Sisolo—2.19.1206
I was right. I did not want to be, but I was. The responsibility of that is nearly more than I can bear...

History books from her most elementary education through university taught her what occurred on Tassry. An ancient feud nearly thwarted the Unification. A Larguessi house with distant claims to the throne had set in motion events that would culminate in the Tassrian Upheaval, a diluted misnomer for one of the greatest victories in Vales Gate history, and one of its darkest moments.

Linhare knew the epic story, and Wait's official part in it. He uncovered the plot. Yerac'ian warships were repelled. Ealiels Bay, the doorway to Vales Gate, was rescued from certain defeat. In the process, Wait saved his king's life, and the lives of thousands that would have perished in a war the archipelago could not have won. He became the hero of an age. But something else happened on Tassry that no history book told—

"Linhare?" His voice accompanied his knock that moment before the door opened and he peered around the jamb. Heart hammering as if she had been caught prying rather than fulfilling a promise, she stuffed the journal under her skirt before calling, "Come in. Please."

Wait stepped into the room, closing the door on the two oafs beyond. Linhare caught a whiff of them and grimaced.

"I've been waiting for you to come all morning," she told him.

"I'm sorry."

"I've been worried."

"There is no need to worry. Not about me."

"Are they keeping me in here, then?" she asked. "Am I a prisoner?"

"You?" Wait shook his head. "No. You are a most honored guest."

"Then Jinna and Egalfo?"

"They belong to me for the time being. I traded for them."

"Trade? What did you trade?"

Wait patted the hilt at his side.

"Oh! You traded your sword?" Linhare jumped up from her chair. The forgotten journal tumbled to the carpet, a crimson stain on the plush buffs and browns. Wait crossed the room. He picked it up and handed it to her. Linhare's hand responded so slowly. When she took it from him, the book felt strangely heavy. Cold. Slipping it into her pocket, she gathered her courage and looked up at him.

"Wait, I—"

"This isn't mine." He patted the hilt. "Mine went down with the tithe ship. This one belonged to Saghan's father."

"Saghan?"

"The Chase Queen. Her name is Saghan."

"Why did she give you her father's sword?"

"In exchange for Jinna and Egalfo."

Linhare shook her head. "That makes no sense whatsoever."

Wait put a hand on her arm, steering her towards the little table where she had earlier taken a meal. He coaxed her into a chair, then sat across from her.

"Of all the strange and impossible situations we have been in so far, this is the most dangerous." Blowing out a deep breath, Wait slumped. He seemed so tired, though morning was barely leaning towards noon. "We can't leave here just yet. Traveling in this sort of terrain is inhospitable at best, deadly at worst. Saghan suggests we wait for tomorrow, see which of her lands presents itself. She's planning some sort of banquet for this evening."

"A banquet?"

Wait shrugged. "Don't ask what that means. I have no idea."

"What about Jinna and Egalfo?"

"When I left her, she said she'd have them brought to me here."

"Good," Linhare said. "Then we can—"

The door opened and two forms were thrust inside. One fair and furious, one dark and graceful, she fell to the ground while he somersaulted to his feet.

"And you smell like the privy behind the groomsmen's barracks!" Jinna shrieked before the door properly closed. Linhare thought she saw one of the oafs outside sniff at himself, but Egalfo was already helping Jinna to her feet. Linhare launched herself at them.

"Oh, Jinna! Egalfo! You're safe! You're awake!"

She hugged them both tightly; they protested and laughed and pried themselves out of her arms.

"You must tell us what happened from the time Longee took you from Weir," Linhare said. "I want to know everything."

"There is not very much to tell." Egalfo pulled a chair closer to the table and sat down. "The last thing I remember is that wretched throg telling us he would take us somewhere safe. After that," he raised his hands, shrugging, "nothing but dreams I can't really remember."

"What about you, Jinna?"

"That's about all I remember, too," she answered unconvincingly. "The madwoman said we belong to Wait until we leave her land, whatever that means."

Egalfo grunted, leaned in to ask Jinna, "Who was that man, do you think?"

"An old lover, sounded like." She shuddered. "Whoever he is, better him than us."

"Better him than you what?" Wait said, just as Linhare asked, "What man?"

WAIT TURNED AWAY FROM THE MIRROR, SATISFIED. No sudden sprouts of wart or mole or goiter; no pointed ears, rat nose or wormy mouth; the boogle remedy for unwanted facial hair was a success. His hair had grown longer than he preferred to wear it, but whether prolonged superstition or a change in preference, Wait left it alone. He was himself again. Queensguard. Clean. Adequately dressed for the first time in weeks. He no longer felt tattered and dirty.

"I'd forgotten what you looked like without the beard," Egalfo said from his side of the mirror. "Very dashing. Linhare will be pleased."

"All this time here, and I've never seen a whisker on a boogle. I just assumed they were naturally hairless." Wait turned his back to the mirror. "And it's going to take a lot more than a clean face to please Linhare. She took the sibbet's trouble too hard."

"Ah, and he changes the subject."

"Pardon?"

Egalfo smiled and shook his head. "Your re-found dashingness. You are quite modest for a hero."

"I'm not a hero."

"There is a whole country that believes otherwise. And so does Linhare. Whatever the creature's trouble, she will appreciate—"

"Enough."

"Fine, fine, fine. I will not go on about your dashingness or hero-ness. I am in maddening good humor. Must be all that...dreaming."

Wait nodded but said nothing. Egalfo came closer.

"Aren't you going to ask me what kind of dreaming?"

"I think I can imagine well enough."

"Not by half, I assure you." Egalfo laughed heartily and did a little dance. "All this time at odds with her and all it took was a desperate throg, a curse, and an eerie twilight world to turn her heart back to me."

"Don't get too confident, Egalfo. Jinna is still Jinna, no matter what you dreamed."

"There you go, trying to spoil my good humor."

"I've known her a long time. Make her feel caught, she'll bolt."

"Then I shall have to craft a net so subtle and so lovely she will not mind."

Wait pretended to inspect himself again in the mirror. Egalfo was not the fool he pretended to be. Whatever his dreams, he knew Jinna too, probably better than Wait ever could. "I'll be in the antechamber. It's too wet in here."

"I'll be along in a few moments. I'm waiting for someone to bring me a comb and the unsnarling cream I was promised."

"Boogles seem to scorn hair in general," Wait called to him. "Beware of whatever lotion they give you."

Egalfo ran a nervous hand along his luxury of hair. Heading for the draped archway leading to the antechamber, Wait startled when a cat or a creature quite like one darted into his path and away. The castle was full of the Chase Queen's servants, fae creatures he had no names for. He wanted this day to end. He wanted night to fall and morning to present hospitable terrain to cross. Being in this place recalled impotent years in the Vale after so much time adventuring.

Flopping into a deeply cushioned chair, Wait stretched his long legs out to the warming hearth, tried to relax. Linhare was likewise preparing for banquet. He respected her wishes and tried not to hover, but kept his senses ever-diligent. Dread Queen Saghan had given her word they were all safe from harm, just as he had vowed to carry her father's sword, but she was as mad as she was cunning. Wait did not trust her beyond that. Not her, her land, or her intentions. And though it occurred to him that her changeable world could potentially open up to one closer to home, he would not ask. Anything outside of their bargain could, most likely would, tip whatever balance she teetered upon for that desperation to see justice done.

"Dread Sir?"

He sat upright. A young boogle stood near, holding a leather pouch out to him.

"You left this in the other room. I assume that you would like to have it back."

"Oh. Yes. My thanks." Wait reached out and took the pouch. Smiling a fanged and unsettling smile, the boogle lad nodded, took a step back and inclined his head before hurrying away. Once the lad was gone, Wait spilled the contents onto his palm. Dolies still left from the stash Ezibah had given him. A bit of thick string experience taught him to hold onto. And the curious blue stone from the forest pool that he had tucked into the pouch when his clothes were taken away and discarded.

Egalfo's sudden protests emanating from the bathing room suggested he was no longer quite as enthusiastic about the unsnarling cream. Wait chuckled to himself. The fire was warm, the balance maintained, and the Therk could take care of himself.

Lifting the blue stone between forefinger and thumb, he held it up to the firelight. It did not pulse or wriggle, even if the dancing flames made the iridescent veins sparkle. Ghosted memory of visions conjured flickered in his mind's eye. His fingers warmed. The sensation oozed up his arm, as if waiting for permission to continue. Instead of falling unbidden into another vision, Wait beckoned, *Come.*

Ellis's weary voice softly replaced his own.

It is no use.

Then the man's image formed, far worse than haggard; he was little more than a corpse now. Emaciated. Filthy. So far removed from the man Wait knew.

We cannot breach the assault. All entrances and exits are ensorcelled. Sealed tight.

All? Yebbe. Her breathing, laborious. Her words, barely audible. *Not all, Ellis.*

It opens into the castle itself, Yebbe. What will we do then? We have discussed this.

Then we must discuss it again! We have no other choice.

There is always a choice, but that is not the right one. What will happen if we escape this trap only to be caught within the inner ward? I will tell you what will happen. She will send her soldiers through to slaughter every man, woman and child in the mines.

Sorcery then, Yebbe growled. *If it is sorcery being used to trap us here, we will use sorcery to get out.*

The mines are unstable. They will collapse if you expend that kind of disparate power. We will all be killed. It is what she wants.

Either way, my friend, it is what she will get. If we must die, let our deaths mean something. Let them be her undoing.

Tears welled in Ellis' eyes. *But there are so many.*

And that is why there will be a great outcry in Vales Gate. She is already losing her grip. If she martyrs us all, even those Larguessi still backing her claim will turn against her. We will die, but we will win.

Ellis looked over his own shoulder to the people there. Wait could see men and women and children all as dirty and haggard as Ellis himself. When Yebbe spoke again, her voice was as soft as death's gentle lure.

There will be victory. That must be enough. This is all that is left to us, my dearest friend. Let us do it together. For Diandra and Ben. For Linhare. For Vales Gate.

Ellis turned away from those he would sacrifice. He nodded. Then he reached out his hand. A smaller one took it. Wait could see Ellis, the Holes, the others to be sacrificed along with them, but no Yebbe. Only a hand. Only a voice.

"Very pretty." Egalfo's voice startled Wait from the images. "What is it?"

Wait closed his hand around the stone. "Just a rock I found. You ready?"

Egalfo spread his arms wide. "Do I look ready?"

Rather than the fire-eater's costume, Egalfo wore clothes more like Wait's. His hair was slicked back and smoothed into a braid. The boots upon his feet were not mismatched and patched but handsome and whole and buffed to shining.

Rising from the chair, Wait tucked away the dolies and the string and tied the pouch to his sword belt. The stone he buttoned into the breast pocket of his new shirt, safe against his heart. It wriggled like a cat into a cushion.

"Wait? Something wrong?"

"Not a thing," he said. "Let's go."

Night settled upon the castle. Hedgehog Chamberlain had been waiting for them in the stairwell just below the entrance leading back into the castle proper while Wait and Egalfo finished in the baths. He nodded approvingly.

"Quite suitable," he said. "This way, gentlemen."

Oil lamps lined the hallways. Now and again a great wheel of candlelight radiated gently from the ceiling. Pushing open the doors to the great hall, the chamberlain preceded them inside. He bowed. "Your guests, my queen."

The Chase Queen and Jinna sat at the table, but Wait only acknowledged their presence in the most rudimentary part of his mind. There was only Linhare rising to greet him. Dressed all in red. Blaring color in a world suddenly melting around her.

Wait took slow and measured steps, forcing himself to breathe normally, holding tightly to the hilt of his borrowed sword. He, who feared nothing, was afraid. This woman, this beloved, this queen he had sworn to protect undid him like no battle, no betrayal, no beast or brute ever could.

He came around to the chair left empty beside her, nearly tripping over a basket tucked close enough to the hearth to be cozy, far enough to avoid singeing the rather large cat sleeping within it. The animal picked up its head and yawned, then it curled in around itself as if the world did not exist. Wait focused on the tawny creature, willing himself calm. When Linhare reached up to cup his hairless chin, Wait leaned into it instead of jerking away.

"Do I know you, sir?" she asked. "I'm not sure I know this hairless face."

Wait smiled. He turned his face so that he could kiss the hand on his chin. Linhare nestled into him. He held her close without the sensation that he was doing wrong ruining it.

"Oh, enough." Saghan was motioning him disgustedly into his seat. "I liked you better with the beard."

Wait did not respond to the Chase Queen now avoiding his glance. Letting Linhare go, he held her chair for her until she sat, then took the one beside her. Egalfo stood beside the empty chair between Chase Queen and Jinna. Saghan turned to him, holding out her hand to him as a queen to her subject. "You may seat me."

Egalfo bowed gallantly over her hand. "I am humbled by the honor, Your Majesty."

"I am certain you are." Hungry eyes worked their way up and down Egalfo's young body. Jinna scowled but Egalfo smiled, not in the least unsettled. Saghan then clapped her hands for the boogle servers waiting along the wall to begin serving the feast. "I understand your desire to be away as soon as possible," she said as plates and goblets were filled. "The morning should present a much more hospitable environ for you to travel in. I will see to an escort to guide you to my border."

"I have been thinking about that," Linhare began. Wait's gut clenched. He tried to tap her foot under the table, and missed.

"Thinking about what?"

"Well, you see, Queen Saghan, when we were set upon the chase, we were actually trying to find our way home, to Vales Gate. Do you know it?"

"Wait told me of your...troubles this morning."

"Then you might understand why I would ask, since your realm exists outside of anything Beyond or Away, if perhaps you might know a way for us to..."

"The Dakhonne has given me his word." Saghan did not look up from cutting her meat even if her knuckles whitened. Then her head lifted slowly. Unblinking eyes fixed upon Linhare. The knife in her hand danced a staccato on her dinner plate. "It is not a matter of opening a door and moving through. Away is everywhere Beyond resides. And Beyond? Away! Do you see?"

"Forgive me, I did not mean to—"

"Ask no forgiveness!" She shrieked, the knife flying from her fingers to clatter against the stone wall. "The answer to your question is no. There is no way from here to anywhere but the Grasslands of Alyria. The Glass King's domain. He lords over the edge of the world. He is also my jailor. It is his sworn task to ensure I never escape. Thus there will be soldiers waiting for you as you depart. Do not be alarmed and do not fight them. They will take you to the Glass King. You will go to him. You must."

"As prisoners?" Wait measured his words carefully. "Or as guests?"

"That will depend upon you." Saghan leaned forward to pick up her goblet, drained it of wine. "The king's Eye sees all," she said. "And it will take you home again, if you ask it properly."

She looked to Wait, her mad and amused grin for him alone; a joke shared that he did not know and could not guess. Setting her goblet down again, the Chase Queen rose. Everyone rose with her.

"Sit. Enjoy the feast. I find myself bored with it all. Living a solitary life for so long has made a recluse of me. Perhaps I shall see you before you leave. Perhaps I shall not. I wish you all a good journey, and good fortune wherever you end up."

Kicking her chair out of the way, Chase Queen Saghan left the table. Hedgehog Chamberlain hurried towards her, but she kicked him out of the way as well and left the hall alone.

THE CASTLE WAS BUSY ALL HOURS OF THE DAY, but deep in the night the silence reigned the same way it did upon the Siren's Curse. Disquieting thoughts born in such silence allowed Linhare no more than a doze.

Do not talk about Rodly.

Wait's warning had drawn a reluctant agreement from her, and Linhare stuck to it despite the longing. Now her mind would not let it go. Where was he? Was he injured? Was he even alive? She had seen nothing of her little pet since the treepiggen in the jungle. What Wait told her, what Jinna and Egalfo said, held no bearing on the bonds night and affection created.

Slipping out of bed, she tucked the blankets gently back around Jinna softly snort-snoring. Red curls splayed across her pillow. Images rushed out of memory, from those days when they were very young. Linhare thought nothing of waking her friend in the middle of a sleepless night then. Jinna thought nothing of being woken. Some of their best conversations happened in the dark, amidst giggles between the sheets. Not tonight. They were not girls anymore.

Tiptoeing across the room to her bag of belongings resting against the armchair, Linhare tried to make herself comfortable, tried to read Wait's journal. The mad words danced in the half-light. The sinister voice behind the scrawled words echoed in the silence of this enchanted castle. Snapping it closed again, Linhare thrust it back into her bag.

She leaned into the chair, eyes on the beckoning door. Maybe, if she were very quiet about asking, she would find a nighttime servant who would tell her what had become of Rodly. Better judgment protested, but Linhare nevertheless slipped quietly from the room. Outside, the two oafs standing guard were asleep, leaning one against the other. Despite their smell, they were quite sweet. A smile had won them over.

Linhare half-expected Wait to come bolting out of his room when she stepped past the guards and into the hallway. Only a smaller version of her darling oafs stood guard at his door. He—*or is it a she?*—likewise slept. Linhare hurried off before she could change her mind.

Empty. Peaceful. Though it was still icy-cold, Linhare feared nothing of the dark. She wandered, almost forgetting the task she set for herself; but no night-time servant appeared to beg answers from. The castle was not simply sleeping; it was dead to the world.

Reaching a pair of great doors she recognized, Linhare pushed them open with a soft *whoosh*. She stepped into the Chase Queen's hall.

It seemed smaller now. Almost cozy. The feasting table cleared and spotless, dishes and cups and cutlery neatly stacked on the sideboard, and a fire's dull, warming crackle burning in the hearth pulled a sigh from Linhare's throat. She sank into the chair set before the fire, unable to recall if it had been there earlier or not. She basked like a lizard on a rock. Wait was right; the sibbet was not her little pet. Rodly was a being capable of loving and choosing and he had done both. What happened between Saghan and him now was their own affair, and none of hers. And though these thoughts caught at her heart and threatened tears, Linhare's eyes batted once, twice.

"Can you not sleep again, dear one?"

Linhare startled from her doze, twisting this way and that. The cat that slept through the feast was awake and gingerly but thoroughly grooming itself. It picked up its head. "I'm afraid I do not have it in me to tell you a story tonight."

"Rodly?"

The animal yawned. He was a big cat; bigger than Kish, though not as fine and fat. Not a housecat after all, but something once feral that might have lived in a tree or a cave. He did not come out of his basket.

"Of course it is me. Who did you think I was?"

"Oh, Rodly!" Linhare fell to her knees beside the basket but startled back again when the cat shied away, hissing.

"Forgive me, dear one," he said quickly. "As I have told you, instinct is bound in the forms I take."

"I've been so worried."

"Worried? Whatever for?"

"Jinna told me—us—" Linhare bit her lip. "She said you were injured."

"As you can see, I am not. Oh, I will admit that my beloved's forgiveness was a bit more than I reckoned for, but worth it in the end. Now come scratch between my ears. I am glad to be able to see you again before you leave. I fear that my Dread Beloved is quite jealous of the love I bear you. I would be surprised if she allowed me to say a proper good-bye."

Linhare reached for the cat. Rodly leaned carefully into her caress. She could feel scabbed-over welts on the skin beneath his fur. He mewled when she ran her hand along his side. "Gently now, dear one. Gently. Oh, yes, thank you. That's very nice."

Linhare began to cry. "Oh, Rodly! I can't bear it!"

"Hush, now. Hush. A good scratch is all I need."

"But how can you love someone capable of doing such harm to you? Don't stay here. Come with us."

"Come with you? After all I have endured to be here? No, my darling-dear. I can't." Rodly lifted his head. "I love her. I would do anything for her. Anything. Even abandon you, who I have loved as well as any sibbet can love."

Linhare smoothed the soft fur between his brows. "I am the one abandoning you, and after you were so good and sweet to me."

"Dear Linhare," he said after a moment. "Believe that to your own peril. I am all she says I am. I am a liar, a deceiver, a betrayer. I tell you this because you mean quite a good deal to me; and even that is a lie I cannot begin to explain to you."

"Don't say such things."

Rodly moved away from her caress to ball himself into his basket again. He lifted his head from his paws. "The only truth I can tell and it is the only one you do not believe. Ah, Little Queen, do not say you were never warned. Now go back to your bed. Morning comes. I need to rest."

Chills slithered up her back. Linhare wiped her eyes with her fingertips. She left the hall-no-longer-a-hall without looking back. She closed the door to a cottage kitchen like Ta-Yebbe's. A shuttered window let sunlight through its slats. Pushing open the shutter, Linhare looked out onto a dewy garden overflowing with pinks and purples and yellows and reds. And green. So much green.

Like the Vale.

But there were no trees, only stretches and stretches of green meadow dotted now and again with color, or another cottage. Chimney smoke rose beyond the hills, proving others she could not spy. Somewhere close by, a cow lowed. If she listened carefully, chickens clucked.

Linhare hurried back the way she had come, through the cottage as vast as the castle, as the jungle compound, to where Wait, Jinna, Egalfo and their guards slept.

There were no guards now. Not her sweet, odiferous oafs. Rather, there were three dogs curled round one another. They picked up their heads as she came near. Tails wagged. Linhare stooped to their level, holding out her hand for them to sniff.

"There now," she said once they were vying for a pat. "Easy, little ones."

Wait's door opened. Though anyone else would have seen a calm and composed man in the doorway, Linhare knew better. His hand grasped the hilt of his borrowed sword. His face fixed like stone. He asked, "What are you doing out here?"

"I couldn't sleep. Look, Wait! We are in a cottage this morning. Outside looks something like the Vale, something like the Farmlands. I don't remember the southern half of the island being so green, though. I remember it being more golden."

Wait's mouth opened, but he closed it again without speaking. Linhare rose to her feet. The dogs whined for her attention. His taut shoulders eased as he took her into his arms. Something of the look glimpsed in his eyes brought the chilling, mad voice scratched into his journal to mind. Then he let her go and he was Wait. Linhare was ashamed to feel grateful.

"It's time for us to leave here," he said. "Wake Jinna."

Opening the door to her shared room, he waited for her to step inside then closed the door gently in her face.

WAIT TOOK DEEP BREATHS. He flexed his fingers, stooping to pet the dogs warily wagging to be petted. He did not feel proud of the control he had displayed; he felt wrong. She was his to protect, no matter what she wanted otherwise. But he tried. For her, he tried. It got harder, each time he succeeded in quelling the fury.

"I see you like dogs."

Wait came slowly to his feet, turning to the deeply feminine voice behind him, to the young woman standing there, hands on hips. Chestnut hair, skin like cream; shorter, curvier, and dressed today like a milkmaid from Urnsy, Saghan's ice chip eyes seemed out of place in a face so soft.

"I am partial to them myself. Good morning, Wait."

"Good morning, Saghan."

"I've come to bid you a proper farewell after all."

"I'll summon the others."

Saghan waved her hand. "You. I came to bid *you* a proper farewell. The others do not concern me. Though you may wish the Little Queen a good journey on my behalf."

The Chase Queen came closer, her hands clenched upon her hips. A masculine stance, once again out of place in this version of her, but it made Wait more comfortable, somehow.

"You sell yourself cheaply, my friend," she said. "Content to be watchdog for so Little a Queen. Does nothing of this Beyond tempt you to take what is your due?"

Wait did not answer. She let her hands fall from her sides.

"Very well," she said. "Our bargain has been struck. Guides and supplies await you outside. Be away as quickly as you are able so that you reach the borders of my land before night falls and the transition begins. Farewell, Wait. May all your journeys lead to someplace better. May my father's sword serve you as well as it did him. And may your visit with the Glass King be all you, and I, hope it will be."

"Thank you, Saghan."

"Do not thank me," she said. Clicking to the dogs, the Chase Queen turned her back on him and said no more. Wait watched her go, the dogs scampering and whimpering at her heels. Besides the three he had petted, there was another dog, a little grey one that did not earlier notice. It nipped at Saghan's skirt as she walked, and she bent to pick it up. It yelped, but its stumpy tail wagged more furiously than the rest.

Stowaway

GIANOSTALIA SLEPT HIDDEN among crates and barrels during the day, and only moved about in the vast belly of the ship to find food and water in the hours between midnight and dawn. Though the thick mist of those hours resembled the substance buoying the Siren's Curse, it was not quite the same. It bore a sentience, a longing, a hunger greater than her own, and kept her below when a breath of fresh air seemed too tempting to resist.

She tried tracking the days but lost count. The meager, half-rancid bits of food she scavenged gave out. Did Moslo forget her? Had he been making a joke when he left the hatch open for her? One he never imagined she would take him up on? Whatever it was, those first urgent pangs threatened to break her. It was death to stow away on the Siren's Curse. The legend was as clear as Hepheo's brutal reputation. Fear kept her in the hold, even as hunger gnawed her to the bone, until it was venture to the galley or die.

Treading the desolate deck, avoiding the mist that clung like fingers, Gia could not reach the galley without passing Hepheo, solid and strong at the helm. Hugging rail and rope, barrel and shadow, Gia made her way past him. She kept low, where the mist drifted heaviest; she stumbled and splayed flat on the deck. The mist gathered thick around her. Hands grabbed at her, or tried, but found no purchase. Gia shook off the hunger hallucinations, listening for any sign of Hepheo's approach. His boots squeaked as he rocked heel-toe, heel-toe. His raspy hum whispered with the mist. Gia relaxed. Crawling to the helm deck wall, she pressed flat against it. Step by silent step, she made her way beyond it before her pounding heart got the better of her.

Victual aroma nearly made her swoon the moment she cracked open the door leading down. Meat. Bread. Savory somethings and sweet nothings. Scent reached her taste buds. Her mouth watered. Gia took slow, careful steps. Would licentious old Moslo still be up and working? Or safely asleep? If he wasn't, Gia was prepared to give him whatever he asked for a single slice of bread and his silence.

Light proved someone's presence. The clink of cutlery and the bump of trenchers hit her belly like a blow. Gia wept. Silently. *So close.* Fisting tears away, she prepared to go through with her own silent promise.

"It is safe, Gianostalia."

The gentle, familiar voice reached out for her, pulling her into the open. Not old Moslo, but Vespe Neciel stood at the enormous washtub, her arms in it nearly up to her shoulders in suds. "Sit," she said. "Eat. There is food on the block for you."

Gia did as she was told, forcing herself to move slowly. Cautiously. Pulling out the stool, she sat down to the trencher full of food, inhaling it like air at first, then slowly and cautiously ate. She remembered the pain of a stomach too long empty, and too suddenly full.

Neciel finished washing dishes. She dried her hands on her apron, hung it on a peg before coming to sit opposite Gia.

"I help Moslo from time to time," she said. "Washing dishes soothes me. It was my chore in the silent village, and one I requested when I began my training as a Keeper. And," she smiled, "it gave me good excuse for being here in the galley after curfew."

"Curfew?"

"The hours between midnight and dawn belong to the mist, Gia. Did you not know?"

Gia shook her head, swallowed the food in her mouth. "Where is Moslo?"

Neciel gestured over her shoulder. "He sleeps quite a lot. He is very old, after all."

Chewing. Swallowing. Eating more. Gia concentrated on her meal, prepared for her by Neciel. How many nights had she set a place for her, only for it to go untouched? Instead, she asked, "How is the throg faring?"

"Well enough. The Keepers see to it that he is not mistreated. Brodic watches over him."

"Brodic does?"

Neciel nodded. She cocked her head, waiting. Gia set down her spoon. "How long have you known I stowed away?"

"Almost immediately," Neciel answered. "Just not soon enough to thwart you, unfortunately."

Gia grimaced. How long had it been since she woke to find the woman's silent face hovering over her like a williwisp delivering a dream? Since that one green eye pulled from her every secret she ever kept? A year or a thousand, no one could know her better than Neciel.

"You could have brought me food," she said.

"I could have."

"Will you tell Hepheo?"

"Only if I want to see you dead."

"I am a Purist and a peacekeeper of rank. He can't—"

"He can," Neciel snapped. "And he will. You are a stowaway on his ship. Hepheo will flog you and feed you to the sea if he finds you. As he *must*. As you *knew*. Why, Gia? Why did you do this foolish thing?"

Gia licked her greasy lips. She picked up her cup, drained it, avoided Neciel's gaze at all costs.

"You know why."

Neciel heaved a heavy sigh. "It has been many years since he left you in my care. Turned his back on you when the cursed loesh was eating you alive."

"Maybe he's yet another curse I cannot resist."

"That is not something to joke about."

Gia set her empty cup down, sopped up the juices and drippings in her trencher with the last bit of bread. "Who's joking?"

"You are a fool," Neciel told her. "One that will stay hidden because I am as big a fool as you. Moslo will keep you here. He is quite fond of you. Hepheo never ventures into the galley. He takes his meals on the deck, or in his habby with Ezibah. When we reach Alyria, I will get you off the ship. What you do after that is up to you."

Gia put her head in her hands, pushing the hair back from her face. *What have I done?* "I'm sorry, Neciel. I truly am."

The Vespe rose from her stool. She placed gentle hands upon Gia's shoulders, a kiss to the top of her head. "I have asked the green what is to become of you. It tells me nothing. Garbled words. Distorted visions. I do not know if it is the lingering loesh still seeped into your blood and bones or your inherent chaos, but all it was once able to see of you is gone."

"Maybe—" Gia turned on her stool. "Maybe the loesh devoured me from the inside. Maybe the green can no longer see into me because I do not exist. Just a shell. Just flesh and bone and poison. Maybe I am dead, and simply do not know it yet."

Neciel wrapped her arms about her, pressing cheek to cheek. She held her close and rocked back and forth.

"A bird is a bird, Gianostalia, even if its wings have been clipped. It remembers flight. It still longs to soar, even if it cannot fly. But feathers grow back. It simply takes time to remember how to use them."

Moslo pressed a finger to his lips when he saw her in his galley, though Gia was close to certain Neciel knew about his hand in her manifestation on the Siren's Curse. She would stay in his habby through the daylight hours. It was a sacred place, the first boards and nails of the ship being hammered in place there, or so he said. No one entered without the permission that Moslo never granted.

"For a taste of that pudding between your thighs, I'll let you share my space," he told her, and then stepped aside and ushered her through, kissing her cheek before sending her to bed alone and unmolested.

No windows. No doors but the one she had come through. A seaman's trunk. A chair. A bed made of leather stretched between posts. Moslo's habby nonetheless exuded the sacredness he claimed. Whether it was so or simply the safety it represented, Gia was grateful for this comfort.

There was not a daylight hour that the blind old cook and his scullery crew were not working. The Everwanderers came to eat in waves, and one meal no sooner finished than the next needed preparing. Being men of open sea and fresh air, most of the crew took their meals above board rather than hunker down in the cramped galley. In the days of her confinement, Gia saw Brodic only once, through a crack in the habby wall. White hair tied back, uniform replaced with a sailor's gear, he appeared younger than he did in Weir.

Through that same crack, she saw all of the crew at one time or another; she came to know their faces if not their names. She glimpsed the throg, stronger and less anxious, often in the company of Neciel's Kept, Danle. Hepheo, she saw not at all; nor the Keepers but for Neciel, whose visits came further and further apart.

"Mind you don't touch the eels I got roasting in the embers." Moslo stumped about his galley, checking pots and prodding the eels wrapped in thick fronds harvested from some tropical tree she never heard of. They had fallen into an easy routine; Gia sleeping through the day, and Moslo leaving her chores to keep her busy through forbidden night. No one came to the galley before the first of the scullery mates in the earliest morning hours, and by then Gia was long hidden in the sacred habby.

"I won't touch them." She grimaced. "They smell disgusting. Do I really have to breathe that stench all night?"

"Mind your manners, woman. They're a special treat for the Captain. If'n they don't stay in the embers all night, they're not going to be worth eating."

"A thousand years in the embers is not going to make them worth eating. I must tell you, old man, that I much prefer your lewd comments to your pecking. Who knew you could be such a hen?"

"Give me something to crow about and I'll show you what a cock I can be."

"One of these days, I am going to surprise you and give you what you ask for."

"Empty promises and cruel teasing. That's all you give me."

"I've never promised you a thing." Gia tugged at the old galley cook's beard, then kissed his cheek. "Go to bed. I'll mind your stinky eels."

"Now who's a hen?"

Alternately grumbling and cackling, Moslo stumped into his habby. In the weeks they had been sharing it, Gia straightened it up some; and though he complained about the fresh bedding and the minty scent of his clothes, he no longer woke raw and bleeding from scratching at the flea bites he endured in his sleep.

Gia set to work peeling, cutting and chopping. If Moslo's scullery crew thought anything of so many of their chores being done in the night, they didn't say anything. She thought she once heard a young sailor remark that old Moslo's kitchen was never so clean and orderly, but she might have been dreaming.

Moving from station to station in the dead quiet of night on the Siren's Curse, storing prepared meats and vegetables in the ice room that neither seemed to empty of food, nor lose its chill, Gia forgot about the pungent stench of roasting eels. If felt good to work. Soothing, the way washing dishes soothed Neciel.

As if thought could summon her, Gia heard footsteps on the stairway leading down into the galley. She smiled, wiping her hands on her apron and setting the kettle onto the fire. Grabbing two chipped mugs from the cupboard, she tossed in a fistful of herbs, calling, "It's about time you came to see me."

"Well, well," a raspy voice answered. Gia spun, and froze. Hepheo closed the ground between them. "Maybe it is at that."

His grip was an iron band clamped too tightly upon her wrist. One good twist, Hepheo would break her arm. Gia did not struggle.

I have done what I have done. I accept the consequences.

Some deep and weary part of herself sighed.

"Y'can't do this Heph. Y'just can't."

"You are sailing stormy seas yourself, old man," Hepheo growled back. "Stay out of this, before I forget what you are."

The Captain yanked harder on Gia's arm. She heard a bone snap. Pain shot through her, but she did not cry out. Moslo's ongoing pleas became dim natterings. Gia heard them only as a whine. Like an insect. Or wind through a reed. She stumbled. Hepheo yanked her to her feet. Again the snapping, the pain. Then oblivion.

When Gia came back to her senses, her wrists were bound. She was lashed to a mast, arms high up over her head and feet off the ground. All her weight pulled apart those broken bones. Her torso was bared. White skin against white mist. She shivered. And then she heard the swish of the cat o'nine tails before it raked across her back. Gia bit back her scream.

"Hepheo! Stop!"

The voice paused him, but Hepheo did not stop. Another swish. Another lash. Another swish, this one stunted. Gia's head lolled. Her vision blurred.

"You cannot do this."

"Go back down to Danle. This is none of your concern."

"She is a Purist!"

"Only half-a-one." Hepheo growled. Gia heard someone stumble. Then the swish again. When the lash landed this time, Gia groaned. "There can't be no exceptions!" *Swish.* "None! Go below. Now. And tell the old man—" *swish,* "—that if he sends anyone else up to interfere, she gets worse."

"If you kill her, it will be a mistake you will regret, Hepheo. By the green I swear it."

"I won't be the one killing her!" he shouted after Neciel as she fled. "The sea will!"

The lashes came harder now. Furious. Hepheo grunted and growled as he beat her. Whether for the draining mist or her draining life, Gia no longer felt anything. She heard the swish and squish as the tails sailed back and again, as it bit into skin already pulped. Her broken arm came apart. Maybe it even fell off. She did not know.

I am ready. Please! Finish me!

One more lash. Just one. *Swish.* No squish. She tried and failed to pick up her head, to see why the blessed end had not come.

"Cut her down."

Brodic's icy voice cut worse than the lash. Gia wept. Softly.

"Get back, Brodic. This is my ship."

"Cut her down."

"She is a stowaway. There can't be no exception. You ask me to betray my ship. My crew. Everything!" Hepheo spoke through labored breath. Perhaps because she was so close to death, Gia heard desperation where she knew there was fury. She felt it in the lash.

"It is not a request. It is a demand. Cut her down, Hepheo. Now."

"You will make me stand down. On my own ship. For what?"

"You brought this on. You could have let her stay in the galley. No one would have known."

"I would have. I am Captain of the Siren's Curse. The penalty to stowaways has been the same since a'fore either of us was born."

"This time, it will be different. Cut her down."

Pain slithered through her body, intensified. Gia was trembling so that she wept strangled sobs.

"Cut her down yourself," Hepheo growled. The pound of boots on boards. Then nothing but the wind and the sound of the Pilfer always churning out the mist keeping the Siren's Curse afloat.

"Help me." Brodic's voice was thick. Two pairs of gentle hands took her down from the mast.

"You had no choice. He'd have killed her."

"That would have been his last mistake."

"But you must understand the burden of this Curse."

"You think I do not?"

Neciel's hands were sure and warm. She touched Gia's splintered arm and instantly, momentarily, the pain soothed. "It is broken in two places, but the bones have pulled apart. I do not know if I can fix this."

"We will do what we can. Help me to lift her."

"It would be better not to move her. I can dress her wounds here."

"No. We must get her out of sight and make her a rumor Hepheo can quell before anyone else knows of her presence. Help me, Neciel. Or leave me."

Excruciating. Agony. Brodic and Neciel lifted her torn and broken body from the deck. They carried her only a little way before descending into stairwell or under the water, or into the Abyss itself.

The haze, the lightness of being, the euphoria—Gia remembered these. Her body had somehow separated into parts. Her head floated in the rafters, her limbs in the far corners, her torso somewhere near the heart of the world. In her mind, a song that these disjointed parts swayed to played.

Pain, too was a separated part. Gia saw it there, bundled on the floor in a drawstring bag. A black bag, velvet and corded with a golden tassel. It looked very heavy, even if it was quite small. It whispered to her.

Fool. What did you hope to gain?

Your favor. Not the bag this time, but a pitcher there on the table just visible in Gia's periphery. *Or your forgiveness.*

Do not put this on me. She was always reckless.

So were you once.

Was I? The bag sighed. Gia saw its sides puff out and deflate like a bellows. *Twice now I brought her to you when I could not help her. Forgive me.*

You did not bring her to me this time. I came of my own accord.

To your own peril.

There is little Hepheo can do to me.

The drawstring on the bag unwound itself. From the velvet lip something like the mist crept out. It fingered its way across the floor, towards the pitcher dripping condensation onto the table.

I would kill him for what he has done. If I could.

But you cannot. And he had no choice. Even Hepheo is bound by conditions he cannot alter. Just as you are. Just as I am.

She isn't. She never has been.

And that is why you love her.

Love? The bag jiggled when it laughed, spewing more of the mist that now rolled along the floor; buoying the pitcher, the table it sat upon, Gia. *If what is between us is love, then it is something I wish to purge myself of as she was once purged of the loesh. It is a dark thing. A destructive one. I want nothing to do with it.*

But it will linger forever in your blood and bones. You can turn it around, though. Love can be made good.

I do not believe that.

The mist from the bag was nothing like that above. It proved no sentience, took no form. Gia could no longer see the velvet bag, the pitcher, her separated body parts. The mist enveloped all. It filled her nostrils, her lungs, her mind. It pulled her back together again. It made her feel her arms, her legs, her torso. The pain. Excruciating. Her back blazed. Her broken arm throbbed. She could not feel the fingers of that hand at all. Somewhere, so far outside of the pain, someone wept.

It is time to dose her again.

Gia lay prone on a cot, her arms splayed from her sides like a sacrifice. Her face poked through a hole in the mattress. Straps held her down. Sobs and pain wracked her body. Writhing made it worse.

"Kill me," she whispered. "Please."

Then Neciel's face appeared underneath the cot. In her hands a cup, a reed poking up from it. "Drink this," she said. "All of it. Hurry."

Gia did not ask what was in it. She knew. Memory was beginning to work out hallucinations. Sucking at the reed, she drank everything in the cup. The taste was sweet, not bitter. The effects instantaneous.

As she drifted away, as the enveloping mist crept back towards the black velvet bag, Gia felt fingers in her hair. She felt a kiss on the back of her head. A whisper.

My own curse. My only love.

Words retreated in the mist. They scrawled long and lovely, elongating as they were sucked in; as if they did not want to leave her; as if she could not let them leave.

Grasslands

THE OAFISH ESCORT PROVIDED by the Chase Queen halted at the fringe of trees. As meadow had abruptly given way to forest, so now did forest give way to plains. Wait looked out to the dusky, unending horizon. There was nothing there. No village. No spiral of smoke to indicate one. No soldiers or Glass King. The oaf grunted, waving them away.

"Your queen said there would be soldiers here to meet us," Linhare said. "How are we supposed to find our way to the Glass King across that?"

The oaf chuffed and shook his massive head. Gentle, gigantic hands pushed her gently forward. Wait's hand went to his sword hilt, but the creature only chuffed again and pointed to the plains.

"We've not enough provisions to last more than a day or two," Jinna protested. The oaf only pointed more insistently.

"It's no use," Egalfo said. "Come on. We might as well get started."

He stepped out of the trees and into the tall grass. Turning, waving them forward, Egalfo vanished with the next step.

"Egalfo!" Jinna shouted, bursting out of the trees and after him. She, too vanished. Wait grasped Linhare's hand before she could follow. "Give your queen our thanks," Wait told the oaf. Bowing its shaggy head, it ambled off into the trees.

"Ready?" he asked her. Linhare nodded, but held tighter to his hand. Walking straight ahead to that place where both Jinna and Egalfo went, Wait heard a popping sound. The forest behind him vanished and they stood surrounded by the vast plains.

"Thank the stars and starlight." Jinna threw herself at Linhare. "I thought we'd gotten separated again."

Wait scanned the darkening horizon from glowing west to darker east. North, then south, and there, upon a rise the deceiving terrain hid, was a rather large creature. And another. One more, and each carrying riders barely discernible against their size.

"There," he pointed just as the last of them started to descend that deceptive rise.

"The Glass King's soldiers?" Egalfo suggested.

"Let's hope so." Lifting his sling bag from his chest, Wait waved it over his head.

A single soldier dismounted from the lead animal. Wait could discern no eyes or ears or legs on the shaggy, bovine creatures. Each one carried three handlers. A rider carrying a long pole perched between its shoulders. Two more, like counterweights, held the reins from baskets on either side.

"Field Ranger Jahvi," the soldier introduced himself, a hand pressed to his heart. Sky-pale eyes were only slightly less eerie than his skin shimmering like sunshine on a still lake. But he smiled when he said, "What keeps the four of you out into the Grasslands at this time of day? You're too far outside the settlement to make it back before dark falls and the tawnies come out."

Wait took Linhare's hand as she opened her mouth to speak, gave it a slight squeeze. *What is your game, Saghan?* Though she looked up at him quizzically, she remained silent. Thankfully, so did Egalfo and Jinna.

"We rode out this morning," Wait told them. "The day got away from us, along with our horses. We were just trying to decide what to do when we saw you coming up over the rise."

"Lucky for you that we did." Jahvi's smile deepened. "And lucky for us you turned out to be lost travelers and not the flash-fire I feared. Let me guess: you're new to the settlement. In from some city on the coast?"

Wait laughed, surprised that it was genuine. "Along that current, yes."

"Where are you from?"

"A small fishing village on the northern coast," he said. "Crone's Hook. Do you know it?"

"If it isn't in the Grasses or Alyria, I don't know a thing about it," Jahvi answered. "Well, then, we were on our way back to camp when we saw the flash. Allow us to escort you there. It's not far. Tomorrow, we'll get you back to the settlement."

"Thank you." Wait stepped forward. "My name is Wait. This is my wife, Linhare, her lady-cousin, Jinna, and our friend, Egalfo."

Jahvi bowed his head to the women, then to Egalfo. "You're a long way from home, friend."

"I am?"

"Did you come down from Therk by sea? Or across the desert?"

"I—uh—by sea."

"I was skeptical when I heard of the caravans wending across the desert. I can't see how it's possible."

"The very reason I came by sea," Egalfo said, glancing sidelong at Wait.

"Come, then. The shigga will carry you from here. You must be exhausted, being out here since morning."

"You want me to ride on that?" Jinna asked. Wait shot her a glance. She amended. "I haven't been able to gather the nerve to do so since we got to—to—the settlement."

Jahvi laughed and the shimmering of his skin intensified. "They are big, but gentle creatures. Most newlings are a little leery at first." One of the shigga lowed mournfully, a deep sound like cattle lowing. The others echoed. Shaggy heads turned and bodies sidestepped.

"Tawnies." Jahvi glanced up at the fading daylight. He motioned them to follow. "We must hurry."

The creature's heavy gait swayed them side to side. Wait felt like he'd been hit in the gut by the time they reached the dun-colored tents only visible for the fire burning in the midst of them. He dismounted gratefully, helping Linhare to do the same.

"Go to the fire with Sal." Jahvi gestured to a man descending from his basket. "Eat. I will arrange a place for you to spend the night and meet you there."

The shigga and remaining Rangers continued on to a holding pen opposite the half-circle of tents, leaving the four of them to make their way to the fire, an area cleared down to soil that billowed around their ankles as they walked. "Isn't it dangerous to keep a fire?" he asked Sal.

"Less dangerous than not keeping one," Sal answered, patting a shaggy-shigga flank as the animal passed. "Tawnies fear fire and nothing else. We are careful. And Rangers are skilled fire fighters."

"I imagine they must be."

Wait's stomach lurched suddenly. Sal grasped his elbow, steadied him. "Nauseous?" he asked. Wait groaned. Sal nodded his head knowingly. "A shigga's gait is deceptive. It seems like a gentle rocking, but it can be unsettling."

Wait took long breaths. The nausea gripping his belly eased. "I've weathered stormy seas on ships no bigger than the shigga and never got sick."

"A shigga is not a ship." Sal laughed. "And the grasslands are not the sea. You will become accustomed to it. You must. Horses are fine modes of transportation in the settlements, but out here in the Grasslands, the shigga are the only reliable way."

"Like camels in the desert," Egalfo offered.

"Exactly like that. A bit of food should help to settle your belly."

Wait did feel better after eating. Sitting around the fire with a dozen or more Rangers, eating food cooked over the blaze contained by a screen that kept down all but the tiniest lifting embers, settled his mind. These men knew nothing of who they were or where they came from. Why had Saghan lied? Or had she? Once they were alone in the tent Jahvi secured for them, he would discuss it with the others. He was enjoying the pretense of being Linhare's husband, the company of men as kin to soldiers as those on Sentry Rock, and watching the curious colors shimmer along their features like Therkian glass when the light hit just right. Soon enough, the crackling fire had more to say than any of those around it. Field Ranger Jahvi pushed wearily to his feet; his men did the same. Standing, offering Linhare a hand, Wait tucked her arm through his and murmured his good-nights.

The tent interior was warm and neat. It housed the gamey scent of the shigga and the sweet aroma of newly cut grass. Signs of longtime use showed; a wearing there in the corner; a patch in the roof. Obviously and recently emptied and cleaned, the interior held nothing but blankets carefully spread over mounds of grass. Wait dropped down among them, gestured the others down, too.

"That was interesting." Jinna spoke first. "Thank the stars and starlight we all caught on quickly."

"But I don't understand why the Chase—" Linhare looked quickly over her shoulder "—why *she* would say there would be soldiers to take us to...to *him*. And it is just a little coincidental that they were right there when we passed through."

"Could she have somehow arranged it?" Egalfo asked. Wait raised his hands for silence, motioned them in closer.

"I don't know why she would lie, or *if* she lied. Maybe that's how it was, once. *She* said something about being forgotten, about centuries passing since her imprisonment. Maybe she has been forgotten. Jahvi said he feared a flash-fire. Maybe he did see a flash, and it was some trigger no one remembers anymore. Or maybe she's just mad and made it all up. For now, we are lost travelers."

"That means tomorrow they're taking us to that settlement," Egalfo said. "What do we do then?"

"We convince them to take us to Alyria instead," Linhare said. "*She* said that the king's eye will show us how to get home if we ask it properly. And Egalfo was recognized as a Therk. It's a long way from here, a long way from Vales Gate, but it exists in both worlds. That means—"

"—that means we can get home. Linhare!" Jinna whispered a squeal. "You're brilliant as a star and twice as sparkling!"

Wait did not tell them that the distance between Therk and Vales Gate was not simply an endless sea. There were maelstroms to weather and sea creatures as big as a boat, bearing tentacles strong enough to drag the Siren's Curse under the waves. The lands in between were not always friendly, and pirates loved nothing more than a queen to ransom. He knew. He'd done it once, when he was very young. Still, it was a chance, the best one they'd gotten so far. If it took ten months or ten years, it was a step closer to home.

LINHARE WOKE DEEP IN THE NIGHT, eyes wide and heart pounding. There it was again; the screech that woke her.

Dreams, she thought. *And tawnies.*

What had she been dreaming? Linhare rolled onto her side. Firelight still burning outside their tent bloomed across Wait's profile, his hands tucked neatly behind his head. The even rise and fall of his chest proved his slumber. Peaceful, even if Linhare knew better.

Her fingers hovered a breath above his cheek, his chin, that scar along his jaw almost hidden by the stubble speckling his chin. She made invisible circles over his heart, gauging the depth of his peace and coming as close to touching him as she dared. She had, on the tithe ship, learned the extent of her power over him. How close they came; if not for the sibbet's call they would have, and all the days and nights thereafter; and she, who thought such things would never again be agreeable, desired it with all her heart. Her hand trembled, dropped back to her side.

"I love you," she whispered, as she did so many nights when he lay sleeping beside her. He never woke, never heard her; yet it always sounded loud to her own ears. Wait would not hear her until she fulfilled her promise.

Rolling up onto her elbows, Linhare took the journal from the bag she'd been using as a pillow. She found that last place where she left off what seemed like an age ago.

Blood on my hands. It burns.

Whose blood? Linhare turned the page.

Vernist-on-Contif—10.30.1206

It is the turn of the year. Tuliel tells me that it is time to put the past to rest. I do not know how I will be able to do this, but for her and for Ben, I will do as I am bid to the best of my ability.

She sits now, in the corner of this tranquil room. Watching me. Her concern makes me love her more than I did a moment ago. It is not love, she says, but a deep sense of gratitude. I am too young—I, who am so, so old—to love her. And she is beyond me. A Purist. One foot in this world; one in another. I'll never be able to reach her. As she told me in that voice like rain and wind, my own and only love awaits me in the future. I have no choice but to trust her wisdom, but I will love her nonetheless.

She watches me, her eyes coaxing me onward as they once coaxed me from madness. I don't remember those first days here on the mountain. I am told that my festering wound made it difficult to distinguish delirium from insanity. Now that I am lucid, now that Violet no longer lurks in the folds of my mind, I know that delirium never had hold of me.

History hails me a hero. A boy of twenty-one discovered a treacherous plot, saved his king from assassination and foiled an invasion begun a generation earlier. Larguessa Violet and her cohorts paid for their betrayal with their lives. Yerac'ian war ships were turned back at sea. Vales Gate remains free.

The scholars have made a good job of recording the Tassrian Upheaval, already analyzing it, putting it into perspective. They say nothing of the innocent blood spilled with the treacherous. They say nothing of a king's transgression. They say nothing of the hero who did not return triumphant, but mad and seeking more innocent blood. Few know those details. Ben and Ellis did a politician's work of making sure of it.

These are the events I must record. Tuliel says that if I do not, they will remain locked inside my head, only to undo all the work she has done to contain it. Instead, this journal that records all that led up to it will contain it, until such a day as Time deems it appropriate to release. There is magic at work, I know, for at the end of each recorded event I must prick my finger and mark it with my blood. I do not understand magic. It is never something I thought too hard on. But here on this mountaintop the Purists have made a believer of me, even if I am no less ignorant.

I am stalling. It is time to begin...

A rusty brown splotch marked the bottom of the page. Blood. Magic. Insanity. A king's transgression. No insight. Only more questions with answers she feared more than the unknown. Linhare closed the journal. She clutched it to her chest. She breathed in the scented grasslands, exhaled thought, until dreamless slumber fell.

PALE DAWN OVERPOWERED THE GLOW OF FIRELIGHT, waking Wait to a silent, dewy world. Condensation rolled from pitched ceiling to low walls. Beneath him, the blankets were damp.

Jinna snored softly beside him. Beyond her, Egalfo slept on. Wait rolled over to face Linhare and found her back to him, shoulders hunched as if she had fallen asleep crying or frightened. Coming up onto his elbow to lean over her, he saw the red journal lax at her breast.

Taking it from her open palms, Wait tucked it beside the bag she used as a pillow. He would not wonder what horrors sent her into slumber. He did not have to.

Rising, graceful and silent, he left the tent. Jahvi and his Rangers were up, trying not to be obvious about loitering near his door.

"Good morning, gentlemen." Wait nodded to each.

"I trust you slept well?" Jahvi asked.

"Very well. Thank you And now I need to piss, so if you could point the way..."

The shimmering men laughed. How easy it was to fall into the camaraderie of soldiers. Jahvi spread his arms wide. "There is no nicety out here in the grasses. Piss away, just don't go too far afield. Tawnies hunt at night, but you can never be too careful. Then join us for a meal. A good bellyful of mash will help with the motion sickness."

"You're suffering for riding the shigga?" Otis? No, Sal, Wait remembered; he had a small, faint birthmark just underneath his left eye. Didn't they discuss it yesterday?

"I suppose I'll find out today if it persists."

Excusing himself, Wait moved off beyond the ring of tents to relieve himself in the grasses as vast as the sea. A contented sound, part purr and part growl, turned his head. Tucking himself in, he slowly crouched to a squat, scanning the tall grass for a break in its uniformity; and there, so close he could scarcely believe he was still alive, was a large feline grooming massive paws. Claws as long as fingers extended when it licked between its toes. Dun colored, like the grasslands. Like the tents. Like the mash waiting for him at the fire. Wait watched the muscles ripple beneath its coat as it groomed itself, rolled contentedly onto its back. A female. Swollen teats attested to kits waiting somewhere. Hidden. Vulnerable.

Wait's brand of invisibility did not fool the animal, for she suddenly rolled onto her haunches, golden eyes pinpointing him, bloody muzzle twitching, smelling. And then she was gone, taking the remainder of her prey with her.

Wait stood upright. All he could see of the retreating tawny was the parting of grasses as she fled. When he was certain she was gone, he inspected the site of her feast. Bones. Blood. And clothing.

"ALL OF MY MEN ARE ACCOUNTED FOR." Jahvi stood over the gruesome pile, grimacing. He nudged a bit of fabric with his boot. "But that is a piece of a Ranger's uniform."

Jinna hugged her arms close about her body. *Killed and eaten. How gruesome.* She let go a deep breath.

"Is there another camp nearby?" Wait asked, pulling her attention away from the pile.

"A few. I'll send word to those nearest. Someone's gone missing. This will not stay a mystery long."

Wait and Linhare stood together over the victim's remains, arms about one another. Jinna wrinkled her nose, moving away from the fire, where those bits and pieces had been gathered. Egalfo was off with some of the Alyrian soldiers in the hopes of glimpsing the magnificent tawny. Jinna was not interested in tempting *that* fate.

Rangers watched her pass, or bowed if she caught pale eyes. Jinna was no fool; she was like a sugar confection in a bakery window to these men. She could have any one of them. Every one of them. In Vales Gate, that notion would have thrilled her.

"Has the tawny attack frightened you?" Jinna turned to the Ranger's voice.

"It's unsettling," she said. "You're Sal, right?"

"As far as I know." He grinned infectiously. "May I ask you a rather bold question?"

"I like rather bold questions."

His grin spread wide. "What are people like you doing in a dull little settlement in the Grasslands?"

"People like us?"

"Women as lovely as you seldom choose a life of such hardship," he said. "The little...one seems a bit unsuited to life in the grasses. She is far too refined. And Wait, he is the large man, yes?"

"Yes."

Sal blew a breath through his lips. "A waste of such power, if you ask me, putting it behind a plow. And the young Therk seems a bit...colorful to take up with the dour settlers. Could it be you are...how to put this delicately...hiding?"

"Hiding? From what?"

"A jealous husband. Bad debts." Sal glanced side to side, leaned in to whisper, "The law?"

Jinna snorted laughter. "No, we're not in hiding, just looking for something we thought we might find here in the Grasslands."

"And you did not."

"Not so far." She gestured Sal closer, spun her tale as close to the truth as she could manage. "Linhare is from a powerful family that would have married her to an enemy to keep the peace. I helped her to run away. Wait followed to fetch her back. Egalfo followed me. Once they found us, they decided to run with us instead of dragging us home. We're not *hiding*, exactly, but we're not looking to be found, either."

"So you chose the most distant, boring place in all the world to settle in."

"Something like that."

Sal laughed softly. "Fair enough, but you are too out of place among those stalwart settlers and their religious piety. Why not go to Alyria instead?"

Indeed. Jinna hid her smirk in what she hoped passed for surprise. "We thought about it, but feared it too well-traveled."

"Ships come and go, but you'd be less obvious there. And it's still at the edge of the world."

"But how would we get there? Our horses ran back to the settlement yesterday, and they were borrowed anyway."

"Several of us are on our way out of rotation," Sal told her. "Too much time in the grasses can drive a body mad. There's a rumor going about that King Atony himself has requested Jahvi for his personal guard. I can, if you'd like, put in a good word for you and the others."

"Oh, Sal!" She gripped his arm. "I could kiss you!"

"By all means—"

Jinna shoved him away, laughing when he laughed. "Thank you. I can't wait to tell the others."

"I'll go speak with Jahvi now. The tawny attack put us behind, but he's already made arrangements to have you escorted back to the settlement."

"Thank goodness for the tawny attack, then!"

Sal's cheerful smile curled wickedly. "Thank goodness, indeed."

Shivers crept up Jinna's spine. Sal's shimmering face seemed suddenly darker, his pale eyes hazy. She stepped back. "I didn't mean— that was not nice of me to say."

"I will speak with Jahvi," he said. Inclining his head, Sal turned and walked away. Jinna rubbed at the chill prickling her arms. She saw Wait and Linhare break away from the morbid gathering as Sal led Jahvi away by the elbow. Shaking off the last of that slithery feeling, she trotted up to meet them, taking Linhare's hands and spinning her about.

"I think I just got us a ride to Alyria."

"DRINK THIS."

Sal slipped Wait a skin bladder.

"What is it?"

"Something that will keep you from getting sick to your stomach. I've been riding these beasties for most of my life and I still get a little queasy before the end of the day. It's eight days to the coast. It'll help. And if it doesn't, I owe you a cup."

"Won't you need it?"

"I have more." Sal patted his chest and Wait could see the outline of a metal flask hidden there beneath his shirt. "Take a good pull now before we set out. When the squizzy feeling in your gut takes a poke at you, take another swig. I'll tell you right now that you'll never taste anything more vile. Like the water your ma washed your dadda's week-old socks and smalls in. But you get used to it."

Wait uncapped the skin and took a sniff. It smelled as bad as Sal promised it would taste. Giving the skin a good squeeze, he tried not react, but his eyes watered, and he gagged and laughed at the same time. "Stars and starlight that is awful!"

"Told you, didn't I? But it'll help. Honest."

"Thanks, Sal. I appreciate it."

"No thanks necessary." Saluting casually, Sal walked away, limping slightly. Wait slipped the skin's strap over his shoulder and headed for the mounting stage. Sal was already climbing gingerly into one of the side baskets, Otis into the accompanying one and Mannit into the saddle. Jinna and Egalfo were being assisted into the litter strapped to the animal's back.

"Exotic, isn't it?"

Wait looked down to find Linhare at his elbow. She smiled and looped her arm through his. "Jinna is a wonder, isn't she?"

"She has her moments." His gut gurgled. Wait could not suppress the need to belch. Linhare giggled.

"Sorry," he said. "Sal gave me a revolting tonic to keep my stomach where it belongs. It's unsettled me some."

"How very nice of him."

"It was. If it works, I'm in his debt."

"We'll see soon enough." Linhare pointed and Wait saw another shigga coming their way. In the saddle already was Jahvi. The baskets carried two men Wait did not recognize. Pointing with his long pole, Jahvi said, "Dorn and Silpa will ride with us."

A platform was brought forward and locked into place. Wait assisted Linhare up the steps, then climbed in himself. Jahvi tapped the shigga's shoulder with the long pole. The animal swayed into motion, and Wait held on to the mash in his stomach as if it were the last food he would ever consume.

Not only did the tonic stave off the nausea, the taste did indeed become more palatable as the days wore on. Wait came to recognize when it was wearing off and sipped accordingly, allowing him to appreciate the lovely but unchanging scenery, the exotic if cumbersome mode of transportation, and the wildlife they came across.

Linhare's eyes were sharp. She sat ever alert in the litter beside him, pointing out bevies of speckled birds that scattered when she shouted to Jinna and Egalfo on the shigga behind them. She was always first to spot the herds of golden, striped deer blending almost invisibly against the heat waves rising, or the deep brown of the wild shigga they came across.

"You can't tell from this distance," Jahvi said when Linhare pointed out a herd to the west, "but those there are quite a bit smaller than our darling Teena here." He patted his mount's shoulder. Dust and hair rose up into his face. "A tawny couldn't take her down, but the wild ones don't get as big. The tawnies keep the grazers from eating the grasslands bare."

"I can't imagine they'd run out of grass to eat," Linhare had responded. "It's endless."

Endless. And deceptive. It hid all manner of animals they would never see. But Wait heard them at night, like he heard the tawnies. Lying awake in a tent with his companions or under the stars beside the Alyrian

Rangers, Wait heard them. Hunting. Growling contented purrs. Fighting over a kill. Slumber became more difficult to grasp, and shallow. It put him on edge.

Six days.

One settlement and four encampments. Three more victims of tawny attack, each one only just before they arrived to inquire. The Rangers speculated that one animal could be responsible for all the deaths, perhaps even following them in the hopes of another easy meal. It was not unheard of, Jahvi insisted, even if it was not common. Wait had his doubts.

"How is the tonic holding out?" Sal dropped down beside him. "You have enough to see you through?"

Wait was lying on the ground, hands tucked under his head, gazing at the stars. There were so many of them. Were there as many in the sky over Vales Gate? He sat up, shaking the skin always slung over his shoulder. "I think so."

Sal eyed the skin skeptically. "Are you sipping it regularly?"

"Whenever I feel the nausea starting to return. You were right, it doesn't taste so bad after a while."

"Good. Good." Sal leaned back on his elbows. "Let me know if you run low. I'd have finished that and then some by now."

"Let me ask you, Sal," Wait said. "What made you become a Ranger if the shigga make you so ill?"

"Ah, good question." Sal looked up at the stars. "I didn't know riding shigga would turn my stomach to gurgling mush when I joined. Like you, I'm a man of the sea. I grew up beside it, and like so many young men, I wanted something different when I came of age. I joined the Rangers, thinking it was glamorous." He met Wait's gaze now. "But there is nothing glamorous about it. I was often mocked for my fragile belly until I was able to hide it. And that reminds me, thank you for keeping my secret."

"I owe you that much, at least. What will you do in Alyria? Go back to sea?"

"Me? No. My dearest love waits for me. I've left her waiting far too long. I can only hope she forgives me for the mistakes I made as a young man longing for adventure. Ah, the forgiveness of a woman is the sweetest thing there is, eh?"

Wait glanced at the tent where Linhare, Jinna and Egalfo were already asleep. "I hope so, Sal. I truly do."

The camaraderie lifted some of the weariness. It felt good. Natural. A sudden longing for the sea, for the Siren's Curse and Hepheo and Danle and the rest of the crew washed over him like mist from the Pilfer. It made him remember Ben. And Ellis. Old sensations surged through him. Wild, youthful sensations. Wait's cheeks flushed. His body buzzed. He wanted suddenly to burst into the tent, take Linhare into his arms and—

"I'm for bed." Sal's voice chased off longing. "You should get some sleep."

"Soon."

Sal moved off, looking once over his shoulder. Those wild sensations chased to the shadows crept back. Memories of Ben and Ellis and those days before Tassry when they were young men on an adventure seemed so real. He could almost see his friends there in the stars. An ache bloomed in his chest, and for the first time since leaving Saghan's domain, the blue stone in his pocket quivered. Fingertips hovered over the pocket. Wait took out the blue stone. He held it up to the firelight, watched those striations shimmer like Alyrian skin. Only just perceptible. A trick of the eye. Or imagination.

What will you show me this time?

He clenched the stone tightly in his fist. It warmed his hand, his body. Wait began to shake. Images assailed him. Ben. Tassry. Ben. Violet. Ben. Her beautiful daughters. One. Two. Three. More. And the Holes. Always, in the end, the Holes. His vision wavered. Wait sat upright trying to breathe through it. He was in the Holes. In the retreat on Tassry. He was on the grasslands Beyond where he was a Dakhonne of old, unharrassed by memories. And the blood. So much blood. It was in his eyes. In his mouth. He was drowning in it. Wait roared and he roared and he roared.

He blinked.

Firelight. Grasslands. The quiet of a camp at rest. He sat beside the fire, blue stone resting on the palm of his hand. It shimmered. A trick of the eye. Or his imagination.

Wait shook his head. He breathed deeply, tucking the stone back into his pocket. Roaring—real roaring and not a stone conjuring—picked up his head.

An answering snarl.

A weak cry for help.

He was on his feet and running. Through the sleeping camp, past the shigga enclosure. Where were the guards? Why had no one else heard the call? Wait was in the high grass, slapping it aside as he ran ever faster, ever farther into empty wilderness.

"Help!"

Ahead, the dark silhouette of a man. Wait pushed harder. He smelled the gamey scent of the tawny. He saw its path in the grass. His own pulse rushed through his ears. Bloodlust rekindled by striations in stone welled. When Wait dove onto the big cat crouched to spring, he felt the impact, the animal's muscles, the heat of its flanks. He felt the claws rip at him. Bloodlust heaved up from his belly and out his mouth in a roar as bestial as any ever heard in the grasslands.

...We were in the Larguessa's retreat on Tassry, negotiating as we had been doing across the archipelago. Relations with this particular isle have always been strained. Ben was most anxious to soothe this animosity once and for all.

I thought it strange to be there rather than the Seat on Sisolo. Violet insisted it was a place more conducive to friendship than the formality of the main isle. Ben agreed. He could not have known what she had been planning since Diandra's mother sat the throne.

The retreat was quite feminine. The only males were the children and servants. I knew the Larguessa was a widow, but felt certain her daughters were mostly wed. At least two were pregnant.

Violet's daughters, even the pregnant ones, fawned and flattered Ben. At the time, he and Ellis believed their goal was a particular trade agreement the Larguessa wanted made, one her own father had vied for—permission to trade fae tears in Yerac'ia and, in the future, Therk.

Ben was considering lifting the ban on trade with the world outside the archipelago. Illegal trade in these stones is as old as Vales Gate itself. By this time, good runners were on the verge of becoming respectable. Crown-sanctioned trade seemed a logical step. A profitable one.

Violet was as brilliant as she was beautiful. While she wooed and wheedled a king who had all but given her what she asked for, Yerac'ian warships were on their way. It was not fae tears, after all, that Yerac'ia was after, but conquest.

As the Sentinels of Ealiels Bay, Sisolo's mighty fleet was the nation's first defense. Her only defense, in truth. In centuries past, it repelled Yerac'ia so often and so well that invasions ceased altogether. There was no greater or more efficient fighting force. But the fleet was corrupted. Those not corrupted were betrayed. And there is always the vast majority so well trained that they cease to think for themselves and simply do what is commanded.

Instead of protecting the archipelago, the mighty Sentinels were escorting the enemy in. Vales Gate was effectively defenseless, and unaware.

I discovered this by chance, not by some genius, as the scholars lead their students to believe. I, too was being wooed by Violet's daughters. As a young man uninterested in (and frightened by) wily women, I escaped their attentions. All but one. She was persistent. And the first to die. I do not remember her name.

There was a boathouse on a secluded lagoon. I remembered it from an earlier escape. Though an initiated Dakhonne, I was not, am still not, in full control of my abilities. I imagine I will be years and years in the making. But I did have some skill in silence, and it was in this silence I entered the boathouse.

Sentinels, perhaps two dozen, were packed tightly into the two long boats there. I kept to the shadows. Silent. Nearly invisible. A moment after I arrived, my pursuer did as well. I thought I'd lost her.

She looked around, as if in shock. Then, I remember, her face changed. It hardened. She asked why they were still there. Were they not supposed to be out at the shipyard already? There was an exchange that I will not record here. The result is, I learned that the Yerac'ian fleet was less than a day out, and that they would capture and sail our own ships into the bay. The crew in the boathouse had been charged to dispense with the Dock Master. A man in the way of the plot afoot.

Treachery wakes the Dakhan. The Dakhonne within me stirred.

I waited for the sailors to start out of the boathouse before slipping away and into the surrounding brush. She stood there on the small platform, watching the traitors row out into the lagoon. Once they were gone, I grabbed her, my blade to her throat.

She struggled at first, until she saw it was me. She could not have known that the boy she frightened from the feast was already sunk deeply into the Dakhonne. I demanded to know her plan. She laughed. I slit her throat.

JINNA AND EGALFO WERE LONG ASLEEP. Linhare turned onto her side. She would not be able to sleep until Wait crawled into the tent. Then she would feign slumber. Once his tossing and turning proved he dozed, she would do her best to soothe it into true sleep. Perhaps this night would be different from all the others.

There was something very unsettling about his sleeplessness; more so than worry for his apparent weariness. There was a sharp edge to it, upon which he was precariously balanced. No one else seemed to notice. To Jinna and Egalfo, Jahvi and the other Alyrians, Wait was his calm, stoic self. But she was the one who knew him best. She could feel it in the hand that jerked when she slipped hers into it. She could hear it in the rumbled quiet of his voice; see it in his lack of appetite, and the way he'd taken to pacing. Linhare believed the grasslands woke something in him—something wild and untamed. Untamable.

Rolling onto her side, she closed the journal and bound it tightly; perhaps it, and not Wait's behavior, was that something troubling her. She had opened and hastily closed it so many times since the first rusty blood print that the cords were falling to pieces. Little pills of broken up leather rolled between her fingers. Linhare wiggled them clean.

She crawled across the tent floor and peeked outside. If Wait had fallen asleep by the fire again, she would join him. He would put his arms around her as he had never done on the tithe ship, and she would listen to his heart beat until they both fell asleep. But Wait was not there. Linhare poked her head out further. Someone was shouting. Other heads appeared.

"Tawny! Tawny attack! Help! Help! Someone help him!"

Sal sprinted the encampment. Sounding the alarm. Linhare's heart rose to her throat. She could not breathe. She could not move. Then she was on her feet. Running.

"Linhare! Linhare, wait!"

Jinna's voice faded into the chaos. Rangers, both armed and unarmed, uniformed and in their smalls, were running with her. Outdistancing her. Moonlight lit the way. Eerie and ethereal. Her feet were too heavy. She could not move fast enough. Her shift caught in the coarse grass, tripping her.

"Linhare!"

Egalfo caught her round the waist.

"Let me go! I command it!"

His grasp faltered. Linhare pushed through the Rangers circled round and shimmering beautiful in the moonlight, fell to her knees in the midst of them.

Wait was on his hands and knees, panting heavily. Blood dripped down his arm. He heaved himself upright. His abdomen was a bloody smear. At his feet, a dead tawny. A big male. Wait took a step backward and dropped again to his knees, head bowed, gaze on bloody palms.

Linhare did not speak his name. She did not touch him. Hands raised, Linhare moved closer to Wait, squatted down beside him. She touched the tawny's warm flank. There was no wound. Only blood— Wait's. Touching him now, sliding her hand across the expanse of taut shoulders, Linhare caught him when he sagged against her.

WAIT DID NOT FEEL THE PAIN. It was there. Pulsing. *That* he could feel. But not the pain. It was buried too deeply beneath the chaos buzzing through his body to slither its way out. His hands, fingers spread in bloody supplication, were no longer his. They had somehow detached themselves to hover, palms up, somewhere near his abdomen. When had they done so? When the tawny first raked claws through his skin? Or was it not until they felt the animal's neck snap?

Linhare was near. He could sense her too, the way he sensed his hands. Detached from him, not part of him. She would never be part of him. He could not allow it. Shouts. Orders called. The encampment was awake and engaged. Wait blinked.

Linhare. Her name, not her voice. Egalfo's.

Wait felt her presence drift away even as it left that fragile thread always between them, always intact. He would follow it. Later. Back to her. Always back to her. Because no matter how he refused to allow her to become a part of him, he would ever be part of her.

It was so quiet there in the night, in the grasslands. Wind and insects and the faraway activity in camp. Wait coaxed the pain up from the depths. It bloomed like dawn from a central point, spreading, spreading until his whole body throbbed and burned. He gasped. Egalfo, the Rangers, they gathered him up. Gentle as they were, Wait passed out before the Alyrians got him back to camp. When he opened his eyes again, he was on his back. A surgeon stood over him with needle and sinew. He felt no pain, only pressure.

"Rest easy." Egalfo was there at his shoulder. Smiling. "It's not as bad as it looked."

"You bled well," the surgeon said. "I've packed the wounds with crushed biddybulbs and stitched them in. They will numb it a bit, as well as prevent festering. Tomorrow, if you run no fever, I'll take them out and stitch you up properly."

Wait turned his head to the side so that he could see neither Egalfo nor the surgeon. Pain would have been better. It would have kept him unconscious. It would have kept him from grasping the enormity of what truly happened out there in the wild grasslands.

The Dakhonne is awake.

The surgeon finished his work and left. Egalfo remained. Wait was grateful. It was dangerous to be alone, even it if was right.

"I shouldn't have killed it," he said.

"You did what you had to."

"Sometimes that is not a good enough reason."

"And sometimes there is no such thing as reason," Egalfo countered. "There is instinct. You are Dakhonne. Protector. Warrior. Your instinct was to save Ben."

Wait turned his head back to Egalfo. "What did you say?"

"I said you are Dakhonne. It is your instinct to protect. You saved Sal's life, Wait. The tawny would have killed and eaten him like that poor Ranger you found the first morning out."

Wait turned his face away again. "Leave me."

"No."

"Go."

"I am your friend. I will not leave."

"Go."

"You are in no position to make me. I'm afraid you are stuck with my company. Like it or not."

273

Wait would not look at him. He was afraid to. It had been a very long time since he wept. He didn't know how, even if he would. He stared at the wall of the tent, the way lamplight shadows played along the slope of it. Whether exhaustion or the effects of something the surgeon stitched into him, Wait felt slumber creeping up on him.

Nothing of what you are can change the love and honor I bear you, my friend. Egalfo's voice came from so far away. *Rest now. I will watch over you. I will keep you safe.*

No one is safe as long as I am near.

Shadows on the tent wall became images. Old images. So many faces. So much blood. A hand pressed his shoulder. A voice said, *Linhare is. And that is all that matters.*

The images burst into flame that became smoke coiling up into the air, and away.

Wait woke to the dimly lit tent, remnants of ill-mannered dreams, and Linhare's breath upon his face. She slept beside him on the coarse pillow, half in a chair, half on the litter. His first instinct was to smile. His second was to touch her face. Both of which he did before sitting up. Carefully. He fingered the bandages for the wounds beneath, satisfied that he could get off the litter without collapsing to his knees. Swinging his legs over the side, he straightened slowly. Cautiously. There were clothes for him slung over a chair. Wait picked up the clean, whole shirt. Whatever the surgeon did, he'd done it well. Wait felt fine.

"What are you doing up?"

Linhare fussed at his side. She took the shirt from his hands. "No one gave you leave to get out of bed."

"I wasn't aware I needed permission."

"Don't you dare be impertinent!" Tears made her voice shrill. "Don't you dare! Do you hear me?"

Something like joy swelled up from his gut. Wait took her into his arms and held her close. "It's all right," he crooned. "I'm fine."

"I was so afraid."

"I'm sorry."

Wait rocked her back and forth, impervious to the pinches and pokes. Something ancient and wild happened, something that thrilled and frightened him. He remembered Sal's cry for help, the snap of the tawny's neck. And blood. But now Linhare's tears were warm on his skin. Her body fit perfectly against his. She was kissing the bandages over and over; kisses he felt deep in his core.

Wait took her chin in his fingers and tipped her face up. He kissed her then, catching her off guard. His lips met her teeth that yielded instantly, gratefully. Linhare relaxed against him, responded to him. He could climb mountains, build cities, raze them to the ground. He could swim across Ealiels Bay, trek the island of Vales Gate from Lerolia to Aughty. Wait could turn back time if he so chose.

"Ah! I stumble upon unruly passions!"

Wait broke away from their kiss even if he did not let Linhare go. He could feel her looking up at him. She was trembling; he could feel that, too. Like the flutter of a bird's heartbeat. Sal entered the tent, followed by Jahvi and a man Wait thought he remembered as being the surgeon.

"Too soon for that, young man." The surgeon removed Linhare from his arms. "Far too soon. Let me take a look at those wounds."

Wait did not fight him. Linhare took his hand, biting her lip while the surgeon unwound the bandages. He wanted to kiss that lip. He wanted to take her back into his arms. He wanted to move. To do. Anything.

"Nice. Very nice. The biddybulb did its work. Tell me, can you feel this?"

The surgeon pressed at his stitches.

"No. Not really."

"Excellent. The effects should last for several days. By then, you should be sufficiently healed to deal with whatever pain lingers."

"And by then we will be in Alyria." Jahvi stepped forward, hands respectfully behind his back. "And privy to a king's store of medicinals."

"King?" Linhare asked. "As in the Glass King?"

Jahvi's smile became laughter. "Of course! King Atony will wish to thank him personally. You are a hero, Wait. Not only did you save the life of a Ranger, but you rid the Grasslands of a rogue tawny with a taste for human flesh."

"Then you've decided that it is the same animal?" Wait asked.

"Given the evidence," Sal said, "yes, we do. Once a tawny has a taste for human flesh, nothing else will satisfy it."

"But is it not too soon?" Linhare asked. "Should Wait travel in his condition?"

"Another man, I might put back to bed," the surgeon answered. "Not this one." To Wait he said, "The stitches will have to be removed in a few days."

"I will see to it personally," Jahvi answered. "When can we leave?"

"I will see to him again this evening. If he remains as he is now, you may leave with my good graces in the morning."

Sal sat on the litter beside him once the surgeon left, nudging him gently with his elbow. "I haven't gotten the chance to thank you for what you did," he said. "Not while you were conscious, anyway."

"How long was I...?"

"In and out for three days."

Wait looked sidelong at Linhare, who was again biting her appealing lower lip. "Maybe that's why I'm so hungry."

Sal laughed. "Maybe."

"We were all so worried," Linhare told him. "Not even the surgeon expected you to sleep for so long."

"Not sleep, dear lady," Sal told her. "Our hero rested in a healing enchantment, brought out of it by the sweetest of kisses. At least, that is the story I shall tell the lads and ladies in the taverns once we get to Alyria. That'll do me for at least a week's worth of courtesy drinking."

Wait laughed, his stitched belly protesting only slightly. He could not remember feeling better, happier, more vital. Snaking his arm about Linhare's waist, he pulled her gently closer. "You can stop worrying. You heard the surgeon. I'm as good as new."

"He did not say that."

"Will you trust me, Linhare?"

"With *my* life," she said, "but not *yours*. Promise you will speak if—"

Jinna burst into the tent, Egalfo in tow. "Look Egalfo! He's up and about, and you worried like a seacow over her pup."

Behind Jinna and Egalfo came Otis and Dorn, Silpa and Mannit. There was no room left in the tent for the medics attempting to herd them out. They all spoke at once, laughing and teasing so that Wait could not make out what anyone was saying. All he knew was that it felt good to be among these shimmering Alyrian Rangers, with Linhare and his friends; and that despite the fact that the first tawny was female, and the one he killed male, his deed was getting them to the Glass King of Alyria—exactly where they needed to be.

Ghost

SHE WAS A GHOST on the Siren's Curse. A rumor unsubstantiated. Elusive as the mist spewing from the Pilfer. Neciel tended her. And Moslo. Dear old Moslo. He bathed her wounds most tenderly. In his presence, Gia could weep without shame.

Brodic did not come to see her; and thankfully, neither did Hepheo. If Ezibah or any of the other Everwanderers she had known for so many years believed the rumors, they did not come looking for her. Gia did not exist. Not on the Siren's Curse.

She healed in this anonymity. Slowly. Painfully. When she could sit upright again, Neciel propped her with soft pillows that she could scarcely feel against the wounds lacing her back. When she was able to lift her arms again, Moslo let her feed herself. Her left hand was useless. Numb. But it was set as well as it could be and mending.

Neciel insisted that Gia walk a little bit every day to prevent her muscles from wasting away and her lungs from succumbing to illness. Bolstered by the Keeper's shoulder when she would stumble, Gia remembered doing the same many years ago when the loesh fog finally lifted. She had been so much weaker then. It heartened her in a strange and terrible way.

It did not take long for Gia to master the walk on her own, around and around Moslo's little habby or in the galley late at night. It hurt, but the pain was good. It calmed her when murderous cravings edged her thoughts. Hepheo was Captain of the Siren's Curse, bound by her ancient rules. A ship of legend. A vessel older than Beyond and Away. A whole world in itself. Stowaways were beaten and tossed into the sea. It had always been thus. No exceptions. Ever. Until Brodic changed the rules. This she could rationalize. She was a Purist and a peacekeeper. She understood the need for absolute discipline.

She could not forgive.

Seated at the block, hands wrapped around a cup of steaming tea, Gia stared at the scarred surface. Years of chopping, hacking and filleting victuals had pitted the hard wood. Moslo lovingly oiled and waxed it every evening. Now Gia did it. She scrubbed it clean of blood and gristle. She oiled it until it gleamed. Then she waxed it, rubbing and buffing and smoothing until her back ached and her right arm was as numb as her left.

Gia blew steam from her cup and sipped at the tea. Doegrass and sweetpetal. Her favorite. She loved the musky scent of it, the way the sweetness lingered on her tongue. Burying her nose in the aromatic steam, she closed her eyes and let it fill her.

"I knew it was true."

Gia scrambled for the safety of Moslo's habby, falling to her knees. Crawling and scuttling like a crab.

"Lady Superior! Please! It is just me. Throg."

Panic surged, gasping through her body. Gia tried to breathe, to calm. She was on the ground. Shaking. She did not scuttle away again when the hairy little half-man came cautiously towards her to squat at her side.

"What have they done to you?"

"How did you know I was here?"

"I listened. And I knew. Foolish, foolish woman." He reached out to push the white-blonde hair from her face. His hand was steady as it was square. Strong. Gia followed his hand to his sinewy arm, to his broad and hairy chest and finally to his face. No more sunken eyes. No more hollow cheeks. But for the sorrow in his gaze, she would not have recognized him. The Siren's Curse had been her doom, but it was Throg's salvation. She managed to smile.

"You look well."

"You do not."

Gia shrugged, wincing. Throg rose and offered her a hand. She took it, even if he was only half her size.

"You're in danger here," she told him. "Should Hepheo find out—"

"I will take my chances. You were kind to me. You took care of me. I owe you nothing less."

"You owe me nothing at all."

"Oh, but I do, Lady Superior. I do."

"Gia." She averted her eyes. "Please."

He nodded.

Gia walked back to the block where her tea was pooled and dripping. Without speaking, Throg cleaned up the mess and made her a new cup, helping her to the stool and moving her hands to embrace the warmth of it.

"There now," he said. "It is like I never arrived."

"Thank you."

Pushing another stool to the block, he sat opposite her as Neciel sometimes did. Throg did not speak. He only sat. In such a position, Gia could pretend that he was an ordinary man. Hairy, but ordinary, his face round and plain and honest.

"What goes on above?" she asked.

"We sail. That's all. There is nothing out here. No ports. No other vessels, though all would flee from the Siren's Curse, I imagine. Alyria is truly on the edge of forever."

"I always believed it more legend than real."

"What will you do when we get there?"

278

Gia blew across the lip of her cup. "I suppose I shall decide when we get there."

Throg visited her nightly. The broom closet that served as his habby was near enough that he did not have to break curfew or brave the mist to do so. He told her of life above board, all the little intricacies that took place on a pirate ship that presently did no pirating. Bored sailors were good storytellers. Throg passed their stories on to her, as well as all their gossip. It was been this gossip that brought him to her in the first place, even while it kept all others away from the galley. The Everwanderers knew the ghost on their ship was no ghost at all. She was a rule broken. Hepheo's shame.

"Look what I have brought you." Throg no longer announced his arrival. He was expected. Anticipated. In his hands he carried a jar containing a golden substance not quite like honey. He handed it to her.

"What is it?"

"Queen jelly."

"And?"

"Oh, right. Sorry." He took the jar back and opened it for her. "Ezibah gave it to me. It is a salve made from the most precious honey in the hive. Of course, she told me it was to lessen the scars I bear beneath my fur, but mine are very old and mostly invisible. This was meant for you."

Gia took the jar from his sturdy hand. She dipped her finger into the salve. It was creamy and sticky all at once. She rubbed it between her fingers. It absorbed almost instantly, leaving behind a warmth as golden as the salve itself. The ache in her back had subsided enough to ignore, unless she moved too quickly or turned too sharply. At the moment, it throbbed.

"Will you help me?" she asked. Throg took the jar, his hand cupping hers and lingering. The compassion of his face unnerved her. Turning her back to him, she sat cross-legged upon the floor and lifted her shirt very carefully. His gasp made her cringe.

"Oh, Gianostalia," he whispered but said no more. Then his creamy, sticky fingertips touched her back with golden warmth. He spread the queen jelly in circles up and down, side to side. It was sunshine on her ruined back, worked deep into her skin by his strong, kind hands. Gia closed her eyes and basked.

"Now your arm," he said. Gia's eyes came open. Throg stood in front of her, jar in hand. She tugged her shirt down to cover her breasts, blushing to realize it was there his eyes had been drawn.

Unwinding the sling and splint Neciel replaced only that morning, she told him, "It is bent and still somewhat numb. The bones knit incorrectly. Neciel said I will probably never be able to use it normally again."

"*Probably* is not *never*," Throg answered. Still sitting cross-legged on the floor, Gia could look up at the half-man as if he were her own size. She watched his face as he worked the queen jelly into her crooked arm. The warmth seeped in deeply, instantly, down to the bone.

"You've very gentle hands," she told him. "You would have made a good healer."

"I would have made many good things had I not been enslaved since childhood. Now that I am free, I will make other good things."

"How did you come to be Longee's slave? Or is that a question I have no right to ask?"

Throg shrugged. He worked more jelly into her elbow. "I don't remember," he said. "Longee always claimed my own mother sold me."

"You cannot believe him. He is a liar and worse."

"True. But it is not uncommon for a family to sell a second son or daughter to keep the others free. It is a sacrifice my kind has been making for so long that it is a given. I knew from birth that I would be sold."

"I thought you did not remember."

His hand faltered in its work, only for a moment. "I remember some."

Gia let the matter rest. No amount of golden salve would heal the scars he bore. Then he was finished, capping the jar again and handing it to her.

"How do you feel?"

"Quite well. Thank you, Thr—" She shook her head. "You are not an anonymous creature. A nothing. You mean a great deal to me. I cannot keep calling you Throg."

The half-man smiled, his gaze lowering and the skin under his hair blushing. "It is kind of you to say."

"No kindness. Fact. Now then, if you will not choose a name, will you allow me to choose one for you? No one else need know, if that makes you more comfortable."

His eyes came up again to meet hers. "That, Gianostalia, would be an honor."

He was good and kind and even gentler with her than old Moslo; than Neciel; both of whom risked nothing by tending her. She said, "I will think carefully about it."

His smile was crooked. Teasing. "Shall I make us some tea?" he asked. "I heard a rather good tale this evening. One of the Unfettered is in love with a sea witch."

"A sea witch, eh?" Gia chuckled. He offered her a hand. Gia took it, amazed as always by the strength in his smaller frame when he pulled her to her feet. Only when she stood towering over him did she realize he had hauled her up by her left arm.

Gia named him Adai. She told him it was the name of a dear friend she lost a long time ago. One she missed every day of her life.

"He was strong and kind and noble and beautiful beyond words," she told him, "like you."

He had blushed then, and thanked her. Gia meant every word, even if it was only half the truth.

Adai rubbed queen jelly into her skin each night. When the first jar was empty, he brought a second. And though Gia offered to do the same for him, he refused every time.

There was little pain, but for the lingering numbness in her arm. Not even the queen jelly penetrated deeply enough to heal that. She could use the limb sufficiently, if not normally. It was her dominant hand; she would never wield a sword again. Gia was close to certain that did not bother her much.

Though he usually arrived just after misting hours fell, this night, he was late. She paced as minutes slugged. Moslo was already asleep in his habby, choking on snores she could hear where she stood. She could not ask the old man if there was some kind of celebration going on to keep her companion away. Moslo supposedly did not know about Adai's visits. Ezibah did, so Neciel must as well; but she never spoke of him when she came to tend her. And he never spoke of her. When she finally heard him coming down the steps, Gia rushed to the entry; but it was Brodic who caught her. Gia could only stare at him. He looked like Brodic, yet nothing at all like him. The sun had done something to the Purist white of his skin and hair. He was golden, like the queen jelly was golden. He steadied her before letting her go. Gia swayed nonetheless.

"What are you doing here?"

"Would you prefer I leave?"

"Do what pleases you," she said. Turning away from him, she walked back towards the block where two cups were already steaming. She picked up one, hoping he did not notice, and set it into the washtub.

"I know that the throg visits you nightly," Brodic said.

"Why have you come here, Brodic?"

"To see you. To make sure that you are well."

Gia kept her back to him. "You could have asked Neciel. Or Moslo. Or Ad—or the throg. It has been weeks, Brodic. Why now?"

He was silent a long time; so long that Gia thought he might have left. But she did not turn around. She would not give him the satisfaction.

"We will reach the Alyrian Sea in three days time. Alyria itself soon after that. A day, perhaps two, depending upon the winds. That is what I have come to discuss with you." But then Brodic fell silent. His head bowed long moments. Gia could almost hear his thoughts churn. When he spoke again, his voice was gentler, if no less cold. "For your defiance, for the dishonor Hepheo was forced to endure, you are hereby stripped of rank, as well as all your rights and protections within the Commonwealth. You may no longer call yourself Purist."

Gia closed her eyes. Tears fell softly, silently.

"You are now the walking dead," he continued. "You may leave the galley if you wish. No one will speak to you or acknowledge you without risking the same. When we reach Alyria, you are to remain on board. When we are finished in Alyria, we sail again for Weir where you will be formally charged. What you do from there is your choice."

Gia leaned her palms to the rim of the washtub. She bowed her head. "You should have let him kill me."

"Perhaps," he said. "But I could not, Gia. I could not."

She knew, through Adai's gentle fingers, the lacework of purple scars still there after all his care. She could feel every rise and divot now as if traced by phantom fingers. Her ruined arm. Her ruined heart. All she had done for the love of Brodic pooled like sickness in her mind.

Pushing off the washtub, Gia forced her shoulders back. She lifted her shirt over her head, pulled the length of white-blonde hair over her shoulder, bared herself for him to see. She spread her arms wide, though the left would not straighten; a crooked crossroads of limbs.

"Take all that is left of me, Brodic. It has ever been yours to claim. But you cannot have my honor. Ever."

Gia did not hear him come closer, but she knew the feel of his hands too well. The flat of his palms bumped over her disfigured skin. Brodic was rid of her at last. Truly and completely. He would finally have his revenge for once loving someone so flawed. For loving her still.

"Gia." He whispered her name. His hands moved to the flawless skin of her abdomen and there clasped together, enfolding and embracing her. Brodic rested his sungolden head to her shoulder. Gia was so cold inside. Too cold to turn in his arms and hold him in return. Too cold and too afraid. His arms fell away.

Gia did not turn to watch him go. Despite the ruination of her back, the queen jelly Adai diligently applied each night had softened the scarring. It let her feel the golden warmth, his gentle hands; it let her feel the moisture drying on her bare back where Brodic's face had rested. Before he kissed it. Before he left her for dead.

The Glass King

DO YOU SMELL THE SEA, my friends?" Sal's arms spread wide; his head tilted back. He took deep, sighing breaths like a maid smitten in one of Sabal's silly plays. "Only the scent of a woman can tickle my manbone as greedily."

"Did I ever tell you that you remind me of someone I know?" Wait asked. He turned in the saddle behind the shigga's head, grinning at Jinna. Linhare's heart skipped. The tawny attack changed this man she loved. Changed. Reverted. More and more she saw the man her father must have known, the man he was in the early pages of the journal she had yet to open since that night.

Jinna called back to him. "I might be as lusty, but I'm not quite as mad as Sal is."

"I am not certain that is a compliment, dear lady." Sal laughed.

"I assure you that it is not."

"Well, then. I am cut to the core. Perhaps you'd be so kind as to assuage my wounds."

Jinna and Wait and, from the balancing basket, Dorn laughed. Linhare's smile only echoed mildly. Then Wait's face paled and he bent forward. Linhare reached for him, but he put up his hand.

"I'm all right."

He pulled out his flask and took a swig. Sal was shaking his head knowingly. "Drink up, my friend. Drink up. We won't be much longer in the grasslands. And that reminds me, you'll want to keep sipping even after we reach the King's Seat. Wean yourself or it'll be worse." He patted his own belly. "I know."

Dorn poked Sal with the long guide pole. "All these years riding the grasslands together and I never knew it made you sick."

"I suppose you will torture me mercilessly now."

"Do not suppose, my friend!"

Sal leaned in. He winked and he grinned. "Do you see why I kept it a secret for so long? I am doomed, I tell you. Doomed!"

SCRUBBY GORSE AND BRAMBLE began to appear here and there along their route. Soon, the bramble was more in evidence than the tall grasses, now green rather than the whispering gold. By the time the sun rested low upon the horizon, this gorse gave way to a planted avenue leading past outlying farms and estates as neat and precise as the model towns Wait remembered covering every surface in Ben's private rooms after the world was won.

"We will reach the city itself before the sun sets," Jahvi had said, and indeed they swayed into the cityseat of Alyria just as the last hump of the sun dipped below the horizon.

Linhare slept curled into the crook of Wait's arm. She would be disappointed to have missed their entrance, but she slept only fitfully since the tawny attack; he didn't have the heart to wake her. There was nothing much to see, after all. Uncluttered streets. Tidy buildings. Alyria was as urbanely sophisticated as Weir was candidly unrefined. Children played, yet not too loudly. The occasional barking dogs that took to following returned obediently when called. Vendors shouted no wares. Patrons did not push and shove their way to the fore. It was perfect. Entirely too perfect; right down to all the shimmering skin and pale blue eyes watching as they passed by.

The nausea gnawed again. Wait grabbed quickly for the flask, gripped instead the edge of the litter against sudden vertigo. He blinked, and Wait was high atop some monstrous creature. The litter seat burned his hands like sunshine. He smelled the sea, his face instinctively turning towards it, and there, punctuating the city like a blade in a dead man's body, was a castle made all of glass. Beyond it, a roiling sea. A bloody sky.

Wait.

His name? Or a command? As suddenly as it had come upon him, the vertigo and the visions faded. He was standing in the litter seat, his hand upon his sword hilt. The shigga passively slumbered on its feet. The red pall and bloody sky was now a soft spectrum of pastels illuminating the castle like Therkian glass. The sea crashed familiarly. Soothingly. Linhare and Jahvi, Sal and Dorn eyed him curiously. Concerned.

Wait exhaled slowly and climbed down from the litter.

THE GLASS CASTLE SEEMED TO FLOAT UPON THE SEA. Like Therkian glass or the shimmer of Alyrian skin, it glittered pink and lavender and blue in the dying sunlight. There was no symmetry to the points and pinnacles; it simply sprawled as if some artist created each piece and joined it later and haphazardly to a whole, yet it was a perfectly sung note, accenting the symphony of Alyria's otherwise precise architecture.

"Remarkable, isn't it?" Jahvi asked Linhare.

"It's like opening the pages of a picture book and having it float out on a bubble."

He laughed. "Yet it has withstood sea winds and storms for centuries."

Dorn and Silpa, having gone ahead to report to their king, stood waiting for them at the great glass doors swinging open as she, Wait and all the others mounted the white stone steps. Thick walls distorted the city, the sea, and the white rocks beyond, as if they existed under water. It would take more than a sea storm to topple the place. More than an army with a battering ram.

Eyes followed them through the halls, falling most often and intently upon Wait. She, Jinna, and Egalfo could have been invisible, and it was a sensation the Queen of Vales Gate had never experienced before. Only then did it occur to her, suddenly and startlingly, that not one of the Alyrians had ever called her *Little Queen*.

"King Atony awaits you in his hall," Dorn said as they reached another set of great doors, these not made of glass but wrought of silver intricately curved and deceptively sturdy when Linhare touched it. Uniformed guards lined either side. None of these pale eyes turned their way. Bodies at attention. Swords at the ready. A decoration guard, certainly, but nonetheless lethal. "And here I must ask you, Wait, to leave your sword with the guard."

Wait tensed. Linhare's heart thudded. Did his hand shake as he unbuckled his sword belt? He handed it to Dorn, who passed it to the nearest guard.

"I thought I was here so your king could thank me for killing the tawny and saving Sal's life."

"There has not been a weapon in the hall since King Pulos sat the throne," Jahvi told him. "And the very reason why none are permitted in there now. It is a long story, and one I'll gladly share, but for now, I give you my word of honor that your sword will be returned to you the moment you step out of the hall."

Wait held his rigid pose as if fallen under some enchantment. Then his body relaxed as he nodded, turning to offer Linhare his hand. "I know something about protocol and kings," he said, and he smiled, and though it should have made her feel better, Linhare's heart thudded all over again.

They entered the King's hall behind Jahvi and the other Rangers, Jinna and Egalfo only a pace behind them. Tables and chairs trimmed in silver, tapestries depicting courtly life, and guardsman dressed so prettily they might move only in doll-like stiffness melded with the backdrop of sparkling walls and a distorted seascape beyond. At the other end of the yawning hall waited an assembly of ladies and gentlemen as fair and light as the Drümbul had been fair and dark. They lined either side of the enthroned Glass King who, unlike his court, was not dressed in some pastel shade, but in grey. As she came closer, Linhare saw that he was not comely, but scarred, plain. His bald head reflected the light coming through his glass walls, but his skin did not shimmer like his people's. Closer still, Linhare realized that he was not squinting in that light as she first supposed, but missing an eye entirely.

King Atony rose from his throne. He was nearly as tall and broad as Wait, though older and more damaged. Standing upon the bottom step of his dais allowed him to meet Wait eye to eye.

"You are the man who saved the life of my Ranger and killed a tawny with his bare hands?"

Wait inclined his head. "I am."

"I doubted the tale until this moment." Atony stood taller. "You are Dakhonne."

Linhare swallowed her own gasp, a feat Jinna did not succeed. Wait only inclined his head again. "I am."

"Your kind has not been seen at the end of the world in a very long time."

"As I've been told," Wait said. "Or anywhere else for that matter."

"Perhaps so; perhaps no." The Glass King's pale gaze flicked over Linhare, Egalfo, Jinna, and came again to Wait. Offering his hand, he said, "Whatever you are, you have my gratitude for saving one of my men, and an untold number of my citizens. A tawny with the taste for human blood cannot be satisfied by any other."

"Sal is a friend. He was in jeopardy. There was no more to it than that. But you are welcome, my lord. It is an honor to be here in Alyria, and in your castle."

"This must be your wife, Linhare." Atony's smile sparkled in his single eye. Linhare offered her hand and he took it as a gentleman, raising it to his lips. "Welcome to Alyria."

"Thank you, my lord."

Likewise greeting Egalfo and Jinna, Linhare did not miss the way his glance flicked back and again to Wait, his smile faltering when their eyes met and locked. Like dogs contemplating a fight.

"It is not often we get Therks here in the city," Atony was saying. "The last time a ship came in we were treated to some of the most exotic spices Alyria has ever tasted. Your people know how to flavor food."

"I would not—" Wait cleared his throat and Egalfo amended, "—have not been home in a very long time. You make me long for my mother's cooking."

"Mahti."

Egalfo's eyebrow rose. "Pardon?"

"Don't your people say *mahti* instead of mother?"

"Oh, yes—I—I have been away from my own kind so long, the tongue forgets."

King Atony's chin raised a little higher, his nostrils flared a little broader, but he said, "I am a man of plain tastes, myself, though I understand my kitchen staff has helped themselves to the spices left in tribute. If you would all do me the honor, stay. Refresh yourselves. We will celebrate this occasion as it should be celebrated." He leaned towards Egalfo. "Perhaps there are spices left that will lessen your longing for home."

"Sounds lovely," Jinna said. "But a bath sounds even lovelier. We all smell worse than my old gran's hunting dogs. I imagine you have some fine bathing tubs in a castle as grand as this."

The Glass King's brows arched, and he laughed as genuinely as he smiled. "That I do, my lady. That I do. Gerda! Timmot!"

From out of nowhere came a purse-lipped woman and a hunched old man. The woman, Gerda, curtseyed to her king, then turned to Jinna and Linhare, hands clasped primly at her bosom. "I would be happy to see to the ladies, my lord. If you will come this way. Gentlemen, Timmot will take you to the men's baths below."

Jinna grimaced, but tugged Linhare from Wait's arm. He stiffened when her hand slid away, but he did not grab her back. Linhare looked over her shoulder as Gerda led them away. He was not looking at her, but at the Glass King.

"I don't like this," Linhare leaned in to whisper. "Wait did not expect to be so immediately brought before the king."

"I was trying to get the two of you a few moments alone," Jinna whispered back. "I didn't think they'd separate a husband and wife from bathing together. What do we do?"

"We keep to our story, and follow Wait's lead. I only hope..."

"Hope what?"

Linhare clutched her closer, slowed their step. "He's not well."

"He's fine, Linhare. You worry too much. That tawny didn't—"

"Hup, hup, my ladies." Gerda stood waiting at the silver door, pinched face even more so for their lagging. "The baths await."

"I didn't mean the tawny." Linhare said. "He's been...tense. Intense."

Jinna shrugged. "Hasn't he always been?"

"Yes. But it's different, somehow."

Jinna walked silently beside her. They caught up to impatient Gerda, who did not wait, but hurried on, leaving them to follow. "Did you consider, Linny, that it is *you* who has changed?"

"I don't understand."

Jinna hesitated; then, "He asked you to learn his truth," Jinna told her. "I've seen you reading his journal. I've seen you cry. Don't deny it, you do. But don't you see, Linny? You're discovering who he is; not the hero your father called friend, but *Wait*."

"I don't know if that's it."

287

"Trust me. It is. Now that I've learned to see beyond all that desirable flesh to the man he is, I see him differently, too. I see the man who loves you like I'll never be loved."

"Oh, Jin—"

"I wasn't fishing for solace." Jinna waved her away. "Egalfo and I are far too mundane to aspire to what you two have. What you *can* have if you ever finish reading that journal like you told him you would."

"It has been so difficult."

"Of course it has." Jinna looped her arm through Linhare's, quickening their pace. "If love were easy, it wouldn't be nearly as much fun."

WAIT STARTLED FROM HIS DOZE, momentarily thrashing in warm water. He could not see more than an arm's length from his face for the steam; and then it came slowly back to him: the old man, Timmot, had left him there with Egalfo. Linhare and Jinna were in the women's baths. They were all in the Glass Castle of the Alyrian King Atony who was missing an eye, like Saghan's husband had been missing an eye.

Sitting higher in the water, wiping the water from his face, he tried to quell the churning in his gut. His belongings sat too far away to reach without getting out of the water. Sinking lower again, he tried to coax his stomach into behaving.

"Not feeling any better, eh?"

Egalfo appeared out of the steam, wrapped in a huge white bathing sheet. Wait blinked until his eyes focused.

"Not yet."

"Sal was here. He said if you woke up before he got back to tell you not to drink any more of your tonic. He's gone to fetch you something better."

"I'm not too sure I want any more of Sal's tonics."

"He got you through the grasslands, didn't he?" Egalfo smiled. Wait blinked when his friend's image wavered; when he suddenly did not seem like Egalfo at all.

"You don't always have to be invincible. Let Sal help you. He's still trying to thank you for saving his life."

Wait only nodded and slid deeper into the warm water where the churning was at least slightly soothed. Voices drifted through the steam. Egalfo's head snapped up at the sound. Wait squinted up at him, but his vision wavered when the nausea welled. Then Egalfo was saying, "I'll go see who it is. If it's anyone but Sal, I'll chase them off until you're feeling better."

Wait did not get the chance to thank him or tell him not to bother. Egalfo darted into the steam as the voices got louder. Wait closed his eyes only for a moment before his friend, now fully dressed in a pair of soldier's breeches and a clean white shirt, returned.

"How'd you get dressed so fast?"

"I've been dressed and waiting for you for quite some time. Are you all right?"

Wait nodded. "I must have fallen asleep again. Thanks. I'll be fine once Sal gets here with whatever new concoction he has for me. I thought that was him with you. I hoped."

Egalfo looked over his shoulder. "That was Timmot. I'm afraid you make him a bit nervous."

"Because I am Dakhonne," Wait said. "Something is trying to work through my head. Stories I've heard...I think."

"What stories?"

"King Pulos. Heph and Brodic mentioned him. Something about him and his daughter wreaking havoc at the end of the world."

"Jahvi mentioned him, too," Egalfo said, "when they took your sword."

"Saghan's father and Saghan? And Atony is missing an eye. Coincidence?"

"We have an explanation for Saghan's longevity, but Atony doesn't look several centuries old."

"Nothing is what it seems here." Wait blew out a deep breath, pushed water through his hair. "Soldiers found us when we came through, but not to take us captive. Did Saghan lie? Or has the story changed?"

"She's mad as a Danessian prophet, Wait. There's little we can do now but go on as we have, see if the king knows about this *eye* that will tell us the way home if we ask it properly. What else can we do?"

"Sail for Therk," Wait answered. "And from there, home, like Linhare said."

"Only if it's the *same* Therk. Things don't work the same way here. It's like..." He shrugged. "It's like time passes differently. Nothing quite connects."

"My stomach hurts too much to try and figure that out." Wait braced himself on the side of the tub to climb out. "Where is Sal with that tonic?" His arms buckled; he splashed, groaning, back into the water. Sal appeared out of the steam that swirled in eddies around him. "Did I hear someone groan my name?"

"Egalfo said you have a new tonic for me," Wait grunted.

"I did?"

Sal and Egalfo exchanged concerned glances. Wait salivated; he swallowed hard. "Well, do you?"

"As it happens, I do." Sal pulled a vial from his breast pocket, turning it round and round, upside down, swirling the thick liquid so that it coated the glass a lovely shade of green. "It's an old Alyrian remedy," he said. "I have to warn you; it's very strong. You might not feel quite yourself for a while after you take it, but it is certain to dispel the lingering effects of the other tonic I gave to you."

Wait reached up and held his hand out for the vial. "How long?"

Sal cocked his head. "An hour. Perhaps two. No more. I'd say by the time you sit to dinner with King Atony, you'll be your charming self again."

Uncorking the vial, Wait tipped his head back and drank it down, prepared for the revulsion to spread across his tongue and down his throat; but the syrup was sweet and not at all unpleasant. Warmth spread through him, starting in his throat, spreading to his chest and shoulders, arms and legs. Wait smiled up at Sal and Egalfo.

"That's not bad."

"How do you feel?" Egalfo asked.

Wait ran fingertips across his face. It tingled like bees droning between skin and muscle, muscle and bone. Down his stomach that twittered girlishly but did not jolt or gurgle. "I think I feel good."

"Rest is what you need now," Sal told him. "Shall I summon Timmot to show you to your quarters?"

A wry smile curled Wait's lips. Something like satisfaction churned in his blood. "He's afraid of me."

"He's old," Sal said. "I'm sure he fears much."

"He'll rest now," he heard Sal tell Egalfo as the soothing drone spread to his head, lured him towards slumber, loosing memory of claws and the teeth, the gamey scent and strength of muscles and the way bones felt when they snapped. A muscle in his cheek twitched.

"I'll stay with him." Sal's voice was so far away. "To make sure he doesn't drown. Have Timmot escort you up to the gentleman's study. The others will be there."

Through slitted eyes, Wait saw Egalfo nod, look once more in his direction, then turn away. His feet slapped on wet stones like a frog trying to walk on two legs. Then he was a frog on two legs, dressed as Egalfo had been dressed in a soldier's attire.

The steam of the baths thickened, congealed like a membrane, contained him. Wait closed his eyes tightly. Rubbed them hard. When he opened them again Sal was with him inside the membranous steam. Good Sal, watching over him. Smiling.

"LOOK AT ALL THESE PERFUMES!"

Jinna's rummaging diverted Linhare's attention from the mirror, where a maid wound her wet ringlets around a finger at a time. "There is quite a collection."

Uncapping and sniffing at the crystalline bottles, Jinna held one out to Linhare. "Oh, smell this one. It's like a summer breeze!"

Linhare wrinkled her nose, pushed it away. "Too sweet."

"You think so?" Jinna sniffed again. She stuck out her tongue. "You're right. It reminds me of your sister."

Linhare tried not to startle, tried to suppress the immediate rage and grief. She hid it by sliding her arms into the long, elaborate dressing gown the maid now held up for her, and tying it tightly closed.

"What's wrong, Linny?"

"What's right is the better question?"

Jinna put an arm around her shoulders, drew her away from the attendants. "Every day brings us closer to home. We have sailed on a pirate ship, broken a spell, survived a madwoman's domain, and trekked across grasslands as vast as a sea. And now, Linhare, we are in a glass-king's castle. Try to enjoy this a little."

Linhare bit her lip to keep the derision in check. For Jinna, this was a wild adventure; she could not fault her for enjoying it any more than she could expect her to understand. Before she ever fell into fae, her experience was trial and test, not adventure; and more awaited her as the journey continued. She glanced at the bag containing Wait's journal.

"I'm going to rest a bit before the feast," she said. Jinna hesitated, but she nodded and let go of Linhare. Sliding her fingers along the opaque walls, perpetually steamed over for the system of pipes running dark as veins in an old woman's hands, Linhare dropped onto a lounging bed set up against the glass wall. She rested her head to the spongy cushion, careful not to spoil the curls the maid had wound so meticulously. She tried not to think about Sabal or Agreth. About home. And Wait. Always Wait.

Fetching the journal from her belongings, she unwrapped those tethers binding the past away. She opened it to that place where she last left Wait—on the beach, a woman dead.

Rusty blood pressed onto the page flaked.

Linhare brushed it away.

And she read.

Dakhonne

...I went immediately to Ben, but he was already abed. I banged on the door of his chamber, but it was Ellis who came out of an adjoining room. I told him what I discovered. Ben did not answer our pounding. There was no time to waste if we were to assemble what remained of the loyal fleet and counter this attack. Ellis and I shouldered Ben's door open.

I cannot judge my friend. We were years away from the Vale, away from his beloved Diandra. He is a man of passions and vitality. I do not know if it was the first transgression, but it is the first I was aware of.

Our moment of hesitation cost Ben some blood. When the woman in his arms saw us, she pulled a dagger from the sheets. The Dakhan are no more swift than when their charges are in danger. Her blade only glanced his arm as I dove into her. She was dead before Ben could bid me spare her.

I had twice tasted blood; twice tasted the fury necessary to kill. There was a yearning inside me. A yearning for more. Until this wrong was righted, it would build. I did not understand that then, as I do now.

There was no time for recriminations, only time to act. Ben sent Ellis to our men outside the retreat. Ben himself went to the shipyard. Later, I discovered that he was too late to save the Dock Master, but was successful in rallying the loyal sailors. This, too will be recorded in the history books, as well as Ellis' success in reaching our men and loyal Sisoloans. They will tell of the rag-tag fleet sent out to repel the invaders, and their victory against the odds. Know that these are all tales to lure history from her facts.

This is what they do not tell.

HOW LONG HAS IT BEEN, MY DEAR, SINCE WE SPOKE?
Wait's eyes startled open. He blinked, and blinked again. Where was Sal? Wait sat higher in the water, looking all around him. Alone, completely alone in that thick steam. Splashing water on his face, scrubbing the sleep from it, he tried to gain his bearings.

You were just a boy when I knew you. Look at you now.

Wait let his hands fall. In the water before him a memory spilled like blood, coalescing, shaping the voice into a woman.

"You are dead."

A minor nuisance here, Beyond.

Larguessa Violet smiled her famed, feline smile, the smile that betrayed a nation. Death had frozen her in time. Her temples white within the luxury of golden hair, her breasts floating full and pink, she was as gloriously beautiful in her middle years as were all her daughters in their brief, fatal youths.

Have you nothing more to say to me?

She was not real. She was strain. She was fatigue. She was illness tampering with his senses and wounds not yet healed. She was Sal's sweet tonic, and she was dead. By his own sword, dead.

I like this place. It so reminds me of my beloved Sisolo. You remember it, don't you? The plains stretching out to the sea. Violets scenting the air through the summer. I do miss that aroma. I do.

He would not blink. He would not turn away. He would challenge her ghost until it vanished.

You glare so! The ghost laughed. *Have you no humor left in you? You were such a merry young man. Shy, perhaps, but merry. Ben loved you, you know; the merriest man I have ever known. How simple it was to manipulate him. How predictable his actions. It was nothing personal, you must understand. I did what I had to do. It was my own ill luck that you foiled all my plans. And my own folly for underestimating you.*

The ghost turned her head, as if hearing someone approach. And then she smiled so that the pearls of her teeth cast a dozen tiny moonglades upon the water.

Truth cannot remain entombed forever, Calryan. Only long enough. The truth is coming for you. It is coming.

Wait blinked. It was as if someone blew into his face, closing his eyes and catching his breath.

"Something wrong?" Sal asked. Where had he come from?

Wait closed his eyes tight to keep them from crossing. *A dream. It was a dream.* "No. Nothing's wrong."

"You sure? Can you hear me all right?"

"I can hear you just fine."

Wait pushed the heels of his palms to his eyes. They were trying to worm out of his head, wiggling in all directions in their vain effort. Sal. Violet. Violet. Sal. Who was in the steam with him?

"Wait?"

The churning in his gut was on fire now; not painful, frenzied. That fire spread. It consumed his heart. His mind. It made him hunger. Wait remembered that hunger.

"Wait?"

Wait struggled to open his eyes. To focus. He was standing upon the edge of the sunken tub, hands clenched. Naked. The steam was rushing away from him. And there was Sal, whose life he saved, smiling a malicious smile. In his hands, offered like a sacrifice, was the sword that once belonged to Saghan's father.

"Avenge my beloved," Sal said. "Free her from her exile. Kill the Glass King."

...Perhaps Ben believed that he was sparing me, giving me the task of rounding up Violet's household and holding them for questioning. Despite the magnitude of her plot, he did not see the Larguessa and her daughters as a threat. They were women, after all. And children. And I was little more than a boy. A boy who had done this tremendous thing. How I wish he gave me soldier-blood to spill.

Violet was my target. I found her on a balcony overlooking the sea, noted her view of the shipyard. A signal went up. She made a triumphant sound into her crystal glass as she sipped down her victory. I did not fear. I did not hate. I did not feel anything. I am Dakhonne. I serve. I protect. I do not feel.

Even after Tuliel's unlocking, I do not remember seizing the Larguessa or drawing first blood. It is all a chaotic splotch of rage and blood. She fought me. I do know that. I bear the scar her fingernails left on my jaw. The Sisters of Rhob gave me a salve to fade it to nothing. I have not used it.

I do remember her words, as the blood drained from the fatal wound in her chest. "As my house lives, Vales Gate shall ever be in peril. I have failed. But they will fight forever."

She died with those words on her lips. Those terrible words that sparked all that came after. Violet surrounded herself with the innocent and the supposed-innocent in some attempt to seem harmless herself. All her daughters. All the children of her daughters. Her whole house sworn to fight forever. How could she not have known?

DEATH STALKED NAKED THROUGH THE CORRIDORS. In his hand, a blade not seen in an age. He did not cut his swath unopposed. Men. Shimmering like Therkian glass. Eyes like pale blue stones. They went down. There was blood. And there was a frog. Coal amid the white rocks of Alyria's shore. A raven on a snowy branch. Death stayed his hand.

Wait! Stop! What are you doing! Someone help him! Find Linhare!

Death heard these words as if he were under water. They meant nothing. If something small and impotent within him were touched by these words, the bloodlust consumed it quickly.

The ground was slippery. The sword in his hand was heavy. Wet. His spectral slain were shouting. A name? Or a command? Death had no name. No conscience. It had only one purpose.

Kill the Glass King.

...When I came back to myself, it was morning, and I was surrounded by carnage as on a battlefield, but cleaner. Quick, efficient kills. There were men piled amid the bodies; and women. Servants. Whatever mighty battle had occurred, they had done their part and died for it.

The silence was absolute. I cleaned my blade so obscured by gore that the black blade was red. There were scarce few wounds upon me: the scratch along my jaw; a cut here or there. The blood drenching my clothes and staining my skin was not my own. I was so weary. Had I truly battled all night?

I walked through the silent house, saddened by all the death. In the room adjoining the balcony where the Larguessa watched for her triumph, all of her daughters lay dead; even the pregnant ones. I vowed that the monsters responsible for such merciless brutality would answer to me. Outside in the trees surrounding the retreat, birds sang. Gulls cried out on the water. I gazed across to the shipyard and all was quiet there. I did not know where Ben and Ellis were, how they fared. I continued through the house, calling. There were no answers. Not a servant. Not a soldier. Not a child. That thought sent me to the nursery, for certainly if the entire house was dead, the children would be on their own. I searched the house and finally came to the nursery, marked only by the dead nurse half in and half outside the doorway.

All the hair of my body stood on end, the way it does in winter. The chill made me shudder. I went inside. The carpet made squishing sounds as I walked. Curtains kept sunlight out and the room in darkness. I opened them, and fell to my knees, vomiting into the gore. Here, like everywhere in the house, the killing was clean. Whoever did this knew exactly where to cut to make the bleeding out quick. And thorough.

All the babies, the children. The oldest could be no more than ten. The youngest was still a nursling. Violet raised seven daughters. Five of her daughters had borne children; thirteen in all. And they were all dead. The Larguessa Violet's line was extinguished.

THE GLASS KING.

Death felt him. Through walls. Through bloodlust. Beyond the door. In that room. Waiting. Waiting for him. For redemption. Or reparations. Waiting.

...There is no need to record the events that followed. It is evident within the pages of this book what was happening inside me. Violet's voice first came to me in dreams, then in waking hours. Tuliel tells me that it was my own voice, my own shame, that spoke and plotted. Again, I will accede to her wisdom, though I have many doubts.

Once in the Vale, my mind no longer occupied by or exhausted from traveling, Violet's voice plagued me more and more. I took to drinking her into silence, but she was never silent. The ale simply kept me from remembering. One morning, Ellis found me slumped against the wall in the hallway outside the little princess' chamber. I had no recollection of how or why I was there; no memory of danger that would have drawn my sword. But it was there in my hand, gripped fiercely in an otherwise inert body. It was then Ellis first asked if I had any memory of Tassry, of the retreat house and of the carnage there.

He and Ben fought terribly. Over me. Ellis wanted to tell me whatever it was they knew that I did not. He wanted to get me help of some sort. Ben wanted me spared. There was no reason to inflict me with memories of something no one could do anything to change. What was done was done. I was a hero, not a villain. Ben was King. Ellis kept his tongue.

I was not supposed to know any of this. I did only because of the silence that I can call upon, and the ale that stripped me of inhibition. But I was remembering. I did not want to remember. I drank the memories away. But I woke more and more often outside the little princess' nursery; more times than either Ben or Ellis know.

I fought Violet's voice. I fought the memories. In the end, I lost both fights. Near the end of Eighthmonth—was it only two months ago?—I succumbed.

DEATH STOOD IN THE DOORWAY. The Glass King did not turn. His back was straight. Strong. Not strong enough. No one withstood Death in the claiming. He spoke, this Glass King, words Death could not understand even if he knew their challenge. Their warning.

Death spread his arms. He roared like a tawny on the grasslands. Deep inside a mind that once belonged to someone else, a protest. Pain. Horror. Death roared again. The protest shattered. The Glass King turned, taking stance. Death met that single blue orb.

...There was no mad rush of memory. No battle-rage or bloodlust. Quite the contrary, it was a serenity that overcame me once I surrendered. I didn't know how completely the madness possessed me. I felt terrifyingly sane.

I remembered killing Violet's daughter and Violet. Ugly as such death always is, I did not lament the duty of a warrior during war. But once the serenity fell, I remembered more.

Violet's daughters. I remember their names now. The woman on the beach was Orania, the third daughter. Orolia, the eldest. Ocisia, the youngest at seventeen. Darocia, the second and most beautiful daughter; the one in Ben's bed. Emalia, the fourth; Urnenia, the fifth and Hortentia, the sixth were pregnant.

The children. Four boys and nine girls. I do not know their names. No one does. They died as anonymously as sheltered children live.

There were no husbands, no fathers, to give names to put upon their markers. Even their nurse was dead.

I killed them all. I was the grimmest of reapers. I collected every life within that retreat house. Violet said that Vales Gate would be in peril as long as her house lived. She spoke such a threat to the wrong man, to the wrong kind of man. The Dakhan do not take such things lightly.

I remembered. I remembered the blood, their fights, their screams. I remembered the children. The silent deaths of those first. The whimpered fear of the infant.

HER BONES WERE COLD. Her breath. Her mind. The profusion of bloody fingerprints on the page turned her belly. Linhare set the journal down and rubbed at her eyes. There was more. She was not finished. How much more horror could one small book contain? How much more could she?

Little by little, the bathing room came into focus. The tubs no longer cascading. The walls steamed with condensation. The maids chatting softly behind the grey curtain. Jinna sitting upon a cushioned stool, brushing out her long, red hair. Watching Linhare in the mirror. Waiting. And there, within the infinite, beloved blue, Linhare realized the truth.

"How long have you known?"

Jinna came to stand behind her, enveloping her like a familiar shrug. "A very long time. Forgive me, Linhare. I was curious, maybe a little jealous that you kept secrets from me, so I swiped it and read enough to make me put it back without reading it all. I asked my mother. She told me everything."

The ache in Linhare's heart caught her breath and held it tight. Her shoulders slumped. Jinna took the journal from her hands, opened it to the page Linhare's finger held.

"You've not finished?"

Linhare shook her head. "I can't."

Jinna shoved her over with a hip, sat beside her. "What do you remember about that summer you spent with mother and me in the cottage?"

Linhare sniffed. She wiped the tears from her cheeks. "It was the best summer of my life."

"It was for me, too," Jinna told her. "But there was a real reason for it. I think it's time you learned the truth."

"All this truth hurts too much."

"Not as much as denying it exists." Jinna put the book into Linhare's lap, took her hands instead. "I am callous and crude and maybe a little unsympathetic, but the only truth I've ever denied in my ill-spent life has been what I feel for Egalfo—a fact I shall rectify starting tonight. But you, my dearest friend, have spent your life denying too much. Face it, Linhare. Face the truth. *All* the truth. It's scary, but you'll be glad you did."

Linhare shuddered, grasped the journal in both her hands and clutched it to her chest. "I told him that nothing between the covers of this book would change my love for him, but it has, Jin. You were right; I have learned to see him as he truly is. I finally know him, and not my vision of him. And because of this book, I know *why*, and I—"

The swoosh and bang of a door thrust open startled the words from her mouth. Jinna gasped and the maids squealed.

"A thousand pardons." Jahvi bowed hastily. "Please, my lady. Come quickly. It is Wait. He's—something is wrong. I will tell you as we go. Just come. Quickly."

Linhare was already on her feet and following Jahvi out the door, wearing only the dressing gown the bathmaid had given her. Jinna was fast on her heels. Jahvi spoke, but she barely heard him for the panic, and for the journal shoved hastily into her pocket slapping rhythmically against her thigh as she ran: a staccato of warning, of doom, and faith.

Ruby floors marked the scene of battle. Many were down; none were dead. Linhare passed them propped against the walls, Alyrian soldiers in castle attire, as well as Otis, Mannit, and Dorn. Silpa was there too, unconscious and deathly pale. He did not shimmer. An overwhelmed herbwife flitted among them. Jinna joined her. And there was Egalfo, standing in the doorway of the hall where so few hours ago they were welcomed by the Glass King of Alyria, where the sounds of battle pulled her forward, past him, past them all to Wait battling, bloody, mad, beautiful. His sword came up and down and up again, nicking and stabbing and jarring Atony, who was a warrior, too.

"Wait," she screamed, but it was Atony who paused. He shouted, "Go back!" and in that distracted moment, Wait found his mark. Atony tumbled backwards. His head cracked like doom on the glass. Dakhonne foot came down upon Glass King chest. The tip of a borrowed sword slid neatly to Atony's throat.

"Wait, no," she said softly. How had she gotten so near? Wait heaved breaths as if there were no air left in the room. Atony growled no dare, begged no mercy; he glared a warrior's resolve, that one pale eye traveling the length of Wait's weapon and back again.

He growled. "You will kill me with my own sword?"

The tip of Wait's blade traced gently from Atony's throat, to his jaw, to his cheek. It hovered over the empty eye socket. Linhare took that step closer, touched Wait's back.

"Wait." She whispered his name and a shiver convulsed through his body. His muscles twitched.

"The blood waits for me. It waits for me."

His voice was the dry graveling of a tomb door. Linhare moved her fingers along his back, to his waist. His arm. Sweat trickled paths through the blood drenching him, proving him human. Dakhonne. Living flesh. Jahvi was moving forward, motioning to her. Jahvi, Egalfo, others she did not recognize. Did they not know? Did they not see how close Atony was to death?

"Wait," she said, this time to them. Over and over, she whispered the word, his name.

Wait. Wait. Wait.

He trembled, violently. His face burned red, then purple. Linhare's fingers glided down his arm, to his wrist, to his hand holding the sword longing to kill. Fighting the need. She covered his hand with hers.

"Come back to me, Wait. Come back to me."

WITHIN THE DARKNESS, THERE WAS A FLICKER OF LIGHT. It came closer. Closer. Mind. Body. Blood. They burned. Yet that single flicker of light crept ever nearer. And then it was beside him. And then it was touching him. And then it was speaking to him.

Wait.

The flicker expanded. Enveloping him. Embracing him. Consuming him. The light beat back mad darkness, strained so near explosion. It did not explode but pulsed stronger, beating like a heart. Floodgates opened, sluicing an eternity of blood in torrents that swept him up.

Come back to me.

She was just a little girl. So small. So trusting.

Wait.

He loved her so. Even then.

Come back to me.

She reached out her hand to him and he caught it before he was swept away.

Come back to me.

She held him, but she could not pull him from the current. She would not let go. She would never let go. She would let the current take them both first.

Come back to me.

He pulled and fought and climbed. And then he was out of it, towering over that delivering child, his hand still in hers. She led him away from the darkness, growing taller, older, more and more beautiful with each step.

Linhare.

Her name burst from his lips like a breath too long held. Wait staggered. Pain descended. His arms, his back, his bloody, shaking hands. And then there she was, taking him into her arms despite the blood.

Holding him. Weeping his name over and again. Wait gathered her close and fierce. Over her shoulder, he saw shimmering soldiers swarm, Egalfo's terrified expression, and he remembered. Wait closed his eyes and breathed the beloved scent of Linhare into his body.

Just one moment more.

"Hold!"

King Atony was on his feet, bloodied but sound. Wait's mind was draining like water through a filter. Images of people and places; thoughts of rage and fear; a past he once locked away in a book, entombed in a rotted out sill all those years ago. The grasslands of Sisolo. The grasslands of Alyria. Castles and kings and queens and soldiers. Friends long gone. Friends newly made. All washed out of him in a rush that left Wait gasping for air. No one touched him. Only Linhare.

"Say something," she whispered against him. "Anything so that I know you are here with me."

Her words soothed. Wait let his grip on her ease. He was bloody and sore from naked shoulders to bare knees. Blood and sweat mingled in his nostrils. His own. The soldiers'. Atony's. His hands slid down her arms.

"I'm here," he said, and let her go to take a safe step back. Alyrian soldiers, Jahvi, Sal and Dorn included, surrounded him. Wait stood at attention.

"Give him clothes," Atony grunted. He was inspecting the sword, running fingers along the flat of the blade and hilt. A pair of pants was thrust into Wait's hands. He put them on. Blood instantly oozed spots into them.

"Where did you get this?" The Glass King stood before him now, the sword thrust between them. "Tell me!"

"The Chase Queen," Wait answered. "Dread Queen Saghan."

"Did she send you to kill me?"

"Apparently."

Several soldiers pulled in tighter. Jahvi's face paled. Dorn's. Sal's cheeks splotched crimson. He started to shake. Linhare tried to move closer to Wait, but they stood in her way.

"She asked him to take it from her enchanted land!" Linhare shouted over them. "She said it was her father's, and that she made a mistake taking it into exile. Tell him, Wait! Tell him!"

"Explain." Atony stood rigid, his hand gripping the hilt so tightly his knuckles paled to white.

"I knew it was a trick." Jinna pushed through the Alyrians unopposed. She stood before the Glass King, hands on hips. "Egalfo and I were tithed on her chase. Enslaved. Wait carried the blade from her prison in exchange for our freedom. She made it seem like an honor only he was worthy of."

"She was right." Atony let the sword fall to the ground. Sal stepped forward to pick up the blade, but Atony stepped on it, glaring his Ranger back into ranks.

"This is *my* blade," Atony said. He took his foot off the weapon, straddled it. "A man, Dakhonne, like Wait, a man like my own father, gave it to me. I did not know she had it. I thought it stored safely away." He turned his back on them all. "After so long, she still bears this hatred. Of course she does. She is his daughter. It is what I wanted."

"Then her story was true," Jinna said. "As punishment for trying to kill you, she was sentenced to the Chase."

Atony nodded once.

"Then you know we are telling the truth." Linhare stepped forward. "She said soldiers would be waiting for us when we crossed into your lands, and they were! But they thought we were lost travelers and we didn't know what to do. We needed to get to Alyria. She said the king's eye could tell us how to get home. So we let them believe—"

Atony silenced her with a gesture. "Home?"

Linhare held her breath, stepped closer to Atony, nearly close enough to grab his hand.

"We are from Away, my lord," she burst in a rush of breath. "I don't know if that means anything here, Beyond and Away, because no one calls me Little Queen..." In a gasp of moments, Linhare grazed over their journey. Taking a deep breath, her voice quavered a little as she finished, "I know it is mad, but you must believe me. You must."

Atony rubbed shaking hands along his scalp. He stepped closer to his throne and nearly tripped over the weapon on the ground. Sal stepped in and took it up, holding it reverently in two hands.

"It is not mad," the Glass King said. "I fear it makes more sense to me than it does to you. Men," he motioned to his soldiers, "take the Dakhonne to the infirmary. Have his wounds attended. Keep Linhare with him. She seems to have a soothing effect on his frenzy. Full guard, but they are still guests. We will convene instead of feast this night. Together, we will—"

Out of the corner of her eye Linhare saw movement. Sal, running his finger along the king's blade, inspecting the blood on his finger. His gaze came to hers that instant his grin faded to grim. Linhare's skin prickled. He hefted the hilt squarely in both hands and shifted his weight...

"No!" she shrieked, surging forward. Wait's arm came out like an iron post, thrusting her back and lunging for Sal, already bearing down on Atony spinning as if caught in a moment. Wait took Sal's legs out from under him, pulling him down, but not before the blade pierced the muscle of the king's calf like a skewer through meat. Soldiers surrounded their king. Shouts went up. Jahvi and Jinna bent over his wound. Sal, unweaponed, thrashed on the ground, caught in Wait's unrelenting grip.

"Vile fool! Let go of me! He must die by his own sword to free her! Let go!"

"Hold him!" Egalfo dove on top of Sal's still wriggling upper half. And then Sal was no more, and in his place a spitting, scratching cat. It bolted, climbing up the back of the throne. Linhare's heart turned cold.

"Rodly?"

The cat hissed, hackles raised.

"It is the sibbet!" Egalfo shouted. "The Chase Queen's sibbet! Do not let it get away!"

He and Wait cornered the cat behind the throne. Soldiers fanned around them, ready to grab it if it should bolt free. Rodly became the tawny, lashing out with claws and roaring the Alyrians back. Wait dove at the cat, knocking Egalfo to the side. They tumbled over and over.

Atony cried out, snapped Linhare's attention to him, to the sword Jinna was trying to ease from his leg. A flutter of wings, a screech turned her back again. Wait held fast to talons despite the beating wings at his head. Egalfo scrambled up, lunging for the bird that was suddenly a snake, it's head whipping around to strike. And there was Egalfo, snatching the reptile from Wait, tumbling with it like the acrobat he was.

"Ah!" Egalfo screamed and fell and thrashed as if on fire. The snake released his bite and slithered quickly away, curled into a swaying and striking coil. Wait danced back, tried to grab it, and back again. The snake—Rodly—inched his way towards the door, to his escape. On the ground, Egalfo twitched spasmodically, his face frozen in horror and pain, pale as new moonlight on white sand. Jinna rushed to his side. Her scream echoed in Linhare's head, and then all sound vanished except for the beating of her own heart, swishing between her ears.

Jinna knelt beside Egalfo. Wait battled the snake, surrounded by Alyrian soldiers. The Glass King writhed on the floor, the sword still sticking out of his leg. A Dakhan blade. And Rodly. Sweet playmate. She had loved him, and he had warned her, and she had not heeded because it hurt too much. Treacherous. Traitorous. A garden. A violation. A trunk. Betrayed and betrayed again. Because she trusted when it hurt too much to be wary.

Never again.

Linhare grasped the sword hilt in both hands, yanked it from the Glass King's muscle. She growled a sound she felt in her throat, a sound that startled the Alyrian soldiers even if she could not hear it above the rush of her own pulse. Shoving her way past Wait, Linhare leapt. She brought the sword down with all her body, all her might, cleaving the coiled snake in two. The creature writhed, its halves changing, changing,

changing, never in harmony, always disparate creatures that could not become whole. It smoldered. Light edged the bleeding halves. Brightening. Brighter. And then it blinked out. The sibbet shuddered, a muddy thing that spread like a puddle, and stilled.

"Never again," she whispered, and dropped the sword.

JINNA'S EYES WERE HORRIFICALLY DRY. Her first and only scream still ached in her throat. Behind her, chaos. King Atony writhing and groaning agony. Battle raging. Not even Linhare's bestial roar turned her eyes from Egalfo, pale and unmoving. She took his hand in hers. His fingers were stiff, but warm. Hot. A sound like rustling leaves made her blink. Egalfo was staring up at her.

He's dying.

The thought settled in her gut, blanketing her in calm. Jinna touched his face. She looked into his grateful, glassy eyes. "The villain is caught," she told him. "The heroes have won the day. No one dies in a bolleytale after all is done and well. Don't you know anything?"

A shuddered breath. The corners of Egalfo's eyes crinkled. The caramel of his skin burned beneath her fingertips tracing tender circles on his cheeks, his brow, his lips. Jinna kissed him, lingering there upon his mouth where life ebbed out and death rushed in. She tasted them mingling on his lips. But his eyes were still open and watching her. *I love you*, they said. *I'll miss you. I wish we had more time.*

Jinna cupped his face in her hands. This was not a bolleytale. It was as real as the Drümbul glade, as the Siren's Curse, as the chase and the grasslands and Alyria. It was as real as this death; as real as squandered love.

"I love you." She blew the words into his open mouth. "I love you." Over and over. Until his heart quivered. Until it failed and eyelashes fluttered and his last breath whispered silent. Jinna drew that breath into her lungs, held it for as long as she could, and let it go.

After All

WAIT COULD NOT WEEP. He lost the ability so long ago. He knew how to continue. He knew how to comfort. He did not know how to grieve; unless that was the constriction in his chest. The disoriented sensation in his mind. Time had so little hold on him. Nausea and madness. Betrayal and death. Had it all happened days ago? Years? Or only moments? Not long enough to have settled into anything resembling acceptance.

In his guarded chambers, blood cleaned away, wounds tended, Wait awaited interrogation. The Glass King and his advisors agreed to leave Jinna and Linhare to their grieving until Egalfo was pyred on the beach in a warrior's rite so old it was the same, Away or Beyond. He, on the other hand, did not wish to be spared; nor had it been offered. Standing at a window—a strange sensation in a castle made of glass—Wait looked out over the sea, wishing for the Siren's Curse to appear on the horizon; but the Curse rode sunrise into port, not sunset. There would be no rescue from Alyrian shores.

The sound of many boots took his attention from the sea. Wait turned, hands behind his back and shoulders taut. The door opened and Jahvi, dressed in castle uniform rather than his Ranger togs, stepped in. He stood aside to allow his king entrance, then placed a bundle on the foot of Wait's bed.

"Your effects," he said to Wait, then to his king, "It has all been searched and found harmless."

Wait inclined his head. Jahvi might have smiled, but whatever began to form on his lips vanished when Atony said, "Leave us."

"But, my lord—"

"I said leave us."

Jahvi met Wait's gaze, but he backed out of the room and closed the door behind him.

Atony made no move but to tug on his lower lip. Wait held his pose as a soldier awaiting orders.

"Saghan's father, my father in heart if not by blood, was Dakhonne," he said abruptly, lifting his head and pacing to the window Wait had just left. "He was Dread King Pulos, feared and loved in turn. I loved him. And I feared him. I battled beside him many times. When you stepped into my hall covered in the blood of my men, I knew the look in your eyes. I knew what was coming. I was Dread King Atony, once; I welcomed it."

That one blue orb met Wait's gaze. The smile on the king's lips turned down. "I claim no Dakhan blood, but I learned Dakhan ways. The mentality. I appreciated the fury within him, the necessity of it. Perhaps I pretended to feel it, or perhaps I absorbed my share. But you, you do not pretend."

Atony waved him into one of the chairs at a small table set under another window. The food and wine brought in earlier remained there still. Atony poured himself a glass. Wait placed a hand over his and Atony set the pitcher down again.

"My advisors want you executed."

"I expected no less."

Atony brushed it away. "They do not understand what I do. Killing you would serve no purpose. Dread King Atony might have thought otherwise, but Glass King Atony does not require vengeance to serve as justice. You are safe, Wait, as are Jinna and Linhare."

"Thank you, my lord."

"Atony."

Wait nodded, slumping back in his chair and mulling over the king's impossible words. Atony touched the rim of his wine glass to his lips, set it down again without drinking. He ran his finger around and around the rim. The whining moan of such musical glass mingled with the muted rush and roar of the sea, mesmerizing. When Atony spoke, Wait startled.

"The only thing I do not know is how she got my sword. Her father's sword."

"It was stored away in a trunk—" Wait fumbled over the word, "—in the foundation of her winter castle."

"Curious." Atony tapped his chin. "When I rebuilt Alyria stone by stone and Dread King Atony became the Glass King, I put it in a trunk I found in the crypt. A symbolic burial, I suppose, of all that I was. I buried *her* away. Perhaps the sibbet retrieved it for her."

Wait's mind buzzed. *Trunk.* Coincidence? He said, "I don't think so. Rodly only got to her by tricking us into taking him onto our tithe ship. I have some experience with trunks that open one place, but what you put in them ends up in another. I'll tell you about it, when we have time. It doesn't matter how she got it, only that she did."

"And I should have known all along she would." The King shook his head. "I dared her to when I made her release from exile contingent upon my death at the end of my own blade. I carried it with me for a very long time. A challenge. A reminder. I gave my Dread Queen nothing but time to plan her revenge. My Saghan proved herself her father's daughter. I think even Pulos would be impressed."

"She told me it was for him I carried the blade from exile. That it was her great mistake for subjecting it to her fate. I believed her. And in a way, I think she was telling the truth."

Pulling at his lip again, Atony settled back into his chair. "What else did she tell you, Wait? I must know everything."

Wait wished he were still standing at attention, hands behind his back. Sitting across from this man he nearly killed, telling the details of the journey Linhare barely touched in the telling, unsettled. His vocal chords tightened so that for the first time in a lifetime he was tempted to sip the wine that would loosen them.

"I trusted that thing," Wait finished. "I thought he was Sal, a friend. I drank the tonic he gave me believing it was aid. I am Dakhonne. I know the fury in my blood. Part of me understood when I killed the tawny, but by then, I was too far gone."

"Perhaps," the Glass King said. "In the end, you proved yourself stronger than your blood."

"It was Linhare, not me."

"It was your love for her, but it was *you*." Sitting back in his chair, twirling the dregs of wine in the bottom of his glass, the king poured himself another. He took a crumble of cheese from the plate and chewed it slowly. "So much makes sense now. Terrible sense."

"I would like to understand," Wait said. "If you would tell me."

Draining the glass of just-poured wine, Atony set it back onto the table. "I suppose that is your right, after what she and her creature did to you."

"I claim no right to anything."

"But it is yours nonetheless. And, truth to tell, Wait, though good men serve me, I have not been among my own in a very long time. I am Glass King now, but Dread King Atony still lives within me. Thank the stars and starlight for that, eh? Or I would be a smear of blood in the hall and a body in the crypt alongside your Therk friend. Forgive me, that was cold."

"It's—" Wait began, but King Atony was on his feet, pacing away from the table and to the window.

"Warrior to warrior, I admit that Saghan did not love me, a fact I have never spoken before. She consented to be mine because her father wished it. She would have done anything for a small scrap of his approval. I did not care about her reasons. She was my heart and my blood. I would have her any way I could.

"Ah, in those days, there was not a shore safe from our havoc. Pulos wanted the world, and for a time, he had it. Until he took a blade to the belly. We both know the horrors of that kind of death. As he lay dying, he put his sword, his Dakhan blade, into my hand instead of Saghan's. *My son*, he called me." Atony shook his head. "And I took it."

The Glass King leaned on the sill, picked at his fingernails. "Even the pretense of love vanished after that. She avoided me as much as she could, instead keeping company with a great number of pets. I never took any great interest in them. They made her happy. They must have all been the same pet. And any man she desired." He grimaced. "I should have known, when she came to me as the wife she had never been, that something was not right. I should have believed her when she said—" Atony blew out a deep breath. "I was young and vain. And I loved her very much, even then. To think that it was not with her I loved, but that—that thing." Atony shuddered. "She lay in my arms, I was the happiest man alive, and then she—*it* attacked me, gouged out my Eye, tried to stab me with my own sword, and fled.

"My soldiers found her in her bed, as if she had been there all along. She said she did not do this thing, but there was blood on her sheets, on her hands. And only now do I know that she was telling the truth." Atony looked up, anguish in his eye, etched into the lines of his face. "Why did she not tell me then? She only said she did not do it, not that her lover did."

"Perhaps she was protecting him."

"But he betrayed her! He let her take the blame for his crime."

"Would you not have done the same for her?" Wait asked, and watched the anguish of Atony's face become agony.

"She truly loved him," he said. "She loved a sibbet, a creature with no true form, when she could not love me."

Wait pushed to his feet, feeling all the aches and pings in his overtaxed body. He stood before the Glass King, not as a soldier before a king, but as a warrior before a warrior. "She was quite mad, if that is any consolation."

Confusion cut through the agony. Atony grunted something like a snort, something akin to laughter. "Her mother was the most beautiful woman in Alyrian history," he said, "and mad as a fisheel at the full moon. Perhaps Saghan was doomed from birth, but what I did to her...of course she is mad. It is what I wanted when I sentenced her to the chase. And because of that madness, I cannot turn her loose to take vengeance upon my people, not even to assuage my own guilt."

"She was not exactly innocent."

"No," Atony said. "And neither was I. Alyria thrives. My people live in peace and prosperity. Saghan must stay imprisoned, and I must live with this knowledge of the great wrong I did that I cannot right. My own prison, eh?"

"I know something of living in such a prison." Wait bowed his head. That was a story he would not tell; not until Linhare read it first. "But, if it helps," he said at last, "someone once told me that a life honorably lived can't undo one really terrible deed, and neither can one terrible deed invalidate an honorable life."

Atony was silent a long time, then he nodded and looked again to the sea. "You said you also know something of trunks that open one place and empty in another."

"I do. It's how Linhare, Jinna, Egalfo and I ended up Beyond."

"Linhare used that word as well. *Beyond.* I am Alyrian-born, but I know nothing of Beyond or Away. I know of Therk and of Vales Gate. I know of Weir and the other end of the world where the Pinewood lies. I knew of the Dakhan only for stories heard as a child—until Pulos. He made a believer of me. And now you."

"I think it might all be part of the same story." Wait glanced at the sunset, now a smear of pink and purple along the horizon. "You want to hear it?"

"I think we could both do with a good adventure tale about now, don't you?"

Wait smiled despite his circumstances, resumed his seat. Lifting the lids on the covered food, Wait breathed in the robust scents of meat and cheese and grainy bread. His stomach growled. Atony grinned and in the lines of his face, Wait saw the Dread King.

This is why the Dakhan stayed behind.

The thought buzzed into his mind, blossomed in his blood. The Dakhan of Vales Gate were not the Dakhan of old. They had evolved into protectors. Guardians. Out of desire or necessity, tamed and diluted through a thousand years. Yet the instinct remained, strong in some, less so in others, all the time buried beneath protocol and training and morals never meant for their kind; like Dread King Atony becoming the Glass King.

From across the room, from the bundle of clothes on the bed, Wait heard a ringing sound, a humming sound, and knew it for what it was. His mouth told Atony of Diandra's death, Linhare's disappearance, his own fall through Sabal's treacherous trunk, but his ear listened to that humming. As it had been those times before, Wait knew he was in his guarded chambers, sharing a meal and a tale with the Glass King of Alyria, even if the part of him attuned to the stone was in another chamber, long ago.

With Dread King Atony.

His face bloody.

His eye socket empty.

And a stone, the same blue as Alyrian eyes, rolling across the floor.

DEATH SHROUDED THE CASTLE. In the crypt, Egalfo's body awaited the pyre that would send him to the stars and starlight. Linhare could not bear thinking of him there, or at all; but she and Jinna had nothing *but* time to think. Escorted to a lovely suite of rooms, they were left otherwise alone.

Jinna ate vigorously when food arrived on Therkian glass plates, under Therkian glass domes, and now slept easily. Linhare looked in on her friend snort-snoring softly in her bed. Tears stung. How could she sleep so soundly? Egalfo was dead. Rodly killed him. And she killed Rodly…

Closing her eyes, Linhare cut those thoughts off so quickly her head spun. She needed Wait, but he was with the Glass King, a notion that made her eyes sting all over again. Jahvi insisted he was only being questioned, and that Atony would see through the chaos to the truth, but Linhare had heard the servants' gossip. Alyria remembered Pulos, and would never suffer another of him on their shores. Whatever Jahvi said or Atony decreed, Wait was not safe here.

Linhare wandered from room to room like a caged tawny. On the table sat the food she'd been unable to swallow, and Wait's journal. She went to the door leading into the corridor, pressed her hand to the surface, opened it.

"Can I help you, my lady?" asked the guard standing there.

"I am restless," she confessed. "I'd like to wander a bit."

"I will summon guards to attend you."

"I would prefer maids," she said. "Like those in the bathing room."

"As you wish," he said, bowing. "Queen Linhare."

The maids, unlike those always following Sabal in Vales Gate, kept their distance. Linhare was effectively alone, and grateful for both this and, after all, their company. The Glass Castle at night was an eerie place of reflected light and shadows. What looked like other restless wanderers turned out to be herself, or the trailing maids; and what she thought reflection often proved servants ghosting those corridors behind walls where the mundane nature of their existence in no way impeded the grandeur of such royal environs.

Walking allowed Linhare to think without tears. Of Egalfo's death. Of Wait covered in blood. Of Rodly's betrayals. Her father's. Her mother's. Sabal's. She could even think about Agreth and what he did. It allowed her to acknowledge the satisfaction of killing; and the grief.

Her belly clenched. Linhare stumbled to a halt. Behind her, a maid squealed. She heard slippered feet hurrying towards her and held up a hand to halt them. Cool fingers of sea air tickled her face, filled her nose with familiarity, with home. Linhare spotted the flutter of gossamer curtain that proved an open window. It drew her and suddenly, there she stood, face to the fresh air and the stars and starlight beyond. Somewhere, out there, Vales Gate waited. For her. Linhare breathed deep breaths. She refused to cry. She refused to long for that place of betrayal. But she did cry, and she did long.

Linhare wiped the tears from her cheeks, rested elbows to the window sill. The window itself cranked outward like a shutter, and she could see her own reflection created by moonlight in the glass. Wraithlike. Eerie. It reminded her of Egalfo's deathly pallor. And then there was another reflection there. Another Linhare looking back. One smiling. One aghast.

The smiling one spoke. "Do not fear me, Little Queen."

Linhare began to tremble.

"Does this form frighten you? I will take another." And in the glass was Sal. "Better? No? Then this."

Her waterfurry appeared. Linhare stifled a sob. "I killed you."

"Killed? Me?" The reflection quivered laughter. "Oh, dear one, is that what you meant to do when you brought that horrid sword down on me? It hurt terribly, you know. But you cannot kill me. No one can. Why would you wish to? I thought we were friends."

Behind the gossamer curtain, Linhare was quite alone. Rodly existed only in the glass, or in her mind. What had Saghan called him? A lie with no true form?

"You killed Egalfo," she whispered.

"But I did not *mean* to," the reflection whispered back. "I was defending myself. It was nothing personal."

"What you did to Wait was."

"The Dakhonne? What is he to me?"

"It is what he is to *me!*" Linhare took a deep breath of sea air. She glanced through the curtain to see the maids had moved a few steps closer. She lowered her voice. "If you hurt those I love, you hurt me."

"I do not understand."

"You say you love me, you love your Dread Queen, but you do not know what love is. You betrayed her. You betrayed me. That is not love."

Rodly sighed. "I failed my beloved, but I did not betray her. It is not my fault her fool of a husband did not believe her innocence."

"You could have stepped forward. You could have taken the blame."

"And then who would have been the fool?" Rodly asked.

Solid cold replaced Linhare's trembling. "You truly do not understand."

The image in the glass wavered, became an indistinct glow of moonlight. "Again and again I tried to tell you, my dearest Linhare, I am what I am. I cannot be what you wish me to be. I came only to say good-bye, because I thought it would make you happy. As it has not, I will go back to my beloved. I found her once. I will find her again. She is going to be quite vexed by my failure, but it will be a very long time before I can form a body she can forgive. Perhaps she will mellow in the interim, and give up on her hope of vengeance. I would be quite happy living in her changeable world, nothing but time and my Dread Love to spend it with. Good-bye, Little Queen."

Rodly shifted through the memories of bodies it had used, fading with each one until it was gone. Linhare stood staring, trembling.

Betrayal does not exist without love.

Treachery was not betrayal; it was cold and it was deliberate. Betrayal was intimate, and far more insidious. The difference was subtle, but there it was. The epiphany slithered through her like cold water in her veins. Pushing aside the curtain, Linhare bolted back the way she came. Past the maids already squealing for her to stop, past guards shimmering at their posts. Past those spectral servants behind glass walls and doorways she hoped she remembered correctly. All the way back to her suite of rooms where Jinna still snort-snored softly. She picked up Wait's journal. Clutching it to her breast, she sank into a chair as far from any reflective window as she could get, and opened it for the last time.

IF THE CONSTRICTION OF HIS CHEST was grief, it lessened during his evening spent with Atony. The guards were removed from his door, though he asked that they remain in place outside of Linhare's, as a visiting queen required. The sword he carried from the Chase Queen's lands and across the Grasslands was already smelted. And though it had quivered the truth of itself into Wait's consciousness, the blue stone—not a stone, the King's Eye—remained in his pocket.

Wait leaned on the slab alongside Egalfo's body, his mind a jumble of conflicts. In the morning his body would burn in a warrior's rite, an honor that the real Sal, murdered at the sibbet's hands, would never receive. Wait could not even mourn the Ranger he never truly knew.

How he ended up in the crypt, he could not say; he had simply started walking, following a pull he didn't know he was following. Standing there, Wait waited for that constriction to tighten, but it didn't. Instead, the corners of his mouth curled. He remembered the day Egalfo hurried into his warrior's hall, spouting dramatics about Jinna; watching him tumble down the trinket mound; stumbling furious into Beloël's glade.

In his shirt pocket, the King's Eye quivered. Wait had been ignoring its quivering. He could not get the image of Atony's bloody face, his eyeless socket, out of his head; but now the stone warmed him like joy, spreading from his heart to his fingers, his toes, the tip of his nose. He felt himself glow with it, and indeed, his fingertips seemed edged with light. The glow spread outward, across the slab, to the body there. For a moment, dead skin bloomed alive again. Wait leaned closer, a hand pressed to his heart, to the stone, half-expecting Egalfo to sit upright.

Nothing of what you are can change the love and honor I bear you, my friend...

311

Egalfo's words whispered from the Grasslands as the glow faded, leaving behind a warmth Wait would keep.

"You were my friend," he said. One of the few. Egalfo believed in him, in the good in him. An honor Wait would live up to.

Taking that proper step backward, Wait bowed to what remained of the fire-eater's corporeal self, and left the crypt for higher ground.

Enveloped in the obscurity that was his to create, Wait made his way to the king's hall. He knew little of Alyria, but quite a bit about kings. Atony would be there.

The Glass King of Alyria sat upon the dais where he had earlier fallen, head in hands. Wait could guess his thoughts, his grief. Letting his obscurity fall away, he approached slowly, waiting to be noticed.

"I saw you come in." Atony picked up his head. "I told you, I learned a few things from Pulos."

Wait dropped down to the step beside the king. Atony opened his mouth, but only nodded. Wait reached into his breast pocket. He held the blue stone in his fist, listening to the song one last time, not sure if he was glad to be rid or it, or sorry to see it go. He handed it to Atony.

"I believe that belongs to you."

A soft hiss whistled from Atony's lips. He held the Eye on his open palm, fingers twitching.

"Before I was Dread King," he said at last, "before I met the man who would become my father and the woman who would become my wife, I had a great adventure. This was the prize. I was warned about the price I would be forced to pay, but I was so young. Invincible. The pain of trading this eye for my own was excruciating. But that was not what the warning meant. It was all that came after that cost me."

Closing his hand around the stone, Atony looked at Wait instead. "Where did you get it?"

"I found it in a pool in the Pinewood when I first fell Beyond. I didn't know what it was, until today."

"And you return it to me because...?"

"Because it is yours."

Atony looked down at his fist. "Is it? I wonder."

"Saghan said it would tell us the way home, if asked properly," Wait told him. "Was that a lie?"

"A lie? No. Not as far as she would know. But is it still true? I don't know." Atony tucked the stone into his breast pocket, jerking his fingers back as if stung. Shaking them out, he asked, "Did it speak to you?"

"It showed me things."

"What things?"

312

What were those events he saw? Past or present? Future possibility? An alternate world Beyond Away where another Ellis and another Yebbe battled for freedom against a foe who was not, after all, Sabal? "Things I did not want to see."

"That does not bode well for it showing you the way home."

Wait blew a breath through his lips. "I figured as much. It might take a long time, but we can get to Therk from here, and from Therk back to Vales Gate."

"A long and treacherous journey," Atony told him. "We get few ships from Therk, send fewer from the Grasslands to the desert. It will take some time to find passage. And from Therk across the sea to your island nation is—"

"Longer and more treacherous," Wait finished for him. "I know. I journeyed to Therk once, when I was a very young man. I don't want to jeopardize Linhare on those seas, but I don't see any other way."

Silence fell.

"It's late," he said, slapping his knees. "I did what I came to do, and tomorrow will happen soon enough. I'm for bed."

"Until daybreak, then." Atony waved him off. "And your friend's sending."

Wait pushed himself off the step, feeling the battle and the tawny-wound pricking pain through his body. He suppressed the groan forming on his lips, bowed to the king, and started away. At the door, he glanced back to see Atony on his feet, holding the Eye up to moonlight streaming in.

...TULIEL HAS BOUND MY BLOODY FINGERS. It is difficult to write with the bandages, but she insists that I finish. There is magic working here; magic threatened by my outburst. Tuliel has forbidden me from doing my own finger-pricking, but will do so whenever I raise my hand. I see the sorrow in her eyes and fear it is revulsion. She must know all that I have done. She must.

I remember now and I am filled with self-loathing. Violet's voice promised that for the price of innocent blood, the little princess' blood, she would leave me in peace. It was a vow. An oath. From killed to killer. It was my absolution. I was desperate.

I went again to Princess Linhare's nursery. Calm. Wrapped in my silence, I slipped past her nurse and to her bedside. I unsheathed my blade. My hand was so steady. She was asleep, her tiny hands curled up on either side of her sweet face. She is a fair little thing. Her skin so white and her hair, ringlets, so dark. A toddler when I left.

I lifted the blankets from her warm little body. She stirred. Her eyes opened. She smiled. "Halloo, Wait," she said, then closed her eyes again. Small and trusting. She undid me completely. Again wrapped in my silence, I left the nursery. Outside the door, the madness fell upon me so hard that the pain was nearly unbearable. But I didn't forget again. It did not spare me that. I knew there was only one thing left for me. To save Linhare, I had to die. I did not hesitate. Outside the nursery door, I fell upon my sword.

Madness. Pain. Delirium. I somehow made my way to the Holes. I would die there in the soothing peace. I brought my journal, this very book, with me. I would leave Ben something so that he would understand. I intended to report what I had nearly done, that if left alive I would kill the little girl. I never got a chance to write that final entry.

What I report next, I do not remember firsthand. I can only trust what those who love me despite all I did told me.

I left a trail of blood. Ben found me. Ben and Ellis. They took me to Yebbe, who then took me to the Sisters of Rhob on Tuscia. They healed my body, but the madness that kept me bound was beyond their herbal skills. I begged for them to kill me. I screamed it from dawn 'til dusk and through the night. Only when they plied me with dangerous amounts of calming herbs did my screams become whispers. Ben sat at my bedside through it all. Ellis spelled him now and again. I do not know what Queen Diandra felt about me then. I still do not. I suppose I shall find out once I return to the Vale. If she allows me to return to the Vale. But I do not believe she subjected herself to my madness. I will hope she did not witness it.

The Sisters urged Ben to send me to Vernist-on-Contif. He took me up the mountain and gave me to Tuliel. It took a long time and much work for her to tame the memories, the madness and the desperation to die. But there was only so much she could do. I had lucid moments, but they were fleeting. I am Dakhonne. My will is great. My body is strong. It took Violet's voice many months to break me. It was going to take a tremendous event to make me whole again.

I recall being in a space so small I could only fit curled up in it, knees to chest and head tucked in. I could not move. I did not want to move. It was as if I had been there so long that my muscles and bones fused into that position, my body molded to the crevice.

There was a scuffle somewhere outside my space. It was as looking through a membrane, but I recognized one figure. Ben. The other was a wild creature. Vicious. Remorseless. It snarled and snapped at the tether binding it to Ben, but it could not break free.

"Calryan," Ben spoke that name he never had. Only Ellis did. But Ellis knew me when I was still that boy. "Come out, Calryan. Please. I can't hold him much longer."

My body did not want to leave the space, but Ben called. I could not refuse. I managed to squeeze myself free of confinement. I was bent and sore but out. Ben helped me to stand. He said, "We have to get him in. There isn't much time. Hurry, or we are both lost."

I am Dakhonne. My will and body are strong. I forced my muscles to work, my bones to un-fuse. I helped Ben force the wild creature into my abandoned space. It bit and scratched. Ben took the brunt of its ravaging. He was bloody and pale by the time we succeeded.

"Close the door, Wait! Close it quickly!"

I did not know how. The creature strained, but Ben blocked its way with his own body. He called out again and again for me to close the door, but never once faltered. I did not know what to do. I was so long in that space, and never noticed a door. But then, I never shut myself in.

It was there, almost imperceptible because it was the same membranous consistency of the space itself, like a flap of skin. I shoved Ben aside, pulling the flap over the opening as the creature tried to snap its way out. The doorway bulged, but it did not give. Ben, bloody and panting on the ground beside me, was still tethered to the thing inside the space.

"Break the tether. Break it!"

I took the tether in two hands and snapped it as if it were a piece of kindling. Ben slumped backwards. I caught him before he hit the ground; but there was no ground to hit. The weight of his body pulled mine and together, we tumbled through the floor.

I do not need to know the magic behind that memory. I understand enough to know what happened in that dream-place. He was weak when I woke, moments or hours or days later. Being Ben, he laughed away my concern and said that now we were even.

That is not so. I saved Ben's life on Tassry. He saved more than my life in Vernist-on-Contif. He paid for that salvation. He denies it, but I fear that the magic he was compelled to perform took something from him. It weakened him. I see him clutch at his chest, and fear. But I cannot undo what he did for me, what his love and friendship were able to do.

I swore the blood oath. Our bond is now doubly strong. For him, for this bond no one but the two of us can ever understand, I am determined to make the most of this life he saved. I swear upon it that my tongue shall never taste liquor again. I swear upon it that I will serve him and his family until I am dead; and if there is something to the stars and starlight, I will serve them even after.

I am done. Tuliel tells me that this is the last piece of the spell begun when Ben contained that part of me in the space. It is all recorded, from merry times to mad, in the pages of this journal. It has become a talisman, of sorts, and a tomb. She has bid me to put it to rest. She says that I will know the proper place when I find it. There it will remain until such time as it is proper for it to be found. Truth, she says, cannot remain entombed forever. Only long enough.

*   *   *

315

WAIT STOOD OUTSIDE THE DOOR TO HIS CHAMBER, a hand upon the lever. It was well after midnight. Most of the castle slept. But someone was in his room. A silhouette paced beyond the thick glass cubes of the wall. His hand trembled. Without the stone to quiver warning or assurance, he could only guess at the reason for her presence.

He opened the door.

"Oh!" His journal flew from Linhare's hand, thumped to the carpet. Wait stared at it. He had guessed correctly. She finished. And now she knew. Everything. He didn't feel himself move towards it or bend or pick it up. But there it was in his hand, pulsing like a wound.

"I remember nothing of the night you came to my nursery." She spoke in a rush of held breath, and the pulsing eased. Wait's eyes drifted from the journal to her face. Small and lovely and more powerful than she could ever imagine—Linhare. A whispered word, the touch of her hand, had tamed his ravening Dakhonne blood not once but twice. Even now, as she moved past him to close the door, her presence warmed him like sunshine on bare skin.

"I pretended that I didn't, but I have always known somewhat of the reason I was sent to live with Ta-Yebbe," she finished, her back pressed to the door. "People talk in front of children, like they talk in front of servants. It's a ridiculous thing, really, to believe they don't understand. I knew my going to Ta-Yebbe had something to do with you."

One step and she was easing the journal from his hands. She turned it over and over, looking at it, not him. "The things within the covers of this book are terrible things, Wait. I cannot pretend to understand what made you capable of—of doing them. You are of a warrior race left behind a thousand years ago to forget what they are. But today...the blood doesn't forget. It can't. You are what you are."

"I understand." He heard his own quiet words and wondered how the frenzy of his thoughts allowed such calm. Wait bowed his head. His eyes burned so that he blinked, and blinked again. Warm, wet tears pooled and trickled, the sensation so alien he did not know what to do with them. Then Linhare was there, taking his hand, looking up at him, waiting for him to speak. But Wait did not know what to do with tears and he did not know how to speak through them.

"No, you don't understand." She placed the book on his palm, covering it with her own. "I told you that nothing within the pages of that book would change what I feel for you, but I was wrong." Linhare's grip tightened when he tried to pull away. "Knowing all you did, all you battle, the silly love I thought I fell into when I was a girl, *that* is what's gone."

His chest tightened. His throat. Wait forced himself to breathe without choking.

"I cannot say it doesn't matter," she told him, her voice so gentle. "It does matter, because you were right; I could not love you until I knew what was in there, until I knew the truth. And now I do. Wait, look at me."

Obeying her command was harder than breathing.

"I give this journal back to you, because it is yours to destroy or keep or entomb again. I love the fisherman's son from Crones Hook. I love the man who saved all of Vales Gate. I love the man who threw himself upon his own sword to save me, and the one who dove into an empty trunk to follow me into fae. Do you understand?"

Linhare's words filled his head, trickled into his heart. His mother had seen the horror and could not love him; but Ben had. And Ellis. Diandra. Yebbe. Tuliel. All of them. And Linhare. The red leather peeked through her fingers. No talisman or tomb, it was just a book after all; a written account of a past and truths that did not belong solely to him. They belonged to Vales Gate. Its history. Its shame. The lies beyond the glory finally revealed for the horror of what they truly were.

"Wait." Her voice yanked him back to the present. Her hand on his cheek made his body burn.

"Whatever happens from here, I love you. *You.*"

The journal dropped to the floor. Wait held Linhare at arm's length, absorbing all she said, all she made him feel. He gathered her to him, breathed her in as if he could draw her inside of him, filling those dark places with the lightness of her. Then he pulled away to thread fingers through pinned curls that came down around her face.

At the end of it all, there is this.

Linhare took his hands from her face. She tugged him gently towards the bed. Wait hesitated, but she shook her head, tugged him more insistently. He saw fear in her eyes, and joy. Wait lifted her into his arms. He carried her to the bed. Resting his head upon her breast, listening to her pounding heart, Wait kissed that spot between, where the sound was loudest. Linhare buried her fingers in his hair grown too long and lifted him from that spot. She brought his face to hers and, forehead to forehead, she told him, "All I am, forever."

"All I am," he echoed. "Forever."

Untying the collar of his shirt, the bodice of her dress, she pressed her skin to his. She shivered, and then she sighed, and then Linhare laughed softly. She kissed him before he could speak. Those pieces of himself incomplete without her filled. His body itched with wanting her. The desperate control vanished. In the Glass King's castle, on the edge of the world, Wait let it go at last.

The Edge of the World

EGALFO OWNED FEW POSSESSIONS to burn with him, these tucked into the driftwood and dried grass already burning. Linhare wept. Wait loomed, shoulders back and brave. Jinna stood dry-eyed between them. Firelight licked her face. The incoming breeze lifted her hair. She clung to no one, only to the tattered cord around her wrist, to the charm she took from Egalfo's body before his bearers set him upon the pyre.

Fire climbed. Consumed. Egalfo's clothes caught. He burned. The romantic notion of this rite hadn't taken into account the crackling, searing, snapping. The stench of burning flesh. There was symbolism. There was honor. There was nothing romantic at all. It was brutal and complete. A cleansing of life she could not quite feel.

Linhare put her arm around Jinna's shoulders, but Jinna shoved her off. Linhare had Wait, and obviously, he'd had her. She could smell it on them. Everything was changed for them, for her. Everything, and it made her feel alone.

The other mourners began to make their way up the beach, to where a feast was spread upon a platform, away from the smoke. Atony and his guard. The herbwives. The soldiers who had escorted them across the Grasslands: Otis, Jahvi, Mannit, Dorn, and even Silpa, his head wrapped in bandages, propped in a chair.

Jinna walked slowly. Linhare and Wait, Queen and Dakhonne, were led to chairs closer to the center of the gathering. Atony was holding out a chair at the head, one beside his own. "Thank you," Jinna said over her shoulder. He slid her chair up to the table, then took his. A server came with a platter of food. Jinna did not know what it was, but it looked like creamed eggs. She waited for the hunger to decorously slither away; instead her stomach grumbled, demanding to be fed. Another server offered fruit. She took some of that, too. Digging into the food, she felt the king's eye upon her.

"Am I using the wrong fork or something?"

"I wouldn't know," he said, pointing to the charm at her wrist. "I was looking at your bracelet."

Jinna wiped her hands. "This? It was Egalfo's." She swallowed. Her stomach protested only slightly.

Atony held out his hand. "May I?"

Jinna slipped the cord from her wrist and handed it to the Glass King. He held it close to his working eye, squinting. "I thought I was seeing correctly. Interesting."

"How so?"

"*Egh Ahl Fo*. It is his name, see?"

"He was a foundling," Jinna said. "It was pinned to his clothes when the woman he called his aunt took him in. She thought it sounded exotic, so that's what they called him."

"Exotic?" Atony chuckled. "Perhaps. Unless one can speak Therk. Let me show you." Atony put the charm onto the table between them, pointing piece by piece. "*Egh* means east. *Ahl* means one. *Fo* is the common term for Therk's famous glass."

"East one glass? That's an odd name."

"Because it is not a name at all. It is a dock tag. It means that whatever crate or barrel this was attached to was a glass shipment going to the east end, dock one."

Jinna took the charm—the tag—back from Atony. She hefted it eye-level.

Egh Ahl Fo.

Grief and love and absurdity rose up, swelling like a bladder near to bursting. "Of course," she said. "Oh, of course."

A last jest, and so like him to make her laugh, even now, even if it was not his jest to make. She could almost see him, standing there just behind Atony, a crooked smile on his lips and laughter caught between the veil separating them. Jinna closed her hand around the bit of etched metal that might have once been nothing more than a dock tag but was indeed a charm. A talisman. Because Egalfo had loved her. Because it was all he had to offer. She accepted it too late, but she accepted it after all.

Looking down the long table to where Linhare sat beside Wait, Jinna's secret smile softened. Her earlier, less than kind thoughts for the obvious changes between them softened too, and Jinna understood them for what they were. The jealousy turned envy had no place in her heart. Not anymore. It caused her too much pain. If loving Egalfo taught her anything at all, it was that giving in to such emotions did nothing but waste time better spent.

"Excuse me," she said to Atony. She pushed out her chair and started towards her friends, but a sound like the wind moaning lifted her attention to the horizon where the sun rose in fiery fingered glory. Jinna shielded her eyes and saw something there, getting bigger. Her grieving heart raced. Slipping the cord round her wrist again, she started running down the beach as the moaning wind keened louder, like the screaming of horses; like scattered plans gathering; like her future come to call.

THE SIREN'S CURSE CAUGHT MORNING'S FIRST RAY as if it were a turn in the road. A cheer went up. Ezibah and Neciel wept. The Curse knew, before any of them could, that the Little Queen lived; it road sunrise rays to her, to the Alyrian coast. The Pilfer surged, the Curse picked up speed and they were careening through the sky like light itself.

Gia and Adai stood at the rail near the prow. Her eyes closed, hair streaming behind her, she could feel the end of her shunning, the beginning of blessed exile like sunshine on her face, even if it was at her back. There was a sound, like horses screaming, rising in pitch. A shrill sound. Somewhat haunting. For Gia, it was the sound of life renewing.

Not even Moslo acknowledged her once she left the galley. Only the throg, in his way. Though he never spoke to or looked at her, he was always at her side. Where she walked, he walked. Where she stood at the rail gazing out to the horizon, so too did he. If she fell asleep in the sunshine, he was there when she woke. And though she was no longer relegated to the galley and forbidden hours, their habit of midnight tea continued.

"Were you not always there watching over me," she told him one such midnight, "I might have thrown myself into the sea."

"Gianostalia." He had spoken her name and the timbre of his voice made it sound like a song. "Why do you think I was there?"

Land ahead. A snow white shore. Gia had heard the legends just like everyone else—Alyria's pristine beaches, and the sand that became the fine glass that gave the mythical castle and the King of Alyria their names. She could see the city there, still sleeping, and the Glass Castle itself. A finger pointed to the sky.

The Curse slowed, then came to a halt where the water darkened to depth. A massive fire burned on the beach. Alyrians stood in the tide.

"Looks like a funeral," Hepheo said. Beside him, Brodic nodded. Ezibah gasped. Vespe Neciel pulled her close. Gia avoided looking directly at any of them while ghosting the ship. It was better for all of them; but this was the end, and she wanted one last image of those she once loved.

Ezibah looked older, tired and worn, while Neciel's ruddy cheeks and bright, mismatched eyes shined vitality. Danle stood beside his Keeper, tall and lithe as any Everwanderer, his hair burnished copper in morning light. Gia let her eyes skim past Hepheo without acknowledging face or form, but in that glance noted the lack of him, as if he were fading away.

Her gaze came to rest on Moslo; the old galley cook's eyes were on the beach but his smile, Gia knew, tilted for her.

Good-bye, you old scab.

She felt the words leave her heart and fly to him as if the loesh hadn't taken all such Purist abilities from her. Moslo twitched, and she knew, at least this once, it had not. The spark of ability shivered through her. She felt Brodic's eyes, those thoughts he was trying very hard not to have. Gia's heart stuttered in her chest. She stilled it. She would not look his way. If she did, she was lost.

Everwanderers brought the ladder out from storage, hooked it in place and tossed it over the side. It vanished into the Pilfered mist.

"Stay here," Hepheo told Ezibah. "If it warrants, I'll come back for you."

"You need me to—"

"I'll be fine for a short time. I en't been in Atony's company since he was Dread King. Or near after. I need to know you're safe."

Ezibah kissed Hepheo's lips. He brushed the tears from his Keeper's cheek. Tenderness from brutal hands. Gia looked away.

Hepheo, then Brodic, then Danle went over the side. Waiting for them to vanish into the mist, Gia bent to Adai, grabbing him by the shoulders.

"This is good-bye, my friend."

"Good—what?"

"I won't live the rest of my life as the walking dead," she told him. "I'm staying in Alyria."

"But—"

Taking his plain, round, hairy face in her hands, Gianostalia kissed him squarely on the mouth. She kissed him hard and she kissed him fast, dashed to the rail and threw her legs over the side of the Siren's Curse. The time to explain her plan had passed through so many cups of tea. It was better that way, she told herself as she fell free, for them both.

The sea was warm and deep; hitting the water still knocked the air from her lungs. Gia bobbed in the waves, only her eyes and nose above water. Hepheo's skiff was already nearing the shore. If she could tread water just a few moments, she would be able to—

A splash startled a cry from her lips and bobbing gulls into flight. Gia turned and turned again in the water, looking for a fin or tail that would indicate a predator eyeing her hungrily. Something broke the surface beside her—not a predator. A throg.

"What are you doing?"

"Why did you jump?"

"Adai! You'll ruin everything!" Gia splashed at him. "The ladder is still down. Go back before it's too late."

"It's already too late." He splashed her back. "What do I have to go back for? A trial? Prison? Slavery? How could you leave me behind?"

How indeed? Sinking lower into the water, her eyes darting shoreward, Gia tried to think through all the thoughts tumbling unwanted in her head; not the least being how she with her crippled arm would be able to swim all the way to shore.

"Come," she said. They swam beneath the surface as far as they could, then made a mad dash for the shore once it got too shallow. The dune left by the last low tide shielded them from view. Flopping down onto the sand, Gia caught her breath, peering over the rise to see Hepheo, Danle and Brodic standing with a tall, bald man further up on the beach. There, the Little Queen and her Dakhonne, and the redhead Gia remembered from the tents. She glanced at the pyre. Who burned there? And then she remembered the handsome young Therk who had performed with the redhead, missing now from the gathering.

The tide was coming in. Soon enough, it would rob them of their hiding place. Gia motioned to Adai, and though her newly-healed body ached from the exertion already expended, she belly-crawled closer to the pyre where the mound and the flames would shield them from view.

It was pleasant enough there, regardless of the fuel. She chanced sitting upright, knees drawn to her chest. Adai stood nearer the blaze. On the beach where the feasting reminded her that she'd not eaten since the night prior, no one seemed to notice them.

"I tithed him to the Chase Queen," Adai's deep voice said. "Were it not for me, he'd not have ended up in Alyria where Death awaited him."

"Longee planned worse for them," Gia reminded him.

"I am still responsible, Gianostalia. Give me my grief while I honor this boy's death."

Gia closed her mouth. She fingered through her hair to help it dry. Adai remained as he was, head bowed and silent, for quite some time. Then Gia realized he was not silent, but singing words unfamiliar, sweet and mournful. As she had known all along, his voice was a minstrel's, enthralling and rich. The whisper of his voice faded. Adai raised his head. Tears caught in the hair on his cheeks.

"Well then," he said, and that was all.

Gia stared at him. "You are a wonder, my friend."

"I am nothing of the kind."

"You are. I'm a fool. I should never have even thought—" Gia bowed her head. "I didn't think at all. I should not have left you, Adai. I am glad you came after me."

"Truly?"

Gia nodded. She held out her arms to him and Adai came to her embrace. He was strong and warm and good, so good, and he loved her. There was something good in her, after all, to earn his devotion.

"Well, Gianostalia, I see death has lowered your standards."

The sudden arrival of Brodic's voice sent tremors through her. Gia let go of Adai to rise.

"I am dead. I do not exist. What do you care?"

"I thought better of you," Brodic said. His gaze fell to Adai, "And of you, throg."

"Adai," he spat. "I have a name, and it is Adai."

Gia's face burned.

"Adai," Brodic repeated. "Is that your birth name?"

"It is the name Gianostalia gave to me."

"Did she now. How nice that was for her to do. I wonder, *Adai,* would you excuse us one moment?"

"It's all right," she said when the throg looked to her. He moved off, but only so far. Further up on the beach, those gathered and mourning watched, even if no one came any closer.

"Adai?" Brodic asked. "I have not heard that name in many, many years."

"Why would you hear it? You forbade me to use it."

"Because you forfeited the honor. A true name is only for—"

"I know what a true name is for. Whatever you say, I am Purist by blood."

"A Purist by blood who has not uttered her own true name in a very long time. Tell me, Gianostalia, do you even remember it?"

She glared rather than give him the satisfaction of truth. Brodic shook his head, amused and angry. "Does your little pet know you've given him my name?"

"He is not my pet."

"Forgive me. Lover."

"He is my *friend,* Brodic. Something you never were."

"Was I not?" Brodic shook his head, tisking. "You will never accept responsibility for what you did to us, to me."

"I accepted it a long time ago, but you will not let me get beyond it. You keep us in this same place. Years and years in the same place. I have changed, Brodic. I have proven myself. But you will not—"

"You've changed?" Brodic choked on his own laughter. "You've not changed. You *can't* change. For a while, I hoped, but hope has never gotten me anything but..." He took several deep breaths, tugged at the hem of his jacket. "I loved you, Gianostalia, to my own peril. Time and again, I forgave, and then I could not anymore. You nearly destroyed me, all the while claiming to love me, just as you will destroy the throg you gave my name."

"You're wrong."

"Am I? Then prove it to me. Go back to the Siren's Curse. Return with me to Weir and pay the consequences for what you've done."

Gia shivered despite the pyre's blazing heat. "If I return to Weir as a ghost, become as despised as Longee, it will prove to you for once and always that I love you? That I have changed?"

Brodic's chin lifted, but he nodded. Gia trembled like sea grass in the wind. Taking his hand, surprised that he did not yank it away, she brought it to her lips and lingered along the pulse hammering in his fingertips. His hand turned in hers to hold her cheek. Gia closed her eyes to this caress she had longed for over the years. Darkened skin and golden hair made Brodic appear more Everwanderer than Purist, but he was still Brodic—*Adai*—the man she loved and always would.

"I nearly destroyed you," she said. "But I did not. In the end, you proved stronger, and I admire you for that." Opening her eyes, Gia looked up into his. She touched his face, drew him to her and kissed his lips so tenderly. His lips responded to hers and for a single heartbeat, Gia nearly yielded; but she could not. He loved her. He could not let her go. Neither could he forgive. Ever. Releasing him, taking a step back, she told him, "I'm staying in Alyria."

Brodic backhanded her before she could raise a withered arm to defend herself. She spun, falling to the sand. She spat out the blood filling her mouth. Her head swam and her vision blurred. Adai leapt up at Brodic, taking him down like a wolf on a stag.

"Enough!"

The voice lifted her head. Arms reached down and gently helped her to her feet. Blinking until she could see properly, Gia found Wait steadying her. The funeral party gathered round: Danle who shook his head sadly, and Hepheo who did not look at her at all; and the tall, bald man whose single eye leveled directly on her. Gia stood up straighter. Wait let her go.

"Striking a woman is a grave offense in Alyria," the one-eyed man said. "Even for Purists who hold themselves above the law."

"Forgive me, King Atony. I apologize for—"

"I am not the one you struck." The man gestured to Gia. Brodic's face crimsoned. His lips quivered with rage.

King Atony. The Glass King of Alyria. Gia said, "Please, Your Majesty. I need no apology. I was a stowaway on Captain Hepheo's ship—" Atony gasped and looked to Hepheo, who still ignored her, "—and was sentenced to living death rather than death itself by Brodic's intercession. Now I seek sanctuary here in Alyria; for myself and for my friend."

"The throg is a criminal," Brodic snapped. "He must return with me to stand trial for his crimes."

"What crime is he accused of?"

Brodic straightened his clothes, composure returning even if his body still trembled with rage. "He is the one who tithed Jinna and Egalfo to the Chase Queen."

"That is not a crime, as far as I know," Atony said. "And I would."

"It was wrong, what I did," Adai said calmly. "No admission or wishing will bring this young man back from the dead. I will not answer to those that made me a slave so desperate that I would do such a thing." He turned to Jinna. "It is she I wronged who I will answer to."

Gia's heart swelled. Adai's lip was bleeding, bruises bloomed on his cheek. *He is good and kind and has paid a thousand times over for the indiscretion that put you on the river.* But Gia could not make her mouth work. It still tasted of blood. She swallowed it down. Jinna separated herself from the others, moved to stand before Adai, who did not cower, but stood tall and proud and ready.

"I should send you down the chase to be the queen's plaything," she said, then shook her head. "But who am I to pronounce judgment on you? I might have done the same, in your situation."

"But the young Therk—"

"Nothing you did caused his death. That's an end to this now. Go. Live a happy life. Linny," she turned, holding her hand out to the Little Queen. Hand-in-hand, they walked back up the beach. Jinna did not turn, but Linhare raised a hand in farewell.

"Come, Adai," Gia said quickly. "Let's leave these people to their mourning."

"That is not quite how it works," Brodic was quick to counter. "As you well know, Gianostalia. I have an obligation to—"

"You are a guest in this kingdom," Atony cut in, "and would do well to remember that I am king. There are no agreements between our people, Brodic. Much as I admire the Purists, I cannot be dictated to in my own land. You would do well to cut your line and let this go."

Brodic stood frighteningly still, his eyes fixed and furious upon Gia. "If you were not dead to me before this, you are now."

"I have been dead to you for a very long time," she said. "Now, you are also dead to me."

Gia would not watch him walk away, even if she could feel every step he took. Then Adai was at her elbow, leading her away.

"Good riddance to you both," Hepheo grumbled; the Everwanderer's glare as she passed him prickled along every scar tracing her back. Silence followed them up the beach. Where would they go? How would they live? Gia had never concerned herself with such things. She was a Purist of the Commonwealth, admired and provided for whether as an acolyte herbwife or peacekeeper; and now she was none of those things. Unmoneyed, unwaged, cast out. *And free.*

"Hold!"

Gia turned to the voice and the man trotting after them.

"I'll not let them take you," Adai whispered. She placed a hand on his shoulder, squeezed it gently as the man came to a halt, bowing his head.

"Kingsguard Jahvi, my lady," he said. "My king bids me tell you that it is a precarious position you have him in. Stowing away on Captain

Hepheo's ship is a grave offense. Until he knows the details of that tale, he cannot offer you sanctuary in his Glass Castle."

"I did not expect to be given such sanctuary."

The man bowed his head again. "King Atony bids you to find an inn called *The Hearthbound Minstrel.* Tell the proprietor that you are there by his request and on his mark."

"Why?" Not Gia, but Adai asked. The guard turned to him, the smile on his lips genuine.

"Hepheo may be Lord of the Curse and the Seas she sails upon, but Alyria is Atony's. He says you are his guest. Will you argue with a king?"

"I suppose not," Gia answered. "Thank your king for us."

"You may thank him yourself. Later, at the Hearthbound Minstrel. He will find you there. He'd like to hear your tale, and how you came to survive not only defying Eminence Brodic, but Hepheo himself." Touching fingers to brow, the man bowed curtly, even if his smile was amused. "I'd like to know that tale myself."

Adai tugged at her hand. Gia turned away, fixing her eyes on the city of Alyria. Back straight and head high, she walked beside him up the beach. In time, she would forget them—Hepheo and Ezibah, Neciel and Moslo. She would forget the Little Queen and her Dakhonne, the halfling and the Therk. And she would forget Brodic. Yes, she would forget him, too. Him most of all.

IT WAS FINALLY DARK. QUIET. Everyone else had left the beach. Wait assured Linhare that he would not linger long, but he did, and now stars were salt spilled on black velvet. There was no moon, just an empty patch of sky, spectral and sleeping, showing its dark side. Wait stared at the patch until he began to see shapes within it. Shadow-shapes, and nothing clear.

Rubbing his eyes, Wait leaned back on his elbows in the sand and looked out over the Alyrian Sea to where the Siren's Curse sat ghostlike on her Pilfered mist. Come morning, it would depart this shore and he with it; first to Therk and then, eventually, the long and treacherous journey across open ocean to the archipelago realm that had spit him Beyond to begin with. Wait was not certain how the leap from Beyond to Away was made, or if the Siren's Curse could make it.

"The Curse en't sailed those waters in all the years I been captain," he said. "But I took the Little Queen's sacrifice. I'm honor-bound. The Curse'll get you there. Never fear."

The Pirate King politely-for-a-pirate refused Atony's hospitality, and returned with Danle to the ship at sunset. Curious as he was about what happened with the Purists on his ship, and if it had anything to do with his sapped vitality, Wait did not ask; he wasn't entirely certain he wanted to know...

"I do not mean to disturb you."

The Glass King of Alyria stood behind him on the beach. Rising, Wait brushed the sand from his pants. Atony nudged the last charred bits of Egalfo's pyre with the toe of his boot. "A good rite, and a fine sending for a fire-eater, don't you think?"

"Egalfo would have liked it." Wait's eyes were drawn again to the Siren's Curse. "He'd have liked it better if he weren't *on* it, but..."

"But, indeed."

"It's going to be strange, boarding the Curse without him. Going home."

"Life continues." Atony grimaced, his eye drawn seaward as well. "I have not seen Hepheo or his ship in a very long time. A good thing, perhaps. We have been rivals. Dread King and Pirate King. We battled many times, but were comrades just as often."

"He seems...diminished."

"You have only a small idea of how much." Atony shook his head grimly. "You stayed on the beach for a reason, and it was not to discuss the health and well-being of the old pirate. I came to give you this." Reaching into his pocket, the Glass King pulled from it a pendant on a chain and handed it to Wait. A bulbous thing like an elaborate cage, or an exaggerated locket. Wait clicked it open.

"I can't—" Wait began.

"It no longer responds to me." Atony stopped him, closed Wait's hand around the Eye. "But it obviously responds to you. See?"

Light edged the creases of Wait's fingers. Already the hum seeped between them—a hum no longer a droning bee but an insistent voice Wait could not hear properly.

"I will give you the advice I was given as a young man, and did not heed: if you attempt to be its master, it will become yours. If you allow it to become yours, you will be lost. Respect it, and it will respect you. My connection to the Eye was made by force, and in blood. Hubris was my downfall. One thing I can be grateful to the sibbet for is taking it from me. I would still be Dread King if he hadn't. Or dead."

Wait uncurled his fingers. The stone pulsed, but did not burn bright. He thought he could decipher some of its words, faint images ghosting in his periphery like ghasty-haints at dusk.

"Thank you, Atony." He closed the locket and slipped the chain over his head. "I will do my best to live up to this honor."

"Hold your thanks. I am not finished yet." The Glass King walked back the way he'd come to retrieve something sticking up out of the sand. As he neared, Wait saw what it was. Dakhonne instincts bent his knees, clenched his fists, prepared for battle, even if the more civilized part of his mind insisted there was nothing to fear.

Atony offered the sword to him, hilt first. Wait's body relaxed. Standing straighter, he took it, inspected it. Lighter than any weapon he had ever carried, shorter, it was nonetheless familiar.

"I ordered twin blades made from the one you carried from the chase," Atony told him. "It seemed a fitting use of so precious a sacrifice. Mine is still with the smith. I thought it safer, considering."

"You have nothing to fear from me. Not now."

"It is not you I feared," Atony told him. "I liked our battle too well, my friend. Far too well. As much as I wish you were staying here in Alyria, the Glass King needs you to leave. But we are brothers in battle, brothers in heritage, and now, sword-brothers."

Wait stepped back, whistled a few careful swipes through the air. The weapon was well-balanced. The hilt fit his hand perfectly. Something like aggression wormed its way through his body, something like excitement.

Sword-brothers. He once thought he had many of those in Vales Gate, among the Dakhan there. On the edge of the world, he learned the truth.

"Good journey, Wait," Atony said. "May the wind be ever at your back, and home in your sight."

Wait watched the King of Alyria trudge back up the beach. Beyond him, the Glass Castle was a twinkling finger pointing up to the sky. It looked nothing like the castle in the Vale, but its grandeur made him think of home.

May the wind be ever at your back, and home in your sight.

An old sea-faring blessing, one known all his life, like Egalfo's funeral rite. Until falling Beyond, he had never heard of Alyria or its Glass King, but somehow, it belonged in the same world; and he wondered if he and Jinna and Linhare were really Beyond, or if there was no such thing after all.

The pendant grew warm against his heart, spread like fingers across his chest. The sensation caught his breath and oozed along his skin. Wait listened to the prickling of energy tingle along his scalp, lighting his mind, opening his eyes, his ears, his thoughts like a book too long waiting to be studied.

The Eye clacked in its case like an angry insect. Pulling the chain from his shirt, cupping the caged Eye in his hands, Wait took deep, sea-scented breaths. *Respect it,* Atony said, and as the Eye eased warmth through him, Wait tried to likewise warm the stone. The insistent whispering softened, slowed. It became combinations of sound Wait recognized. Soothing and ingenuous as a child's first hushed promise, the

Eye asked. Wait answered. He eased it from its cage. He pinched it between forefinger and thumb. He held it up to the light.

Show me.

In his mind's eye, he saw the Glass King walking up the beach; the feast, the pyre, the Siren's Curse rushing shoreward. Wait was in his chambers, learning every curve and rise of Linhare's body. He was standing outside his door, hand on the lever. Being questioned. Being cleaned. Being Dakhonne. Back and back through the days flickering behind his lids like a picture book flipped too quickly; back to the Pinewood, to Beloël's glade, to the trinket mound not a trinket mound any longer, but a trunk like the one in Saghan's castle, like the one in Sabal's room, that he and Linhare stood beside, hand in hand.

Back, Not Backwards

THE MISTY MOMENTS just before dawn were Jinna's solace. The first time she'd come above before sunrise, Hepheo opened his mouth, then closed it again with a nod. Jinna respected his accord and did not abuse it. Moments. That was all she needed. It was all she took.

She was surprised and disappointed to learn they would travel back to the Pinewood, rather than north to Therk; in the end, it did not matter to her. Wherever they were going was away from the chase that gave her back Egalfo, and Alyria that took him away. Wait's stone vision of ending their journey where it began, of himself and Linhare standing before a trunk that had once been a trinket mound, irked her into arguing its reliability. But the Vespe Neciel said the green agreed with the pale blue stone. It was all a lot of guesswork, as far as Jinna was concerned, and in the end did not matter to her enough to argue further. Somewhere between falling through the bottom of Sabal's treacherous trunk and Egalfo's death, she lost all desire to go home again. And if anyone noticed she was never once mentioned in Wait's stone vision, no one said it aloud.

Dawn pinked the sky. The mist swirled overboard. The Siren's Curse came about. Any moment, it would catch dawnlight rays and ride them screaming to Beloël's shore, ending Hepheo's obligation to Linhare.

"Still time t'change your mind."

Jinna turned to face Hepheo. Brightening dawn silhouetted him, lighting only his edges even here, on his own ship, becoming indistinct. They had not spoken, but each morning spent together in the mist created the conversation now coming to a close.

"I've made my decision," she said. "Just tell me what I have to do."

"Say the words."

"What words?"

"Any words. It's more the intention what binds you to the Curse." He left the helm, came to put his hands on her shoulders. Firm and strong, his grip comforted. "But words is power. Once you speak, you can't take it back. You're an Everwanderer, bound for eternity. You must be certain."

Underneath her feet, the deck lurched. The Pilfer groaned. The Siren's Curse began to pick up speed. Crew clambered topside and into the riggings.

"Jinna! Jin!"

Jinna spun out of Hepheo's grip. Linhare was trotting towards her. Fingers clenched into fists. Eyes fixed on her friend coming closer and closer, Jinna murmured, "I bind myself to the Siren's Curse. I will serve out my life, and then after death. By my oath, I swear it."

"Didn't you hear me?" Linhare grabbed her hands and spun her about. If there was any sensation to go with the binding, it got lost in the lurching of Jinna's heart and the speed of the Siren's Curse careening over the sea.

"Sorry. I was…talking to Hepheo."

Linhare leaned over the rail. "It's not nearly as dramatic as watching it from land."

"I suppose."

"Something wrong, Jin?"

"No, not really."

"Yes there is, I can tell."

Of course you can. Jinna found herself smiling, and for a moment she regretted the oath she could not take back. Then Linhare's face brightened that instant before she waved. Jinna turned to see Wait coming their way. *It's best. For all of us.*

Jinna let go a long, slow breath, her heart throbbing against her ribs. Wait met her eyes over Linhare's head. The colorful, sailcloth bags crisscrossed his chest. His, and Linhare's.

"Are you ready, Jin?" he asked.

Jinna smiled up at him, tears brimming. She held out her hand and he took it, squeezed it gently, and let it go.

"Ready or not, it's time," she answered.

"I've already said most of my good-byes." Linhare was glancing at the faces gathered to see them off. "If you want to see Moslo before we disembark, Jin, you should—"

Jinna pulled Linhare into her arms, kissing her soundly silent. She pushed her off again. Linhare stumbled backwards, hand to lips and cheeks blushing.

"What was that about?"

"The only good-bye I need to make," Jinna told her.

Linhare's brow furrowed. She shook her head, pointing shoreward. "Look there! Someone awaits us on the shore. Perhaps it is Beloël, or Liloat. Where is your bag, Jinna?"

"In the Keeper's room, where it belongs. Linny, I'm—"

"Oh for pity's sake, Jin!" Linhare turned to Hepheo. "Would you ask one of your men to fetch it for her?"

"Linhare!"

Linhare spun to face her, face flushed and tears glistening. "No! No, Jinna. Don't say it! Do not say the words!"

"I already have."

Color drained from Linhare's cheeks. She stumbled a step closer to Jinna. Wait's steadying hand caught her elbow. Linhare shook off his grasp.

331

"What about your mother?"

Jinna's jaw clenched. "If you believe the way home is here in the Pinelands," she said. "If you believe anything Wait's blue stone has told us, then you know my mother is dead."

"Is this—is it because of Egalfo?"

His name on Linhare's lips hurt somehow. Anger and jealousy and grief churned, but Jinna choked them down. "Yes and no." She took her friend's hands, surprised and grateful that she did not pull away. "You left me behind when you went to university," she said at last. Linhare opened her mouth, but Jinna gave her hands a squeeze. "You were right to. I knew you were then, but I wanted to be angry with you, and I was, Linny, for a very long time. But the truth was, I didn't want to go to university with you. I wanted you to stay in the Vale with me."

"I couldn't. You know that."

"I do. And I also know that you didn't want to, either. We have been on different paths for a very long time, probably since birth. I didn't realize it until Egalfo…" She blinked back tears. "When Egalfo asked me to come away with him, I let him, and you, believe that I could not bear to leave you. That I was too loyal a friend. It wasn't true, not really. He scared me, Linny. He scared me so much."

"Because you loved him."

"Because I *could* love him," Jinna corrected. "And then I did love him. And then he died. But that isn't why I'm staying on the Siren's Curse."

"Then why?"

"I'm staying because this is *my* path." She put Linhare's hand into Wait's, pointed shoreward. "There is yours."

Thumbing the tears from her friend's cheek, Jinna kissed her one last time.

"Go," she said. "Go home. Make everything right."

"Oh, Jin."

Linhare pulled her into her arms, held her so tightly. Jinna held Linhare as tightly. *This is right. This is right.* But she could not let go. It was Linhare who did, lifting a hand as if to wave. Jinna pressed palm to palm.

"I love you, Linny. No matter what. No matter how far apart we are."

"No matter how far apart," Linhare said, and hurried away.

Jinna did not watch her go. Instead she went to the rail facing out to sea where the mist swirled and spread. Out there existed other seas and other lands she never dreamed of, even if she wished. Drawing deep breaths of sea air, Jinna let the brine and the roar fill her.

*   *   *

HEPHEO CAUGHT AN INBOUND WAVE, riding it expertly to shore. He and Wait leapt from the skiff to pull it up onto the beach. Liloat, for it was indeed the gobbet-man awaiting them on the beach, was offering his hand, excitedly chattering words Linhare did not hear. Then Wait was there, taking her hand from the gobbet's. Sound returned. Linhare could breathe without choking. She could speak without vomiting.

"Where is she?" Liloat's voice pitched too-high. "Where is my halfling?"

"Out there." Linhare pointed to the Siren's Curse.

"He was right! She did come back! I must go to her."

"Hold on there." Hepheo looked up and down the beach, to Wait. "Something's not right. Do you feel it?"

Wait nodded.

"Feel what?" Linhare grasped at Wait. "What is it, Hepheo?"

"I don't know," he said, then to Liloat, "Where is Beloël?"

"He's gone," Liloat answered. "They're all gone. Only I stayed behind, because he said she would come. And she did! Please, I must go to her. Give me leave, Captain, to—"

"What do you mean *all gone?*" Wait asked. "Where did they go?"

"Away!" Liloat moaned. "Please! All this time so alone in this Pinewood. For her! For my halfling. I beg you, give me leave to go aboard the Siren's Curse!"

Hepheo's fading form blinked like a ghasty-haint at dusk. He looked out to sea, to his Curse. Linhare thought it seemed lower in the sky than it had been, the mist thicker.

"I have to get back," Hepheo said. "Something is very wrong here, and I 'ent strong enough to fight it. If you're coming, come. If you're staying, stay."

"The Eye said this is the way home," Linhare said. "Wait, could you have been wrong?"

"I know what I saw," he said. "And Neciel agreed. Maybe we should get her ashore and—"

"Look at me!" Hepheo's voice warbled like a bird's. "Look at my ship! This 'ent no place for me or mine, and I 'ent waiting for sunset." Reaching into his pocket, Hepheo pulled out a silver whistle, the mouthpiece forged into a bat-like shape and the pipe like folded wings. He placed it onto Linhare's palm. "Take this. If it turns out Wait was wrong, give it a blow and the Siren's Curse will come for you. I got to get out of these waters afore I can't no more."

"Go," Wait said. "Hurry."

Hepheo hesitated, or his wavering form made it seem so. Nodding once, he closed Linhare's hand around the whistle. "Good luck, Little Queen. You," he pointed to Liloat, "help me row." Floating, wobbling, fading down the beach, Hepheo climbed into his skiff and shoved it into the waves. Liloat followed fast on his heels.

"Beloël left something for you, Little Queen!" he called as he ran. "He made me promise I would see you got it!"

"Where?" Linhare shouted after him as he dove in after the skiff. But if there was an answer, it got lost in the rumble of the tide. Hepheo pulled Liloat on board and together, they rowed out to sea, to the Siren's Curse.

"I don't understand," Linhare murmured. "What just happened?"

Wait's arm came around her shoulders. He pulled her in close. "We'll find out soon enough."

Birds sang. Insects chirped. Vines and leafy trees displayed autumn's bright presence. The Pinewood was otherwise abandoned. No bolleys flitted from branch to branch. No gobbet fluff drifted on the breeze. Not a single Drümbul lord or lady sighed from the shadows. No ghasty-haints sparkled in the night.

Linhare walked through the days, following Wait and whatever instinct propelled him toward home. The abundant stores Ezibah packed for them, supplemented by the wild fare Wait found along the way, sustained them. Several days—Linhare lost count—after leaving the beach, they came upon a familiar glade one late afternoon when the sun slanted through the pines. Beloël's antlered chair held its honored place at the head of the table set with domed platters, silver goblets and plates made of wood so fine they looked like glass. Linhare lifted a dome.

"Still hot," she said, dipping her finger into the gravy drenching the roasted meat. "And delicious. But Liloat said he'd been alone for a long time. And we're days from last seeing him."

"This is fae." Wait stood behind Beloël's chair, his eyes on it and not the impossible feast. He bent to retrieve something from the seat there, held it up to show her a silver box the size of his palm. "And I think this is that something Beloël left for you."

Wait handed it to Linhare. Upon the lid, and above a scene of fae revelry, her name was etched in sweeping letters more swirl than line. Raised images of woodland creatures bumped the polished sides. The box opened with a flick of a latch.

"It's empty." She held it up for Wait to see.

"A keepsake?"

"Maybe." Linhare turned it over, feeling every bump and groove. "Look at this." Moving into a sunbeam, Linhare read the words engraved into the bottom:

* * *

"Old wrongs are righted;
Old ways, made anew.
For time moves forward;
And though, sometimes back,
It never moves backwards.
"What does it mean?"

"Maybe it doesn't mean anything," Wait told her. "Maybe he just wanted you to have it."

"Somehow," Linhare said, tucking the box into her bag, "I don't think so."

Linhare and Wait ate in the Drümbul glade, slept in the sleeping basket waiting for them as the feast had been. In the morning, the glade was as deserted as the rest of the Pinewood; but for Beloël's antlered chair.

They walked.

And slept.

And ate.

And loved beneath the stars and starlight, beside the forgetting pool where Wait had found the Eye, at the edge of the meadow they had come to separately, and would leave by together, and wherein stood the trunk like, but not identical to, Sabal's.

Evidence of the once-imposing trinket structure existed only in a lack of thick bramble and high grass. Not a shoe, not a thimble, not a shard of pottery or scrap of cloth. Linhare and Wait stood over it, side by side, hand in hand.

"Is this what you saw?" she asked him.

"It is." Still holding her hand, Wait lifted the lid. Nothing came out of it. No ominous cloud. No deadly horde. Not even a foul stench. It was as empty as Sabal's. He said, "Let's eat."

Linhare dropped his hand. "Now?"

"It's one of the first things you learn as a soldier," he said. "Eat when you know you can, especially when you don't know what's coming next. Now, we are safe. We have food. Once we get into that trunk, neither of those things are assured."

So close. Home. The Vale. Answers to questions she denied even asking herself until this moment. Despite the unknown dangers they faced, Linhare felt the longing so desperately she sighed without meaning to.

"All right, Wait," she said. "We eat."

Flopping onto the ground beside him, she grabbed her bag packed well and efficiently with papery, bark-wrapped packages. After however long they spent in the Pinewood, it still seemed as full as it had been the first time she opened it, and Linhare thought perhaps Wait was right; the fae food could well vanish once back in Vales Gate. Digging in, she found a loaf as fresh as the day it was baked. Breaking a piece off, she savored the nutty goodness as she rummaged through the contents for some of the dry, salty meat she enjoyed.

Her hand landed upon a silky something her fingers knew that instant before her mind did. She pulled out the scrap of cloth as blue as Alyrian eyes, as blue as the stone at Wait's throat: the wrap her father once brought her from Left Foot, lost and found again on the trinket mound.

Linhare set the bread aside, spread out the blue cloth. Her eyes filled. She felt Wait's eyes on her, but she would not look his way as she rose to her feet, held the cloth out before her. Holes and dirt and pulls marred what had once been a father's gift to the daughter he missed. She did not remember taking it from one place to the next, but there it was, the tattered evidence.

Linhare pressed it to her face and breathed in the scent of the chase, the Pilfered mist, the sea, and the scent of fae food. In her mind's eye, she saw them all. Beloël and Liloat, Hepheo and Ezibah, Brodic and Gianostalia, Queen Saghan and King Atony. She saw Rodly as the waterfurry, and as Sal, as the snake that killed Egalfo who appeared there behind her lids, alive and happy and laughing. And Linhare saw Jinna on the deck of the Siren's Curse, wind in her hair and sun on her face. They were all there in the scents mingling on this piece of home she had carried across fae and back again.

One last deep inhale and Linhare pushed a little way through the grass to a copse of brambly-thorns that had once borne flowers. The bulging, seedy hips weighed heavily at its branches. Roses, perhaps. Wild and fragrant and tough. Placing the cloth upon the thorns, Linhare gave it a good tuck to make sure it would wind into the bramble rather than blow free. Going back to Wait, already on his feet with their bags, Linhare held out her hand.

"Just a moment," he said, yanking loose the chain Hepheo gave him, the one he had used to keep them bound out on the chase. He looped it around both their wrists, made sure they were secure. "Now we're ready." They took hands. Wait lifted the trunk's unadorned lid. "At the same time."

They each put a leg over the side, then the other. Hunkering down into it, bound hand still holding bound hand, Wait grasped the open lid with his free one.

"Ready?" he asked.

"Ready," she answered.

The lid came down. All went dark. Nothing happened. Linhare could hear herself breathing, and Wait. Her hand in his started to sweat. The air in the trunk became hot, moist, thin.

"I don't think—" she began, and in that same instant, her body lightened, Wait's hand tightened, slipped from the sweat, but held. Her words became light falling like a star in the pitch black of night.

And she fell, and she fell, and she fell...

Beyond the Gate

NO CAREENING FALL INTO OBLIVION. No bump onto a mound of old treasures. Wait smelled earth and woody musk. He could feel the confined space all around him, and Linhare in his arms. Burying his face in her hair, he asked, "Are you—"

"I'm fine. Where are we?"

One arm holding her to him, he felt around with the other. A wooden box. A curved lid. Pushing it open, Wait was instantly aware of the thrumming earthsong beyond the box. Soothing. Humbling. Sacred.

"The Holes," he said.

"How can you tell? I can't see a thing."

"There is a feel to the place." Taking hold of her hand, Wait rose to his feet. He legged over the side of the trunk, rummaging about in his pocket for his tinderbox. Pulling Linhare down with him, he struck sparks and fed them some of the thin bark from the wrapped packages inside his bag still full of food.

They were in a small room, one with a heavy door propped open by skeletons still held together by their clothes. Behind them, the trunk they fell through twice. The magic once invisible now fairly pulsed in the soft firelight.

Linhare reached up, her bound hand lifting his as well, and closed the lid firmly. "Someone must have put that down here. Someone who didn't want anyone falling in."

"Or coming out." Wait tugged free his chain and refastened it to itself. He moved to the edge of light and tried to see out. "This is the deepest part of the Holes, where the worst or most dangerous enemies were kept."

He nudged the skeletons with his foot. They toppled. "Forgive me," he breathed, and fished a femur from the tattered clothing. He wrapped it tightly with cloth, brought it to the dwindling bark fire and lit it. Dust crackled, but it caught quickly.

"It will do until we find a proper light," he said. Taking Linhare's hand and whatever loose cloth he could gather from the pile of bones, he led her away from the trunk, out of the cell, and into the Holes themselves.

The floor crunched beneath their feet. Debris. Bones. Years and years of decay. Cobwebs hung like Aughty-moss. Great spiders skittered away from the light. The Eye trilled as it hadn't since stepping foot in the Pinewood, as Wait led Linhare through the Holes, into the mines themselves, but it showed him nothing.

"Just up ahead," he told her, "is the hub. If there's anyone down here, that's where they'll be."

Wait drew her closer. The absolute silence ahead, the unmistakable scent of dust and death, the images he had pushed aside as possibility coalesced into reality. They stepped into the hub. The light shafts drilled deep into the mountain illuminated the grisly truth of what the Eye told him before he truly knew how to listen.

Bodies. Everywhere. Skeletons still wearing clothes like those propping open the door to the cell. And rubble. Huge chunks of rock had fallen from the ceiling above. The staircase that once spanned six stories lay in sections amid the bodies it broke when it fell.

The mines are unstable. We will all be killed. It is what she wants.

Ellis' voice whispered as if in his ear. What sorcery had Yebbe known to cause or attempt to prevent this?

"Wait, look."

Linhare stood several feet away, motioning him to follow. At a section of crumbled stairway, she halted.

"Most of these people did not die when the roof came down," she said. "See? They are huddled here, as if for warmth or comfort."

Indeed, skeletal arms entwined. A small skull rested upon a lap. Another body propped up in the arms of another. On down the line of bodies, it was much the same.

"Did they starve?" she asked.

"Not likely," Wait answered. "Starving people don't huddle together for comfort. The scene is too peaceful. Maybe suffocation? Exposure?"

"Or sorcery," Linhare said. "Perhaps my sister was not as untalented as her tutor claimed."

She nudged a skeleton. It toppled with a macabre clack. Wait reached for her, but she was bending down, reaching for something within the bones.

"A lantern," she said. "Like we used to take camping in the Pinelands when I was little. Feels like there might be a bit of oil left in it."

Wait took it from her, lit it with the rag-wrapped femur.

"Looks like you're right," he said. "See what else we can find."

Linhare turned up a few stubs of candle and one fine taper, never lit. Wait found several jars of what might have once been peaches or apples but had long ago turned black.

"I think we should try to make our way out of here," he told her. "These people have been dead a long time, but there's no saying what killed them is gone."

Linhare nodded. She retrieved their bags, hesitating when Wait took her hand to lead her away.

"Could Ellis and Yebbe be here among the bones?"

339

Wait squeezed her hand. "Possibly. Probably."

"Does the Eye tell you anything? Has it showed you more visions of what might have happened here?"

"No, Linhare. I'm sorry. It stopped doing that before we reached Alyria."

"Oh."

He felt her body tremble through their joined hands.

"Come," he said. "This way."

"But all the stairways are fallen. Are we not as trapped down here as they were?"

Wait held the lamp higher. Their shadows were giants on the far wall. "I know another way," he told her, and led her back towards the Holes.

FRESH AIR HIT HER FACE; fresh air scented by summer lingering, a chill coming, and the ever-present, permeating aroma of *green.*

Wait reached back for her hands, lifting her easily from the rain well in the inner ward where she and Jinna and Sabal once played snow war. His step never faltered. He never once lost their way on that wormhole path the deepest, darkest parts of his mind still knew. Linhare simply followed, trusting him as she always had. As she always would.

Dawn's pale glow stained shadows purple. Wait led her through the servant's alley and into the gardens themselves. The beds once lovingly tended were tangled with long-dead flowers, bare shrubs, spindly trees. And there, where the topiaries once stood so meticulously trimmed, were only hewn stumps; and a grave marker.

Chira. Beloved nurse.

The ground around it was dry. Cracked. The paving stones heaved out of the earth, jumbled like shells on the shore. Tough vines snaked unopposed. Victorious. Then Wait took her hand again, hauling her along and away from her silent mourning, toward the solarium doors that looked more like the gap teeth of an old man than the pristine panels in her memory.

"Could the castle be deserted?" she whispered. "Like the Pinewood?" But Wait motioned her silent. He pointed to light spilling from a window partially hidden by a dead bush.

My room.

How many times had she flung open those windows to sit upon the sill? Breathed in the heady scent of the jonqui vines trained to grow around that window? The bush obscuring the view now had always been clipped to stay below her sill so that the yellow flowers popped open in the fall, perfectly offset the blazing orange of the jonqui.

Linhare tried to walk as silently as Wait, but dry things snapped and cracked beneath her shoes. No one came to the window. Nothing stirred in that spilling light. She squeezed in between Wait and the castle wall to peek inside.

Mother?

She gasped. Wait put a finger to his lips. They crossed the inner ward, stepped through the broken solarium and into the wing that was more home to her than any other place in the Vale. The floors did not shine. Lamps gave no light; only one outside the door once hers. Draperies still hung, the same deep blue velvets that always adorned autumn windows, just as the lace always replaced them in the spring; but these were faded and drab. Even in the pale dawn light Linhare could see the streaks where the sun had bleached color away.

No guards stood sentry in this most royal of halls. No nightly serving staff in sleepy attendance. Wait motioned her forward, to that lone light. There he paused. He put a finger to his lips, touched the door. Linhare nodded her head. When he placed his hand upon the lever, she held her breath.

The door opened with a sigh of untended hinges. The woman impossibly her mother, spied through the illumined window, was not alone. In a chair all colors of pale gold, an old man slept, slack-jawed and drooling, spittle glistening on his chin.

"I did not call for anyone."

The woman's husky voice was not Diandra's even if the face was her face. Older. Harder. Lined with angry ill-temper. A scar on her cheek stood out like a pale flower in a brilliant patch of green. Narrowed, gem-blue eyes pinned Linhare where she stood. Deep in the pit of her stomach, dread thrummed. Wait remained silent, unseen. The woman's jaw worked back and forth. Her lips twitched.

"I had a sister once," she said at last. "She looked a bit like you. Who are you, child? And why have you come here at this forsaken hour?"

"I—I am newly assigned to you, your—Your Majesty. I saw your light and thought you would like an early breakfast."

"Assigned to me, eh?" The woman laughed scornfully, familiarly. "Oswin must be feeling more kindly towards me as I age into decrepitude, to send a serving lass to my prison. Very well, then. You may pour my water. It is all I require for now."

Linhare dipped a curtsey and hurried to the table where a pitcher and cups sat ready; where they had always sat ready. Unlike the state of the inner ward and the hallway, the room was tidy, if shabby. She recognized all her own furniture, even her quilt, tattered but still neatly covering the bed canopied in the same lace curtains there since childhood.

The woman took the cup. She sipped, sharp eyes never leaving Linhare's face. The dreadful pang became a certainty.

"All these many years and you come back to haunt me now?" The woman spoke into her cup, the sound as haunting as it was haunted.

"I beg pardon, Your Majesty?"

She handed the cup to Linhare and turned towards the window. Long moments passed: silence and breathing and sunlight brightening. Linhare looked to Wait, still hovering in the shadows of the room. He was closer to the sleeping old man now, but he shook his head and pointed to the woman now leaning at the windowsill.

"I never meant for it to go so far," she said at last. "Do you know that, child? Do the history books that paint me such a villain teach that to you? Do they tell how I saved her from all I have since endured?"

"I—I have never been schooled, Your Majesty."

"Never been schooled?" She turned from the window. "I thought the Senate put an end to all that long ago. Are you from Esher, then?"

"One of her harlotries."

The woman laughed. "Yes, you must be. Only so remote an isle would still use that old crass term. I should have known that Oswin would send me an illiterate little barnacle like you."

"Forgive me if my ignorance offends."

The woman waved her apology away, her face pinching in distaste. "I prefer ignorance, if truth be told. I was happily ignorant once. Content to play with magical things and flirt with all the young men who came to call. But they did not interest me then. Only one man did, and he did not want me." The old woman's chin came up. She said, "If I could not have love, I would have power. And it was mine, for a time."

The woman tossed her head as if to shake such thoughts from it. She came closer then, close enough for Linhare to see the fine lines of her face, the veins underneath translucent skin and the scar marring her cheek. A stranger's face. But in the gem-blue intimacy of her eyes, Linhare saw her clearly.

Oh, Sabal. My little sister.

The woman thrust a finger under Linhare's nose. "Listen well, child; remain ignorant. There is no happiness in wisdom and certainly none in power. That," she flicked her hand towards the old man in his chair, "is the price one pays for power. Wisdom comes harder yet. I don't recommend it. I don't recommend it at all."

Sabal turned away from Linhare then. Her hands were clenched upon her hips, her body so bony that shoulder blades jutted against the worn fabric of her gown. The old man in the chair snored, sputtered awake. He blinked rheumy eyes that went instantly to his wife.

"Is there someone else here, my dear?"

Linhare shuddered, an involuntary reaction to that voice unchanged. *Did she ever tell you? Did you know it was you I asked for?*

She backed towards the door, despite the fact that he was old and shriveled and could no more touch her than rise from his chair. Then Wait was standing behind him, his face composed. Assuring. Linhare stood taller.

"You startled me, sir. I didn't see you there."

He blinked and blinked and blinked, his mouth still slack and open. Shouldering higher in his chair, he sat forward just a little and whispered, "Linhare?"

"Fool!" Sabal's voice cracked, making him flinch. "Linhare is dead. You killed her. I killed her. We killed her, the two of us. This is just a serving girl from Esher, given to us by our beloved Senator. Go back to sleep, Agreth. Or die. Whichever you prefer today. If you choose the latter, I'll give you my biscuit at dinner."

"A serving girl, you say?" Agreth slumped back. "Come closer, my dear, so that I may look at you."

Wait shook his head, gestured to the door, but Linhare moved closer to Agreth. The once-clear blue of his eyes had been robbed away by the filmy cloud obscuring them. His hair, what remained of it, was pure white. Knobby, veined hands shook. Clothes hung on his skeletal frame. He smiled wetly, nearly toothlessly. Faraway as that smile was, clouded as were his eyes, he saw her. Linhare knew that he did. But it was into the past he spoke, to a young woman who no longer existed.

"She told me that you loved me. She said you were too ashamed to say, your mother so newly in her grave. Give you time, she said, a little bit of time, and you would find the courage to speak. But I was impatient, my beloved. I wanted you. I took you. And then you left me. Forever left me."

Bile rose in her throat. Linhare would not flee. She stood over the old, impotent monster and wished she had it in her to laugh; but she did not. Backing away, she met her sister's angry glare, and knew that Jinna had spoken truly. Again revulsion threatened to undo her, but Linhare refused it. She dipped a stumbled curtsey, turned and headed for the door. The old man's weeping intensified, his scrawny shoulders shaking, hand outstretched. Sabal watched her, but did not stop her from leaving. Wait was already in the hall, ready to take her into his arms.

"I loved her so," she said into his chest. "My little sister. Jinna was right; it was she who told him I loved him. Jinna was right."

"And she has paid for all her treachery." He put her from him just enough to look down into her face. "This all happened so long ago. They lost. They're prisoners here in this place left to rot."

"But how? We were not gone *this* long?"

"I really don't know," he said. "The Eye showed me, but I didn't understand. I still don't, but—"

Linhare gasped up at him. "Old wrongs righted, old ways made anew," she repeated the words etched into the bottom of the silver box Beloël left for her. "This is what the poem meant."

"Maybe you're right, but we won't find out standing here."

"Where do we go now?"

"Up the mountain," he said. "To Vernist-on-Contif. The Purists will tell us—"

"Ghosts and more ghosts."

Linhare spun. Wait tensed. Sabal grasped at the door. In the dawnlight, she was young again, beautiful again. The roundness of her cheek returned, for that moment, with the pale spun gold of her hair.

"Am I as enfeebled as my husband?" she whispered. "Will I now cry out to you as he cries out for her?"

Her eyes then fell upon Linhare tucked into the curve of Wait's arms, and narrowed again. She stood straighter.

"You all cry for her. Vales Gate cries for her. Always her. Always Linhare. Even I cried for her. Night after night after year after year I cried out for her, but she never came. When I wed Sisolo as she should have done, I cried out for her. When he tried to get me with child, again and again and again, I cried out her name just as he did. No child ever came. I stopped crying."

Sabal stood straighter then. Sunlight found its way through thin patches in the heavy draperies and made her old again. She smoothed her dress, her hair. She raised her chin in that same way she did as a young woman always too good for the company she kept.

"Tell Oswin that I will not be needing a serving girl after all."

Sabal stepped back into the room once Linhare's; the room now a prison so fitting. Linhare stepped out of Wait's embrace. She took several steps back towards the door and stopped.

"Back, but never backwards," she whispered. "Oh, Sabal."

What is Done

LOWER DOCKSIDE SMELLED OF FRESH FISH, cooking spice and sunshine seeped into old wood. Linhare breathed in those blessed scents, cleansing her mind and her heart, grateful for this ageless place where seagoing vessels creaked and bumped at their moorings; where gulls shrieked and fishmongers shouted out the day's catch; where everything remained as unchanged as the sailors returning from sea, ruddy-skinned and boisterous as the girls come to greet them.

They left the castle by deserted servant corridors and taken their time walking the length of Littlevale. Yebbe's cottage stood yet, maintained with love, and in honor of that heroine of *the Republic*. Linhare and Wait had taken a meal with the wife there, and her flirting, fleeing toddlers. From her they learned that the Republic of Vales Gate ruled itself, not the monarchy. She wrinkled her nose when she mentioned the imprisoned queen, believed the king long dead and chattered eagerly about Senators and councils and how difficult it was to get those from the furthest islets in the archipelago to the Vale for the yearly sessions. Her husband, a sailor aboard one of the ships assigned to Esher and Siys, spent more time carting Senators back and forth than he did in his own home. Linhare held in her grief all the while, held it until she and Wait left the cottage, then wept until they passed through the Gate and into Upper Dockside. Titles held since her family first set foot on Vales Gate, a crown her father fought to maintain, the crown her mother ultimately died for, no longer existed; only an aging captive festering in a castle fallen to ruin.

In Upper Dockside, handbills tacked to every storefront declared the yearly council of Senators would convene in nine days' time, in the amphitheater where she and Jinna watched the Thissians eat fire. Linhare and Wait temporarily abandoned their quest to go up the mountain in favor of discovering firsthand the changes in Vales Gate, as they might have had Sabal never tricked them both.

"Maybe this all started back then," Wait had said, reminding her of the note Ellis sent. "He and Yebbe were going to bring me into it, and that means you, too. Maybe if we hadn't—"

Linhare placed a finger on his lips then, fighting thoughts she was already having and tears she was tired of fighting. "And maybe it wouldn't have mattered," she told him. "Maybe Sabal would have worked some other mischief. Maybe I'd have married Agr—" She could not say it. "—Sisolo after all, and events would have gone differently still. Maybe doesn't matter, Wait. All that happened, happened. And here we are."

They camped in the wood just beyond the Gate, living on the stores no longer infinite, but giving out. As they did, they moved camp to the dunes just south of Lower Dockside where Wait could fish and Linhare could dig clams while they waited for the ships bearing the Senators to arrive. After nine days spent sorting and pocketing her losses, her gains, and the obvious prosperity of the archipelago she loved, Linhare sat on the docks, drinking in the scents and the sights familiar and beloved, watching those ships pull to port. She experienced the excitement of her people, *as* one of her people. The grief of a lost crown slipped from her brow.

A shadow momentarily blocked the sunlight. Wait lowered himself to the piling beside her and handed her a warm, wrapped parcel. Linhare opened it.

"Fried sugardough? Where did you get this?"

"From the baker, of course."

Linhare nudged him with her elbow. "I mean, where did you get the coin to purchase it?"

Wait pulled her into his arms, laughing. He laughed often since returning from Beyond. Some of the ferocity found there had faded; very little of the somberness once shrouding him had returned. This, Linhare understood, was Wait. *Calyran.* And she loved him all the more.

"The baker was cursing a pile of bricks for his new oven," he let her go to say, "and the boy he'd hired to stack them in his yard. Apparently, the bricks arrived but the boy didn't, and he was stuck. I moved the bricks. He paid me. I bought you a treat in celebration."

"My stalwart provider."

"A man does what he can."

A fanfare of horns and shouts turned their heads. Five great ships now bobbed in the harbor. Smaller boats filled with red-garbed figures were being lowered to the sea.

"Look, Wait! The Senators!"

Her own shout got caught up in many others. A surge of humanity hurried for the appointed dock. Shoving the sugardough into her mouth, Linhare tugged at Wait's hand, and they followed the crowd.

THE AMPHITHEATER WAS THE SAME, yet not the same at all. No bigger, but grander. The stands glowed as white as the Alyrian coast. Ancient reliefs worn by time and the sea air had been replaced. Sturdy new columns held up the tiers rather than those carefully preserved, but crumbling ones Wait remembered. Crisp, sun-warmed autumn made sitting in the sunshine comfortable, a good thing since it took so long for the theater to fill and the thirty or so dignitaries on the stage to arrange themselves. Linhare dozed on his shoulder by the time an elderly gentleman dressed all in deep blue raised his hands for silence.

Wait gasped. Linhare's head came up.

"What is it?" she whispered. Wait leaned forward. It was no mistake. The man, tall and straight and strong despite his obvious years, was unmistakable.

"It's Oswin," he told her. "My Firstman. Oswin."

Linhare's eyes went round. "Sabal mentioned his name," she said. "I didn't make the connection."

"Neither did I."

Silence fell; Firstman—*Senator*—Oswin spoke.

"As elected Speaker of the Senate, I thank you, Senators, for making the long journey here." He turned to the gathering of red-clad dignitaries, then to the audience. "And you, people of Vales Gate, for bearing witness to this council."

Oswin bowed his head while those gathered applauded. Wait imagined he could hear his thoughts gathering, clicking into place, and realized the Eye was wiggling in its case. He covered it with his hand and it eased.

"It has been a very long time," Oswin began when the clapping faded, "nearly twenty-five years since the mines collapsed and took Mine Officer Ellis from us. Longer since our beloved Queen Linhare vanished, and with her all the hope of sparing Vales Gate from what was to come. Every person here over the age of thirty remembers how dark a time it was, but no amount of treachery could put out the spark of the great Republic Ellis conceived, fought for. Died for. Forestwife Yebbe, bless her to the stars and starlight, carried his ideas and principles out of those mines. She gave them to us. She continued the fight. And in the end, won the peace all the queens and kings of Vales Gate had never been able to attain. Let us offer a moment of silence for their sacrifice."

Everyone bowed their heads, everyone but Linhare. Hers was raised proudly, defiantly. Wait took her hand.

"Brother and sister Senators." Oswin turned sideways to acknowledge those dressed in red. "We gather to vote, at long last, on reopening the mines. The wounds are old and scarred over. Debates have been argued and decisions made. Moreover, it is time to commemorate the sacrifice of that ill-fated rebel and all those who stood with him to the end. It is time to send those who lost their lives in that pivotal battle to the stars and starlight."

A massive round of applause burst from the audience, and from the Senators on stage. Oswin held up his hands again; it took a long while to quiet the crowd. "I will consider that a vote of approval from the people," he said. Laughter rumbled about the amphitheater. "Senators? A call to vote."

Each Senator stood in turn, answering with an *approve*.

"We are unanimous. Proposals will be presented during closed council three days hence. Next for open council, we are hearing arguments for and against opening Vales Gate to trade with Yerac'ia and Therk. Senator Violetti of Sisolo will speak first in favor. Senator?"

The woman stepping forward was small and plump and dark-haired. If she was related to that ill-fated Larguessa, a generation or two had thinned the blood. Wait did not listen to her arguments. He heard them all before, so many years ago when he did not quite understand about trade agreements and piracy.

The debate on stage droned between his ears, like the Eye when it was humming. Wait leaned back on his elbows, scanned the robed Senators on the stage and wondered what his part in this might have been, had he not fallen Beyond. Linhare did not want to think about it, but Wait could not help running those scenarios through his head. Would it have been a bloodless revolution, sanctioned by Linhare herself? Would she have resisted, forcing him to act against his friend and mentor? Would she have married Agreth, like Diandra did, to patch the peace crumbling far too long to ever be mended?

Wait glanced at Linhare, her attention fixed on Senator Violetti, and knew: Linhare would have saved her people a revolution. She had her father's head for diplomacy, his interest in matters of state. Wait could imagine her among the Senators, more than a figurehead, better than a monarch. Coming out of Beyond where his blood beat fiercest, thrust into this world decades older than when he left it, Wait acknowledged that he would have been better suited to the past that was rather than the one that wasn't. He was a warrior. A Dakhonne made for battle. The thought alone made his blood surge, and Wait did not try to banish it.

The Eye clicked softly in its casing. Wait did not silence it this time. It gave him no images. It spoke no truths. It simply hummed, curious as a kitten and taking in the gathered Senators through Wait's eyes. Obliging its curiosity, Wait scanned those on stage one at a time, letting the Eye absorb all it wished to. Red uniform after red uniform, men and women. Young and old. And there, all the way in the back, another someone. Not a Senator. She was not dressed in red, or even in Oswin's blue.

Tall and slender, hair long and features angular, her skin was the color of moonlight on white stone. And though she was too far away to see the color of her eyes, Wait knew that one was evergreen, the other earthy. Warmth spread from his chest to his extremities. No one else seemed to notice Tuliel standing there; no one ever did. He understood her now as he could not when she was his salvation. A Purist left behind to watch over wilder kin, she had tamed the blood duty sparked. He could not have been the only Dakhonne to lose the control bred over a thousand years. Like his own past buried in a rotted out windowsill, there were others. There would be more.

Reaching into his bag, Wait pulled from it the journal there and mostly forgotten since Linhare released him from its spell. Pride welled; and sorrow. It was the past, his past, but it belonged to Vales Gate, not to him.

"Linhare," he whispered. "Can we go now?"

"Now? But they're not done—"

"And they won't be for days. I still have to fish our supper out of the sea."

Linhare looked longingly at the stage.

"Unless," he said, "you are thinking about claiming what is rightfully—"

"No!" she said a little too loudly. Several heads turned, eyebrows raised and lips pursed. On the stage, Oswin squinted their way. Wait hunkered down as low as he could.

"Come," she said, and tugged at his hand. Wait followed her in a crouch along the line of scowling spectators, down the steps, through the culvert and out into Dockside. Wait did not look back. Not at Tuliel or Oswin. Not at the Senators. Not at the appropriately red, sufficiently scarred journal on the seat where he left it.

THEY SAT TOGETHER ON A DESERTED DOCK, eating the fish Wait caught and the vegetables Linhare purchased with the coins from the baker. They would not last long. As always, Dockside was an expensive place to be. Wait had already found work on the docks loading and unloading cargo, while she agreed to help the baker in his shop. A month in Lower Dockside, they decided, to earn enough money to move on. Already Wait's size drew unwelcome attention. Linhare had even seen cadets from Sentry Rock watching him and whispering among themselves. If they were to stay anonymous in this Vales Gate, they needed to get as far from the Vale itself as possible.

"Are you certain it's what you want?" Wait asked, tossing bones into the sea. "Oswin will know me. Sabal recognized you. We could go to the Senators. You could claim your rightful place, work with them and this new Republic."

"No," she said again, this time less vehemently. "The time for that has passed. I thought I was fighting to get back to right all that went wrong. But it all happened without me, Wait. Without us. The crown is no longer mine. I did not earn it. I did not fight for it. I did not make a stand and hold it against all odds. The people of Vales Gate, those Senators, Oswin and Ta-Yebbe and Ellis, they fought. This is their Republic. I fought to get home, to Vales Gate. I am here. It is what I've earned. And to be honest, my love, it is what I want."

"But you lived your whole life preparing to be queen."

"I did." Linhare took both his hands in hers, kissed them one at a time. They smelled of fish. As a boy, he'd been a fisherman with his father. It made her smile to know he was once again.

"Oswin was right," she told him. "This is the peace my family could not forge. What Vales Gate was meant for. At the end of it all, I can think of no better life than living in this Vales Gate with the man I love. We can do anything, Wait. We can be anyone. That is exciting, is it not?"

Wait pulled her into his arms, rested his chin on the top of her head. Linhare burrowed into him, lingered in his scent. Wait tilted her face up, kissed her lips. Linhare's blood caught fire. Destitute, living in the dunes outside of Lower Dockside, within this Vales Gate no longer hers, Linhare was truly happy.

"And now what, my queen?" he said against her lips. "Where do we go?"

"Anywhere." She pulled away. "Anywhere at all. The Pinelands. The furthest islets of Esher. We can go to Therk. Yerac'ia. Now that the Senate will open trade with them, there will be plenty of sailing ships going . . . oh."

"Oh?"

Linhare pulled back further. She reached into the neck of her dress, pulled out the whistle Hepheo had given to her. Holding it on the flat of her hand, she waited for him to understand.

The sun was mostly set. Only a thin sliver and the purple-pink light it offered lit the world in eerie light. Wait looked at her a long time, the eyes as blue as Ealiels Bay tearing at her heart for the longing in them. But he smiled, caressed her cheek, kissed her trembling lips. He curled her fingers around the whistle.

"Save it," he said. "You never know if we'll actually need the old pirate to come to our rescue again, or if it even works here. What I have wanted most in my life is right here on this beach, on this dock, in my arms."

"Then Crone's Hook." She kissed him. "Where you were a boy. We can settle there for a while. What do you think?"

"I think it sounds about right."

Rising, Wait pulled her to her feet. Together, they walked down the dilapidated dock, to the pier through the grassy dunes. Linhare tucked the whistle back into the neckline of her dress. Gazing out to sea, she conjured a pirate ship on its Pilfered mist. It blinked and sparkled, as if trying to form. Her heart thumped. She blinked it away, but the horizon still sparkled.

About the Author

TERRI-LYNNE DEFINO is a fantasy writer living in rural Connecticut. Her first novel, *Finder*, was published by Hadley Rille Books in 2010. Her second novel, *A Time Never Lived*, released in May, 2012. *Beyond the Gate* is her third. Her original fairy tale, "Jingle," was published as an ebook in February, 2013.

When she is not writing, Terri-Lynne wields her red pen like a ninja, editing for Hadley Rille Books since 2011. She has edited seven novels to date; and though her authors curse her ninja-editor skills now and then, they always thank her in the end.

She attended the Viable Paradise Workshop in 2007, under the mentoring of Teresa Nielsen Hayden, Patrick Nielsen Hayden, James Macdonald, Debra Doyle, James Patrick Kelly, Cory Doctorow, Steven Gould, and Laura Mixon. The experience changed her life, and continues to do so.

CPSIA information can be obtained at www.ICGtesting.com
Printed in the USA
LVOW12s1833141113

361320LV00008B/1359/P